Rangers Roadsend

What Reviewers Say About BOLD STROKES' Authors

∂✅

KIM BALDWIN

"Her...crisply written action scenes, juxtaposition of plotlines, and smart dialogue make this a story the reader will absolutely enjoy and long remember." – **Arlene Germain**, book reviewer for the *Lambda Book Report* and the *Midwest Book Review*

∂✅

ROSE BEECHAM

"...a mystery writer with a delightful sense of humor, as well as an eye for an interesting array of characters..." – *MegaScene*

"...her characters seem fully capable of walking away from the particulars of whodunit and engaging the reader in other aspects of their lives." – *Lambda Book Report*

"...creates believable characters in compelling situations, with enough humor to provide effective counterpoint to the work of detecting." – *Bay Area Reporter*

∂✅

JANE FLETCHER

"...a natural gift for rich storytelling and world-building...one of the best fantasy writers at work today." – **Jean Stewart**, author of the *Isis* series

∂✅

RADCLY*f*FE

"Powerful characters, engrossing plot, and intelligent writing..." – **Cameron Abbott,** author of *To the Edge* and *An Inexpressible State of Grace*

"...well-honed storytelling skills...solid prose and sure-handedness of the narrative..." – **Elizabeth Flynn**, *Lambda Book Report*

"...well-plotted...lovely romance...I couldn't turn the pages fast enough!" – **Ann Bannon**, author of *The Beebo Brinker Chronicles.*

"...a consummate artist in crafting classic romance fiction...her numerous best selling works exemplify the splendor and power of Sapphic passion..." – **Yvette Murray, PhD**, *Reader's Raves*

Rangers at Roadsend

by

Jane Fletcher

2005

RANGERS AT ROADSEND

ISBN 1-933110-28-7
THIS TRADE PAPERBACK ORIGINAL IS PUBLISHED BY
BOLD STROKES BOOKS, INC.,
PHILADELPHIA, PA, USA

FIRST EDITION: MARCH, 2005 BOLD STROKES BOOKS, INC.

CREDITS
EDITORS: CINDY CRESAP AND STACIA SEAMAN
PRODUCTION DESIGN: J. BARRE GREYSTONE
COVER IMAGE: TOBIAS BRENNER (http://www.tobiasbrenner.de/)
COVER DESIGN: JUDITH CURCIO

Rangers at Roadsend

DEDICATION

To the memory of
Lizzy Evans

my best friend
my world
my love

PART ONE

Chip Coppelli

16 September 533

CHAPTER ONE—A NEW GIRL IN THE SQUADRON

The new recruits to the Rangers were gasping as they stumbled up the road at an unsteady trot; many looked as though their legs were turning to rubber. Wisely, Sergeant Chip Coppelli stopped to let them pass, rather than relying on rank to grant her right of way. The recruits were clearly in no state to undertake evasive maneuvers. A grin spread across Chip's face at the sight of the exhausted women. It was not smug or malicious; an easygoing smile was merely her normal expression. Initial training for the Rangers was hell, as she well remembered, but sending out ill-prepared recruits would be verging on murder.

The trainees tottered to a halt in an open space nearby. Chip watched them form up in a line, swaying noticeably. A drill sergeant strutted forward slowly. The heavy, menacing steps made Chip's grin grow still broader. She wondered whether newly appointed drill sergeants were given lessons in swaggering or whether their gait was assessed for suitability before they were offered the job. And the voice! There must be a knack to sounding sarcastically ironic at full bellow. Chip could see the recruits flinch. It was a fair bet that they were all bitterly cursing themselves for applying to join the Rangers. Chip knew she had done so during her months as a trainee, but not seriously or for long. And the eight years since she had become a proper Ranger had been the happiest of her life—although it was fair to say that the preceding nineteen did not offer much in the way of competition.

With her path clear, Chip continued walking across the site, through the collection of barrack blocks, admin offices, stores, stables and training fields known as Fort Krowe. Her eyes took in the surroundings. The paths between the buildings were worn bare of grass, the ground still damp from the previous day's rain. From its hillside perch, the site commanded a view of the roofs of the town below and beyond them the lowland pastures, cut by the Landfall road heading southeast. The sun shone in a cloudless blue sky, but the weight had gone from its heat. The wooded hillsides held the first tinge of red and orange. Autumn was on the way.

It had been a busy summer for the 23rd Squadron, chasing from one side of the Homelands to the other. The missions had been successful, and the only losses from the squadron were two women who had completed their period of enlistment and decided not to rejoin. The one from Chip's patrol had gone only two days before and was probably still nursing her hangover. Chip was not sure whether the woman was wise (in leaving rather than celebrating). While out on assignment, Chip always looked forward to returning to Fort Krowe for the chance to take things easy. It was only when she got back that she remembered how dull it was. Leaving the Rangers might well be the same.

The barracks allocated to the 23rd were on a gentle slope, slightly detached from the rest of the site. Chip looked at the wooden buildings fondly. Fort Krowe felt like home, far more so than her parents' house had ever done. She was just approaching the C Patrol bunkhouse when a voice called out, "Sergeant Coppelli."

Chip stopped and looked around. "What is it?"

The Ranger who had hailed her jogged closer. "Ma'am, Captain LeCoup wants to see you in the briefing room. Your new recruit is here."

"Already? That's great." Chip switched direction.

The briefing room was in the block housing the officers' quarters. In a normal barracks, it would have fulfilled a range of administrative functions, requiring desks, bookshelves and cabinets, but at Fort Krowe, there were divisional offices to take care of such things. The only furniture in the room was a large central table and benches pushed back around the walls.

When Chip entered the room, Captain LeCoup was half sitting on the table, with one foot dangling free. LeCoup was short and square, with a face that epitomized determination. In Chip's opinion, it would be a brave brick wall that dared stand in her way. LeCoup was looking displeased, which was not a rare expression for her, although her fairness and competence meant that it did not stop her troops from generally approving of her. The current focus of her displeasure appeared to be the woman standing at attention in front of her.

LeCoup's eyes shifted as the door closed. "Sergeant Coppelli, the new member of your patrol is here. Private Katryn Nagata." Her voice was clipped.

Chip covered her surprise. Everyone managed to annoy LeCoup at some time; however, doing it within minutes of arriving in the squadron was both unusual and unwise. Chip took a few steps forward until she was standing beside the newcomer and then turned to look at her.

She was almost exactly the same height as Chip, her body lightly built but too well balanced to appear weak. Her head was small and neat, with a finely cut profile. The first thought to strike Chip was that Katryn Nagata was incredibly good-looking. The second thought—that the woman was older than she had expected, in her mid-twenties—was followed immediately by a mental double take. LeCoup had given the woman's rank as private, not Leading Ranger. A quick glance at Katryn's shoulder badge confirmed it. The shield was blank.

Promotion to Leading Ranger was a formality granted when a woman had completed two years of service and was marked by a single bar on her badge. It was possible for an officer to recommend that the promotion be delayed, but it was exceptional for that to happen, and certainly for no more than a year. In Chip's experience, you only met someone the newcomer's age who had an empty badge if she had been busted to private for a disciplinary offense.

LeCoup's next words supported this inference. "Private Nagata has been transferred to us from the 12th."

Chip mentally completed the story. The offense had not only been serious enough to merit demotion, but also had made Katryn so unpopular with the other members of her squadron that it had been necessary to move her. Gross cowardice would have done it, or stealing from her comrades, and either would probably have earned her a flogging as well. Whatever the crime, she was unlikely to be an asset to the 23rd. Chip could understand LeCoup's annoyance.

Chip studied Katryn's face in profile. The new arrival's gaze was fixed on the wall; her jaw was clamped shut. She was trying to look impassive, but the line of her mouth gave her away. She was miserably nervous, and she was very beautiful. Chip knocked the thought away and turned back to LeCoup.

The captain was glaring at Katryn, but then she sucked in a deep breath. "Okay, Private. You're not the person I'd have chosen, but I suppose someone had to have you. I'll assume that all appropriate action has been taken and we can draw a line under the past. You're in the 23rd Squadron now, and this is day one. Behave yourself, and things will be fine. Step out of line, and you'll regret it. Understood?"

"Yes, ma'am."

"You'll be in C Patrol, under Sergeant Coppelli here. She'll be watching you very carefully. Make sure she sees only good things." LeCoup paused, glaring. "She's all yours, Sergeant. Dismissed."

Chip led the way to the C Patrol bunkhouse. The dormitory layout was standard. An unlit iron stove was close by the door. A single bed for the corporal and double bunks for the other six members of the patrol stood in the corners. The door to the sergeant's room was at one end. All remaining wall space was taken up with lockers to hold the Rangers' possessions.

Chip pointed out the vacant top bunk and spare locker. "They'll be yours."

"Yes, ma'am." Katryn's voice was taut to the breaking point.

Chip looked at her. Katryn's hands were shaking visibly. Her eyes were bleak and despairing. "Trapped" was the word that came to Chip's mind. A ripple of sympathy flowed through her. Everyone made mistakes. You should not have to pay for them more than once. In a lighter tone, she said, "Don't be too worried by Captain LeCoup; she doesn't do the chummy act, but she's not vindictive, and she means exactly what she says. She's given you a clean sheet in the squadron. The rest is up to you."

"Yes, ma'am. Thank you." Katryn sounded no happier. She looked like a condemned woman on her way to the scaffold.

Chip stepped closer and put a hand on her shoulder. "It's okay. You're over the worst bit with LeCoup and me. The rest of the patrol can do reasonable impersonations of human beings—on a good day."

On cue, the door opened, and Lee came in. Chip accosted her and made the introductions. "This is Private Katryn Nagata, who has joined C Patrol, and this is Corporal Lee Horte, who is going to sort out your horse in the stables, show you where everything is and trot you around to say hello to everyone while I go and put my feet up in the approved fashion for sergeants."

Chip shot a warning glance at Lee before heading out through the door. Lee would be a good person to help Katryn settle in. It had to be stressful to be dumped in a group of strangers who were going to distrust you. Lee was the calmest person Chip had ever met. In five years in the Rangers, fighting their way out of countless dangerous situations, Chip had never heard Lee lose her composure enough to mutter an oath stronger than "Oh, dear." Lee was far more diplomatic than the average Ranger and could be counted on to not overplay a drama. Lee would also protect Katryn from too much tactless curiosity from the other patrol members.

Standing outside the bunkhouse, Chip paused and thought. It was not just her and the captain who would add things together and draw conclusions. For the sake of unity in the patrol, it would be nice to have the facts; no matter what, they would be better than rumor. While Lee sorted out the practical details, Chip decided to go back for a talk with Captain LeCoup and see whether she could find out exactly what Katryn Nagata had done.

❖

General mail arrived at Fort Krowe once a week. Rather than have the staff pestered by every woman on site, it was the responsibility of sergeants to collect and distribute mail to their patrols. It was Chip's next task after leaving Captain LeCoup—no wiser than before. The captain was not withholding information about the new recruit; there was simply none to be had.

"You're early; you'll have to hang on!" the clerk shouted as Chip entered the mail office.

"You mean you're not ready yet?" Chip's tone was teasing.

"That was the general implication."

"You'll have to start taking shorter lunch breaks."

"I haven't had a lunch break today."

"You mean your morning tea break overran so much, there wasn't time to fit one in?"

In reply, the clerk merely glared at her tormentor, but there was no real animosity on either side. The mock arguments were part of a traditional baiting game between divisional staff and those on active service in the squadrons.

Most of the office was taken up with desks and cabinets, but in a corner were a few stools. Chip selected one and sat down. After a few minutes, the door opened again, and Sergeant Aisha O'Neil of A Patrol entered, with Kimberly Ramon close behind. They were, respectively, the oldest and youngest sergeants in the 23rd. Ash O'Neil had been a sergeant when Chip joined the squadron. It was known that she had repeatedly turned down promotion to lieutenant, claiming that she preferred to stick with what she was good at. And there was no one who would deny that Ash was an exceptionally good sergeant.

Kim Ramon of B Patrol was also well respected. Reaching the rank of sergeant at twenty-four was fast work, and there was little doubt she would go much farther. She had been tipped as captain since her first month in the Rangers. Chip felt no resentment at knowing she would be overtaken on the promotion ladder, especially because Kim was her best friend.

"You can tell who hasn't got enough work to do," Kim teased, seeing Chip already there waiting.

"I'm merely maintaining good morale by making sure my patrol get their mail promptly," Chip answered in kind. Then she raised her voice. "Or at least they would if the staff didn't fart about so much."

"Sod off!" The answer was shouted back.

"What has happened to witty repartee?" Chip shook her head sadly.

"You weren't expecting wit from divisional staff, were you?" Kim spoke in mock innocence.

The three sergeants grinned at the harassed clerk and then settled down to wait. Ash rested her back against the wall and said, "I hear we've got a new girl in the squadron. I take it she's in your patrol."

"Yes. Turned up about an hour ago," Chip confirmed.

"You frowned when you said that."

"Mmm." Chip hesitated—not because she had doubts about the discretion of her fellow sergeants, who would soon learn everything via the grapevine anyway, but because she was uncertain what to make of the information she had to give.

"There's a problem with her?" Kim prompted.

"Well, she's not a new recruit. She's a transfer," Chip began. "Her name's Katryn Nagata. She must be twenty-five or so, and she's got the rank of private."

There were a few seconds of silence while the other two added things up. "What did she do?" Ash asked eventually.

"We don't know, which is really winding up LeCoup. I've come here straight from talking to her. Apparently, the transfer papers have got no information on them at all."

"Isn't there a record of the court-martial?"

"There must be—somewhere, but it hasn't got here yet. She's been transferred from the 12th, which is in Western Division...I think."

"Eastern," Ash corrected.

"Whatever." Chip shrugged. "The legal documents are probably still doing the rounds in Landfall."

"It's not a good situation," Kim said, shaking her head.

"No, not really. I've been trying to think of all the things you can get busted for." Chip pursed her lips. "I suppose blasphemy wouldn't bother me too much."

"It's not being busted to private that's worrying." Ash gave her opinion. "It's having to be transferred. Upsetting the authorities can be a matter of bad luck. Upsetting your comrades points to something nasty."

"How did she seem to you?" Kim asked.

"I didn't talk to her much."

"First impressions?"

"Well..." Chip caught her lower lip in her teeth, working to hide her grin. "I don't know how to tell you this, Kim, but she may well take your place as pretty girl of the squadron."

Kim laughed. "She's welcome to it. The bonus pay for the post is abysmal."

Chip tilted her head sideways. "She may be trouble, but at least she'll be ornamental."

Ash joined in the joking. "Don't knock it. When you've been a sergeant as long as me, you'll know the value of an ascetically pleasing patrol. Remember, for one reason or another, you have to spend an awful lot of time looking at them."

"Okay, the mail is ready!" the clerk shouted over, interrupting the discussion.

The three sergeants picked up the appropriate piles of letters and wandered back to the barracks. "So what are you going to do about your new Ranger?" Kim asked when they were outside.

"What can I do? She's been assigned to the 23rd. Anyway,

maybe she's learned her lesson. It's not fair to assume we need to do anything."

"I meant about finding out why she was court-martialed. You don't want to leave it to rumor."

"Oh, that," Chip said cheerily. "I've worked out just what to do. I'm going to ask her."

❖

A small town had grown up next to Fort Krowe. Initially, it had existed solely to supply the needs of the Rangers, but over the years, it had acquired a life of its own. Unsurprisingly, from the first, the town had attracted bowyers and swordsmiths, who no longer confined their trade to the military. Blades and bows from Fort Krowe were prized throughout the Homelands. The weekly market in the main square was the center of this trade.

Kim looked around as she and Chip wove their way between the crates and half-dismantled stalls. It was the end of another frenetic day of buying and selling. Crowds were thinning, and the stalls were being taken down for the night. No one spared a second glance for the two Rangers in their uniforms of green and gray, strolling across the cobbles. The indifference brought a wry smile to Kim's lips. Anywhere else, they would have attracted a lot of attention, if only from wide-eyed children, but this was Fort Krowe, home of the Rangers.

As they reached the far side of the market, Chip tapped Kim's arm and pointed down a side street. "Do you mind if we go to the Cat and Fiddle tonight?"

"No," Kim agreed easily and changed direction. "Any particular reason?"

"The rest of my patrol are going there. I'm hoping the new girl will tag along so I'll get the chance for a little off duty chat."

"To try and find out why she was court-martialed?" Kim put a teasing edge to her voice.

"Of course. Why else?"

"Well, you did say she was attractive."

"I said she was prettier than you."

Instead of answering, Kim directed a sideways look at her friend. Chip laughed. "Don't tell me you're worried."

"About what?"

"That she might take away some of the adoring hordes that chase after you."

This time, it was Kim who laughed. "There are enough women mesmerized by a Ranger's uniform to go around."

"And around and around." Chip grinned. "Well, you should know."

Kim made no attempt to deny the gibe. It was true that some women were fascinated by Rangers, and Kim was quite happy to admit that she made full use of the allure of her uniform—as did many others in the squadron. Maybe there was comment on her unrelenting pace as she worked her way through the stream of infatuated women, exceptional even among the free-living Rangers. However, she did not intend to get defensive about her behavior, especially not with her best friend. Chip knew her, and her life history, well enough to come up with some painfully sharp conjectures about the underlying causes, and it was not a subject that Kim felt ready to reflect on.

Their arrival at the tavern put a temporary end to the conversation. The taproom of the Cat and Fiddle was busy. Even so, it was not hard to spot the group of Rangers in the corner. Chip led the way, with Kim half a step behind. As they sauntered over, loud voices hailed the two sergeants. Both were well liked and, off duty, welcome drinking companions. Kim immediately identified the newcomer at the back of the group. The woman was clearly uneasy, although making an effort to fit in. The other members of the patrol were being polite, but they were also unsure how to react to the new addition to the squadron.

While they were still out of earshot, Kim whispered, "I take it that's her?"

"Yes."

"Not bad," Kim said appraisingly. Chip had not exaggerated her appearance. "But you don't need me to tell you to be careful."

"I said I thought she was good-looking. I didn't say I planned on doing anything."

"I heard what you said. I also heard how you said it."

"Don't worry. I'm not about to do anything daft." Chip rapped her knuckles gently on Kim's arm. "Anyway, there's no chance that someone who looks like that would have the slightest interest in anyone who looks like me."

Kim managed to stifle her sigh. It was an old point of contention. Chip often claimed that her adolescent delight in being able to pick up lovers at will had gone with the knowledge that the women were attracted purely by her uniform. If Kim argued, Chip would cite the mirror as evidence, saying that the most flattering word she could come up with to describe her own face was "interesting." Chip said it without bitterness or false modesty, but in Kim's opinion, that still did not make it correct.

Kim had tried unsuccessfully to explain that only when Chip was studying her own reflection was her face inanimate, humorless and critical, which made all the difference. Many women had told Chip that she had a nice smile; Kim just wished Chip would take what they said seriously.

Yet now was not the time for a fresh attempt to change Chip's opinion of herself. The new squadron member was a far more immediate concern. Just before they reached the group of Rangers, Kim caught hold of Chip's shoulder and pulled her around so that their eyes met. "Friendship" was too weak a word for the bond between them. Each had risked her life for the other on countless occasions. The vigilance did not stop when they were off duty, and something about Chip's reaction to the sight of Katryn set off alarm bells in Kim's head.

She lowered her voice to an earnest whisper. "Just remember, she's trouble."

❖

It was late in the evening before Chip got the chance for a private chat. The tavern was clearing slowly. Kim, true to form, was homing in on a soft-faced trader from Landfall. Katryn was sitting alone at a table in an alcove. Chip took her drink and slid in opposite.

"How are you doing?" Chip opened the conversation.

"I'm fine, thank you, ma'am."

"We're off duty. You can call me Chip."

"Yes, ma—" Katryn swallowed and looked anxiously toward the bar, as though searching for advice. Her eyes dropped to her almost-empty tankard. Chip pointed at it.

"Can I buy you another one?"

"Oh, no…I…" Katryn was floundering for words. "I don't drink much, but thank you."

Chip studied the downcast face. She had tried to work out a tactful way to approach the subject, but everything she had thought of sounded contrived. It did not seem hopeful that Katryn was going to volunteer the information, so blunt honesty was going to have to do.

Chip settled back slightly in her chair, in order not to appear too intimidating, and asked, "Why were you court-martialed?"

"Pardon?" Katryn's head shot up.

Chip did not repeat her words, judging that Katryn's response was not due to mishearing.

Katryn met her gaze for a few tense seconds and then shook her head. "I haven't been court-martialed."

"So why aren't you a Leading Ranger?"

"I haven't been in the Rangers long enough to qualify. I only completed initial training in January."

Chip opened her mouth and then shut it again. Her eyebrows drew together in a frown. Of course, it was possible. Before a woman could apply to the Rangers, she had to complete two years' probation in the Militia. The full term of enlistment was fourteen years. Those whose applications were successful spent the last twelve years in the Rangers. After that, it was possible to reenlist in seven-year extension periods, as long as the woman was not too old. Forty-four was the cutoff point for active field duty, sixty for divisional staff and seventy for command. To enlist in the Militia, a woman could be between sixteen and thirty, but in practice, it was extremely rare for anyone to join after the age of twenty. A fair proportion of the squadron had applied for the Militia and then the Rangers on the very first day they were eligible. Chip had not been quite so prompt, but she had still entered the Rangers before her nineteenth birthday. She had never heard of anyone very much older even wanting to transfer to the Rangers, let alone being accepted, but it was not prohibited by the rules.

"I didn't...er...I..." Now it was Chip who was lost for words.

"I haven't been charged with any crime, let alone found guilty." Katryn's voice was soft, with a bitter undertone.

"I'm sorry. I'm afraid I made assumptions from your age."

Katryn bit her lip and then nodded. "That's all right. I know it's unusual."

The question of why she had been transferred remained, but

Chip felt that she had blundered into enough awkward mistakes for one evening. She decided to retreat to another subject, and it would be safest to let Katryn choose it. "Right. Well...um...is there anything I can tell you? About the squadron or whatever?"

"I don't know much about Central Division, what the postings are like or..." Katryn's voice trailed away into a shrug.

Chip nodded. It was a safe subject. "Varied, very varied. Northern, Eastern and Western Divisions have their section of border to protect. Central has to cover everything else."

"The coast to the south?" Katryn suggested.

"Technically, yes. But though I've heard tales of sea monsters, they stay in the water and don't cause us problems."

Katryn's face fell slightly. "A shame. I've always wanted to see the ocean."

"Oh, you'll get to see it, all right, and everywhere else in the Homelands as well. Whenever a local Militia has a problem too big to handle, they call on Central Division. We're the smallest division— only five squadrons—and we cover the largest territory. On top of that, we are sometimes loaned to other divisions as reserves, particularly in winter, when snow lions get troublesome. We think of Fort Krowe as our base, but we don't spend much time here."

"It sounds like the 23rd sees a lot of action."

"Oh, we do. Of all sorts." Chip's grin returned. "The other divisions rotate around the garrison towns on the borders. We get to visit places where they don't normally see Rangers. You won't believe how enthusiastically women will grab their once-in-a-lifetime chance to examine the contents of a Ranger's uniform."

Chip glanced across the tavern. Once-in-a-lifetime chance or not, Kim's trader was clearly eager to undertake the investigation.

"I'm not into...I mean, if that's what other Rangers want, it's okay, but for myself, I don't..." Katryn mumbled.

Chip yelped with laughter. "Now, that's not the proper attitude for a Ranger."

The humor missed Katryn. "I had a lover before, and she..." Her voice failed her. Katryn's expression had been starting to open. It snapped shut, but before it closed, Chip saw into a raw pit of pain.

Chip slipped down in her chair, letting her gaze rise to the blackened beams of the ceiling. It would explain the transfer. Affairs between

Rangers were not approved of, but they were impossible to forbid. In the closed world of barracks and field duty, many Rangers slept together, generally expressing no more than the intense camaraderie of active service. On a daily basis, your life lay in your comrades' hands, binding you closer than sisters. The authorities would take no action unless the relationship got out of hand, threatening the military discipline of the squadron, but then they would step in—hard. It was particularly likely in the case of an affair between an officer and her subordinate.

Katryn was attractive enough to make any Ranger forget herself. It would not be surprising if a sergeant, or someone of even higher rank, had fallen for her. Separating the lovers was the quick, ruthless answer, and Katryn, as the new recruit, would be the one to be moved.

Chip's face softened in sympathy. As she had thought before, it had to be hard to be dumped in a new squadron, in circumstances that guaranteed distrust. And it was so much harder to do it with a broken heart.

CHAPTER TWO—A BAD NAME

The practice blades were blunt but could still provide a painful jolt, even through a thick leather jerkin. Katryn gasped and staggered back a step but kept her grip firm on her own sword and her eyes on her opponent. Chip followed up the advantage, thrusting forward again. This time, Katryn managed to block—just. However, after a few more parries, Chip again got through the defense with a hard swipe to the stomach. Katryn doubled forward, ending up wheezing with both hands braced on the ground.

Chip stood back and pursed her lips. It was not the point to leave people black and blue, but you did no one any favors in playing patsy during weapons practice. When Katryn had recovered her breath, Chip offered a hand to pull her back to her feet. Katryn stood shamefaced under Chip's appraising stare.

"I've known worse," Chip conceded at last. "But I expect better." In fact, Katryn was average, or would be with a bit more practice.

"Yes, ma'am."

Chip bent down and picked up the dropped practice sword. "What are you like with a bow?"

"Better."

Chip tilted her head to one side. "Really? Well, we'll give it a go after lunch." She turned to look around at the other pairs sparring on the grass. The weather was colder than the day before and overcast. The tops of the mountains were lost in clouds. Despite this, all eight women of C Patrol had worked up a sweat.

Chip was about to reassign partners when a shout echoed over the field. "Sergeant Coppelli!" She looked up to the top of the field. A Ranger from D Patrol was charging toward them. The urgency in the woman's tone prompted Chip to meet her halfway.

"What is it?"

"Captain LeCoup has summoned all the sergeants."

Chip did not need to hear more. The 23rd Squadron had another mission. "Corporal Horte, weapons practice is finished for today. Take the patrol back, and check out their gear." Chip threw the order over her shoulder and raced off without waiting for a response.

As she got close to the officers' quarters, Chip saw the other sergeants converging on the building from different directions. Kim caught up with her by the door. "We're off again."

"Looks like it."

Captain LeCoup and Lieutenant Ritche were waiting in the briefing room. Seconds after Chip and Kim took their places, the door opened, and the other two sergeants came in. LeCoup ran her eyes over the small group and began.

"I've not got many details to give you at the moment. A convoy was ambushed in the forest north of Redridge and the cargo stolen. Three women were killed. We have to get to Redridge as soon as possible and liaise with the local Militia captain. There's an hour before lunch to get ready. We'll stay to eat and ride out straight after. Any questions?"

There were none.

LeCoup gave a crisp nod. "Dismissed."

❖

Late afternoon, three days later, the squadron arrived at the outskirts of Redridge. From a long way off, the Rangers could see the toylike silhouettes of houses stuck atop the sandstone hill that gave the town its name. Redridge was situated high on the flanks of a long mountain chain. To the south was a pass leading to Landfall. In summer, there was steady trade on the road. Winter closed the route, however, and those who could not avoid traveling at that time had to take the long detour by Fort Krowe at the western end of the range. North of Redridge, the road went through dense forests until it reached the rich farmlands around Fairfield.

Captain LeCoup called a halt at the bottom of the hill. There was no need to drag the entire squadron and their horses through steep, winding streets. With only Lieutenant Ritche beside her, she set off in search of the town mayor and Militia captain. The other Rangers made the most of the chance to rest after the hard ride, stretching tired muscles and talking. Before long, a messenger came back down the hill with directions to a field where the squadron could set camp.

The work of erecting tents and digging latrines went smoothly, watched by a curious group of locals. The Rangers paid little heed to their audience; they were used to receiving attention from excited civilians. Of more concern was the suitability of the campsite they had been allocated—something that was often an issue—but this time, there were no grounds for complaint. The field was large enough and had been left fallow for summer grazing. There was still plenty of good pasture for the horses. A stream ran nearby, with woods behind for fuel. By the time the two senior officers returned, the camp was finished and preparations for the evening meal had started. The first trails of smoke rose into the evening sky.

Chip stood with her back to the tents, watching birds squabble in the nearby trees.

"Briefing for the whole squadron in ten minutes outside the captain's tent." The Ranger from A Patrol passed on the message.

Chip glanced over her shoulder to check that all her patrol had caught the news. "Any indications?" she asked the messenger.

"LeCoup is fuming."

"Surely not over the robbery?" one of the newer members asked.

The messenger laughed. "Outlaws are what we're paid to deal with. It takes the Militia to get the captain screaming for blood."

"A wild-goose hunt?" Chip suggested.

"I fear so."

As soon as the briefing started, it was plain from LeCoup's expression that the messenger had been correct. The captain looked at the ring of uniformed women seated on the ground and ran a hand over her face as though she were trying to rub away the scowl. It did not work.

"Okay. This is the story." LeCoup's tone was scathing. "There was a shipment of gold jewelry from Landfall to Fairfield. Rather than pay a fortune for lots and lots of guards, the merchant decided she'd disguise the cargo as something else. So the jewels were hidden inside bales of wool, and everyone on the crew tried to look as ordinary as possible. The outfit was made up of just two wagons, each with a driver and a guard, with one extra mounted scout. They got as far as Redridge without any problems, but a few kilometers to the north of here, they were ambushed. Three of the crew were killed. Two managed to run like hell and get away." LeCoup paused, glaring. "And this happened over a month ago."

Groans from around the circle greeted the last announcement.

"Yeah, I know. The Militia have obviously mistaken the Rangers for some relatives of the Tooth Fairy. I asked how they thought we could track down anything now. Perhaps they thought we'd brought our magic wands with us."

"Why did they wait so long to send for us?" a Ranger from D Patrol asked.

"The Militia assumed it was a local gang who didn't know what was in the bales. They were expecting the wool to show up in town." LeCoup shook her head in disgust. "If it had been one bale swiped off the back of a wagon, maybe, but nobody is going to steal two whole wagons of raw wool." Her voice died in disgust. "I'm surprised the Militia didn't leave the door of the lockup open and hope the thieves would walk in. And even if it was an ambitious bunch of petty thugs, they'd have repacked the wool into new bales, with a different stamp on the seal. Once the goodies started dropping out, they'd have forgotten the wool. But wherever the gang came from, I think we can safely assume that the jewelry has been melted down by now and the thieves are drinking their way through the profits on the other side of the Homelands."

"Since the thieves were so quick to murder three women, it implies they were very determined, which in turn implies they knew what was in the cargo." Lieutenant Ritche gave her opinion.

"You're probably right," LeCoup agreed.

"Is there any clue as to how the thieves found out about the real cargo?" This time it was Kim who raised the question.

"Nothing the Militia picked up on, but there was something." LeCoup pulled several sheets of paper out of a pouch and riffled through them. "It's in the statement from one of the survivors. Let's see…" She unfolded one. "Yes. From a Clarinda Wright, who was the scout. She says here…" LeCoup scanned the paper. "One of the drivers who was killed had a one-night stand with someone she met on the other side of the pass. And Wright thinks, but can't be sure, that she caught sight of the same person again in Redridge, hanging around the back of the inn. The implication would be that the driver mumbled more than sweet nothings in her sleep."

"Any description of the woman?"

"Quote, a bit rough-looking for my tastes, unquote." The dry delivery prompted scattered laughter. "Unfortunately, since Wright doesn't give any information on what her tastes are, we can't even use the description to eliminate suspects—if we find some. And Wright's now gone back to Landfall, so we can't ask her." LeCoup folded the paper again. "Any other questions, suggestions, bright ideas?"

There were a few whispered remarks, but nothing anyone chose to say aloud.

"Okay, briefing over. I'll try to think of something sensible for us to do tomorrow. My big regret is that we rushed here so quickly. We could have gone easier on the horses and had a chance to look at the nice scenery on the way."

❖

Dusk was settling by the time the evening meal was over. Chip and Kim stood at the edge of the camp, looking at the packed mass of buildings huddled on the hill. As the light faded, lanterns glimmered in the windows. Beyond, on the skyline, white peaks of mountains caught the last of the rusty sunset.

"Do you feel like popping in to check out a tavern or two?" Chip asked.

"Just for a drink?"

"It's all I intend, though I don't suppose you'll limit yourself to that."

"I meant you might want to try to catch any local gossip about the robbery."

"And if we find a good-looking woman who might know something, you'll volunteer to question her at length?" Chip teased.

Kim gave her a playful shove. She opened her mouth to speak but stopped at the sight of someone approaching. Chip followed the direction of her eyes and saw Katryn coming to an uncertain halt a few steps away.

"Yes, Private?" Chip asked.

"Ma'am. Could I have a quick word?"

Kim backed away. "I'll catch you shortly."

"It's all right, ma'am. It's not personal," Katryn said quickly.

"I've got a few things to sort out." Kim pointed at Chip. "And I will have that drink." She headed off in the direction of her tent.

"What do you want?" Chip asked when she and Katryn were alone.

Katryn hesitated. "The woman the captain named…the survivor of the ambush…were there any other details about her?"

"I don't know. I haven't seen the full statement. Why?"

"It's just…the name." Katryn spoke uncertainly. "When I was in the Militia in Woodside, there was a Clarinda Wright. The last I'd heard of her, she'd moved to Landfall with her cousin. But it might not be the same person; it's not so unusual a name."

"And if it was the same person?"

"No one would be at all surprised to hear her name in connection with a robbery. Her being the victim is the unexpected bit."

Chip thought for a moment. "Come on. We'll go and talk to the captain."

Katryn looked even more unsure of herself but followed Chip.

The captain's tent was large enough to hold a dozen women but was almost empty of contents. A lantern hung from the central pole. A pile of bedding was heaped at one side, with a few domestic items dropped on top. A board balanced across two saddles served as a low makeshift table. A map lay on it, its corners held down with stones. No other kit was visible. LeCoup stood, glaring at the map as though she was considering the possibility of setting fire to it.

Lieutenant Ritche was just leaving as Chip and Katryn arrived. Chip forestalled her departure. "Excuse me, ma'am, but I think you might like to hear this as well."

LeCoup looked up at the sound of Chip's voice. Seeing Katryn trailing behind, her expression became even sterner. "Yes, Sergeant?"

"Private Nagata has some information that might be useful."

LeCoup had obviously expected Katryn to be in some sort of trouble. She looked confused for a second but then asked, "What is it, Private?"

"Ma'am, you gave the name of one of the survivors of the ambush. I wondered…was the other one called Nosheen Paulino?"

The captain's confusion returned, but she picked up the pouch beside the table and flipped through the assortment of papers inside, holding them to the light. Eventually, she stopped at one and studied it in more detail. "Yes, she was." LeCoup faced Katryn. "I assume there's more to this than an announcement that you wish to perform a mind-reading trick to entertain the squadron."

Katryn swallowed visibly. "Yes, ma'am. I told Sergeant Coppelli that I recognized the name of Clarinda Wright. She's a troublemaker from my hometown of Woodside. The same goes for Nosheen Paulino, who's her cousin. The last time I saw either, I was pushing them into the station lockup in Woodside. After the magistrate finished with them, they both headed off to Landfall—or that's what the rest of their family said. Our captain sent a letter, advising the Militia there to watch out for them. I didn't hear if there was any reply."

"You think these are the same people?"

"Yes, ma'am. If it was just Wright's name, it might be a coincidence, but not with Paulino there as well."

LeCoup nodded as she leafed through the papers. "There's no mention here of them being related." She looked up. "Tell me more about this pair."

"The whole family has a bad name. Some are no worse than aggressive drunks—stupid with it. Most have been caught at some stage with property that doesn't belong to them. It's all been small-scale stuff to date. There was talk that Wright's gene mother was involved in a bungled robbery at a warehouse some years back, where the owner got killed, but it was never proved. Wright and Paulino, though..." Katryn paused. "Wright is considerably brighter than most of her family, and Paulino has had a vicious streak ever since she was a kid. They're a bad combination." Katryn's face twisted in a frown. "I'm just surprised any merchant would hire them."

"But you say Wright's smart," LeCoup said thoughtfully. "It's surprising the places a smart crook can talk herself into." She walked to the door of her tent and stared out for a long time. No one else said anything until the captain turned back. "It's obviously worth having a talk with the merchant to find out more. Wright and Paulino might also make for an interesting conversation, but they'll probably be a good deal harder to find. Private Nagata, since you know the pair, you're an obvious person to send, and I'd like Sergeant Coppelli to go as well. You can leave after breakfast tomorrow." LeCoup nodded to Katryn. "Dismissed...but I'd like a few more words with Sergeant Coppelli."

LeCoup waited until Katryn had left the tent. She turned thoughtfully to Chip. "Either we've had a big stroke of luck, or our new private is playing some sort of game. I admit I can't see what or why, but that's one of the reasons I wanted you to go as well—keep an eye on her."

"You could simply write to the Landfall Militia, asking them to investigate," Chip said brightly.

"I wouldn't trust them to be able to read the letter, let alone act on it." LeCoup snorted. She directed an uncompromising look at Chip and went on. "I know you have your own reasons for wanting to stay away from the city; however, you know the place and can find your way around. You also have a better understanding of the way merchants work than most of the squadron, and I'm sure you can use your name to pull strings, if needed."

Chip opened her mouth to protest. "Ma'am, I don't think my—"

LeCoup cut her off. "I said your name, not your family."

"Yes, ma'am." Chip sighed.

"Stay as long as you need, and take whatever steps you think necessary. I trust you to use your head. Corporal Horte should have no trouble leading C Patrol in your absence. It will be good practice for her. The rest of the squadron will stay around here for ten to twelve days. I'd like to leave tomorrow, but we have to go through the motions of hunting the gang. It won't be worth your coming back here when you're finished in Landfall, so go straight to Fort Krowe." LeCoup gave her the nearest thing to a smile that she had displayed all afternoon. "Dismissed."

❖

"I'm sorry. I know you thought you were owed a few days' rest." Chip tightened the girth strap and patted her horse's neck. As the animal huffed, two clouds of white steam blossomed in the still air. Chip could feel the icy nip in her own fingers and toes; summer was gone from the mountains. She looked up at the crisp blue sky and the fading pink wisps of dawn.

"You're about to be off?" Kim's call made Chip look around.

"Nearly."

Kim stepped closer and dropped her voice, although the smile stayed on her lips. "Okay, you were stalling last night, but now tell me how you wrangled it."

"What?"

"I know you're interested in Katryn. How did you talk LeCoup into giving you this little jaunt off together?"

"She's a Ranger and my direct subordinate," Chip pointed out, her tones uncharacteristically rigid.

"I just thought…a bit of companionship on the road." Kim's tones were playful.

"I don't think Katryn is into that sort of companionship. I know I'm not."

"Ha," Kim jeered. "I know the descriptions of at least twenty women who'd dispute that. And I only stick at twenty because I was too busy myself at the time to make a note of all the rest."

"That was all some time ago."

"And now you're too old? Or have you worn it away? I did warn you not to—" Kim yelped and ducked back from the dig aimed at her ribs. Her expression became more serious. "You're not happy, are you?"

"You know how I feel about Landfall. I was hoping never to go near the place again," Chip said glumly.

"You could try to avoid your family."

"I could try to avoid breathing. It would have the same chance of success." Chip's face twisted into a wry grin. "But I guess I'll survive. And it will be a chance to get to know Katryn better."

"Mmm." Kim agreed as her own smile returned.

"Talking—nothing else. There's something about her that doesn't fit. Maybe I can find out what."

"It's—" Kim broke off. "Here comes your traveling companion now."

Katryn jogged up. "I'm sorry, ma'am. I got delayed."

"No problem," Chip said. "You're ready to go now?"

"Yes, ma'am."

The pair swung up into their saddles. "I know you'll be miserable and bored without me, but try not to let it get you down too much." Chip addressed Kim with mock earnestness.

"Don't knock it. It's a lot safer than fun and excitement… particularly the sort you've got in mind."

Kim had to duck to avoid the playful swipe aimed at her ear, but the jibe had succeeded in putting a genuine grin on Chip's face. The two friends exchanged an amiable, informal salute; then Kim stepped back and watched as Chip and Katryn rode off around the edge of the campsite. After reaching the open gateway, they joined the track bordering the field. Then the riders turned toward town, the first stage on the route that would take them over the pass and on to Landfall. As the figures dwindled, Kim lost her smile, and a frown crept in.

"Is there a problem?" Ash appeared at her shoulder.

"I'm worried about Chip," Kim said.

"She's a big girl; she can take care of herself."

"In most things, yes." Ash's eyes prompted Kim to continue. "I've got doubts about her judgment when it comes to the new girl in her patrol. Katryn."

Ash nodded. "I know. I've wondered myself. Chip swallowed the story of late enlistment much too easily—and the explanation of why she was transferred. I'm not sure why Chip was so quick to take the woman's word on it."

"She's fallen for her," Kim explained.

"Oh," Ash said softly.

"I don't want Chip getting hurt."

"You think she might?"

"Yes. Just now, I was teasing her about being attracted to Katryn. Chip did everything except deny it. I've had this nasty feeling growing for a year or so that Chip's about to get serious about someone. Which would be bad enough in itself, but when you add it to the questions concerning Katryn…" Kim let the sentence hang.

"It's awful when a Ranger starts getting serious about someone." Ash spoke ironically.

"I know. If ever it happens to me, I'd like to be put down humanely."

"I might remind you of those words someday."

Kim grinned by way of an answer. The two sergeants watched the distant riders disappear around a bend in the road.

"I've got some contacts in Eastern Division," Ash said at last. "I think maybe I'll make a few inquiries."

Kim glanced at her and then away. "Yes. Why not?"

CHAPTER THREE—BACK IN LANDFALL AGAIN

The city of Landfall was a sprawling maze of buildings on the banks of the river Liffey. It was noisy and crowded. Despite the sewer system, it stank in high summer. Its inhabitants were habitually rude and impatient. There were back alleys where Militiawomen were frightened to walk alone—and the Militia in Landfall was the toughest in the Homelands. It marked the spot where the Elder-Ones had first set foot on the world, the spot where the Blessed Himoti had lived, worked and died. It was the holiest place in the universe, and it was a monument to money, politics, ambition and greed.

Chip stopped to study the city in the distance and could not prevent her lip from curling. She could not remember when she had started hating the place—sometime far back in her childhood. The city still felt like a deep, dark trap, and she had the irrational fear that if she entered its streets, she would be snared. Chip took a deep breath and straightened her shoulders. It was silly to feel this way. She had escaped once, and she could do it again. She urged her horse forward. Katryn kept pace beside her.

It had taken them seven days to make the journey from Redridge, a fair pace without pushing the horses too hard. Chip had fought the incompatible urges to delay, putting off the moment of arrival, and to press ahead and get the visit over with as soon as possible. Now, as she rode the last kilometer, Chip was suddenly aware of a strange eagerness to see the city, if only to confirm that it was as bad as she remembered.

"Have you ever been to Landfall before?" she asked Katryn.

"Yes, ma'am. Twice. The first time, I was quite young, and I don't remember much of the city itself. The other time, I passed through on my way to Fort Krowe when I applied to the Rangers. I'm afraid I had my mind on other things then as well."

The corner of Chip's mouth twitched at the "ma'am." Riding together, Katryn had opened up and would talk amiably to pass the time, but she never lapsed into anything that might be considered disrespectful. It was true that they were technically on duty, because they were in the process of obeying orders to go to Landfall, but few Rangers would have stood on rank—not so much because they were lax on military protocol, but because they adapted it to the conditions. Unlike Militia members, most of whom went to their homes each night, the Rangers lived in the closed community of the squadron. It would be unnatural not to form friendships with all your comrades. The lines between the ranks would blur, only to snap into focus when the situation demanded.

"So what do you remember?" Chip prodded.

"The council room inside the joint military command building and eating in the officers' mess."

"They let an applicant to the Rangers eat in the officers' mess?"

"Oh, no, ma'am. It was the first time I went to Landfall." Chip's expression of surprise grew, prompting Katryn to grin and continue. "My gene mother had been a lieutenant in the Militia. There was an award ceremony for her."

"She took you with her?"

"She was dead. That's why she got the award."

"Oh...I'm sorry," Chip murmured.

"It's okay. It was a long time ago, and I don't remember her very well."

Katryn did not seem distressed. Chip considered her thoughtfully. Although they had chatted on a range of subjects, this was the first time Katryn had offered information about her family or any other part of her life before she joined the 23rd. Chip's lips pulled into a wry grimace; of course, she had not been giving away much of her own life story, either.

There was something decidedly enigmatic about Katryn. Over the previous days, Chip had found a dry, understated sense of humor, coupled with quick wits and sharp observation skills. It was a description that could apply to many Rangers, but Katryn was quiet and unassuming—and that was unusual. Rangers tended to bravado. It was not easy to earn the right to the green and gray uniform, and most Rangers took every opportunity to flaunt it.

Katryn's behavior was atypical of Rangers in other ways. Chip had not seen Katryn drink more than two tankards of beer in an evening. The women who were drawn by her good looks and uniform wasted their time. The nearest Katryn had come to showing anger was when a groom gave soiled oats to her horse, and the anger had shown itself only in her clipped tone as she watched over the replacement of the feed. It was an awkward fact that Chip's initial attraction to Katryn's appearance had been strengthened by knowing her better as a person.

They rode on in silence until they reached the first outlying buildings of the city. The road squeezed between the crooked, overcrowded shanties of the poorest laborers. These constructions looked as though they could be washed away in a storm, but soon, the houses became more substantial. As they approached the river, they occasionally saw run-down mansions—relics from the days when the north side of the Liffey had been a prestigious neighborhood, before it had been swallowed by the expanding slums. They reached a band of docks and warehouses; then the buildings fell away on either side to be replaced by a view over the river. It was slow progress making headway on the overcrowded bridge, but at last, they crossed into the heart of the city.

Ahead, the great temple to Celaeno dominated the skyline. The street was wide and crowded. Waves of screams, shouts and laughter rose on all sides. Women, children and crones swarmed over the cobblestones. Chip's eyes took in the scene. Her stomach churned. It was so familiar, and the most awful thing was that she could almost feel she belonged there. It was so tempting to search out the memories: the tavern where she had first gotten drunk; the small upstairs room where she had first made love; the cold doorway where she had cried and slept on a wet, miserable night.

"Um...ma'am. Do you know where we're going?" Katryn asked hesitantly.

"Yes." Chip forced her thoughts to the present.

Even without Chip's knowledge of Landfall, their first destination was easy to find. All the main roads converged on the old market. Just before they came to it, Chip turned aside into a smaller street and then through an archway leading to a gravel square. Around it were the offices of the joint military command complex. The two Rangers slipped from their saddles, hitched their horses to posts and went through the nearest door.

They had to repeat their story several times, but eventually, they were shown in to see a Militia lieutenant seated at a desk. She listened to what they had to say, read the dispatch from Captain LeCoup and scribbled a note. "Of course we'll do what we can to help. We can give you billets and stables, and this will get you fed in the mess." She offered the sheet to Chip. "I'll have someone show you where everything is."

"Thank you, ma'am."

The lieutenant walked to the doorway and called to an orderly. She glanced at LeCoup's report once more before returning it to Chip. "Coppelli? You know that's a distinguished name in Landfall?"

"Yes, ma'am."

The orderly arrived and led them outside to reclaim their horses. The stables were the first stop, followed by a short tour of the site. Conversation was limited to the practical, most of which Chip already knew. The room they were finally shown into was on the third story of a block behind the mess hall. It was small but very clean, with scrubbed wooden floorboards. The only things in it were two unmade bunks and a chest. A tall window was opposite the door.

When the orderly had gone, Chip threw open the shutters and leaned her shoulder against the frame. Late-afternoon sunlight flooded in; with it came the sounds and smells of the city…and memories. She was back in Landfall again. Chip stuck her head out, taking in the full panorama. Little more than a view of rooftops was on offer, but if she twisted her neck, she could just catch sight of one corner of the temple.

Katryn dropped her saddlebag on the chest and stood in the middle of the room. "What do we do now, ma'am?"

Chip turned around. She felt tired and sticky after the days on the road, and if you could not avoid civilization, you might as well make the most of what advantages it held. She knew exactly what she wanted to do.

"There is a really first-class bathhouse around the corner. I want to get clean." Chip spoke with feeling.

Katryn smiled. "That sounds like a good idea."

It then occurred to Chip that maybe it was not.

❖

Chip sat on the bench with her back against the wall, feeling the sweat bead and trickle all over her skin, taking with it the dust, odors and muscle aches of the journey. Her eyes were closed. It was safest that way. A fine mist of steam filled the hot room of the baths, condensing on the mosaic wall tiles and occasionally dripping from the ceiling. It carried a clean lemon scent. And it did very little to obscure visibility. Chip had tried not to make too obvious a point of not looking in Katryn's direction—and not to make her response too evident when she did.

Three other women who had been sitting nearby got up and waddled off toward the cold pool, feet slapping, still gossiping about the affairs of their acquaintances. Katryn took advantage of the space left by their departure to lie face down on the bench, her head buried in her arms. Chip took advantage of Katryn's pose to stare at her. She could not help herself; the rest of Katryn's body was as perfect as her face. Chip's examination started at the ankles and traveled slowly upward, pausing only briefly at the bottom. The skin of Katryn's back was flawless. Whatever else, she had never been flogged. Chip felt painfully guilty about the shameless ogling—and even more guilty about wanting proof that Katryn had not been court-martialed.

Katryn turned her head. Chip tried to pretend that she had been staring blankly into the distance.

"What the lieutenant said about the name 'Coppelli,'" Katryn began, "I've been trying to think where I've heard it. Wasn't it the name of the previous mayor of Landfall? The one who held the post for years?"

"Yes." Chip closed her eyes, but for a different reason than before.

"I don't suppose you're related?"

Chip bit her lip. "My birth mother."

"What?" Katryn's head shot up. "Aren't the family incredibly rich? Don't they own half of Landfall?"

"No, no, you're thinking of the Tangs. They're the really wealthy ones—my gene mother's family." Without looking, Chip knew that Katryn's jaw would be hanging open. She went on. "Now you're going to ask what someone from my background is doing as a sergeant in the

Rangers." Chip met Katryn's astounded gaze. "It's simple: I'm running away from home."

Katryn dropped her eyes. "I'm sorry, ma'am. I didn't mean to pry."

Chip laughed, happy to have something else to focus on. "For the love of the Goddess, drop the 'ma'am.' We are *definitely* off duty at the moment."

Katryn smiled and laid her head back on her arms. "We could discuss mission plans for tomorrow."

"Not much to plan. First, we'll talk to the merchant, Mistress Drummond. I've got her address. Then we'll talk to the local Militia captain. And then we'll pick up on any leads we get." Chip settled back against the wall. "How far is it to Woodside from here?"

"A day and a half to the south. Why?" Katryn suddenly sounded defensive.

"We might need to go there. Talk to more people who know the suspects." Chip glanced over. "It would be a good excuse for you to visit your family."

"I'm not too bothered about that." Katryn's voice was muffled by her arms, but her unease was unmistakable.

Chip pursed her lips; obviously, she was not the only one who lacked fond memories of home. "On the short-term plans, when we leave here, we can get a meal. I know I've got a chit for the mess, but there are some wonderful eating places in Landfall, and they won't even make too big a dent in a Ranger's pay."

Katryn turned her head on one side, smiling again. "Great. I could do with getting something inside me."

Chip thought about that statement for a few seconds. Then she got up and jumped in the cold plunge pool.

❖

Early the next day, they set out on foot. The merchant had a large property in the slightly less fashionable part of town. It was on one of the older streets, close by the temple. For years, the area had been in decline, but as Chip led the way on the short walk, she noted signs of money flowing back. Several facades were freshly painted; repairs on one rooftop were under way.

Their destination looked much like its neighbors. Chip and Katryn were led into a large open hallway and asked to wait while a servant went in search of Mistress Drummond. Chip looked around. Like its surroundings, the inside of the building had the air of a place undergoing alterations. She guessed that Drummond's fortunes were changing, but whether the direction of the change was up or down was harder to tell.

It was not long before the two Rangers were escorted into a counting room. A middle-aged woman rose from her ledgers to greet them. She was overweight and overdressed and made the expansive gestures of a market trader. "Ladies, how may I assist you?" Her eyes narrowed. "I assume your visit has something to do with the appalling events in Redridge?"

"Yes, ma'am." Chip spoke formally. "We have a few questions."

Chip did not get the chance to go further. Drummond leaped in. "It was shocking. Business has been going well, but there's no way I can afford losses like that. And three of my employees dead! What do I tell their families? When the news came, I couldn't believe it. Nothing like this has ever happened to me before, and it wouldn't have happened this time if Grosskopf had listened to me."

"Grosskopf?" Chip queried.

"The buyer in Fairfield. Going via Redridge was her idea. She said it would be cheaper to take the river to Petersmine and cut down on the land part of the journey, even though it meant crossing that high pass. I'd have sent the shipment via Fort Krowe. You don't get bandits hanging around there. When Clarinda told me the Militia was trying to find the murderers on their own, I knew it wouldn't work and they'd have to call in the Rangers."

Chip managed to get a word in. "That would be Clarinda Wright?"

"Yes. Praise the Goddess that she survived. My business has suffered enough without losing one of my best workers."

The description of the suspect clearly astonished Katryn. Her eyes narrowed as a disbelieving frown creased her forehead. The response was noticed, and Drummond faltered, her own expression less confident.

"Has she been with you long?" Chip asked in the sudden silence.

Drummond's eyes flicked between the two Rangers. "Just over a year." The abrupt cut-off in the flow of words was conspicuous.

"And she has been a reliable worker?"

"Yes. I don't employ people I don't trust."

"I wonder if it would be possible to talk to her? Or the other survivor?"

"I'm afraid not." Drummond's composure and talkativeness returned in a rush. "After what they'd been through, it was only right to let them take a short holiday. In my experience, it pays to treat your staff sympathetically. You can't expect loyalty if you don't act like someone it's worth being loyal to. When Clarinda came to me last week and asked for a month's leave to go and visit her relatives, I agreed, of course; and Nosheen went as well."

"Her relatives? That would be in Woodside?"

Again, Drummond hesitated, but she recovered quickly. "Yes... yes, I think that's where she said. It was definitely to the south of here. But my foreman in the warehouse spoke to them at length before they went. Maybe she could answer your questions about the robbery. I'll send—"

Chip cut in before Drummond got going again. "I'm afraid it was those two we really wanted to get in contact with. It seems as if we might have to follow them to Woodside. If they return early, could you send word to us at military command?"

"Yes, of course, Sergeant Coppelli. And I'm not going to forget that name. You know that the last—"

"Yes," Chip interrupted. "Well, thank you for your time, ma'am."

The two Rangers said nothing until they were out of the building, surrounded by the midmorning bustle on the street. Katryn voiced their joint impression. "I don't trust her."

In response to their request for a meeting at the Militia station, the Rangers were asked to come back after lunch. After lunch, they were asked to return again still later. When they were put off a third time, Chip lost her patience and announced that they would wait by the captain's door until she was free. She selected a chair and threw herself down with an uncharacteristic scowl on her face.

"Must be an epidemic of lost dogs today." Chip made no attempt to keep her voice down. Katryn took a seat beside her in a calmer fashion.

The military was comprised of three branches: the Militia, the Rangers and the Temple Guard. All three sections disliked the other two. Bitter rivalry existed between the Rangers and the Guards. Each saw itself as the elite service, for different reasons. And although everyone started in the Militia, the opinion was frequently voiced that only the second-rate stayed there—an attitude that did not endear itself to the Militiawomen any more than the trivializing of the work that they performed. It was a distortion to claim that even in rural districts, the job of the Militia amounted to no more than rounding up drunks and stray animals. The gibe was particularly unfounded in Landfall, where the Militia saw more violent encounters with more criminals than most squadrons did.

It was half an hour before Chip and Katryn were shown into the room. The thin-faced captain in the black uniform scarcely bothered to look up from the papers on her desk. "Good afternoon, Sergeant. I am Captain Gutmann. Can I do something for you? But you'll have to be quick."

"Yes, ma'am. We're investigating a robbery and three murders that happened just north of Redridge. We're trying to locate two suspects," Chip said crisply.

"You think they might be in Landfall?"

No, we just came here for the pleasure of seeing you. Chip restrained her first sarcastic thought. "This is where they said they were going."

"You've spoken to them already?"

"We have copies of statements they gave."

"And you let them go?" The captain's voice was smug. "That was careless."

"They had been released before my squadron arrived in Redridge. I'm afraid it was the Militia that was careless...ma'am."

"You're saying the Militia made a mistake?" The captain's voice held a dangerous edge.

"An error of judgment, ma'am."

The two antagonists glared at each other—or, more accurately, the captain glared at Chip while Chip glared at the wall a few centimeters above the captain's head. Eventually, the captain drew a sharp breath and snapped, "So who are these two?"

"Their names are Clarinda Wright and Nosheen Paulino, ma'am."

"I've never heard of them."

"They work for Mistress Drummond in Upper Street."

"If you have questions about her employees, I suggest you go to Mistress Drummond herself." The captain's tones implied that the meeting was over. She returned to the papers on her desk.

Chip was speechless in frustrated anger, but Katryn entered the debate. "Ma'am. If I may, I have some more information."

"What?" the captain barked.

"Before I joined the Rangers, I was in the Militia in Woodside, which is where I came across these two. As a member of the Militia, I personally arrested them both, and they were picked up on other occasions as well. Clarinda Wright was a particular problem. After we in the Militia had done our job, half the time, she'd talk her way around the magistrate and walk out of court free. We're concerned that she might have duped Mistress Drummond as well."

Some of the hostility faded from the captain's face. After a few seconds' thought, she pulled a sheet of paper out from a pile. "What did you say their names were?"

"Clarinda Wright and Nosheen Paulino from Woodside, ma'am."

The captain scribbled a note quickly. "I'll see if anything is known about them." She glanced up, her eyes still glittering angrily. "And if that's all…"

This time, there was no avoiding the dismissal. Outside on the street again, Chip could finally give vent to her irritation. "Yet another bloody waste of time, courtesy of the Militia."

"She said she'd ask around," Katryn pointed out.

Chip sighed bitterly. "Yes, she did, and that was only because of you. Thanks; you did well. I'd lost my temper and couldn't think straight." Chip kicked a loose pebble across the cobbles. "I noticed you didn't try to confuse her with doubts about Drummond's honesty."

"I just tried to keep things as simple and calm as possible."

"Well, you obviously knew how to handle her."

"It was just knowing that Militia captains hate gullible magistrates even more than they hate arrogant Rangers."

Chip stopped short. There was a definite hint of criticism in the remark. "You think I could have been more tactful?"

"Um…" Katryn hesitated, searching for words. "I'm not sure blaming the Militia for letting them go was wise."

"The captain was the one who started making accusations of carelessness."

Katryn shrugged. "How would LeCoup react to a Militia sergeant who told her the Rangers had gotten things wrong and then asked a favor from her?"

Chip opened her mouth and then closed it again. Actually, it did not bear thinking about—if you were squeamish.

CHAPTER FOUR—OLD ARGUMENTS

A bay-fronted inn stood at the corner of the road a short way from the military command compound. Noisy groups of Landfallers crowded the front, but the rear of the taproom was quiet and half empty, occupied mainly by inn guests taking an evening meal. Yellow lamplight brought out the warmth of the wood-paneled walls. The low-beamed ceiling made the large room feel snug. Chip and Katryn found an empty corner table and sat down with their drinks.

"I suppose the day hasn't gone too badly," Chip conceded. "We've probably made more progress than they have up in Redridge."

"I think it was all worth it just to hear Clarinda Wright described as a reliable worker. I was so impressed by the way Drummond kept a straight face while she said it. I was waiting for her to add that little Nosheen is kind to children and old ladies." Katryn's voice held amused disbelief.

"You don't think it's possible they've become reformed characters?" Chip joked.

"Not unless the Goddess has paid a personal visit to Landfall this past year. Because I can't see anything less than her physical intervention doing it."

"And it would be too ironic if they became victims of bandits immediately after they've joined the side of the righteous."

Katryn's face became serious. "Drummond has to be involved in some way. Wright and Paulino have never done an honest day's work in their lives. Even if it were part of an elaborate plan to defraud, they couldn't have kept it up for a year. Drummond has to know what they are like and is lying to protect them. I just can't see why, since she's the one who loses."

"That's if she is." An idea suddenly hit Chip.

"How?" Katryn asked when the silence dragged out.

Chip's gaze focused on the distance. "Something Drummond said has just registered on me."

"You'd trust her word?"

"Oh, yes, because I don't think she realized that she'd given herself away—or that I'd understand the significance."

"What?"

"When she said Grosskopf in Fairfield was the one who insisted on the route via Redridge." Chip smiled at the incomprehension on Katryn's face. "You obviously don't come from a family of merchants. Usually, a trader goes where she can get the thing she wants, pays for it and takes it away with her. But for some items—and custom-made jewelry would be a good example—the trader has to go to a supplier, put in an order and have the goods sent to her when they are ready. When she pays is subject to negotiation. A really reputable supplier will take cash on delivery, but I think we're agreed that Drummond isn't reputable."

"You think Grosskopf paid money up front?"

"That's where Drummond made the slip. The buyer must have had some financial stake in the cargo to have a say in the route, else it would have been entirely up to Drummond how the jewelry got to Fairfield. My guess is Grosskopf paid half on ordering, with the rest due when she got the goods."

"So Drummond would still have lost half the value of the cargo."

"Not if it never left Landfall. Consider whose word we've got that the bales contained hidden jewelry."

"Three women died..." Katryn started to protest but then fell quiet.

"Drummond said the three were her employees but didn't say for how long. With Wright and Paulino in on the fraud, the others could have been expendable dupes, stabbed in the back when they weren't expecting it." Chip paused and then asked, "Do you think Nosheen Paulino is up to murdering in cold blood?"

"Yes, if the money was right," Katryn said slowly. She looked troubled, and her eyes were fixed on the tabletop. "So what do we do now?"

"Information about the robbery should be held at Joint Command. From it, we can get the names and addresses of the women who died. It would be interesting to find out whether they were long-term employees or casual hands Drummond picked up the week before; although it doesn't mean she'd have put any value on them, even if they'd been with her for years." Chip frowned. "Basically, we need to get enough evidence together to persuade a magistrate to give us a search warrant for Drummond's place."

"We'll need to get the Landfall Militia behind us."

Chip sighed. "True. I think we'll have to visit Woodside." She glanced across. Katryn's face had fallen. "I know you're not keen on it, but a report from the Militia there about Wright and Paulino could be vital in building our case—and persuade the Militia here to take us seriously."

"Oh, I understand. It's just that there are some people in Woodside I'd rather avoid." Katryn shrugged. "I'll survive it, though."

"I can sympathize, because I'm not looking forward to the other thing we need to do."

"Which is?"

"We need proof that Drummond could make a profit out of faking the robbery. A copy of her contract with Grosskopf will be logged with the merchants' guild. We need to see it."

"What's the problem?"

"To view a contract without written consent from one of the parties, we'll need the personal authorization of the guildmaster. Her name's Prudence Tang." Chip grimaced. "She's my sister, and we didn't part happily." Chip's mouth was suddenly dry. She picked up her tankard, only to discover that it was empty. Waving it toward Katryn, she asked, "Do you want another drink?"

Katryn pulled a half smile and shook her head. "I've still got most of mine left."

"You'll never get drunk like that."

"That's my intention."

"I'll just get myself another half." Chip slipped out from the table. She had barely reached the bar when a woman sidled over. Chip was not surprised; she had already noted the woman smiling in their direction.

"Good evening, Sergeant. Could I buy that drink for you?"

Chip tried to excuse herself politely. "No, but thank you…it's… I'm okay."

The woman looked disappointed, but she continued. "I'm a trader visiting Landfall. A drink would be the least I could do to show my appreciation of the women who keep our roads safe for commerce." Her voice was low; her tone implied that other ways of showing her appreciation were also on offer.

"No, really."

"Maybe another time?"

"Maybe."

"I'll be here tomorrow night as well." The woman would not give up.

"I'll keep that in mind."

Chip got her drink and returned to the table in the corner. On the way, she risked a quick glance back at the trader. The woman was pretty in a mature way, with a well-shaped body. There had been a pleasant lilt to her voice. A Ranger could do far worse for a night's entertainment. However, Chip was not tempted—not with Katryn waiting for her.

❖

The clerk at the merchants' guildhall did a double take when Chip gave her name, but her expression immediately settled. No doubt she was marking it down as a coincidence. She listened to the request for a meeting with the guildmaster, muttered, "I will see what can be arranged," in tones implying that the middle of the next week was the time scale the Rangers should expect, and trotted away.

When the clerk returned, her face looked as though she were trying to perform compound-interest calculations in her head. She beckoned the two Rangers to follow her. "The guildmaster can see you now." The words were devoid of emphasis, but the Rangers could see the sums whirling around behind her eyes.

Chip and Katryn were led along a wide tiled hall. The décor was plain but unmistakably expensive, intended to whisper quality rather than shout it. No hanging drapes deadened the sharp clack of footsteps; even sound was used to bolster the impression of purposeful progress. The door the clerk stopped outside was carved from solid wood. The panels were without ornamentation, but the proportions were perfect. Chip tried to ignore the tension building inside her.

"Guildmaster Tang's office." The clerk pushed open the door. "Sergeant Coppelli and Private Nagata of the Rangers to see you, ma'am." She backtracked out, allowing Chip and Katryn to enter.

Prudence Tang sat behind a huge desk. She had put on a little weight since Chip had last seen her, and her face was showing the lines of middle age, which further hid any family resemblance—not that there had ever been much, except maybe in their noses. Her frozen expression also did not help. She looked as though she were rooted in her chair. It was some seconds after the door had closed that she found her voice.

"By the Goddess...Piety! It is you, isn't it?"

Chip ignored the unorthodox greeting. "Thank you, ma'am, for seeing us so promptly. I'll try not to take too much of your time. We're investigating a robbery and multiple murder, and we need information concerning one of your members."

Prudence Tang's jaw sagged. She shook her head sharply and pinched the bridge of her nose. "You...you just reappear after....And now you...what?" She sounded dazed.

"I said, ma'am, we're investigating a robbery and multiple murder, and we need information concerning one of your members." Chip could hear that her own voice was less steady than at first.

"And that's all?" Prudence's composure had solidified in disbelief. "No 'Hello, sis, how are you doing?' No word about where you've been the past ten years?"

Chip's gaze dropped briefly to the floor. "I assumed that if you'd wanted to know that, you've have tried to find out for yourself. You do have the resources."

"You just walked out on the family and—"

Chip cut her off. "I was thrown out. Remember? You were there."

"Mama Izzy was angry."

"Oh, surely not!" Chip said in savage irony.

"I couldn't have done anything to help you."

"So you didn't bother trying."

"I thought...we all thought that you'd go back to the sanctum."

"That I'd just knuckle under like the rest of you and do what our mothers wanted?"

Prudence slumped in her chair. "No. I knew you'd find a way out. I just wish you'd...come to me. Or at least let me know where you were."

"You really had no idea?"

"Some years back, Sandy finally told me you'd called to see Mama Izzy a few days after the row. She said you'd been wearing the black uniform. I checked with the Militia. I was told you'd transferred to the Rangers."

"Then you knew where I was."

"That was years later." Prudence's voice intensified. "But back when we first learned you'd abandoned the temple. Mercy, Constance and I were distraught. We all were. You could have been lying dead in a gutter, for all we knew."

"Then you should have searched the gutters on the night I was thrown out." Chip was implacable.

"So you've come here to dig up old arguments?" Prudence spoke with a flash of anger.

"No. As far as I'm concerned, it's over and finished. I've come here to get information on one of your members who we think might be involved in robbery and murder."

Prudence took a deep breath, visibly reining in both her confusion and irritation. "All right, we'll play it that way. Who is the merchant you want to know about?"

"Mistress Drummond of Upper Street."

"Really?" Prudence retreated behind a mask of businesslike authority. "It's awful to say, but I'm not totally surprised to hear you name her. She doesn't have a good reputation. Her accounts balance; however, they don't tie in with her visible expenditures. There have been rumors, but no proof. I'm afraid there's nothing definite I can tell you unless you have a specific question."

"What I'm interested in is a recent contract between her and a trader called Grosskopf, from Fairfield. It concerns jewelry that was supposedly stolen in transit. I suspect it never left Landfall, but I need to be able to show that Drummond could have made a profit from faking the robbery. Since I don't want to ask Drummond's permission to see the contract, I've come to get your authorization."

Prudence nodded crisply. "I understand. I'll get someone to check the archives. A certified copy of the contract will be ready for you to pick up here tomorrow afternoon."

"Then I won't take any more of your time. Thank you for your assistance." Chip retreated toward the door.

"Wait…please." Prudence's aloofness slipped again. She

scrambled out from behind her desk.

Chip looked down to meet her sister's eyes. Prudence was the shorter of the two by a good ten centimeters. The guildmaster put her hands on Chip's upper arms and examined her face. She spoke softly, almost whispering, "Just tell me everything is okay. That you're happy now. And that you'll forgive me for not standing up to our mothers. You know I was never very good at it."

Chip flushed softly. For the first time since entering the room, she felt a trace of her usual grin return. "I know, and it's okay. I'm happy. Give my love to anyone you think deserves it."

❖

As soon as they were outside the guildhall, Chip set off down the street, with Katryn trailing behind, but after a hundred meters she halted abruptly and rubbed her face with her hands, Then she gave Katryn a shamefaced grimace. The interview must have been a confusing experience for the onlooker. "I'm sorry to have dragged you through that."

Katryn shrugged. "It's okay. I don't get along very well with my sister either."

"Oh, Prudence is all right. She just..." Chip sighed and stopped. "I...er...I need to take a break and get my head back in order."

"Fine."

Chip started walking again, this time an aimless stroll. Nothing was said until they reached a small empty square overlooking the river Liffey. The flagstones had been washed clean by the overnight rain; damp patches remained in the shade of tall buildings. A waist-high wall ran along the embankment, and steps led down to a mooring jetty. Chip rested her forearms on the wall and stared out over the water, watching the river barges and wading birds. Katryn took a place beside her.

Chip felt the need to talk. "It was odd seeing Prudence again. She was always my favorite sister, which was what made it so hard when she wouldn't stand up for me. I never expected much from the other six."

"You've got seven sisters?" Katryn exclaimed.

"Oh, yes." Chip grinned. "I was the youngest. It was all part of my parents' plans for world domination."

"I was thinking of the imprinting fees."

"Remember, we're talking Tangs."

"Of course. They're rich."

"Forget rich. Did you hear of the golden chapel extension on the temple fifty years back? The Tangs paid for it as proof of their devotion. In gratitude, the Sisterhood waived all their imprinting fees for three generations."

"Who got the better deal?"

"Financially?" Chip wrinkled her nose. "The Sisterhood. I doubt the Tangs took advantage of the exemption. They're landowners; half of Landfall pays them rent. They don't think in terms of money; they just sit there and rake it in. But the Coppellis...they're merchants. Waving the word 'free' in front of one of them is like waving a bone in front of a starving dog. It went without saying that my birth mother made full use of the exemption when she had a Tang as a partner. I'm only surprised that they stopped at eight. Maybe after me, they ran out of suitable careers."

"Pardon?" Unsurprisingly, the last sentence had lost Katryn.

"My mothers' alliance marked the union of boundless ambition with money. My birth mother, Isabel Coppelli, was the one with schemes for the future. My gene mother just let her get on with it—and provided the funds. Mama Izzy had this idea of a large family of sisters, each of them taking a key role in the city. Of course, we didn't get a say in it; our future was decided for us. Prudence was marked down as guildmaster before she was born. My oldest sister, Constance, has had a bit more of a struggle, but she should achieve her destiny and become mayor in another few years."

"What were you supposed to be? Or are the Rangers...?"

"Hardly." Chip paused and then said bleakly, "I was headed for the Sisterhood. I don't know if my mothers thought they could bribe my way to Chief Consultant, but it was their chance to see how far money could push a woman up the temple hierarchy. But I was completely unsuited to the role—the only flaw in the plan. All my sisters were taught suitable subjects at home by tutors; I was enrolled in the temple school when I was four. One of my parents' bodyguards, either Sandy or Jez, would escort me across town. The Sisters would spend the day trying to drum theology into my head, and then I'd be taken home again. I hated it. The lessons were so boring, and when I realized that my mothers expected me to become a Sister and spend my whole life in the temple…" Chip fell silent at the memory.

"But the Sisterhood is a calling; you have to make your vows freely before Celaeno."

Chip gave a cynical grunt. "I don't think it ever occurred to my birth mother that her daughters could have minds of their own. Certainly, my sisters never gave her reason to consider the idea. When I finally told her I didn't want to enter the Sisterhood, I think she was genuinely astounded."

"What did she say?"

"I was told not to be silly. So I tried to get myself expelled from the school. All I got was a few good hidings. My mothers kept bribing the Sisterhood to let me stay. I felt trapped. I was actually pushed as far as becoming an initiate when I turned sixteen. I entered the outer sanctum at the temple, white robe and all." Chip's eyes were no longer focused on the river before her. "I'd been there five months, but I hadn't taken full vows, so I was allowed home for my gene mother's birthday, and I knew I couldn't go back. All hell let loose when they realized I meant it—threats, screaming. Mama Izzy tried to box my ears. I pushed her away. I didn't hit her, but she fell over. So she called Sandy and Jez to throw me out of the house—literally."

Chip could feel her eyes filling at the memory. "And that hurt. Sandy, particularly. She'd been around for as long as I could remember; playing with me when I was little, taking me to school, looking after me. I just took it for granted that she was there to protect me, and she physically threw me out of the house while nobody else said a word. I couldn't believe it. I walked the streets in a daze. It was pissing down rain. Eventually, I found a dryish doorway and tried to get some sleep."

"They left you to…" Katryn sounded dumbfounded.

"My birth mother is rather good at politics. Outmaneuvering opponents, things like that. It was one of her rare miscalculations. She thought if I had nowhere else to go, I'd have to return to the temple. I'd rather have died, and I nearly did. I woke in the middle of the night, freezing cold, with a couple of thugs sizing me up. Then the Militia appeared and scared them off. I don't think the Militiawomen even noticed me huddled in the corner, but they gave me the idea. The next morning, I went to Militia HQ and signed the next fourteen years of my life away. And that's when I nearly died." Chip could not restrain an ironic laugh at her own expense.

"I was sixteen and a half years old, and I'd never been outdoors in the streets without a bodyguard before. I'd never handled real money. I'd never been in a tavern. And there I was, dealing with thugs and crooks and drunks. I don't know how I survived the first week. I may have the height, but I had the muscles of a Sister. I can't believe I passed the physical exam to get in. I suspect the Militia was short on recruits and accepting anyone that month. I was the joke of the division."

"You've obviously..." Katryn looked Chip up and down and then blushed faintly.

Chip shrugged. The implied approval of her physique was gratifying, although the military training program would have to take the credit for it. "It was shape up or die. I had to work a bit harder than anyone else. No one would overlook any mistake I made. As far as most of the division was concerned, I was a spoiled rich kid playing soldier, and they all knew my mother was mayor, which didn't help."

"Did she know where you were?"

"Yes. I went to see her the day after I'd done my first night patrol, realizing what I'd let myself in for. She said she'd buy me out of the Militia if I'd go back to the temple." Chip pursed her lips thoughtfully. "Actually, if she'd phrased it as an offer, I might have accepted, but she declared that it was what was going to happen, whether I wanted it or not. I threatened that if she tried to get me back to the temple, I'd re-enlist. For once, she missed the chance to call my bluff. We had another screaming row, and she formally disowned me."

Chip pushed away from the wall and began to pace along the flagstones. Katryn fell into step beside her. They left the square and entered a narrow riverside passageway. "What made you join the Rangers?" Katryn asked after a while.

"Partly to get away from Landfall and the daily reminders of my family. Like the time I arrested a woman stealing bread in the market. She only had one leg. I found out later that she'd lost the other in an accident in one of my mothers' warehouses." Chip's shoulders twitched uncomfortably. "Their lawyers had managed to wrangle the family out of paying any compensation."

"You weren't responsible."

"Some thought I was, although by the time I'd completed my two years' probation, things were getting better. I'd done my exercises and lost my naïveté. I'd like to think I was quite good at the job, but I still didn't get along with my colleagues, except for two friends. They were both desperate to join the Rangers. It was the only reason they'd enlisted in the Militia to start with. I didn't want to be left alone in Landfall when they went, so we agreed we'd all apply to the Rangers at the same time. We went for appraisal together." Chip sighed at the memory. "I was accepted. They weren't. That's how it goes." She turned her back on the river and leaned on the wall; then she tilted her head to one side and looked at Katryn. "I know it's early, but I think I could do with a drink. We could take an early lunch in the mess and track down the relatives of the murdered women after."

Katryn nodded her acceptance, and the pair set off along the crowded streets of the city.

CHAPTER FIVE—LIES

S ergeant Coppelli!" a voice called out as they returned to the command compound.

Chip looked around. One of the orderlies was waving to her through an open window. There was a piece of paper in the woman's hand. Chip crossed the gravel. "What is it?"

The orderly held out the paper. "This message came for you just a few minutes ago. I was going to have it sent to your room, but then I saw you come in."

"Right. Thanks." Chip took the folded note. The orderly smiled and swung the window shut.

Chip took a few steps before opening the sheet to read.

Sergeant Coppelli
Rangers, 23rd Squadron

Following our discussion yesterday, I learned that Captain Kalispera of the Woodside Militia is currently in Landfall, attending a regional meeting. I was able to talk to her last night. She confirmed the highly dangerous nature of the two women you are seeking. It was her opinion that they should be taken for questioning as a matter of urgency. She has asked that you get in contact with her in the officers' quarters at the JMC to coordinate our effort in tracking them down.

Captain Gutmann
Landfall Militia

"Typical. Now that someone in a black uniform has agreed with us, the Militia will take what we say seriously," Chip said angrily

"Are you going to try to speak with Captain Kalispera now?" Katryn asked.

"Might as well. Come on."

"Do you want me to…go with you?" Katryn finished weakly.

It occurred to Chip that the captain might be one of the people from Woodside whom Katryn wanted to avoid. Chip hesitated, disconcerted by the idea that Katryn might have been in trouble with her superiors in the Militia. However, Katryn had evidently decided that the answer to her question was obvious and started walking toward the senior officers' accommodation block without waiting for further debate.

The entrance hall was a chilly, dim chamber with long corridors leading off on either side. They were looking around, hoping to find someone to ask directions of, when three Militia captains appeared in the corridor to the right and began walking toward them. Katryn froze and then whispered, "That's Captain Kalispera on the right."

Chip nodded and moved forward to intercept the women in black. "Excuse me, ma'am. I'm Sergeant Coppelli of the 23rd Squadron. I believe Captain Gutmann has spoken to you concerning our visit to Landfall. Would this be a convenient time to talk?"

Captain Kalispera was staring over Chip's shoulder at Katryn. A hostile frown crossed her face; then she pulled her eyes back to Chip. "Um…yes, Sergeant. I've got a few minutes free before lunch." The captain nodded at her two colleagues, who continued on their way without her.

Chip and Kalispera stepped a little to the side. Katryn hovered in the background. "Okay, what can you tell me about this reported robbery?" Kalispera asked.

Chip quickly went through the details, known and conjectured. She finished with their request for a copy of the contract and plans to learn more about the murdered women. The captain nodded frequently but asked no questions. When the account was complete, she said, "Wright and Paulino hadn't shown up in Woodside when I left three days ago. I think we can be skeptical of claims that they've gone there. I agree this Drummond seems suspect. Because she's an associate of known criminals, there should be no trouble getting a warrant, although I'm not too sure what we'll find."

"I think the merchants' guild would be very happy to loan us a couple of competent accountants to look through all of Drummond's paperwork—not just the bits she chooses to show to their auditors," Chip said. "And if we put the pressure on, maybe one of Drummond's women will tell us where Wright and Paulino really are."

Kalispera gave another sharp nod. "That might produce results. Do you want to apply for the warrant?"

"I think it would be better if the request came from the local Militia. I'll contact you once I've got the copy of the contract."

"Yes, I think you're right." Kalispera's lips pulled into a tight smile. "The case isn't proved yet, but you've done well to be onto it so quickly."

"We were lucky to have someone in our squadron who recognized the names of Wright and Paulino." Chip beckoned Katryn forward. "I know that you're already acquainted."

"Yes." Kalispera's smile became sour. "I hadn't expected to see you again so soon, Sergeant Nagata....Oh, but of course, you're not a sergeant anymore." The slip was blatantly deliberate. "Well, Sergeant Coppelli, *Private* Nagata, I will hope to hear from you shortly." The captain moved away.

"Ma'am." Chip snapped to attention to acknowledge the end of the meeting. She stared after the departing captain, her face blank but her thoughts in turmoil. She realized that Katryn had lied—about being court-martialed, about being demoted and possibly about much more.

❖

The crowd at the inn seemed identical to the one the night before, including the obliging trader, who was still casting hopeful eyes in Chip's direction. The Rangers managed to get the same cozy corner table, and the beer was just as good, but Chip took no enjoyment from it. She was in a miserable mood.

The afternoon had been productive, but in a negative way. After hours of hunting through cramped streets on the poorer side of town, they had not succeeded in tracking down any grieving relatives. They had found only two women who would even admit to having seen any of the deceased, and they had little to tell except for the names of people who might know more. By default, it seemed to prove that the three dead women had not been established figures in Landfall and, therefore, were unlikely to be longstanding employees of anyone.

Now Chip and Katryn sat in silence at the table. Katryn had made an effort to talk, but Chip had lacked the desire to reply; her short answers had died in her mouth. She felt like a fool to have taken Katryn so quickly on trust, yet it had made no sense for her to lie when the truth must come to light. Chip knew that she had desperately wanted Katryn to be innocent of any wrongdoing—or, more truthfully, she had desperately wanted Katryn. She dared not poke around at her own feelings to see whether she still did.

Captain Kalispera had made "Sergeant Nagata" sound like a slip of the tongue, but it had been a pointed dig, a reference to Katryn's past. Obviously, Kalispera knew the story. No wonder Katryn had wanted to avoid meeting her. The urge to go in search of the Militia captain and ask just what Katryn had done was almost irresistible. Chip clenched her teeth and swallowed. It could wait until they got back to Fort Krowe, when she would have the chance to read the full transcript of the court-martial.

Chip drained her beer. Getting drunk was not wise, but she did not want to sit looking at an empty tankard all night. "Do you want another?" she asked, offhand.

"Um…yes…okay." Katryn also sounded distracted.

Chip's eyebrows rose slightly in surprise. It was the first time she had known Katryn to match her in finishing a drink. Maybe now that Kalispera had broken Katryn's game of lies, she would reveal her true colors as a drunken lecher. It was not a nice thought.

Chip headed to the bar, her lips compressed tightly. She was waiting to get served when there was a voice at her shoulder.

"Well, Sergeant. What are my chances *this* night of getting you to accept a drink from me?" It was the trader.

Chip twisted her neck to see the woman standing, smiling, behind her. She took a deep breath. "It's…um…" Then Chip's expression changed slowly to a grin. "A lot better."

"Good. I was also hoping that I could…er…chat with you."

Why not? Chip asked herself. It might be the very thing to disentangle her emotions from Katryn. Aloud, she said, "I was getting a drink for my comrade as well."

The trader laughed. "I'll buy one for you both. I can afford it. Business has gone well this visit."

"That's awfully generous."

"I'm a generous person." Her eyes flicked across the room. "Do you want to go back and sit with your subordinate?"

A hint in the trader's tone on the last word made it clear that it was not only the Ranger's uniform that attracted her. She obviously took note of the rank insignia on the shoulder badge as well. *Of course, if she was looking at the woman wearing the uniform, there's no way she'd hit on me rather than Katryn,* Chip thought bitterly, and for a moment, her intention wavered. But the trader was merely being honest, and wasn't that what she wanted?

"I'd rather stay here and talk to you." Chip grinned again. "But I'll carry her drink over. I'll be back in a second."

Chip placed the full tankard in front of Katryn. "It's a present from my friend at the bar."

Katryn looked across the room at the smiling trader. "Friend? You know her?"

"Not quite as well as I'm expecting to in the next few hours," Chip whispered. "You don't mind me leaving you here, do you?" It was not Chip's usual practice to ditch another Ranger in this fashion, but Katryn was in no position to claim a comrade's loyalty.

Katryn looked uncomfortable and mumbled, "Oh…no. Of course not."

Chip took a half-step back. "I…er…should see you tomorrow morning."

Katryn nodded.

Back at the bar, the trader had wedged herself into a corner. "So, Sergeant, what exciting missions have you been on recently?"

"How gullible are you?" Chip asked.

"Why?"

"It makes a big difference in the story I tell."

"Which story is the most entertaining?"

"The one for the gullible—no question."

Chip started a tale of a bandit raid. It was soon apparent that the trader would have been just as interested in discussing fluctuations in the price of copper ore; the two did not have anything in common to talk about. But before long, the trader made the expected suggestion that they continue the conversation in her room upstairs. As they left the taproom, Chip glanced toward the table in the corner. Katryn's tankard was still there, but there was no sign of Katryn.

As soon as they were in the trader's room, all pretence of dialogue went. Chip put her arms around the woman and pulled her close. The trader's lips molded against hers, her breath coming fast and ragged. The kiss was long and forceful. In businesslike fashion, Chip removed the trader's clothes and then undressed herself. It had been a warm day, warm enough that there was no rush to get under the bedclothes. They stood naked in the center of the room. Chip nuzzled the trader's neck while her fingers traced the outline of shoulders, ribs and hips. The woman was very nicely constructed.

By the time they slipped between the sheets, they both were fully aroused. Passion would carry them over any hurdles of clumsiness with a stranger's body. It was going to be very easy, Chip knew. It was what she wanted—what she needed—a simple cure for heartache. All she had to do was stop herself from imagining that the woman in her arms was Katryn.

❖

"When you find the bitch, remind her she owes me ten dollars," the bricklayer snarled, peering down from the scaffolding.

"I'm afraid she's dead," Chip called up.

The brickie put down her trowel and swiveled around so that her legs dangled over the drop. Her face was as stony as the building she worked on. "I suppose that means I'm not going to get my ten dollars?" The woman snorted. "My own stupid fault for lending it to her. She had the room under mine, said she was new in town, needed a bit of cash to tide her over until she got work. Last I saw of her or the money. Jo said she got a job as guard on a wagon…was going to pay me when she got back."

"She was killed when the wagon was attacked."

"Was that it?" The woman's face became regretful. "Oh, well, best not to think ill of the dead. Perhaps she would have repaid me."

"Do you know anything else about her? Where she came from? Who are her relatives?"

"Not a clue."

"Do you know of anyone else who might?"

The woman shook her head. "Like I said, she was new in town."

"Okay. Thanks for your time."

The brickie returned to her work. Chip and Katryn left the building site. It exhausted the last of their leads on the dead women, but they had learned something. All three women had been new to Landfall. None of them had any relatives, lovers or close friends to start asking questions.

"You know, Drummond thought it all out very well," Chip conceded.

Katryn nodded but said nothing. She had been subdued all morning and had hardly eaten at lunch.

Chip went on. "She had the Militia—and us—wasting our time searching for the jewelry up by Redridge when it had never been anywhere near the place. A report of the robbery would have been sent back here, but there was no reason for the Landfall Militia to take any action on it. I'll bet Drummond offered to inform the relatives, knowing that nobody was going to give a damn that they were dead."

"Umm," Katryn agreed dejectedly.

Chip glanced sideways and felt her stomach flip. It was not that Katryn looked any more attractive when she was miserable—just that Chip felt the overwhelming urge to hug her. The night with the trader had not worked at all. Chip set her feet to a crisp march. She had to get a grip on her emotions.

Nothing else was said until they reached the merchants' guildhall. The porter by the door told them that Prudence Tang was not in her office and directed them to a nearby room, where a tired-looking clerk greeted them. The woman listened to their request as though she were being subjected to personalized victimization. Her posture gave the impression that it took vast amounts of energy for her to walk to a cupboard, take out the rolled sheet of paper and hand it over—not forgetting to shut the cupboard door after her. Then she returned to her work as though she had already forgotten the Rangers' existence.

Chip unrolled the sheet.

"What does it say?" Katryn asked, sounding livelier than she had so far that day.

"That Grosskopf is a fool." Chip smiled. "Well, maybe not in so many words. She paid a third of the money on order and another third on dispatch. The final installment was to be made when the jewelry arrived. The money was to be refunded only if Drummond was unable to ship before the end of the year, with some nicely artistic penalty clauses built in."

"Grosskopf didn't get a refund if the jewelry was stolen before it got to her?"

"Oh, no. In fact, that possibility is specifically mentioned in the contract. There's a financial-jeopardy clause, taking account of the unorthodox method of transport." Chip rolled up the paper. "And I think this concludes our investigation for today. I need to get back to our room and write out a report to hand on to Kalispera. The Militia can get their bits together and apply for a search warrant tomorrow."

"Is there anything for me to do?"

"No. You can take some time off. Look around the town."

"I think I might visit the baths."

"Good idea." *Especially if I don't go with you,* Chip added in her head.

The two left the guildhall and walked on until their routes separated. "Have a nice time. I'll see you at dinner," Chip called out. Katryn gave her a halfhearted smile and turned away.

❖

When she entered the room Chip saw that two letters had been slipped under the door. They lay, corners touching, on the scrubbed floorboards. Chip scooped them up, sat on her bed and broke the seal on the larger with her thumb. It was a dispatch from Captain LeCoup, written two days after she and Katryn had left Redridge.

Sergeant Coppelli:

Some information that may be of use to you.

Apparently, the thieves did not steal the wagons and horses, which were all left standing on the road with the bodies. It's something that the Militiawomen had not thought worth mentioning during their initial briefing. They considered it proof that the thieves were local women who did not need transport to remove their loot to a safe place—an interesting assumption, given that the wagons were ambushed in the middle of a forest.

Today, two of the Militiawomen took Sergeant O'Neil's patrol and me to see the site of the ambush. I did not expect to find much; however, O'Neil made an interesting discovery. Fifty meters from the road was a burned circle. It looked the right age for the robbery. Turf had been cut and replaced, and an attempt was made to hide the patch under dead leaves, but there was no excuse for the Militia's missing it.

Taken together, it seems obvious to me that the thieves knew the jewelry was inside the bales and were not interested in anything else. After killing the three women, the thieves took the jewelry from its hiding place and then destroyed the wool to cause confusion. That they felt they had enough time for this is pretty good evidence Wright and Paulino weren't racing back to Redridge to get help. I would say there must have been at least one more woman involved, to take away the small sack of jewelry, but possibly no others.

I sincerely hope that you are making more progress than we are.

Captain LeCoup

Chip smiled with satisfaction. More circumstantial evidence, but it tied in very neatly with the case she was building. Wright and Paulino waited until they were on a deserted stretch of road, murdered the other three women in the crew, removed the bales of wool and burned them to make it look like a robbery, and then ran back to Redridge with stories of an ambush. Chip shook her head at the idiocy of the Militia. Whoever heard of thieves leaving perfectly good horses behind? The animals provided their own transport and were extremely easy to sell.

Chip turned to the other letter. The address was written in Kim's handwriting. Chip looked at the outside apprehensively. Experience warned her that it would contain more teasing on the subject of Katryn, and she did not feel up to dealing with joking innuendoes. However, it would be better to read the letter now than when Katryn was present. Chip broke the seal and flipped the paper open.

Chip:

Just a quick warning. Your new girl has not been honest with you. I was talking to Ritche, and I mentioned the story about her being a late joiner. Ritche disputes it. She hasn't seen Katryn's full records, but she does know she's only got four more years of her enlistment period to go. When you add everything up, it leaves seven years to account for.

Sorry to be the one to pass on bad news. Look after yourself. If you get emotionally attached to her, you're going to be hurt.

Kim

Chip put down the piece of paper. The warning had come too late.

❖

Neither Chip nor Katryn suggested going out to find dinner, so they ended up eating in the mess. The food was not bad by military standards, but Chip could muster little enthusiasm. Katryn also spent more time looking at her meal than eating it. Chip talked about the contents of LeCoup's letter, but it was Kim's she was thinking of. It confirmed that she had not misheard, or misunderstood, Kalispera's words.

Afterward, they wandered back to their room. Katryn opened the window and stood staring out over the rooftops. "Are you going to meet with your trader again tonight?" She spoke without looking back.

"No. She left Landfall this morning, heading downriver." Chip lay slumped on her bunk with her arm over her eyes.

Katryn turned around and leaned on the windowsill. "I...er...I feel I've done something to annoy you. I thought at first, this morning, you were preoccupied with the trader, but you don't seem to be...happy with me." She bit her lip. "What have I done?"

Chip took a deep breath; then she sat up and swung her legs around. If Katryn wanted to force the issue, it was okay by her. "You've told me lies." She spoke bluntly.

"I...no, never." Katryn sounded genuinely bewildered.

"Okay. I asked you once informally. This time, it's an order, and I want the truth." Chip snapped out the words with a vehemence LeCoup would have been proud of.

Katryn sprung upright, her eyes fixed on the wall. "Yes, ma'am."

"What did you do to get court-martialed?"

"I swear I haven't been court-martialed, ma'am."

"Kalispera called you Sergeant, yet you told me you hadn't been demoted. You said you were a private because you hadn't been in the Rangers long enough to reach Leading Ranger. You enlisted ten years ago."

Katryn's cheeks were flushed. "I wasn't demoted, ma'am. I gave up my rank voluntarily."

"What?" Chip shouted in outraged anger.

"I told you the truth. I have only been in the Rangers for a year, but before that, I served nine years in the Militia. I was a sergeant in Woodside. The rank was forfeit when I joined the Rangers, which I knew when I applied."

Chip stared at Katryn, who was shaking visibly. "Why didn't you say that before?"

"Permission to talk informally, ma'am."

"Yes," Chip snapped.

"Because I know that not applying for the Rangers the day after you become eligible is proof that you're a fool and a coward, only fit for rounding up stray dogs."

"That's..." Chip's voice died. Maybe you did not have to apply bang on the day after, but some Rangers would see nine years in the Militia in those terms.

Chip bowed her head and interlaced her fingers behind her neck. It all sounded too glib. She did not know what to think, and for once, her instincts could not help her. She desperately wanted to believe Katryn and, for that very reason, distrusted her own judgment. Chip tried to work her way forward. "So why was Kalispera displeased to see you? It wasn't exactly a happy reunion when you met."

"Captain Kalispera didn't want me to leave the Militia. I can't prove it was her, but someone pulled strings to get me a promise of promotion to lieutenant if I withdrew my application to the Rangers." Katryn's lips compressed in a tight line. "She made a personal appeal to me to stay, but I ignored her. Now she feels angry, and I feel like a fool, because she was right. I shouldn't have left."

"And that's your story?"

"It's the truth, ma'am. You don't believe my word, but you could go and find Kalispera and ask her about it."

Chip got to her feet and stood directly in front of Katryn. She stared into her eyes; they were filling with tears, but they held no faltering, no deceit and no sign of bluffing. Chip did not know what to do or what to believe. The situation was hard enough, made impossible by her intense desire to kiss Katryn. Chip felt her arms starting to move of their own accord.

"I'm sorry. I shouldn't have…" Chip could not find the words she wanted. She stepped over to the window. Katryn remained at attention. "Oh, dismissed…stand down…whatever."

Katryn relaxed but stayed where she was. "I should have told you that I'd spent so long in the Militia, but I wanted a chance to prove myself…before I got prejudged."

Chip shrugged. She was partly convinced that there was something more that Katryn was not telling her, but she lacked the certainty to probe. Going in search of the Militia captain was not a good idea. Trust was vital to a patrol. How could she ever ask Katryn to trust her if she was not prepared to trust Katryn's word? It would be totally unjust if Katryn was telling the truth, and even if she were still lying, Chip did not want to deal with it until they were back in Fort Krowe. Or better still, let Captain LeCoup deal with it.

"Do you want me to come with you and find Kalispera?" Katryn asked.

"No. I want you to come with me to the inn and let me buy you a drink."

Katryn flinched but then nodded.

Outside the building, the air was fresher, and Chip felt calmer but no less unhappy. *Kiss and make up.* The words echoed in her head, along with the mental picture of giving Katryn a big hug and saying, "Sorry." The idea was not a safe one to play with. Chip glanced sideways. Katryn looked understandably subdued.

Chip cleared her throat. "While the Militia sort out the warrant tomorrow morning, we can take it easy. I can show you the sights."

"You don't think we should be there with the Militia at the magistrate's?"

Chip pulled a wry grimace. "Probably best if my face doesn't get seen. My sister, Honesty Coppelli, is the city's chief magistrate, and we never got along, even before I left home."

CHAPTER SIX—THE FIRST TIME

The great temple of Celaeno was awe-inspiring, or so Chip had been told. She could not remember it ever inspiring awe in her, only boredom and despair. However, in showing Katryn around the cavernous central hall, she felt that she was seeing a different aspect of the place. It was amazing what knowing you were free to walk out did for your perceptions.

The shrines to the Celaeno's servants, the Elder-Ones, filled every centimeter of wall space. Still more were clustered around the supporting pillars. The Blessed Himoti, greatest of the Elder-Ones, had her monument in the very middle of the hall. Her eternal flame danced in its crucible; its light flickered over the faces of worshippers.

Katryn appeared to be genuinely moved by the temple. Without going into religious rapture, she kneeled, bowed her head before Himoti's flame and prayed silently. She also paused to offer a short prayer to her namesake, Katryn Novak, the Elder-One who was patron of bakers. Chip waited for her to finish and then carried on around the perimeter of the hall.

Next, they stopped at the alcove housing the military shrine. In the middle stood the statue of Natasha Krowe, patron of Rangers, with her iron-gray hair and green skin. She was flanked on either side by Su Li Hoy of the Guards and David Croft of the Militia. Again, the colors reflected their followers' uniform. Su Li Hoy had yellow skin and bright red hair; David Croft's skin and hair were both jet black, making her the most monochromatic of the Elder-Ones. Chip could not restrain the grin that spread across her face; she knew how much it rankled the Guards that the Rangers' patron took the central position, but the Rangers were the oldest branch of the military.

The two women went on and paused again outside the entrance to the sanctum. Six Guards stood on sentry duty by the hanging drapes that hid the secret inner part of the temple from view. The women stood stiffly at attention in their dazzling red and gold uniforms, long swords drawn and held upright. Candlelight glinted off their helmets and braid.

"Don't they look pretty?" Chip spoke just loud enough for the Guards to hear. She was rewarded by seeing a flush darken the face of the youngest. The jeering was part of the ritual contest played between Rangers and Guards. Chip did not push things any further. It was unfair to taunt when the Guards could not retaliate and, at odds of six against two, unwise to do it when they could.

"Did you used to go in there?" Katryn whispered, pointing to the curtains.

"No. That's the inner sanctum. Only full Sisters and Imprinters are allowed in. As an initiate, I got no further than the outer sanctum."

A faint stirring disturbed the hall behind them. Chip glanced over her shoulder and drew Katryn out of the way. A small group was marching toward the entrance to the sanctum, an escort of six more Guards. Chip knew that they would take particular pleasure in shoving Rangers aside if they got the chance. In the center was another woman, clad in simple blue: an Imprinter.

For the first time, something like awe did sweep over Chip. Imprinting was the one great mystery that the Sisters could not reduce to tedium. Imprinters were the ones chosen by the Goddess to receive Himoti's gift: the gift of calling new human souls into existence. They were the ones so strongly blessed with the healer sense they could not merely cure sickness and injury or induce cloning in farm animals, but also imprint genetic patterns on an embryo. It was the gift of Imprinters to copy DNA sequences from a gene mother to the cloned cell inside her partner's womb, creating a new life that was not a soulless clone but a true human, a daughter of the Goddess.

Chip felt her mouth go dry as the woman in blue was ushered by and disappeared through the hanging drapes of the sanctum.

"Did you ever meet an Imprinter?" Katryn asked.

"Who, me? You're joking. Despite my parents' money, I was the lowest of the low—especially after I entertained my schoolmates by demonstrating my scoring ability at basketball, using the Chief Consultant's knickers as a goal."

"You did what?"

"It was one of my failed attempts to get expelled."

"How…?"

"She wasn't wearing them at the time. I raided the laundry."

"But…"

Chip laughed and pointed to the exit. "Come on. We'd better go if we want to be on time for the briefing."

They passed under the high arched doorway of the temple and into the day outside. A soft drizzle was falling, but the weather showed signs of brightening. The gardens surrounding the temple held the first misty suggestion of sunshine.

"You don't seem very devout," Katryn began hesitantly after a few steps.

"The Chief Consultant's underwear isn't mentioned anywhere in *The Book of the Elder-Ones*, so it can't be that sacred," Chip joked. Then she became more serious. "But you're right. I tend to be a bit of a skeptic."

"But you were educated by the Sisters."

"That's why." The pair reached the exit from the temple grounds and strolled into the street beyond. "Most people in the school wanted to be there. I didn't, so I wasn't quite so ready to believe everything I was told, without question. And then, when I became an initiate, I got to read some of the books that aren't revealed to the general public. Which is when I realized that 90 percent of what's in the temple is a load of rubbish."

"Like what?"

"The statues of the Elder-Ones, for example. All the green skin and blue hair. The Elder-Ones weren't that different from us. I've seen old pictures of them."

"But it says in *The Book of the Elder-Ones*: 'Their skins were diverse in tone, and their hair was yellow and red and black, and all the shades between. And some were tall, and hair grew on their faces.'"

"But not that diverse. All the Elder-Ones had conventional brown skin. It was just that the shades varied far more than you see today. Some were so light-colored that they were even referred to as white, though they were really a pale beige, and others were very much darker. We'd all fit somewhere in the middle of the range."

"And the hair?"

"Some did have yellow hair, but it was a bit rare. The Elder-Ones usually had dark brown hair, just like us. Most of them could walk down the street today and not attract a second glance from anyone."

"Except for those with hair on their faces?"

Chip laughed. "They might. However, those who had it often shaved it off."

"I'd always wondered if it got in the way when they were eating." Katryn matched Chip's smile. They walked a few more yards in silence before she continued, "If it's in the books, why don't the Sisters sort the statues out?"

"Because Sisters who rock the boat don't get promoted, and life inside the temple sanctum is the most ruthless, cutthroat, backstabbing battlefield I've ever had the misfortune to witness."

"The Sisters are supposed to be the guardians of truth."

"The Sisters are also supposed to be compassionate, meek and celibate."

Katryn looked shocked. "You mean they're not?"

"No. On all three counts. And the Chief Consultant is probably—" Chip broke off sharply. It was not a wise conversation to have in the middle of a street in Landfall. She fought the impulse to look back over her shoulder to see who was listening. "Er…perhaps we should discuss it another time. This isn't really the place. We could just manage a quick look around the market before we need to get to the briefing."

Katryn opened her mouth as if to ask another question; then she, too, seemed to realize the risk of being overheard and nodded her agreement.

As ever, the market was crowed. Sounds, smells and gaudy colors fought in a riot for the senses. The two Rangers sauntered between stalls laid out with goods from all over the Homelands. If something could not be found in the market at Landfall, it probably did not exist. Neither bought anything, although not for lack of effort on the part of the traders they passed.

"Do you think the Militia will get the warrant?" Katryn asked.

"Kalispera seemed confident, and they stand a better chance without me there. Honesty and I always used to enjoy irritating each other. She'd probably ask for extra information just for the fun of watching me run around."

They walked on farther, leaving the market square and heading toward the Militia station. Katryn's face was creased in thought. At last,

Chip asked. "What are you thinking?"

"I'm trying to work out what 'Chip' is short for."

"It's not short for anything. It's a small fried piece of potato."

Katryn gave a yelp of laughter. "I think not. I've just got the handle on your parents' idea of names: Prudence, Constance, Mercy, Honesty. I just can't see how 'Chip' fits in."

Chip bit her lip to hide her smile. "I'll give you a clue. 'Chip' has nothing to do with what my parents called me. I got the nickname when I was six, and I've clung to it. It's a big improvement."

"That isn't much of a clue."

Chip's smile escaped. "How about…my mothers picked names to help us in our careers. They felt the merchants would like entrusting the guild to someone called Prudence, and you couldn't doubt the fairness of a magistrate called Honesty. Now remember, I was headed for the Sisterhood…"

"I know," Katryn exclaimed. "Faith."

"Oh, they probably would have liked to, but I'm afraid Great-Aunt Faith disgraced the family some while back, and the name has been out of bounds since."

The lines on Katryn's forehead deepened. "Chastity, Devotion, Diligence…"

"She's the tax auditor," Chip interjected.

Katryn dissolved in stifled giggles. "No, I can't guess."

"You don't have to. Prudence called me by my name when we met. Obviously, you weren't paying attention. They named me Piety." Chip was fighting with her own laughter. "My parents were cruel bitches."

Chip felt light-headed standing close by Katryn, sharing laughter. She did not know whether she totally believed Katryn's story but could not bear to let the doubts surface. She suspected that there was more to come out, and Katryn was still holding back on her for some reason. Yet Chip knew, in the depths of her being, that she trusted Katryn as a Ranger should trust a comrade: with her life.

❖

More than twenty women were crammed into the briefing room at the Militia station. Captains Gutmann and Kalispera stood at the front, giving the necessary background and assigning roles. Most of the assembled squad of black-clad Militiawomen were squashed onto benches; others lined the walls. The two accountants from the merchants' guild sat to one side. Their faces looked as though they were trying to project "serious professional" but were at risk of lapsing into "kids on a picnic." Chip and Katryn were in a corner at the back. Chip was resigned to the Militia's taking control, because it was providing the manpower, but she had been angered by initial suggestions that the Rangers would play no part in the raid at all. In the end it had been an unexpected piece of news that had settled the issue.

Gutmann was moving on to the discovery. "Wright and Paulino have kept their noses clean since they've been in Landfall, so we haven't had dealings with them. One of our regular informants is a delivery girl who works in the area. We decided to tap her to see if she could tell us anything interesting. She knew who we were referring to, couldn't say much about the pair—thinks they've made several lengthy trips out of town. But one thing she could say is that they aren't out of town at the moment. She saw Wright at Drummond's place yesterday morning. So much for their visit to relatives."

Gutmann gestured toward the back of the room. "Since they know our colleagues from the Rangers are in town looking for them, we think they'll be staying out of sight, so we've got good hopes of finding them in Drummond's house. But they might try to bolt when the raid starts. There are two rear exits. We want to have people waiting outside both, and we want someone there who will recognize our suspects. Unfortunately, their faces aren't well known in Landfall, but we have Captain Kalispera from Woodside and Ranger Private Nagata, who are familiar with the pair. Captain Kalispera will be on the gates to the stable block. Private Nagata will be on the scullery door. Ideally, we don't want anyone to leave, but our top priority is to catch Wright and Paulino. If they are spotted, make damn certain they don't get away."

The Militia captain went on to name the members of each group and to allocate specific duties. "We go on the first strike of the noon bell. Any questions?"

"Are they likely to be carrying weapons?" one of the Militiawomen called from the center of the floor.

Gutmann turned to Kalispera for an answer. "They'll both fight if cornered, and Paulino often carries a knife. Wright usually relies on talking her way out of things. If they're forced to make a run for it, they won't have time to grab anything nasty on the way out."

"Why didn't they use false names in Redridge?" someone else asked.

Gutmann snorted. "We'll ask them when we catch them. My guess is that it kept the paperwork aboveboard. Remember, it was a real long shot that they were recognized."

"Do we have a description of what this jewelry is supposed to look like?"

"It's in the contract. The accountants have it. But it's likely the jewelry never existed and Drummond just pocketed the money."

Chip looked around the room as the questions continued. The only one that interested her was the first. The Militia traditionally went armed with long batons, although swords and bows were issued when necessary. Because of the triple murder, this was judged to be one of those occasions. It probably was what had prompted the question. However, Chip wondered how proficient the Militiawomen were with the weapons. She would have liked to have had a few more trained Rangers. Her sweeping scan of the room finished on Katryn, who was passable with a sword—just.

Chip leaned over and whispered, "You said you're better with a bow?"

"Yes, ma'am."

"A lot better? A little better?"

"A lot better, ma'am," Katryn said confidently.

"Take your bow with you."

❖

The scullery door to Drummond's kitchen opened onto a small yard, which in turn provided access to the side street via an iron gate. Currently, both gate and door were ajar, although nobody had gone in or out for a while. Chip waited with Katryn and three Militiawomen in the shadow of a nearby alley, at a point where they could see the gate without being visible from the house.

The Militiawomen fidgeted with their weapons while they exchanged comments, excluding the two Rangers from their conversation as much as possible. Chip considered them. The sergeant appeared to be competent, but like her subordinates, she was overeager to show that she was just as good as a Ranger. The risk was that this attitude would push them to do something stupid in a crisis. Katryn looked calm but preoccupied. She had checked her bow and arrows once and now stood with her eyes fixed on the gate.

The side street was no more than three meters wide and virtually deserted, although the sounds of passersby echoed from the main thoroughfare at the end. The cobbles were worn, and some were missing. The walls on either side rose high, with few windows and less ornamentation. Signs of the area's new prosperity had not yet spread down this back way. A group of laborers had been busy at the junction with the main street, although they were gone now, presumably at lunch. Several of their larger tools were leaning against the wall.

The temple bell struck the hour of midday. Like runners in a sprint, the Militiawomen surged forward. Chip and Katryn followed more slowly, and by the time they reached the entrance to the yard, the three Militiawomen were lined in front of the scullery door, swords drawn. Chip stood in the gateway. The enclosed area was four meters square, empty apart from two broken barrels and a small heap of rotten sacking. She looked up just in time to catch someone leaping back from an upstairs window.

Chip turned her head to speak to Katryn, who was directly behind her. "Our friends can mind the door. I'll stay here. You would be better some way back, where you can get a clean shot if necessary."

"Yes, ma'am." Katryn retreated several steps.

Chip continued standing in the gateway. For a while, there was no sign of anything happening. Then she heard shouts inside the building, but it was impossible to make out any words. The Militiawomen were getting twitchy again.

Abruptly, the scullery door was wrenched wide open; a head poked out, saw the Militia and ducked back in again. The door slammed shut. The Militia privates seemed unsure whether to pursue the attempted absconder, but the sergeant ordered them to stay put. Chip mentally nodded her approval. The waiting went on.

"Sergeant!" Katryn called urgently.

Chip twisted around. Katryn had positioned herself on the other side of the street, in the mouth of the alley. She was pointing past Chip's shoulder, up toward the junction with the main road. Chip's head turned, following the direction of her outstretched hand.

Figures were moving on the roof, from which a rope had been lowered. One woman was just reaching ground level, and a second was clambering out over the edge of the roof, preparing to follow. Two others were there assisting, although it was unclear whether they would also try to climb down or merely remove the rope and other evidence after the escapees had fled.

"It's them!" Katryn shouted.

Chip didn't need the confirmation. She yelled to the Militia and charged up the street.

The first woman was standing on the ground now, holding the rope steady and looking up. At the sound of Chip's cry, she backed off a step; then she turned and ran. The second woman flung herself down the rope, using her hands merely to slow the speed of her descent. She let go two meters from the ground and dropped the rest of the way.

The woman hit the cobbles hard, her foot twisting, sending her staggering sideways. She recovered her balance immediately and turned to follow her companion—but too late. Chip made a diving tackle and hurled the fugitive to the ground. The impact must have driven the air from the woman's body, but desperation gave her strength. She struggled violently, reaching for her waist, and then Chip saw the knife.

Chip cracked the heel of her hand up under the woman's chin, snapping her head back. She grabbed the wrist and smashed the hand gripping the knife down onto the cobbles. Still the woman clung to her weapon and fought on, but Chip had gained the mastery. She sat astride the woman's chest, pinning both of her wrists against the ground. From down the street came the sound of the Militiawomen racing to her aid. Then Chip heard other, closer footsteps. She looked up. The first woman was returning, brandishing above her head a long iron crowbar, no doubt taken from the laborers' discarded tools.

Time slowed to a crawl. Chip watched the attacking woman seem to float closer; at the same time, she was aware of the woman beneath her, who was also armed and struggling. There was no way to avoid the iron bar without releasing the hand holding the knife. *I've got a choice*, Chip thought. *I can sit here and get brained or move away and get stabbed.* She had hours to make up her mind but could reach no sensible conclusion. The sound of the Militiawomen was very close but not close enough to matter.

Suddenly, feathers sprouted on the chest of the woman who was wielding the bar. She shuddered to a halt, looking just as surprised as Chip. But Chip's confusion faded faster; she had seen such things enough times before. She did not need to wait for the patch of red blood to seep through the woman's clothes or for her ears to recognize the hiss as the flight of an arrow. The shot woman still looked bewildered, unable to work out what had happened, but her legs were failing her. The crowbar twisted and slipped from her fingers. It hit the ground at the same time as her knees. And then the Militiawomen arrived. Two of them needlessly hauled the dying woman back; the third joined Chip and tore the knife from the hand of the woman on the ground.

The Militiawomen were shouting to one another in three disjointed conversations. The sergeant shouted the loudest. "This one's finished! Help Sergeant Coppelli get the other tied up!"

The captured woman was dragged to her knees, and her arms were pulled behind her back. For the first time, she saw the state of her companion and screamed, "Clary! You fucking assholes! I'll kill you. I—" She broke into sobs.

"Too late; you've missed your chance." The sergeant was smug. She looked at the dead woman lying on the ground and then at Chip. "I hope that wasn't just a very lucky shot by your private. I felt the arrow go past."

Chip turned her head. Katryn was still standing by the gateway, her bow hanging loose in her hands. It was a distance of, at most, twenty meters—a close-range shot. But the sergeant was right. It was not what Katryn had hit that was impressive; it was what she had missed. With three women running up the narrow street and Chip kneeling in front of the target, shooting the woman must have been like threading a needle by throwing cotton at it. Chip remembered the confidence in Katryn's voice when she had said, "A lot better." She had not been idly boasting.

Chip's gaze narrowed to Katryn's face. What she saw prompted her to stand, leaving the captive in the care of the Militiawomen, and walk back down the street. Katryn did not move. Her eyes were fixed on the dead woman, her face a mask of horrified disbelief. It was an expression that Chip was also familiar with: the spontaneous gut response of a woman who, for the first time, has killed another human being.

CHAPTER SEVEN—RUMORS

K atryn still appeared to be disorientated back at the Militia station as the initial reports were gathered. She answered questions when they were put to her but volunteered nothing. Her first spontaneous words came during the walk to their quarters, when she said she wanted to visit the baths. Chip nodded, understanding the common and futile wish to metaphorically wash the blood from your hands.

Afterward, they again took dinner in the mess. There was no point in paying for food that Katryn would not taste. She ate each mouthful as though she were having to concentrate on working out how to swallow. Chip kept an attempt at conversation going, confined mainly to issues within the 23rd Squadron, although Katryn did little more than nod in the right places. Chip watched her in sympathy, remembering the first time she had killed someone. She had been five months in the Rangers, a private in Sergeant O'Neil's patrol.

It had been high summer. The patrol had spent four days on the trail of a gang of cattle thieves and had finally overtaken them at dawn. Ash had called on the gang to surrender, but they had come out fighting. Chip, inexperienced, had been caught on her own when one of the gang rushed at her, waving an old sword that looked better suited for use as a meat cleaver. Chip had avoided the bandit's clumsy swipe easily. Then she had moved in, ducking the backswing and driving her own sword into the woman's body.

Chip could not forget a single detail. She had used the classic stroke that the Rangers taught new recruits; the point of her sword had entered under the bandit's ribcage and angled upward to slice the heart and lungs. She imagined that she could still feel the texture of the flesh transmitted through the hilt of her sword to her hand. Fixed in her memory were the odd sound at the back of the dying woman's throat and unrelated details: the smell of mint-grass and cattle, the pattern of stitching on the woman's shirt, the taste of dust in her mouth. The only thing Chip could not recall was the woman's face. In her dreams for years after, it had been a faceless corpse that had fallen against her and crumpled to the ground.

But Chip could remember her state of mind that night—the unrelenting rerunning of the fight through her head, the pointless questions. The Rangers had handed the surviving members of the gang over to the Militia in the nearest town. Afterward, Ash had dragged Chip to a tavern, bought a bottle of rough spirits and poured most of it down her throat. Years later, when Chip had also become a sergeant, the two had spoken about the incident. Ash had said getting drunk was not a good way of coping with the reaction, but it was better than anything else she had come up with.

It had been a long time since the dead bandit had intruded into Chip's dreams, but she still had only to close her eyes to revisit the scene. Chip flexed her hand, trying to dispel the tactile memory of the sword hilt and the feeling of resistance as the blade slid into the body. She looked across the table. Katryn's eyes were fixed on her plate, although it was doubtful that she saw it or anything else in the mess hall. The remains of her food were starting to congeal. It was obvious that she would eat no more.

"Come on. I'm taking you to the inn," Chip said as she stood.

Katryn looked up. "I don't know. I'm not sure I want—"

"Believe me. You want to come to the inn with me."

Katryn lacked the will to protest further until they were seated in the taproom and Chip had placed a large shot of brandy next to Katryn's tankard of beer. "I don't drink spirits."

"You do tonight."

"No." Katryn shook her head. "You don't understand. My gene mother...I swore on her grave I'd never...She was murdered by a drunk. It wasn't an outlaw, not even a petty crook—just an ordinary woman who drank too much and lost control and killed someone...like me today." She was rambling.

"You weren't out of control."

Katryn showed no sign of hearing. "It was like hitting a straw target. You'd think a woman would be different. I can still feel the string on my fingers, feel the bow jerk as I loosed the arrow. And when it hit, I felt that"—she clenched her fist—"that…flash of triumph…like waiting for a judge to call bull's-eye. Then she fell down and died. It was just like target practice. But a woman should be different."

"A woman *is* different. That's why you're sitting here with your head in pieces."

"It was so easy."

"I wouldn't have said it was an easy shot. I couldn't have managed it."

Katryn's face twitched in a quick grimace. "The Militia in the way didn't help, but I couldn't have missed at that range. She didn't stand a chance."

Chip considered Katryn. She had said the words far too matter-of-factly to be boasting. It might be worth finding out just how good she was with a bow, but that could wait.

"Katryn, I know how you feel. We've all been through it. Drink the brandy. It blurs the mind so you can't think straight, and when you've had enough, you'll sleep. You'll wake up tomorrow feeling like shit. You'll be sick and have a headache. It will be lunchtime before you'll be in a fit state to worry about anyone else. By then, Clarinda Wright will have been dead a whole day, and you'll have enough distance to be able to cope with it." Chip picked up the glass of brandy and held it out. "If your gene mother were here tonight, she'd tell you to drink this."

Katryn met Chip's gaze. For a while, neither moved. Then Katryn's lips twisted as her eyes filled with tears. She reached for the glass.

❖

At the end of the evening, Chip had to half carry Katryn back to the room. They staggered out of the inn and along the road. Katryn babbled some story from her childhood about a game of football that had become a fight. Clarinda's name was featured, though the recounting was so disjointed, it was not clear whether Clarinda was the hero or the villain. *Of course,* Chip thought, *that is one big difference. I had never met the bandit before. I never even knew her name. But Katryn grew up with the woman she killed.* Chip was not sure whether that made things better or worse. At least there would be fewer unanswered questions.

Their irregular footsteps took them through the archway and across the main square of the compound. Their room was not much farther.

Katryn was still rambling. "Her fam'ly won't wanna buy any more bread...Mama won't be pleased...she never is w' me...she and Cy..." Her voice ground to a halt, and she slumped against a wall.

Chip stood protectively close to ensure that Katryn did not fall. Abruptly, Katryn's shoulders started to shake with sobs. Without hesitation, Chip wrapped her arms around Katryn and hugged her close, stroking her back. It was what she would have done for any Ranger in similar distress, but Chip could not shake off the awareness that it was Katryn she was holding. She tried to ignore the effect it was having on her, tried to stop herself from enjoying the feel of Katryn's body filling her arms, and she partially succeeded.

After a while, Katryn calmed down, but she still leaned against Chip. Her face was buried in Chip's shoulder, and at some stage, her arms had wrapped around Chip's waist. *Cuddling like a pair of lovers.* Chip mentally stamped on the thought. She tried to pull back slightly, ready to suggest that they carry on walking, but Katryn's grip remained firm, and she began talking again. "I shouldn't have joined the Rangers. I can't cope with it. I don't like killing people."

"There's no place in the Rangers for anyone who does," Chip said firmly.

"I'm no good as a Ranger."

"You're doing fine."

Katryn moved her head slightly, burrowing into Chip's neck. "It's better in the 23rd. In the 12th...my sergeant there, she and I...we..." Katryn broke off, gulping air.

She was the affair that got you transferred, Chip surmised, but Katryn's next words went in completely the opposite direction.

"I didn't get along with her...not like you. I like you. You're nice."

Katryn's arms tightened around Chip, who was caught so completely off guard that she failed to react as one of Katryn's hands slipped up under her jacket while the other dropped down, pressing their hips hard together. Katryn's head twisted; her lips brushed Chip's throat and started to climb toward her mouth. The hand on Chip's back was trying to pull her shirt free from her waistband. It was something that had to be stopped, Chip knew, if they were not to regret it deeply the next day. She did not know where she found the willpower, but somehow, Chip mustered the resolve to peel Katryn off her.

Katryn stood swaying, fighting to focus her eyes. Her expression was surprised, then upset, and then surprised again. The final shift was one that Chip recognized very well after eight years in the Rangers. She was just able to direct Katryn's head in a safe direction and get out of the way in time as the drunken woman threw up in the gutter. It was, Chip thought, a pretty good summing-up of her love life in general.

Afterward, Chip maneuvered Katryn into the latrine block and got her cleaned up. Katryn sat on a water butt, looking dazed. "I'm sorry, ma'am, I didn't mean..."

Chip patted her shoulder. "I know you didn't mean it. Come on. Time for sleep."

In the room, Katryn collapsed on her bunk. As Chip removed Katryn's boots and outer clothing, she kept a firm grip on her thoughts, letting her eyes focus only on each button in turn. There was no way that Chip would let herself sink to the level of getting an emotionally vulnerable subordinate drunk and then seducing her. Chip folded the clothes into a neat pile beside the bed.

"You don't have to stop there," Katryn mumbled indistinctly.

Chip turned her head, but Katryn's eyes were closed, and within a few seconds, it was obvious that she was fast asleep. Chip tugged the blankets free and arranged them over Katryn; then she stood, staring down at the sleeping face. For herself, Chip felt quite sober; she had not attempted to match Katryn drink for drink.

Eventually, Chip turned away and pushed open the window. She hitched one leg up onto the sill. Wisps of thin cloud obscured half the sky, shielding the stars over Landfall, but the auras of both moons were visible through it. The fuzzy crescent of Laurel was low, brushing the rooftops, while the larger glowing orb of Hardie hung high overhead. The air was crisp. Chip leaned her head back against the window frame and considered the town of her birth.

She was pleased that she had returned to Landfall; it had given her the chance to put her past in context. It was a process not so much of laying ghosts to rest as of finding out that they no longer existed. The spirits had been exorcised years ago; she just had not noticed until she went looking for them. Her family had no hold on her, and the temple had no hold on her. She might have been running away from them to join the Rangers, but she had ended up where she belonged.

Meeting Prudence had been the point of illumination. Chip had spoken to Katryn afterward to prove to herself that she could, with a swelling sense of freedom. And Prudence had asked her not if she was financially solvent, or in line for promotion, but if she was happy. It was a choice of question that said much about Prudence's own situation.

Of course, happiness did not mean that she had no problems. Chip shifted around, turning her back on the rooftops. Katryn was now snoring. Chip studied her outline in the moonlight. She remembered Katryn hugging her, trying to kiss her—and she had stopped Katryn. Chip groaned softly, but she had no regrets. Katryn had been drunk and upset, probably not even fully aware of who she was with. If Chip had taken advantage of Katryn's situation, she would never have forgiven herself. It would have been deeply wrong—an abuse of trust.

Chip sighed and let her eyes return to the scene outside the window. Of course, it was just as well that Katryn had been drunk and had not meant it. If, by the grace of the Goddess, Katryn should ever come to return her feelings, they would be doomed. It would be blatantly obvious to everyone it was more than a comradely sharing of a bed, and the Ranger command would simply separate them. That would go badly against Katryn, to be transferred between squadrons twice.

A bitter grin at her own expense spread over Chip's face—adding things up like there was ever a serious chance of it happening. With Katryn's looks, she could have just about anybody she wanted, and Chip had no expectation of ever coming toward the top of anyone's list. It went without saying that someone like Katryn would have to be blind drunk to take the slightest interest in someone like her. And there lay the only hope for a solution. Unrequited love would not last forever. Someday, it would fade. But until then, Chip knew that she did love Katryn with every scrap of her being.

It was several days before Chip and Katryn were free to leave Landfall. They had to give evidence at the preliminary hearings against Drummond and Paulino, and to provide sworn testaments to the magistrate (fortunately, not Chip's sister) who would try the case. There was also a brief inquest into the death of Clarinda Wright.

When they were not occupied with these matters, the pair spent their time in a wandering tour of Landfall. Chip even discovered an odd affection for the city as she showed Katryn around. They accepted an invitation to dinner with Prudence and her family, to the delight of Chip's young nieces, who were overwhelmed to have two real live Rangers in the house. Chip called in on three more of her sisters, the favorite ones, and ignored the rest—including her parents.

The best bit for her was an unexpected appearance by Sandy, her mother's retired bodyguard. The elderly woman met Chip with tears in her eyes, words spilling from her mouth. "I was sorry to throw you out. You know I didn't want to, but your mother ordered, and I couldn't say no. But you shouldn't have made off that night. You should have waited round the back. I came looking for you as soon as I could—searched half of Landfall. I knew you wouldn't return to the sanctum. You always were too damned stubborn." The two had hugged and headed to the inn for an evening of drunken reminiscences. That night, Katryn was the one to carry Chip back to their room.

October was half gone by the time they left for Fort Krowe. Chip and Katryn made haste to rejoin the rest of their squadron, but rain and bad weather slowed them down. The trees along the road were covered in red and orange. As they got closer to the mountains, they could see the snow already beginning to creep down the slopes. It was going to be a long winter.

As they rode the last few kilometers to Fort Krowe, Chip studied the cluster of buildings on the hillside above the town. "I wonder if the rest of the 23rd will be there waiting for us."

"Surely they'd have gotten back weeks ago," Katryn said.

"I was thinking they may have been sent out again. We'll never get to stay here all winter. I'll bet the border divisions have already put in requests for reinforcements."

"Will they need it?"

"They will by spring." Chip turned to look at Katryn. "Have you had any encounters with snow lions yet?"

"Yes, once." Katryn's tone implied that once was enough. "They're nasty."

"I know. A Ranger in another patrol was killed by them."

Chip's face became grim. "It can happen."

They learned that the 23rd was still billeted at Fort Krowe and had been back from Redridge for two weeks. Chip and Katryn arrived just in time to unsaddle their horses and give a full briefing to Captain

LeCoup and Lieutenant Ritche before dinner. Their arrival in the mess hall was greeted by friendly shouts and lighthearted banter.

Chip slipped into her place at the C Patrol table with strangely mixed feelings. It was good to be surrounded by all her comrades, and it would be less strain now that she would no longer be forced into such close personal contact with Katryn, but she was not sure that less strain was really what she wanted. Katryn's company was the most enjoyable torment she had ever known. However, she was so busy talking that she did not have time to think about it. Everyone wanted to hear what had happened in Landfall.

After the meal, Kim caught up with Chip by the door. "I need to have a word with you."

"In the tavern of your choice?" Chip suggested.

Kim shook her head. "Not the right venue."

"What is it?" Chip was apprehensive at the expression on Kim's face.

"Not here. Come over to my room."

Chip followed her friend across the parade ground to B Patrol's bunkhouse. As sergeant, Kim had a small private room at the end. Kim closed the door and sat down on the edge of her bed, leaving the padded lid of the chest opposite for Chip. Her expression was serious.

"You got my note about Katryn?" Kim asked.

"Yes, thanks. But she hadn't, strictly speaking, been lying. I challenged her, and—"

Kim interrupted. "Yes. I know. When we got back here, Ritche looked at her records. I admit it was something I hadn't thought of." She paused. "Nine years in the Militia. Did she tell you why she left?"

"No. I didn't ask."

Kim looked faintly uncomfortable. "Did you get along well?"

Chip could not help smiling. "Are you trying to find out if we slept together?"

"Not quite that simple. But since you've raised the issue…?"

Chip shook her head.

"Do you still want to?"

"Kim!" Chip protested, mainly from confusion. "Where is this going?"

Kim combed her fingers through her hair. "I just wondered how you got along. What you made of her as a person. How you would sum her up."

"I like her." Chip caught her lip in her teeth. "And since you asked, yes, I do still want to sleep with her, but I'm not planning on doing it."

"She didn't tell you why she left the Militia after nine years?"

"No. I've already told you that."

"Did she tell you why she was transferred from the 12th?"

"No."

"Do you think she's been completely honest with you? Is she trustworthy?"

Chip hesitated before answering. "I think she's still holding something back. But I trust her."

A frown appeared on Kim's face. She pinched the bridge of her nose as though she were trying to ease it, or to muster her thoughts. At last, she began. "Ash has some contacts in Eastern Division. She's got contacts everywhere. She sent a letter to a friend there, to see what was known about Katryn...why she was transferred. Ash got a letter back yesterday morning. What it said was..." Kim sighed and looked at Chip. "It said she murdered her patrol sergeant...stabbed her in the back."

"What!" Chip shouted in disbelief and then slumped back in her seat. "Oh, come on, Kim. Be sensible. If she'd murdered someone, she'd have been strung up by the neck, not transferred to another squadron."

"What Ash's friend said was that everyone knew she'd done it, but it couldn't be proved. She'd have been lynched if she'd stayed in the 12th, so they had to move her."

"How could anyone *know* she'd done it if there was no proof?"

"Apparently, there was no direct evidence, but the sergeant was found with a trail knife in her back, and Katryn was the only one with the opportunity to put it there."

"If there had been any sort of case to answer, they wouldn't have let her go."

"Logically, you're right," Kim conceded. "But we don't know the circumstances. That's why I asked for your impression of her."

Chip closed her eyes and covered her face with her hands, thinking. Eventually, she dropped her arms and looked up. "She didn't do it."

"You sound very sure."

"I am."

"Why?"

"You heard she killed one of the bandits in Landfall—a pretty neat shot with a bow. I saw her reaction. It was the first time she'd ever killed anyone."

"Are you sure it wasn't just a prod to a guilty conscience?"

"Yes," Chip answered simply.

"It's not exactly conclusive proof."

"That puts it level with the evidence against her. She didn't do it. I'd stake my life on it."

"It might come to that if she's in the habit of sticking knives into her patrol sergeant."

"I owe her my life as it is. That thug would have killed me if Katryn hadn't shot her first. But you weren't there. You didn't see how it affected her. I tell you, she's never killed anyone else."

Kim pursed her lips. "The letter also said there were rumors she'd left the Militia to escape some trouble that was catching up with her."

"Rumors?" Chip made the question a challenge.

Kim gave a dismissive wave of the hand as a reply.

"Who else knows what was in the letter?"

"Just Ash and me. We wanted to wait until you got back."

Chip stood up. "Okay. I'll try to get some answers."

"How?"

"Like before. I'm going to ask her."

"You already have," Kim pointed out.

"This time, I'm going to ask for the complete story. Nothing less than the whole truth."

❖

Katryn was in the C Patrol bunkhouse when Chip entered, talking to Lee Horte and some others from the patrol. They were asking about the raid on Drummond's, and Katryn was clearly being modest about her archery skills.

"Here she is at last," Lee exclaimed, spotting Chip. "We were about to head off to a tavern but thought we'd see what you were doing."

"It's okay. I have something I need to sort out up here."

"You're trying to tell us we needn't have wasted valuable drinking time waiting for you?" Lee joked ironically. "Okay, let's go. We'll be in the Cat and Fiddle if you have time later." She went to the door, with the rest of the patrol trailing behind.

"Um...Private Nagata," Chip spoke up. "I'll need you to stay here as well."

"Yes, ma'am." Katryn stopped immediately. Like the others, she had a Ranger's thick winter cloak around her shoulders. After a quick questioning glance at Chip, she took it off and hung it in her locker.

When the others had gone, Chip indicated the door to her room. "We'll talk in there."

All four of the bunkhouses were identical in layout, including the sergeant's accommodation. The room was not large; the bed completely filled one wall. The only other furniture was a cupboard; a low chest with padded lid that served as a seat; and a small folding table, which currently was collapsed against a wall. Chip pointed Katryn to the chest. She considered remaining standing, but in the end, she sat on the edge of her bed, reversing her position from the conversation in Kim's room. Katryn waited for Chip to start talking. Her expression was mystified, but Chip thought there was apprehension as well.

It took some time for Chip to find the words. "It's just occurred to me, although I've twice accepted your assurance that you haven't been court-martialed, that I've never actually asked you why you were transferred from the 12th." Katryn's eyes widened slightly, but she said nothing. "And now I've heard some rumors concerning a dead sergeant."

"I didn't murder her," Katryn interjected.

"Was it murder?"

"Yes, ma'am, but it wasn't by me."

"You make it sound as though someone has accused you."

"Someone did. But I wasn't charged."

"You haven't mentioned this before."

"No, ma'am." Katryn clenched her teeth but then went on talking. "I didn't think it was a good way to introduce myself—to tell people as soon as I met them that I'd been transferred because some people thought I'd murdered my previous sergeant."

"It was going to come out eventually."

"I know." Katryn's eyes dropped to the floor. "I've not been wasting much effort worrying about my long-term future."

Chip studied Katryn's face. She remembered her first impressions of Katryn, the hopelessness and the fear, which she now understood.

It had not merely been apprehension about meeting strangers in an unfavorable situation. It was the knowledge that things would get worse, not better. The rumors would catch up, and no squadron was going to respond well to a murderer in their midst—certainly not one who had killed another Ranger.

Chip decided to push things a little bit farther. "I've also heard you had to flee from the Militia, which is why you applied to the Rangers."

This time, Katryn looked confused. She shook her head. "No, ma'am. That's just people making things up." Then despair swept over her face. For a moment, it seemed that her composure would collapse completely, but she brought herself back under control.

"So why don't you tell me the full story?" Chip spoke more softly.

"It isn't straightforward."

"It doesn't matter. Take your time. But this is your chance to tell me everything. I don't want to be back here in another month, asking for explanations of the next set of rumors."

Katryn turned her face and stared at the darkened glass of the window. Her expression held the hopeless despair of their first meeting. Her hands were balled in fists in her lap, but after several ragged breaths, she nodded unevenly. "Okay, but I'm not sure where to start."

"Why don't you start with why you left the Militia after nine years?"

Katryn nodded again. Her face was now calm, resigned, almost relieved. "That would go back to August last year. There was a heat wave at the start of the month. I guess it all began with me doing a night patrol with another colleague…"

PART TWO

Katryn Nagata

2 August 532

CHAPTER EIGHT—A JILTED LOVER

As midnight grew near, the streets of Woodside were so silent, it seemed that not only the inhabitants but even the houses themselves were sleeping. The dark ranks of buildings were huddled in the light of the moons, the walls slowly oozing out the heat they had absorbed during the long, hot summer's day. The only sounds were the whooping of a night bird and the dull clop of two pairs of Militia boots striking the cobbles in a steady, unhurried rhythm.

The women in their black uniforms paused their round at the edge of the market square. Militia Sergeant Katryn Nagata gazed around thoughtfully. The time to hunt for lawbreakers was when the market was in full swing, with pickpockets preying on the unwary and traders giving short measure. During the day, the square would be the scene of as much illegal activity as was to be found in Woodside (which still was not saying much), but now it was utterly devoid of life—law-abiding or otherwise.

Katryn's eyes lifted to the upper stories of the buildings. The heat had prompted many occupants to leave their shutters open, which might attract the attention of thieves. However, even the most stupid burglar would have the sense to wait until the Militia was out of sight before scrambling up a wall. The chances of stumbling across any criminals were very slim, but the rules decreed that two members of the Militia must patrol the streets each night, and that was what she and her colleague were doing. It was true that pounding the beat in the cool of night was less unpleasant than it was during the sticky midday heat, but Katryn would rather have been at home, asleep in bed with Allison.

She glanced at the woman standing beside her, a new recruit to the Militia, just past her sixteenth birthday and still in her probation period. Private Dekker was stifling a yawn. Judging from her expression, the yawn owed as much to boredom as tiredness.

"Are you finding life in the Militia as exciting as you hoped?" Katryn asked dryly.

Dekker's mouth turned down at the corners. "Well...shall we say no worse than I feared? I reckon I can put up with it for two years."

"And then you'll apply for admission to the Rangers?" Katryn guessed as she began walking again.

Dekker fell into step beside her. "Oh, yes. I'm applying the day I finish my probation. Just one year, nine months and three days to go."

Katryn laughed and said nothing to crush the young woman's hopes. However, she knew of too many others who had joined the Militia, intending to transfer to the Rangers after they completed their two-year probation, only to fail the rigorous entry test for the elite service and be forced to complete all fourteen years of their enlistment period in the Militia.

"It is so dull here, I don't know how you stand it. Did you never think of joining the Rangers?" Dekker asked curiously as they left the market square.

"Not really." Katryn scrunched her nose a little as she replied. "It crossed my mind once or twice, back when I was your age, but I'm happy in Woodside. I've got family here and a partner." Her expression shifted to a contented smile. Meeting Allison just before her probation was complete had put the final block on any ideas of applying for the Rangers, and never once in the following seven years had Katryn regretted her choice. "We've been saving money. This time next year, we'll have a place of our own and a child."

"You've got enough for the imprinting fees?"

Katryn grinned at Dekker. "Well, I'm not expecting the temple to imprint us a baby for free."

"Your partner must be quite something to keep you here in Woodside."

"She is," Katryn agreed. "But even without her, I don't think I'd have joined the Rangers. I'm not the adventurous sort. And I always wanted to be in the Militia."

"Because of what happened to your gene mother?"

Katryn glanced sideways. "You've heard about her?"

"Someone mentioned her back at the station—the last Militiawoman in Woodside to be killed on duty. They weren't too sure about how it happened, though."

"It was a stupid accident. She stepped in to stop a tavern brawl and got stabbed in the back by someone too drunk to think or see straight. The killer was probably aiming at the person standing beside my gene mother."

"That's bad luck."

"Even worse luck that it was her first month back at work after giving birth to my sister."

"How old were you?"

"Just turned six."

"So your birth mother lost her partner and was left with two young children. That's rough. I guess the widow's pension wouldn't begin to compensate."

Katryn nodded and said nothing, but she suspected that her childhood would have been far happier for everyone had both her mothers been present. She hoped that Dekker's curiosity would not set her off probing any deeper and was saved by a sudden outbreak of shouting in the distance. The two Militiawomen spared only a sharp glance at each other before breaking into a run toward the sound of the disturbance.

They charged into an alleyway and emerged onto a wider street at the far end. The shouting was louder, although it was still impossible to make out the words. With Katryn in the lead, they rounded the last corner. Standing in the middle of the road was a woman, clearly the worse for drink. She swayed and staggered as though the cobblestones under her feet were the deck of a pitching boat. From her mouth came a string of abuse, screamed at the closed front door of a house.

"Bitches! You're just a pair of fucking bitches!"

Katryn's initial thought was that the shouter was an adolescent troublemaker, unable to hold her drink. However, when she got closer, she saw that the woman was closer to forty than fourteen and, from the cut of her clothes, not a destitute alcoholic. The woman seemed to be unaware of the Militiawomen's arrival, but it was possible that the occupants of the house had been watching from a window. As the Militiawomen reached the angry drunk, the door opened, and two other middle-aged women emerged. One held a small lantern aloft; the yellow light flowed out over the cobbles.

At the sight of the pair, the drunk made an indecisive lurch forward. Then her face crumpled. "Why?" Her voice cracked as she spoke. "Why? I love you. You know I do. I love you. Why d'you leave me? Come home, please."

"Elli…" one of the women in the doorway began, but the other cut her off with a hand on the arm.

A jilted lover, Katryn thought, sizing up the situation. A depressingly common occurrence, and one that would require tact. The rowdy woman was probably an honest citizen who had made the mistake of trying to drink away her grief. Katryn stepped between the antagonists, with her face toward the drunk. "I think, ma'am, it might be best if you went home. Sleep it off. It will be easier to sort things out in the morning."

The drunk ignored Katryn and stared instead, with tears in her eyes, at the women in the doorway. "You promised you'd love me forever."

From behind Katryn came a snort that sounded halfway to a laugh. Katryn glanced over her shoulder. It was impossible to say what the rights and wrongs of the situation were, but from the patronizing expressions of the two women in the doorway and the distraught misery on the face of the other, Katryn knew where her sympathies lay. It was a shame that it was not against the law to stand on your own doorstep looking unbearably smug.

Katryn turned back to the drunk. "Come on now, madam. Why don't you go home?" She pitched her voice low and reassuring in the hope that the tone, if not the words, would register.

The drunk's eyes fixed on Katryn for the first time. "You're on their side."

Katryn met the combative glare. "I'm not. I'm on the side of the law, and you can't stand in the street at midnight, shouting and waking the whole neighborhood."

Their eyes locked for several seconds; then the other woman dropped her gaze. The fight went out of her, and her shoulders sagged. Katryn put a hand on her arm and gently steered the unsteady woman away. With her other hand, she gestured for Dekker to join them. "If you tell us where you live, we'll see you safely home."

The drunk went along meekly for the first few steps, but then a mocking voice rang out behind them. "By the Goddess, if you could see yourself now, you wouldn't come around asking why."

The drunk tensed and jerked free of Katryn's grip. Katryn gave her a firm shove in the right direction; then she turned back to face the two women in the doorway, trusting Dekker to keep control of the other.

"You aren't helping matters. Could you both please go in and close the door? We will deal with the situation," Katryn said sharply. She glared at the women, waiting for them to obey her instructions.

Without needing to look, Katryn could tell that the drunk had staggered on for a few steps before regaining what she could of her balance. Now the sounds of her uneven footsteps were approaching; she had outmaneuvered the inexperienced Dekker. Katryn put out an arm to stop the woman from lumbering past, but instead, the sounds came directly behind her. Then the back of Katryn's head imploded. The buildings jolted sideways and blurred. The cobblestones of the street turned to water and raced up to meet her. A whirling cartwheel of sparks was swallowed by darkness.

❖

Katryn awoke in the Militia station with one of the town healers bending over her. The woman's eyes were unfocused as she concentrated on the mysterious other senses of the healer's craft. Lieutenant Rashid's anxious face wavered in the background. The window beyond was dark, so it was still night. Katryn's head felt hollow, but she could detect the soothing influence of the healer's talent flowing out from the hand on her brow. She let her eyelids close and drifted in the ripples of well-being while vaguely wondering how she had gotten to the station and what had happened to the drunk.

Eventually, the healer sat back and announced, "I guess you'll live. You've got a thick skull. It didn't crack as easily as the bottle."

"Was that what she hit me with?" Katryn asked slowly. "From the way it felt, I'd have guessed it was a slab of granite. Except I didn't see how she'd kept it hidden."

The healer's smile broadened. "And the blow obviously hasn't shattered your wits. You should go home now and get as much rest as possible, but I'd like to see you again first thing tomorrow."

The healer patted Katryn on the shoulder and rose to her feet. She gave a respectful nod to the lieutenant and bustled out through the door. Katryn sat and swung her feet over the side of the bench she had been lying on. The motion left her a little queasy and light-headed, but her eyes had no trouble focusing—which, as she was experienced enough to know, was the most important thing.

Lieutenant Rashid slipped into the chair vacated by the healer. "How do you feel?"

"Like a fool. Of all people, I should know not to turn my back on a drunk."

"Is that what happened? The report I got from Private Dekker was a bit confused."

"That's not surprising," Katryn said ruefully. "If Dekker had been more aware, I wouldn't have gotten hit. But again, that's my fault. I should've made allowances for her inexperience."

The lieutenant's lips pursed into a thin line. "Maybe. But I'm not going to question you about it now. Are you okay to walk, or shall I get someone to help carry you home?"

"I think I'm okay. The healer would have warned me otherwise."

"Fair enough. But I'll come with you. We don't want you passing out in a gutter."

Katryn had no problems on the short walk, and the lieutenant parted company with her at the doorstep of her mother's shop. Inside, it was dark and silent. The lantern was in its place beside the door. Katryn hesitated for a second before lighting it. Normally, she had no fears negotiating the house in the dark, but the last thing she wanted was to trip on an unexpected obstacle and bang her head again.

The four walls of the baker's shop sprung up around her as the wick flared into life. Katryn looked at the familiar room with mixed emotions. The shop had been her home all her life—but not for much longer. Katryn was eager to be gone. It was not that she could accuse her mother of anything serious. There were no examples of malice or physical cruelty to point at—merely a lack of affection and the constant sense of being on the outside. Throughout their childhood, her sister, Cy, had been cuddled and indulged, while Katryn had mainly been ignored.

As a young girl, Katryn had been hurt and confused by the favoritism. As an adolescent, she had gotten the idea that her mother was overcompensating for the loss of Cy's birth mother, so the neighbors could not say that Delia Nagata was neglecting her gene daughter by comparison with the one she had borne. Now Katryn suspected that the truth was far less convoluted: Her mother simply liked Cy better than she did Katryn.

The money for the temple imprinting fees had been ready for more than a year, but Katryn had wanted to put off having the child until she and Allison could also afford to move out from her mother's house. She wanted to raise their child somewhere she felt she belonged.

Katryn walked through the back of the shop and past the ovens. Even this late at night, she could still feel the unwelcome heat radiating from them. Then she climbed the twisting rear stairway to the upper floor. She paused on the landing and looked at the three closed doors. Of course, the smallest room was hers. Her mother had explained that Cy needed the bigger room because she worked in the shop and, therefore, spent more time in the house. Katryn's lips tightened at the memory. Cy did not have more possessions or spend more time sleeping, and she did not have a permanent partner. However, logic did not come into it, so Katryn and Allison were squeezed into a tiny cubbyhole.

Katryn pushed open the door to her room and stepped inside. In the light of the lantern, she saw at once that the bed was empty. Katryn ran a hand over her face; the aftereffects of shock were catching up with her, and she just wanted to go to sleep without delay. Obviously, someone— probably Dekker—had brought news of the assault, and Allison had gone out to meet her. Katryn was not keen to start wandering around the streets, especially as she would doubtless miss Allison on the way to the station. With any luck, if Cy were awake, she would know how long Allison had been gone.

Katryn did not wait for an answer to her knock on Cy's door. It would be nice to think that Cy cared enough for her to go out looking with Allison, but in any case, Katryn was too spent to bother with formalities. She felt as though she had been through a mangle, and the beginning of a headache was pounding at the back of her skull.

The sight of two figures in Cy's bed did not surprise Katryn. With her nineteenth birthday less than a month away, Cy was well into the stage of casual relationships. In fact, she was a year older than Katryn had been when she met Allison. And then the two women jerked awake and sat up, staring toward the door and blinking in the light of the lantern.

Nobody spoke. There was not much to say, although Katryn found herself desperately hoping for some innocent explanation. It was a forlorn wish; the expressions said it all. Allison had the grace to look guilty, but on Cy's face, for the second time that night, Katryn found herself looking at a smug, triumphant sneer.

❖

The anteroom outside the captain's office was empty apart from Katryn. She sat staring at the door and trying not to cry any more—for what good it did. She knew that her eyes were as red as they were going to get. The healer had clucked over Katryn's condition when she had called in that morning. Screaming rows were not a recommended treatment for head injuries, and despite the healer's instructions, Katryn had had very little rest, finally bedding down on the floor of a friend's house just before dawn.

The angry words had been predictable and pointless. Their mother had felt that although Cy had been a little inconsiderate, Katryn was making too much fuss, and obviously, it was all Allison's fault anyway. Cy had been defiantly provocative. Allison had said very little and settled into a mood of sullen bravado, doing no more than occasionally muttering, "So what?"

Katryn had mainly wanted to get away. It had been Cy, with an appalling sense of timing, who had tried to draw out the confrontation. But then, confrontation had probably been Cy's main motive from the start. It was not that Cy disliked her older sister; rather, she was continually driven to prove her favored position. Katryn was coldly certain that Cy did not want Allison because she was attracted to her; Cy wanted Allison because she was Katryn's. It had been the same since they were children and their mother had encouraged Cy to think she had a right to anything she wanted.

Katryn remembered a rag doll she'd had as a child. Cy had taken a fancy to the doll, making so much fuss that in the end, their mother had declared eleven-year-old Katryn too old for dolls and given her loved toy to her younger sister. For two weeks, Cy had taken every opportunity to flaunt her prize, but once the satisfaction of victory had faded, the rag doll was forgotten. Katryn had found it some months later, filthy, rain-soaked and discarded in the yard in the back of the house.

To her dismay, the memory of the doll's pathetic remains brought fresh tears to Katryn's eyes, and she pinched the bridge of her nose between her thumb and forefinger, trying to fight them back. At that moment, the door to the captain's office opened, and Katryn's name was called. She took a deep breath, squared her shoulders and marched in.

Captain Kalispera was sitting at her desk. She looked up as Katryn entered. "Sergeant Nagata, I'm pleased you've asked to see me. I'd have wanted to talk to you anyway about last night. I trust you're feeling well." Her voice sounded uncertain as she examined Katryn's appearance.

"I've got no problems as a result of the blow, ma'am."

"But you have some other problems?" the captain suggested.

"Yes, ma'am."

"I haven't seen the report yet, but with your record, I'd think it went without saying that no blame was attached to you."

"Thank you, ma'am."

"So what's your problem?"

"I wish to transfer to the Militia in another town."

"Which one?"

"Any one. The farther away, the better."

The captain looked at her in surprise. "Surely not because of what happened last night?"

"Not the incident with the drunk."

"Then why?"

"Personal reasons." Katryn had to fight to keep her voice steady.

Captain Kalispera sat back and considered her shrewdly. "Can I assume that your early return home last night caught someone by surprise?"

"Yes, ma'am." Tears were burning in Katryn's eyes again.

"I'm sorry. I'm really sorry," Captain Kalispera said softly. "And it wasn't telepathy on my part in guessing. I've seen it happen far too often before. Which is why I can be confident in telling you that running away isn't the right response. Someone has taken your lover. If you run away, she'll have taken your friends, your family and your home as well. In a few months, you'll be feeling stronger and will regret having given her so much. You need to stay and overcome your difficulties."

"I don't think so." Katryn could not bring herself to say more. "I can't stay in Woodside."

The captain shook her head. "I'm afraid I can't help you. The garrison is understrength. So by the rules, I'm allowed to transfer people out only in certain exceptional circumstances, and your situation doesn't qualify."

Katryn hung her head. It was not just losing Allison. Cy would be wanting to wring as much out of the situation as she could. Even if Katryn used her share of the savings to move away from her mother's shop, Cy would track her down and lay siege to the front door. If she could not see Katryn suffering, then half the fun would be lost. Cy would make sure that Katryn could not avoid the sight of her parading her new toy through town. The thought of months of torment ahead was unbearable.

There seemed to be no way out. But then a new idea launched itself into Katryn's head—something Dekker had said the previous night. It was every Militiawoman's right to apply once, and once only. Katryn had never availed herself of her right. She had never wanted to before. She looked up. "I wish to apply for admission to the Rangers."

CHAPTER NINE—WELCOME TO FORT KROWE

Katryn's lungs were burning, her heartbeat was pounding in her ears, and the shoulder straps of her weighted backpack were biting deeper into her shoulders with each stride. Sweat stung in the chafed cuts. Her legs were both leaden and rubbery. Every muscle in her body was in agony. Her life was reduced to the effort of throwing one foot in front of the other on the rough woodland track.

Birds whistled in the branches, and the rich scent of firs filled the air. The warm sunlight would have been pleasant on an afternoon's stroll but only added to the torment of the assessment run. A slight breeze stirring the tops of the trees did not reach the forest floor to dry the sweat on her face. Stones and roots broke the surface of the path. Twice, Katryn stumbled and nearly fell as the trail climbed the wooded hillside.

At the top of the incline, the track emerged onto coarse pastureland. Sheep were dotted over the slopes. The sun was hotter, but now the wind could offer some relief. In wordless agreement, the applicants for the Rangers paused to try to regain part of their breath.

Katryn rested her hands on her knees, sucking in lungfuls of air. Stopping was probably not a good idea; she could feel her body trembling, but she could not afford to give in to weakness yet. She had to keep going. The sun was dropping toward the horizon, and the finishing line at Fort Krowe was still kilometers away. The team of applicants had to complete the run by sunset if they were to be considered for the Rangers. The timed endurance run was the last, and most grueling, of the entrance tests.

Katryn looked at the seven other women. They were all eighteen or nineteen, making her the oldest by several years, but their youth did not seem to be conferring any advantage. Most of them appeared to be just as exhausted as she was, and one looked an awful lot worse. The struggling woman, Laura, was shaking visibly. Her skin was blanched, and her eyes were glazed. She had been the pacesetter for the first two hours of the run and had obviously pushed herself too far.

"Are you all right?" Katryn asked in concern.

Laura nodded but could not speak.

"Come on. We need to get moving," one of the other applicants called out.

Katryn glanced across. The speaker was Gitana, the tallest and strongest of the applicants. Throughout the series of tests, her manner had made it clear she felt a place in the Rangers was hers by right. She was so arrogantly sure of herself that she had managed to convince most of the other applicants as well. Many of them now looked to her for leadership—a role that Gitana also seemed to feel she deserved. But a leader must take responsibility for her followers. Katryn opened her mouth, about to express doubts concerning Laura's condition, but Gitana had already set off running, and Laura was trotting after. Katryn tagged on at the rear.

For another two kilometers, the route kept to the highland; then it dropped again into a valley. At the bottom, a wide stream rippled over stones. Katryn's boots splashed down into the water, which barely covered her toes. In three strides, she had crossed the stream and scrambled over the undercut ledge on the far side. Three of the applicants struggled awkwardly on the waist-high bank. The weakest woman did not make it. Laura collapsed against the edge of the stream and then began to slip sideways into the water.

Katryn jumped down and, with two other applicants, got Laura onto dry land. They laid her on the ground virtually unconscious. She was not going to run any farther. Someone took her pulse while the rest stood around or collapsed on the grass, exchanging anxious looks.

"What do we do?" one of the applicants asked the group.

"We'll have to carry her," Katryn answered.

"Then we'll never make Fort Krowe in time," Gitana objected immediately.

"We can't leave her here," Katryn spoke up again.

"I'm not giving up my chance to join the Rangers just because someone else isn't up to it."

"We're supposed to be a team. We should carry her."

Most of the group hung their heads, too exhausted or too unsure of themselves to voice their thoughts. Gitana glared at Katryn, trying to intimidate her into backing down. When that did not happen, Gitana scowled and looked away, thinking of fresh arguments.

"The people at Fort Krowe need to get a healer out here as quickly as possible. Therefore, we need to get to them as quickly as possible. Which means we run flat-out. If you want, you can stay here and keep an eye on her." Gitana's delivery made it more an ultimatum than a plan.

Katryn looked at the others. None of them would meet her eyes. It was obvious whose side they took. They were not happy about abandoning Laura but would not risk failing the test for her sake. Katryn finished with her gaze on the woman on the grass. She pursed her lips, trying to keep the sarcastic anger from her expression. Was it really fair to judge the other applicants? Maybe they were simply more committed to the dream of joining the Rangers than she was, or maybe her added experience made her value team unity more. Whichever it was, there was no way she could desert a colleague in need. She raised her eyes again to meet Gitana's and shrugged. "Okay. It's on your conscience."

"Right." The woman smiled, ignoring the implied criticism. "Keep an eye on her. We'll let them know where you are." Already, Gitana was back on form, making it sound as though she were the one giving orders. She turned to the other applicants. "Come on, now. Let's get going." At a steady trot, she led the remaining women up the trail.

Katryn kneeled down and slipped the backpack from her shoulders. It hit the ground with a heavy thump. She fumbled to remove the collapsed woman's pack as well and loosen her clothes. Laura groaned; her legs were starting to shake spasmodically. Katryn lifted one of Laura's eyelids with her thumb and saw mainly white. The woman was clearly in a very bad way.

Katryn turned her head. The other applicants were about to disappear over the brow of the hill. Katryn felt angry at their self-serving callousness and irritated at her own impotence. In applying to enter the Rangers, she'd had to forgo her rank of sergeant. Now she found herself missing the three stripes on her badge. If she had been in charge, she could have insisted that the others carry Laura.

Katryn's expression became even more grim. Perhaps if she had been applying to the Rangers out of real ambition, rather than as a refuge, she would have had the determination to challenge Gitana's lead.

But there was no point wasting time on ifs. The sick woman needed her help.

Katryn dragged one of the packs over. Most of the weight was made up of sandbags, but there were some useful items as well. It did not take much digging around to find the salt rations, a tin cup and a blanket. Katryn filled the cup from the stream and added the salt. She took the first draught and was surprised by how good it tasted. Then she got Laura into a sitting position and tried to get her to drink—with only partial success. Much of the water dribbled down Laura's chin.

The sun was still warm, but now that they had stopped running, Katryn was starting to cool, and Laura's skin felt icy. Katryn wrapped her in the blanket and then lay down, hoping to recover her strength, but it was impossible to rest. Tingling cramps clawed at her legs. The sun was sinking lower, and the temperature was falling with it. Lying on the cold ground was not a good idea.

Katryn shielded her eyes to stare along the track, wondering how long it might be before a rescue team arrived and whether it would arrive in time for Laura. Katryn examined her again; there was no doubt that her condition was worse. She might be suffering from exhaustion, salt loss or some other medical condition. Laura was fully unconscious now, and her pulse was weak. She was in real danger, and a few minutes either way might prove to be crucial. It would be a good idea to minimize the distance the rescue party had to travel from Fort Krowe.

Katryn got to her feet. She felt weak and shaky. Her legs ached, and she was nauseous, but her life was not the one at stake. After strenuous effort, she managed to get the sick woman up and over her shoulders. Then, resolutely, Katryn began to walk along the trail.

The light had gone, and stars glittered in the deep blue sky. The wind had increased, with a cold, stinging edge. Katryn had lost all sense of who or where she was. It was hard even to focus her eyes on the ground. Her feet kept to the trail mainly out of instinct. No thought remained in her head except the determination to keep going, although she could no longer remember why or where.

Lost in exhaustion, Katryn was unaware of the sound of approaching horses or the shouts when she was spotted. The riders reined in their mounts and dropped to the ground, surrounding her. Katryn stared at the circle of faces in confusion. Her feet came to a standstill, and then, without warning, her knees gave way. Hands caught hold of her, and Laura was lifted from her shoulders. Something was said. Katryn thought it was a question, but she was unable to make sense of the words and shook her head. The night sky whirled when she did so. Katryn felt as though she were simultaneously drunk and hungover.

A horse was positioned in front of her. Katryn stared at it as though she had never seen one before. More words were spoken. She was hauled up like a sack of potatoes and placed in the saddle. A second rider swung up behind her, reaching around her to take the reins and holding her so that she would not fall. A period of confused milling-around followed; voices called out. Then another rider—a healer—brought her horse alongside, close enough to reach out and put her hand on Katryn's brow. For a moment, the fog lifted from Katryn's mind. Then she drifted off into a gentle, healing sleep.

❖

It was late afternoon the following day when Katryn had the formal meeting to be told the result of her application—not that she had any doubt what the decision would be. Via the camp grapevine, she had already learned that all the other applicants had been rejected, even those who had completed the run inside the time limit, whereas she had not even finished the course.

However, her attempt to join the Rangers had not been a complete waste of time and effort. A month away from Woodside had given her the space to regain her self-control, sufficient to face down Cy, and their mother and maybe even Allison. Also, the post that morning had contained a letter from the regional Militia HQ. In nearly so many words, it had promised her a lieutenancy within the year if she stayed in the Militia. It was nice to think that someone did not want to let go of her.

The room Katryn was shown into was furnished with a single large desk and was clearly someone's office rather than a general admin room. It was also surprising that the woman sitting behind the desk was wearing a major's badge. Katryn had been expecting a far more junior officer for the routine interview.

The major treated Katryn to a long, thoughtful stare before she started to speak. "Applicant Nagata, I'm hoping that you can help me sort things out."

"Ma'am?"

"Do you realize what an awkward decision you've given us?"

"With regard to...?" Katryn was confused.

"Your application for the Rangers."

"I would have thought it was quite straightforward, ma'am." At Katryn's words, the major raised an eyebrow, her expression inviting Katryn to continue. "I failed on the timed run. I didn't get back in time."

"Yes." The major gave a drawn-out sigh, tapping the knuckle of her forefinger slowly against her chin, her eyes fixed on Katryn. Abruptly, she sat up straighter, her manner more decisive. "However, we do have a degree of discretion in interpreting the results when unusual events occur—although I'll admit that someone's collapsing is not as rare as I'd like. We screen everyone to make sure that they're fit enough. Still, accidents happen—or, like yesterday, errors of judgment. The woman was capable physically but made the mistake of burning herself out in the first part of the run."

"I'd heard that everyone else on the team had been rejected," Katryn blurted out.

"Yes, because you *were* a team, as was made quite clear at the start. You were not timed as individuals. It was the last person in who counted. But as I said, things like this have happened before, and we don't fail an entire team because of one member. We can make allowances for unfortunate events, except that the rest of your team carried on as though nothing had happened. Since they didn't let the incident affect their actions, they disqualified themselves from any special consideration as a result of it. But you gave a remarkable performance, and the tests are more about character than fitness. We can rectify the latter with exercise, but we can do nothing with a woman who'll abandon her comrades for personal gain."

Katryn felt her pulse kick as a thought shot through her head: *They're going to accept me. Or are they?* The major's attitude was not that of someone giving good news.

The major carried on talking. "The allowances that can be made aren't formally specified, and they are at the discretion of the senior recruiting officer. What it boils down to is this: It's up to me whether you're in or out. I'll be quite blunt. If you were an eighteen-year-old who'd applied to the Rangers the day after she'd completed her probation, I'd accept you without a second thought. But you aren't, and this gives me a problem on two grounds. First, your commitment to the Rangers is in question. I have the impression that you made your application to escape some unpleasantness back home, rather than as a positive choice." She settled back in her chair, her eyes boring into Katryn. "Do you have anything to say?"

Katryn felt a blush rise on her cheeks, but she could not deny the accusation. "My reasons for leaving the Militia had nothing to do with any trouble relating to my work."

"I wasn't suggesting that they were." The look in the major's eye hinted that she was fully aware of the truth.

"Also..." Katryn paused, hunting for words. "Just because a woman is eager to join the Rangers doesn't mean she's doing it for the right reasons. In my experience, many young women apply because they're bored in the Militia and are expecting life in the Rangers to be full of excitement and adventure."

"And you're not?"

"I'm expecting it to be hard work."

A suspicion of a smile flicked at the corner of the major's mouth. "A good answer." She took a deep breath. "My second concern is about the length of time you have left to serve. You've spent nearly nine years in the Militia. By the time you finish your basic training, you'll have less than five left to go. We would like to see some return on the investment we'd make in training you."

"I've always intended to re-enlist," Katryn said. In fact, she had planned on completing both of the permitted seven-year extensions to active duty and following them with an administrative post, if she had reached a sufficiently senior rank by the time they expired.

"You might, but we can't count on it." The major picked up a few sheets of paper from her desk and began to scan through them, although she clearly was already familiar with the content. "You have shown good general aptitude, and you scored very—no, you scored *exceptionally* high in archery. That's always a good skill to have in a Ranger."

The major turned her head to look out the window, tapping

the papers on the desk. Katryn allowed herself a faint grin as she remembered the expression on the face of the Ranger who had assessed her marksmanship when she produced one of the highest scores ever recorded for an applicant. Archery had been her favorite pastime since she was a child. She had won the town competition a record six times in a row.

The waiting dragged out as the major mulled things over, but at last, she turned back, her decision made. For the first time, a true smile showed. "Welcome to Fort Krowe, Ranger."

❖

Katryn spent the next four months at Fort Krowe, going through the initial training program for the Rangers: wilderness crafts and weapons practice. It was four months of hell, exceeding her worst expectations of hard work. Most nights, she stumbled into the bunkhouse with the other trainees, too tired to see straight. She developed an intense personal dislike for all the drill sergeants and devoted much of her spare energy to wishing something nasty would happen to them. However, she knew she was having an easier time of it than many of her co-trainees were.

The assessor who had written that she had "good general aptitude" obviously knew what she was talking about. Katryn was well toward the top of the group in everything except swordsmanship, which she more than compensated for with her skill at archery. It was predicted that she would end up as a squadron's sharpshooter.

It was shortly after Midwinter's Day when Katryn completed her training and was issued her kit. The senior drill sergeant personally signed her papers and shook her hand, smiling. This stunned Katryn. For a second, the woman had looked as though she might just possibly be human.

Back in the bunkhouse, Katryn laid the new uniform out on her bed. Unlike the plain green clothes issued to trainees, the shirt and trousers had gray piping to match the gray Ranger's leather belt and the sleeveless reinforced jacket that offered protection without sacrificing maneuverability. The sword and trail knife were her own personal weapons, rather than the general issue used for training. She also had the wide-brimmed gray Ranger hat.

Katryn lifted up this last item and examined it. A steel cap was sewn inside the crown, with further reinforcement in the brim to protect the face from slashing attacks. Katryn knew that in parts of Landfall, the Militia was also given helmets—but nobody bothered in places that were safe, like Woodside.

Her thoughts slid back. Suppose that she had been wearing a helmet during the encounter with the drunk. She would not have been knocked out, would not have gone home early, would not have found Allison where she did. And would she have been any happier?

Katryn shook her head. Ignorance had never been an option. She was sure that Cy had wanted the affair to come out and had probably pre-planned some big scene. Cy always had gone overboard on drama.

In her new uniform of green and gray, Katryn reported to the main administration office for her posting. Woodside was on the boundary between the regions allocated to Central and Eastern Divisions. Katryn had been asked whether she had any preference and had chosen Eastern out of a desire to get as far away from the drill sergeants as possible.

The clerk in the office riffled through various papers and eventually slid a form toward her. On top of it, the clerk placed two shoulder badges. The insignia was the empty green square worn by privates; beneath it was the designation *12th Squadron*.

Katryn picked up the embroidered cloth badges, which she would sew onto her uniform that night. On the paper underneath were her orders.

Ranger Private Katryn Nagata will report to Captain Dolokov of the 12th Squadron, currently posted at Highview Barracks, by 1 February 533.

CHAPTER TEN—A LOT OF BAD FEELING

The town of Highview was the northernmost posting in the region covered by the Eastern Division, and as its name implied, it was situated in the highlands. It was the center of the timber industry for the area upstream of Landfall. In summer, the Liffey would be filled with rafts of logs floating down to the sawmills and timber yards of the city. Now the river was icebound, and the surrounding countryside was smothered under a thick coating of snow, but the roads had been kept clear, and Katryn reached her destination by the specified date.

It was midafternoon when the road finally emerged from the forest and Katryn saw the town perched on the hilltop ahead. The skies were clear, but the smell of more snow carried on the wind. The thought of resting with a hot meal beside a fire was enticing, and even canteen food in a mess hall did not sound too bad.

In her uniform, Katryn drew a fair number of looks as she rode through the streets, although they were less marked than she had become used to on her journey to Highview. Presumably, Rangers were a common sight for the local population. The face of the woman Katryn stopped to ask directions of showed little curiosity. However, it did show a mixture of emotions that set Katryn musing as she rode on.

The black uniform of the Militia was met with fear from those who had a guilty conscience and with relief by people who needed aid. The rest of the time, people simply looked blank, in an attempt not to attract attention. The green and gray uniform of the Rangers produced a markedly different response. The Rangers were respected, of course, particularly in the borderlands, where they risked their lives protecting the ordinary citizens. Katryn was still taken aback by the effect she'd had. The locals had looked at her with admiration, almost deference, and had acted with childlike eagerness to be helpful. Katryn grinned at herself when she realized that without thinking, she was now sitting straighter in the saddle.

The Ranger barracks were set just beyond the town, inside a high wooden stockade. Katryn dismounted at the gates and led her horse by the reins. No sentry was on duty, but her unfamiliar face attracted attention immediately. Another Ranger hailed her, and after a brief discussion, she was escorted farther into the site.

On one side of the road were stables; on the other, buildings that Katryn guessed to be the bunkhouses. After a dozen meters or so, the road opened out into a central parade ground. Directly ahead was a single-story building, which the other Ranger identified as the admin block and officers' quarters. Katryn tied her horse outside and followed her guide up the short flight of stairs to the open balcony.

Inside the doorway was a long room, the walls lined with books and maps. A desk took up a fair proportion of the floor space. Two officers were seated there, leaning over a report. From their shoulder badges, Katryn saw that one was the 12th Squadron's lieutenant and the other, a staff sergeant. They broke off their conversation and looked up.

"Ma'am, it's the new recruit," Katryn's guide announced.

"Good." The lieutenant got to her feet. "Go and find Sergeant Ellis."

"Yes, ma'am." The Ranger departed.

Katryn stepped forward, holding out her orders. "Private Nagata reporting, ma'am."

The lieutenant took the offered sheet and glanced at the contents. Then she raised her head and studied Katryn thoughtfully. It was a two-way exercise. The lieutenant was a thin-faced woman in her early thirties whose air of crisp efficiency struck a slightly false note, as though she were consciously working at it. Katryn wondered what lay underneath.

After a few seconds of silence, the lieutenant put the paper on the desk and began speaking. "Captain Dolokov is currently out on patrol with half the squadron. I am Lieutenant Bergstrom, and I'm in charge of the barracks in the captain's absence. You are assigned to B Patrol, under Sergeant Ellis, who'll be here in a moment. She'll see that you're allotted a bunk and stabling for your horse. She'll also instruct you in local procedures and restrictions. If you have any problems, you should report them to—"

She broke off as the door opened again. Lieutenant Bergstrom looked at the new arrival with an involuntary expression of distaste but suppressed it so quickly that Katryn half thought she had imagined it. The woman in the doorway was a sergeant. She was short, stocky and a few years older than Bergstrom. She projected an air of belligerence— which, Katryn realized, was utterly genuine.

"I understand my new recruit has turned up..." The sergeant paused for a fraction of a second. "...ma'am."

Katryn managed to hide her surprise. The effect of the hesitation was blatantly insolent; however, Lieutenant Bergstrom acted as though she had not noticed. It was obvious that the dislike between the two women was mutual. "Yes, Sergeant Ellis." Katryn detected an emphasis on the rank. "Private Nagata has just arrived from Fort Krowe. See that she is settled in." Bergstrom stared coldly at Ellis and then snapped, "Dismissed."

Katryn followed Ellis out of the building and collected her horse. Obviously, a lot of bad feeling existed between her new sergeant and the lieutenant, which could lead to all sorts of complications. Katryn was determined to keep well out of it.

They were halfway across the parade ground before Ellis spoke. "This your first posting?"

"Yes, ma'am."

"You look a bit on the old side for a new recruit."

"I served nine years in the Militia."

Ellis came to a standstill as though she had run into a wall, contempt on her face. "Oh, Himoti's tits. And they thought they'd dump you on us?"

Katryn also stopped, stunned by the speed and vehemence of the reaction. Although the Militia was not held in high regard by the Rangers, she had not expected her long service to be held against her. However, Ellis was acting as though it was an admission of cowardice and incompetence.

Ellis poked her finger into Katryn's shoulder. "Right. Listen. You're in the Rangers now. We don't find lost dogs, and we don't arrest kids who've swiped a few apples from the neighbor's orchard. If you make a mistake, people are likely to die, yourself being the most probable candidate. You sharpen up. You do what I say, when I say it, and we'll get along fine. Understood?"

"Yes, ma'am," Katryn said, reining back her flare of anger. She prayed that Ellis' response was partly displaced hostility from the encounter with Bergstrom; otherwise, life in B Patrol would not be pleasant.

Ellis snorted as though she also foresaw a stormy future and led the way into one of the stables. Two other Rangers were working there. "Sivarajah, Wan, this is—" Ellis broke off and looked to Katryn. "What was your name again?"

Katryn took a deep breath. "Private Katryn Nagata, ma'am."

The sergeant's lips showed a faint sneer as she turned back. "Right. Well, our new patrol member is straight out of nine years in the Militia. So she'll have lots of experience in helping drunks get home, and we all know who that'll be useful with. Only the Goddess knows what other good she'll be. Show her where to put her horse, how to take its saddle off…things like that. Sort her out in the bunk room, and I'll have another chat with her before dinner." Ellis gave a last, exaggerated sigh and left.

The older of the two Rangers had been standing at the back of the stables, her eyes flitting around nervously, as though she were looking for somewhere to hide. Only when Ellis had gone did she walk forward and stare at the doorway where Ellis had disappeared. The woman's face held an expression that was hard to read beyond a degree of relief. Her gaze shifted to Katryn.

"Hi. I'm Jan Sivarajah…corporal in B Patrol." A trace of defensiveness marked her tone as she stated her rank, as though it might be open to dispute. She was at least fifteen centimeters shorter than Katryn, and her build verged on scrawny, giving the impression that she could be knocked over by a stiff breeze. But she had to be tougher than she looked, both physically and mentally, to have lasted in the Rangers. She pointed to the other woman. "That's Nikki Wan."

The other Ranger had also wandered over. She was young, barely twenty, and her shoulder badge was blank like Katryn's. Her face was square, with an adolescent blandness. She nodded in response to her name but said nothing while subjecting Katryn to scrutiny.

Jan Sivarajah combed her hands through her hair, as though she needed to straighten her thoughts, and then dropped her arms with a sigh. "Okay. These are B Patrol's stables. There's room for your horse on the right. I assume it was issued to you at Fort Krowe with your kit and isn't a relay…?" She broke off at Katryn's nod of confirmation. "Your tack goes in that box there, and brushes are on the shelf above."

Katryn led her horse to the side of the stables and tied its reins to a ring on the wall. Nikki came up, stood to one side and then spoke for the first time. "You need to loosen that buckle first and then—"

"I know how to unsaddle my horse." Katryn snapped the words through clenched teeth.

Nikki took a step back, confused. "It's just…the Militia don't use horses much, and Sergeant Ellis said—"

"I know. I heard. Basic training must have become more extensive since whenever you went through it. Now they give lessons in things like caring for horses." Katryn tried to control her anger, but the sarcasm in her words came out more biting than she had intended.

"Oh, you've been through basic training?" Nikki spoke with naïve surprise.

"No, I bribed the major to let me off it."

The expression on the face of the young Ranger switched from confusion to embarrassment to anger. She squared her shoulders and muttered, "Fine." Then she turned on her heel and marched away, slamming the stable door behind her.

Katryn set her jaw and returned to her horse. Jan came over and patted her shoulder. "It's okay. Take a deep breath, and count to ten. If you're going to survive in B Patrol, you can't afford to let Ellis wind you up." The corporal's voice was a conspiratorial whisper.

Katryn opened her mouth to speak sharply and then closed it again. Jan was right. Nikki had been trying to be friendly, and now she was probably feeling stupid that she had taken Ellis' words at face value. A moment's thought would have told her that Ranger Command would not send out someone who was untrained. Katryn wished that she had also thought before speaking. With a sergeant like Ellis, she knew that she could not afford to start antagonizing the rest of the patrol.

❖

Katryn met the other four members of B Patrol at dinner. The Rangers' mess hall held one long table for each patrol and a smaller one for the officers. With half the squadron gone, two tables were empty. Katryn would have preferred not eating with Sergeant Ellis, but no one showed any wish to spread out; possibly, the rules forbade it. Fortunately, the sergeant finished eating her food quickly and left. In her absence, the atmosphere at the table eased. After a few questions about Katryn's background, the conversation settled down to banter about longstanding issues, giving Katryn the chance to observe the rest of her new comrades.

All four had served long enough to merit the single bar of a Leading Ranger on their badges. The tallest was Tina Agosta, a huge slab of a woman. She gave the impression of being slow and easygoing to the point of torpor, but as the conversation progressed, she made a series of sharp comments that caused Katryn to reconsider her evaluation. It was apparent that Tina's sluggish demeanor masked a critical, dry sense of humor. It was also apparent that Tina thought far more than she said.

Bo Hassan was the patrol joker. Her voice was the one heard most often around the table. Her stream of gibes, puns and innuendoes was directed at everyone. The witticisms were of variable quality and frequently crude, but nobody took offense—probably due to Bo's willingness to make herself the butt of her own jokes and the total lack of malice in her tone. Jan Sivarajah, the corporal, was the only one to show a trace of impatience with Bo.

Pat Panayi had well-formed features, and she knew it. She smiled frequently, but there was no warmth in her expression. She sat back at the table, tossing in the occasional remark. Her eyes shifted from person to person without regard to the flow of conversation. When she caught Katryn's gaze, she raised her eyebrows slightly, as though they were sharing a private joke, but Katryn had no idea what it was supposed to be.

The oldest and quietest was Sal Castillo. She sat hunched over the end of the table, staring at her knuckles and playing little part in the talking, despite attempts by the others to draw her in. Her eyes kept shifting to the door. She was the one who eventually broke up the gathering when she stood and announced her intention of going into town. After a fair amount of dithering, the others, as a group, decided to join her.

It was a short walk to the patrol's favorite tavern in Highview. The seven women straggled along the road in an untidy bunch. Sal led the way purposefully; there was laughter and playful shoving in the rear.

Katryn tagged along in the middle, walking next to Nikki, who ignored her. Apparently, the young woman was someone who nursed a grudge. Katryn could only hope that it would not last long.

The tavern was a two-story timber construction, much like every other building in Highview. It was identifiable by the beer keg hanging outside and the volume of noise within. As the door came into sight, Bo Hassan sidestepped over and put her arm around Katryn's shoulder. "Now, this is probably the first time you've been out for an evening's entertainment in a Ranger's uniform."

"Um...yes," Katryn replied cautiously.

"You are in for a very interesting learning experience."

"I..." Katryn's voice trailed off in confusion.

"You may have heard the world is full of women who are dying for the chance to examine the contents of a Ranger's uniform. Tonight, you can get to see how many and how much." Bo pulled away slightly and looked at Katryn's profile. "In fact, with your looks, you might even get to challenge Pat's position as the squadron's champion clit tickler."

Pat Panayi was only a few steps ahead and heard the remark. She paused with her hand on the door of the tavern and looked back, smiling. "I reckon I can cope with the competition."

"You want to make a competition of it?" Bo laughed. She mimed the actions of a race official. "Okay, first one to reach ten, starting... now."

Katryn tried not to look offended. Luckily, the disruption as the group shifted around to file into the tavern gave her time to recover. Of course, she had heard of the Rangers' reputation for promiscuity, but she had not thought of it in relation to herself. Casual sex had never interested Katryn, and she certainly was not in the mood to start, with her heart still raw over Allison. For some women, it might have provided a temporary salve for the pain. For herself, Katryn knew, it would merely be a reminder of what she had lost.

As she stepped through the doorway, Katryn was hit by a wave of heat and noise. Several voices called out as the Rangers were recognized. The tavern was doing good trade, but the Rangers managed to find a relatively clear spot in the corner. Katryn squeezed onto a bench at a table next to Jan. Bo and Sal also sat down, while the other three remained standing closer to the bar. Tina ordered the first round.

The drinks arrived quickly. Sal drained hers immediately—something that Tina evidently had expected, as a second tankard was ready. For a while, the conversation flitted over a disjointed succession of subjects before Bo and Jan got stuck in a debate about stable-duty rosters, which began lightheartedly but became more touchy. It was obviously something that Jan thought was important, while Bo was being deliberately provocative.

"Give her a rest, Jan." Sal spoke up at last, smiling to remove any sting from her words. "She gets enough earache from Ellis."

Katryn peered at the speaker. It was the most animated response she had heard yet from Sal. Then she noticed the three empty tankards by Sal's hands. Katryn was still on her first drink and had not seen the third arrive. She looked back at Sal, for the first time picking up the signs she had learned to recognize from her work in the Militia. Sal Castillo was not yet lost to alcoholism, but she was well on the way. Surely, the others must know, yet nothing was being said. Katryn looked away to hide her surprise. She had expected the Rangers to be stricter about such things. Ellis had been so dogmatic about the high standards of the elite service.

The conversation had just started to move on again when angry voices erupted at the bar. Katryn jerked her head around to see an unknown woman squaring up to Tina Agosta. Tina was taller by a head, but the other woman was either too drunk or too furious to care. Almost before Katryn had noted the details, Jan was out of her seat and between the two adversaries. She put her hands on Tina's shoulders. Not that the slight corporal could have restrained the larger Ranger physically, but she clearly had a calming effect, and Tina made no move as a couple of the other woman's friends wisely bundled her away.

Jan returned to the table with Tina in tow. Katryn gave up her seat to make room. Bo also stood, and the two wandered over to the bar.

"What was that about?" Bo asked.

Pat shrugged. "That local thought Tina had been ogling her girlfriend. She said something, and Tina gave it back, with a bit added on for good measure. You know how drink can get Tina sometimes."

"Was she ogling?"

"I don't know about Tina, but I certainly was. The sweetie is well worth watching," Pat said, grinning. She raised her tankard to her lips.

"Where's Nikki?" Bo switched tack.

Pat pointed to two figures wedged into a dim corner nearby. "She's found a friend. I think they're cleaning each other's tonsils."

Bo glanced at them and then back. "It's not usual for Nikki to get into action before you. Aren't you being a bit slow tonight?"

"I'm being sporting to the competition. I thought I'd let Katryn get a head start. But if she doesn't make a move soon, I'll have to do something."

Katryn blushed faintly as Pat and Bo both smirked in her direction. She shook her head. "It's not my game."

"Oh, come on! You're a Ranger now." Bo protested. "Say, I know what. Why don't you make a play for that local's girlfriend? Don't worry if the woman gets nasty; I'm sure Tina would love an excuse to flatten her."

Katryn started to smile and then realized that Bo wasn't joking. Her blush deepened, now partly the effect of anger. She was saved from the need to answer by a loud voice at her elbow. "I knew I'd find you layabouts here." Sergeant Ellis had arrived.

Flustered, Katryn turned and spoke without thinking. "Ma'am, it's my round. Can I buy you a drink?"

Ellis looked her up and down as though she had said something absurd. "No." Then she snorted and relaxed slightly, "And you're off duty. My name's Mel." Ellis turned to the group at the table. "Jan, I need to talk to you back at the barracks. Something's cropped up. But there's no rush. Finish your drink in your own time."

Despite Ellis' words, Jan drained her tankard immediately and stood up. "I'm ready."

"Oh. Right." Ellis seemed a little put out by the speed of the response. Her eyes scoured the group and finished on Pat Panayi. Her expression became softer but no less intense, and after the briefest hesitation, she beckoned Pat to one side with a jerk of her head. The two exchanged a few whispered sentences. Then Ellis stepped away and headed toward the door, with Jan hurrying to catch up behind her.

Pat watched them go and let out a long sigh. "I'd also not been making a move on anyone, since I had a feeling this would happen."

Bo looked uncomfortable. Obviously, she understood what Pat meant; however, it did not take much tact for Katryn to know not to ask questions. Tina and Sal left the table and joined them at the bar.

Tina turned her head to look sideways at Katryn. "A word of

advice. Ellis may have implied that you can call her Mel, but I wouldn't recommend trying it. 'Sarge' is a safer bet if you can't avoid her off duty."

"Thanks," Katryn said, trying to look more at ease than she felt. She could not afford to start judging the other members of the patrol; neither was it wise to isolate herself. She slipped her purse free from her belt. "Anyway, the offer still stands; it's my round. What do you want to drink?"

Katryn turned to the bar, waiting to get the attention of the bar staff. Behind her, Bo started talking. "Now that Auntie Jan has gone, we can have some fun. Pat and I were just saying that Katryn ought to prove she's up to the standards of B Patrol."

"You had something in mind?" Tina asked.

"We certainly did. That woman who was annoying you..." Bo indicated with her thumb. "Katryn should give her something to really get upset about. Try to score with her girlfriend."

Sal yelped with laughter and leaned against the bar. "And she deserves it. I can't stand jealous women."

Katryn clenched her teeth as the last remnants of fellow feeling for her comrades vanished. At the other side of the room was the couple in question. It did not help that the disputed girlfriend had a passing resemblance to Allison. Their smiles were identical.

Bo patted her back. "There you go, Katryn. A unanimous vote. Are you up for it?"

"No." There was ice in Katryn's tone, but no one seemed to notice.

Pat chipped in. "Why not? She isn't that bad-looking."

"Don't worry; we'll back you up if fists start flying," Tina added.

"It's nothing to do with the woman or her partner. I'm just not ready to..." Katryn's voice died as she bit back her rising anger.

"Oh, you're not going to tell us you're nursing a broken heart for the woman you left behind, are you?" Bo screeched with laughter, oblivious to the accuracy of her taunt.

Katryn bit her lip.

"Do you know your problem?" Pat said. "You drink too slowly. If you'd been keeping up with Sal, you'd have lost all your inhibitions by now."

"And probably the contents of your stomach as well," Tina tagged on the end.

Bo leaned on the counter and looked at Katryn. The woman would not let things drop. "So…when are you going to make your move?"

"I'm not," Katryn said grimly.

"Why not?" Pat said. "There's no need to be nervous. With your looks and a Ranger's uniform, you could have any woman in the tavern. Five dollars says the girlfriend falls into your arms."

Katryn snapped. She spun around. "I don't flirt with other people's partners, certainly not on a bet. I don't get drunk. I don't pick fights for fun. And I don't want to stay here any longer." She slammed her money down on the counter. "When you get the bar staff's attention, you can buy yourselves a drink on me. I'm going back to the barracks." She started to stalk off, elbowing her way through the groups of drinkers to grab her cloak.

Behind her, Tina said softly, "Then you should have joined the Temple Guard rather than the Rangers."

Katryn did not look back. The door of the tavern swung closed. Outside, it was cold, and a soft fall of snow had started. Katryn's mood faded from anger to bitterness as she walked up the street, shoulders hunched. She stopped on the bridge and stared down at the ice-bound river. Things were not going well. All she had to do was say something unpleasant about Jan Sivarajah's mother, and she would have set the whole patrol against her.

The cold wind attacked the tears that spilled down Katryn's cheeks. Six months before, she had been happy, with a job she was good at and enjoyed. She'd had friends, a partner she loved, plans to become a mother. How had everything gone so wrong? It had to be a nightmare. The trouble was, she showed no signs of waking up.

❖

The next day started with the bell ringing out over the barracks. Katryn rolled over and sat up. She had heard the other Rangers return some time during the night, but when she looked around the bunk room, she saw that two of the beds were empty. It did not take long to find out who was missing. Even before the chimes had died away, the door opened and Nikki trotted in, grinning broadly. Her appearance was greeted by a few ragged cheers and other, less polite noises.

The far door to the sergeant's room opened, and Ellis emerged. "Wakey-wakey! Rise and shine!" Ellis' voice made the words sound like a threat. She stopped by Katryn's bunk and looked up. "Parade in twenty minutes. And Militia…" She used the word as though it were a name. "Look tidy. Make sure you get the buttons in the right holes—your sword belt not twisted. Get someone else to check your kit before you set foot outside."

Katryn might have felt annoyed by the patronizing tone, but her thoughts were distracted by the sight of Pat Panayi slipping out of Ellis' room and heading for her locker. Nobody else showed any surprise, though they all must have noticed. Ellis flung out a few more caustic comments and left the bunkhouse.

Tina wandered over and threw Katryn's purse up onto her bunk. "Thanks for the offer, but we didn't pay for the drinks with your money." Tina's expression and tone were both utterly blank, but Katryn already had enough of a feel for the woman to sense the underlying scorn.

Katryn merely nodded in reply. If she wanted to fit in with the rest of the patrol, she was going to have to make concessions, but there was no time for explanations, and Katryn was not sure whether she wanted to give them anyway.

Pat was standing by the wood-burning stove, warming herself before venturing out. She rolled her head back and pulled an expression halfway between a pout and a smile. "I think a good long wash is called for this morning." She cast a further sideways look around the room, eyebrows raised, and left.

At first, it seemed that there would be no comment. Then Tina said calmly, "And we all know which Ranger won't be shoveling shit out of the stables this month."

❖

Sergeant Ellis shouldered her way through the door of the barracks, grasping a fistful of letters. "It seems as if your mommies haven't forgotten about you after all!" Ellis shouted. Her face held a wide smile, but it was artificial—no more than a mechanical device to show that she was not currently angry with anyone. Even that much of a concession to friendliness fell away when she stopped by Katryn.

During the ten days Katryn had been in the patrol, their relationship had not improved.

Ellis' lips twisted in taunting scorn. She held up a letter. "Do you reckon that this is for you?" There was something challenging in the tone; however, Katryn scarcely noticed in the shock of seeing the handwriting. In Allison's slanting scrawl were the words

> *Sergeant Katryn Nagata*
> *Ranger Headquarters*
> *Fort Krowe*

Katryn only just remembered to reply, "Yes, ma'am," as she took the letter. Ellis continued to glare at her, but the others were waiting for their post, showing as much impatience as they dared, and the sergeant eventually turned away.

Katryn jumped up onto her bunk and sat cross-legged, staring at the outer sheet of paper, oblivious to the noise and laughter in the barracks. Someone had drawn a squiggle through the bottom two lines and written *12th Squadron, Highview Barracks* instead. Katryn wondered how long it had taken the redirected letter to reach its destination; presumably, it had only just missed her at Fort Krowe. She toyed with the idea of returning it unopened, but not seriously. She had to know what the letter said.

Her hands were shaking as she broke open the seal with her thumb. The three sheets of paper were densely covered in Allison's handwriting. Katryn spread them flat and began to read.

> *My darling Kat:*
>
> *I've been stupid; I know I have. Can you ever forgive me? How could I have thought your sister was in any way a match for you? I feel as if I have lost all right to say this, but I love you...*

Katryn put down the letter. Tears—partly of pain, partly of anger—blurred her vision. She did not need to read any more to know that Cy had tired of another rag doll.

CHAPTER ELEVEN—MISUNDERSTANDINGS

"Hey, Militia."

Katryn looked up from putting the finishing touches on polishing her boots in acknowledgement of what had become her nickname. Sergeant Ellis was standing over her. "Yes, ma'am?"

"Captain Dolokov wants to see you right away in her office."

"Yes, ma'am."

Katryn quickly pulled her boots on and headed toward the door of the bunk room. Just as she reached it, Ellis spoke again. "Someone's reported a lost dog."

Scattered laughter rippled around the room. Katryn looked back, wondering whether the summons was real or whether Ellis was merely pulling her leg. "Does the captain really want to see me, ma'am?"

Ellis did not speak but waved her away with a gesture like swatting a fly. Katryn stalked out of the building and across the parade ground. If it were a joke, Ellis would have to run after her—either that or explain to Dolokov why she was playing silly tricks on her subordinates. However, when Katryn arrived, it turned out that the summons was genuine, and she was immediately directed toward the captain's office.

Captain Dolokov was waiting for her, arms crossed, perched on the front of a battered old desk. Lieutenant Bergstrom was also there, standing to one side. As Katryn entered, they both fixed her with hard, accusing stares. Something was clearly very wrong. A knot was forming in Katryn's guts as she came to attention. "You wanted to see me, ma'am?"

Dolokov examined her in silence for nearly a minute. Katryn felt the pulse hammering in her throat. The captain had been back from patrol for only three days, and this was the first time Katryn had met with her, but she had heard a lot. Dolokov had been promoted to captain less than six months earlier. It was predicted that she would soon be making changes in the squadron. Jan Sivarajah had implied that some changes were long overdue. Dolokov was said to have strong ideas that did not always fit with the rule book. "Arrogant," "callous" and "bitch" were three words often used to describe her. She made many people nervous. Katryn could understand why.

When Dolokov finally spoke, it was so sudden that Katryn jumped. "Are you aware that it is a severe disciplinary offense to impersonate someone of a higher rank?"

"Yes, ma'am."

"And have you ever done that?"

"No, ma'am." Katryn relaxed a little as she guessed where the conversation was going. It should not take too long to get there.

Dolokov leaned back and studied Katryn for a few more seconds. "Then can you explain why you've been receiving mail addressed to 'Sergeant Nagata'?"

"Yes, ma'am. I was a sergeant in the Militia at Woodside. I relinquished the rank when I joined the Rangers. The letter in question was from someone who knew me when I was in the Militia and used my old rank, unaware that it was no longer appropriate."

Captain Dolokov looked startled. "You were a sergeant?" There was a faint edge of skepticism in her tone.

"Yes, ma'am," Katryn answered. "It should be in my records."

Dolokov's gaze became thoughtful but no less stern. Abruptly, her posture eased, and she gave a small nod, presumably satisfied that Katryn would not be stupid enough to make up a lie that could be disproved so easily. Her head tilted to one side as she continued to examine Katryn. "You must have been very keen to join the Rangers."

"Yes, ma'am, I was." Katryn tried not to emphasize the past tense.

"When you next write home, impress on people your new status, so that there are no grounds for misunderstandings in the future."

"I'll try, ma'am."

"Try?" Dolokov challenged her.

"I can't guarantee it won't happen again."

"Why not?"

"My grandparents were very proud of my rank as sergeant, and their memories can be conveniently lax at times."

The faintest suggestion of a twitch pulled at the corner of Dolokov's mouth. "Yes. I've got a grandmother like that as well." Her expression hardened again. "Very well. Dismissed. And Private, I'll leave it to you to explain the situation to Sergeant Ellis."

"Yes, ma'am."

Katryn stepped outside the office and drew a deep breath. Surprise and alarm were giving way to anger. It had not taken the last sentence from Dolokov to work out who had reported her. Katryn thought of Ellis with contempt. As a sergeant in the Militia, Katryn would never have accused one of her subordinates without talking to the person involved first. She would have made sure that she had uncovered all the facts and would have supported her junior if there were any possible doubt of the woman's guilt. Further, if the accused were guilty, she would have taken no pleasure from the consequences.

Ellis had wanted Katryn to be in trouble. In hindsight, Katryn realized that it was obvious from Ellis' face when she delivered the message. She stared across the parade ground, trying to compose herself before she returned to the bunkhouse. The captain had told her to explain the situation to Sergeant Ellis, but Katryn doubted her ability to talk to the woman in a civil fashion.

Ellis was still there when Katryn entered the bunkhouse. The sergeant stood back smugly as Katryn pulled open her locker and kneeled to rummage through her belongings at the bottom, no doubt assuming that Katryn had been sent to collect the evidence of her guilt. It took a few seconds for Katryn to find the item she wanted: the letter from Militia divisional headquarters. She scanned it quickly, refreshing her memory of the details. It was an official dispatch with an authenticating seal. It made clear reference to her rank in the Militia and warned of forfeiture—as though she might have been unaware of the rules. It also contained the carefully worded promise of promotion to lieutenant if she abandoned her attempt to join the Rangers. *Let Ellis chew on that!*

Katryn stood up and closed the door of her locker. She walked over and held out the letter. "I think, ma'am, that this will make the situation clear."

Ellis' face froze in confusion. Neither woman moved. Then Ellis snatched the paper. Katryn turned and left. The anticipated pleasure of watching Ellis' face as she read was still not enough to keep Katryn in the same room with the sergeant an instant longer than necessary.

❖

From the hills above, the buildings looked deserted. Not even a guard dog roamed in the snow-covered yards around the six cottages. Then Katryn noticed the soft trickle of smoke from a chimney stack and heard the bleating of sheep inside a barn. When she got closer, she saw footprints in the snow. Yet only the sheep and the wind disturbed the utter silence as the column of Rangers rode into the center of the hamlet.

Suddenly, a door opened, and an elderly woman rushed out. "You're here! Praise the Goddess!"

Three more doors opened, and other women emerged. Some had red eyes. All looked frightened. Katryn heard "Too late" muttered more than once.

Lieutenant Bergstrom halted by the first woman. "You've seen them?"

"No, but..." The woman broke off, fighting for control of her breath. "My two daughters went out to the East Woods early this morning, and they haven't come back."

"They went out?" Bergstrom repeated. "Haven't you heard there's a pride of snow lions in the area?"

"Yes, but we were running low on fuel, and we've got a woodpile already cut and stacked back there. They took the sledge. They should only have been gone half an hour." The woman's face started to crumple.

A baby cried, too young to understand the words but old enough to sense the fear. Katryn looked around at the villagers. In a tiny community like this, they would all be related to the missing women: nieces, cousins, aunts. The expressions of grief and dread on some faces were hard to bear; even harder was the desperate hope on others. They stared at the Rangers as though they were a miracle from the Goddess. It would be a miracle if the missing women were still alive.

After a few more questions, Lieutenant Bergstrom got directions to the woodpile and led the column up the valley. Once they were out of earshot of the huddled family group, Ellis said, "Looks like we're closing in on the lions." After the misery they'd just left behind, the cheerfulness in Ellis' voice grated on Katryn.

Bergstrom was also disapproving. She turned her head to glare back at the sergeant. "We don't know yet that it is the lions. There may be another reason for their delay."

Ellis shrugged and dropped her voice. "True. A fool can always get into trouble. And you know what they say: 'Only fools and Rangers go out when snow lions are around.'" She glanced purposefully at Katryn and added in an even lower mutter, "Of course, some folk belong in both categories."

The Rangers advanced as quickly as was safe, which was not very quick. Stumbling into the jaws of the snow lions would help no one, but many were clearly chafing at the delay as each clump of undergrowth was checked. It had been ten days since word of the snow lions had reached Highview, and Lieutenant Bergstrom had taken B and D Patrols out to hunt down the dangerous predators. They had followed the trail of sightings and dead farm animals, steadily gaining on their quarry. Now they were closing in. It would be tragic if they caught up with the pride a few sorry hours too late to prevent the deaths of two women.

Unfortunately, the tragedy was not to be averted. Before they got halfway to the woodpile, they came across the abandoned sledge, piled high with logs. Not far away was an area where churned snow was stained red. Jan Sivarajah swore under her breath. Others were not quite so restrained.

"Quiet!" Ellis' biting undertone silenced the outcry. "They're close. We don't want to make enough noise to scare them away."

Belatedly, Bergstrom appeared to realize that Ellis had given the order she should have issued herself. With a show of reasserting her authority, the lieutenant beckoned Ellis and Sergeant Takeda of D Patrol to her side. After a few minutes of talking, the two sergeants returned to their patrols with orders.

"Agosta, Hassan, keep watch over to the right. Castillo, you and Panayi clear the logs off the sledge. Wan, stick with me. Sivarajah, check out the tracks; see what you can learn. Nagata…" Last of all, the sergeant turned to Katryn. "We're going to have to take the bodies back with us. See if you can find all the bits and load them on the sledge."

The Rangers dispersed to their tasks. Katryn walked over to the blood-stained snow. "Bits" was a fair description; Katryn was not sure she could even identify some of the lumps of flesh as human. Her stomach heaved, but she fought back the spasm and glanced over her shoulder. Ellis was watching her, smirking. The sergeant would love it if she threw up or fainted. Katryn gritted her teeth, determined not to give Ellis that pleasure.

Katryn knew it was not simply the luck of the draw that she was the one given the job of collecting the bodies. Ellis always assigned the most unpleasant and menial tasks to her. At first, Katryn had thought it was some sort of apprenticeship for the newest member of the patrol, but since the incident with the letter, it had gotten worse. Ellis seemed to have a personal vendetta against her. Not only was Katryn treated as the patrol drudge, but she was also continually criticized and ridiculed in front of everyone else. Her relationship with the rest of the patrol had gotten off to a poor start, and Ellis was doing her best to isolate Katryn still further.

The parts of the dismembered bodies were strewn over a wide area. Katryn bent down and grabbed hold of the nearest large section— a torso. As she pulled on it, the guts spilled out into the snow. Katryn kneeled and took four deep breaths, building herself to scoop up the intestines with her hands.

There was a voice at her shoulder. "I'd say this one was caught by an old male. You can tell from the distance between the incisor marks on the shoulder." Katryn turned her head to see that Jan was crouched down beside her. Somehow, the corporal's footsteps had not even squeaked in the snow.

Jan met her eyes and then spoke in a whisper. "If I help you pick up the bodies, Ellis will get mad, but I was told to examine the tracks, and the best place to start is here. I know it can be rough, the first time you come across victims of snow lions. You have to learn to be detached. For one thing, getting emotional won't help, and for another, there is important information to pick up here. It might save someone else from the same fate. So don't think; just watch and listen." She raised her voice again slightly. "Those prints there would be the male, and there are at least two adult females. One has a weakness in her back left paw. You do know what I mean by 'male' and 'female'?"

Katryn nodded, focusing her attention on the impromptu lesson. The assignment of Jan to investigate the scene had also not been random. Everyone knew that she was the best scout in the squadron. Her observations were astute, soon catching Katryn's interest enough to let her step back mentally from the gruesome task she was performing. In fact, a faint smile touched her lips once. If she could have only one ally in the patrol, Jan was easily the best choice.

❖

By late afternoon, the Rangers were again on the trail of the snow lions, heading toward the crest of a ridge. Dusk was not far off. Normally, they would have stopped and returned to their lodgings for the night, but dark clouds were building on the eastern horizon. A storm was blowing in. If they did not overtake the pride that day, the tracks would be lost, and then they would have more days of scouring the countryside for sightings—and maybe more bodies.

Katryn was positioned in the rear of the column. Ellis had implied that it was the place where she would be least likely to get in the way. With nothing to do except tag along, she could allow her thoughts to wander. The place they went most often was to memories of the dead women. Jan had assured her that most of the damage had been inflicted after the women were dead, the lions mauling the bodies in frustration once they found that they were unable to eat their prey, but it could not have been a pleasant death.

Jan had asked whether she understood the terms "male" and "female" in relation to the lions. The Rangers' basic training had covered the topic briefly, as far as was necessary to understand the composition of a pride. And of course, Katryn was already familiar with the teachings of the Sisterhood—that the Goddess had to provide an alternative method of procreation for wild animals, because Cloners could not get close to them. Dual-sex reproduction meant that snow lions were genetically unique, like imprinted humans; so by the teachings of the Sisterhood they had souls. To prevent the sacrilege of eating anything with the divine spark, humans and wild animals were mutually inedible. It still left questions, such as the ethical status of wild animals eating one another and why lions could not eat cloned farm stock. The main question in her mind, however, was why Celaeno had not completed the job and given snow lions the sense to know that humans were not a source of food.

The brow of the hill was only a stone's throw away when Katryn's thoughts were interrupted. A signal rippled down the line, and the Rangers came to a halt. The horses stamped their hooves in the snow. At the front, Bergstrom, Jan and the two sergeants slipped down from their saddles and walked the short way to the top of the hill on foot. Katryn waited with the rest in silence. After a few minutes, the four Rangers returned, and the signal was given to dismount and gather around.

Bergstrom started to talk softly. "We've caught up with them.

They're settling down for the night on the other side of the hill. There are six in all, one a juvenile. A couple look unwell; they probably ate a mouthful of the women or some farm animal. We're going to split—B Patrol left, D Patrol right. Follow your sergeant, and stick to cover. I'll stay up top. When both patrols are in position, I'll give the signal to attack. Three short whistles. Nobody must break cover until then. Okay?" She looked around. "Right. Go."

Katryn slipped into file directly behind Jan. Ellis led them on a wide sweep, crossing the skyline behind the shelter of an outcrop of boulders and then down into dense undergrowth. By the time the signal to stop came, it was starting to get dark. Katryn crouched beneath the straggly branches of a bush and drew her short Ranger's sword. There was neither sight nor sound of the snow lions. She almost wondered whether this was another of Ellis' stupid wind-ups. Then she heard a low, rumbling growl. It was closer than she had expected.

Katryn's mouth went dry. She braced her hands on the ground to hide the sudden shaking. Still, there was no signal. The waiting was a nightmare. Katryn found herself longing for something to happen. Action would be easier than thinking.

Without warning, there were shouts, and the roars of snow lions broke out in a frenzy. Confused, Katryn looked at Jan. Had D Patrol attacked before the signal, or had something gone wrong?

Ellis was standing a little way to one side, peering through the branches at a point that offered a better view down the hillside. She was shaking her head with a smile that owed more to malice than to humor. Her only other movement was when Tina rose and started to advance. Ellis held out her hand. "Remember the lieutenant's orders. Wait until the signal." Ellis' voice was a low growl.

The sounds of fighting got louder. Then, above the shouts, came a long scream. Katryn stared at Ellis. D Patrol was in trouble. Was Ellis really going to keep them there in deference to a plan that had clearly gone astray? But at last, Katryn heard the signal, three short whistles. As one, the eight Rangers of B Patrol burst from the bushes and hurtled down the slope.

Once she was in the open, Katryn was able to see what was going on. Forty meters away, in the gloom at the bottom of the hill, three snow lions were prowling around a huddle of women. A juvenile was hanging back, and one other beast already lay dead on the ground. The largest lion was closer at hand, crouched over something, but at the sight of the new group of Rangers, it leaped up and began bounding up the slope.

The animal was huge, nearly the size of a horse. Its shaggy white pelt hung like a mat of knotted rope, stained red around the muzzle. Saberlike fangs slotted into grooves in its square lower jaw. The beast headed straight for Jan, probably selecting her as the smallest target—a mistake. As the lion sprang, Jan sidestepped. The dull light hit her sword in a silver blur. The lion either did not see or did not understand the danger. Its momentum carried it on, impaling itself on the blade. Too late, its body twisted aside and crashed down onto the snow. Even before Jan had torn her weapon free, Sal had come to her aid and embedded her own sword in the snow lion's throat.

Meanwhile, Tina had reached the juvenile and dispatched it with ease. The young lion, hungrier and less experienced than the others, had obviously forced down a mouthful from a body and was suffering the effects of iron poisoning. At the bottom of the hill, the attack from B Patrol had distracted the other beasts, and the defending Rangers seized on their confusion. Two more lions went down. The last remaining animal turned to flee—straight onto the swords of Bo, Nikki and Ellis. It was over.

Katryn skidded to a stop. She stared around in confusion, realizing that she had drawn her sword in earnest for the first time and done nothing more than run down a hill, waving it about. Ellis would make a joke of it. Even as the thought went through Katryn's head, the sergeant's eyes turned in her direction. But before Ellis could say anything, Sergeant Takeda charged over. "Where the fuck were you?"

"Obeying orders. What were you doing?" Ellis snapped back.

"Why didn't you attack on the signal?"

Ellis paused. "We did."

"No, you didn't. I know you, Ellis, and how you hang on to your record among the Rangers. You let my patrol—"

Ellis cut in, raising her voice. "You went too early, hoping to claim all the kills. And now that you've been chewed up, you want to shift the blame."

"Chewed up!" Takeda almost screamed in outrage. "Yes, some of my girls have been chewed up, and I swear, if any of them are seriously hurt, you'll pay for it."

Lieutenant Bergstrom, her face gray, arrived to hear the last exchange. "Ellis! Takeda!" Her voice cut through the argument. "This will be discussed at the proper time and in the proper way. Take charge of your patrols."

The two sergeants became aware of their audience. They both stepped back and looked around. Most of D Patrol was clustered around the spot where the large snow lion had been crouched. Takeda stalked over to join them. A short way off was another Ranger from D Patrol, swaying on her feet, her uniform soaked in blood, her eyes glazed. Takeda directed two Rangers to her assistance, but at first, the women of D Patrol seemed to be unwilling to disperse. Takeda literally had to push her subordinates into doing her bidding. As the tight knot of women separated, Katryn saw a figure lying unmoving on the ground.

Jan had been standing close by the group, watching intently but making no move to intrude. Now she walked away, shaking her head. As she came closer, Tina muttered, "Who?"

"Fitz. Dead." Jan gave the terse answer.

"Shit." Tina stared down at the blood on her own sword, her lips compressed.

Katryn stood to the side, feeling like a detached observer. She remembered Fitz from D Patrol complaining about her breakfast that morning, yawning as she saddled her horse, adjusting the collar of her cloak to keep her ears warm. Katryn's eyes fixed on the bar of red clouds lining the horizon. The sun had dropped out of sight. The day was over.

Jan came and stood close by Katryn. "Are you okay?"

"Oh...yes, sure," Katryn answered distractedly. "I didn't get anywhere near a live lion."

Jan glanced back. Several members of D Patrol were crying. "It's not a good start to active service."

"What went wrong?" Katryn needed the answers.

"You were there. You've got as much idea as me."

"What did Takeda mean about Ellis' record in the Rangers?"

Jan's mouth twisted. "Ellis has a lot of faults. But one thing she does well is keep her subordinates alive. Her patrol has the lowest injury rate in the entire Rangers." Jan patted Katryn's arm. "You may not have a nice time serving under her, but you stand the best chance of someday collecting your pension."

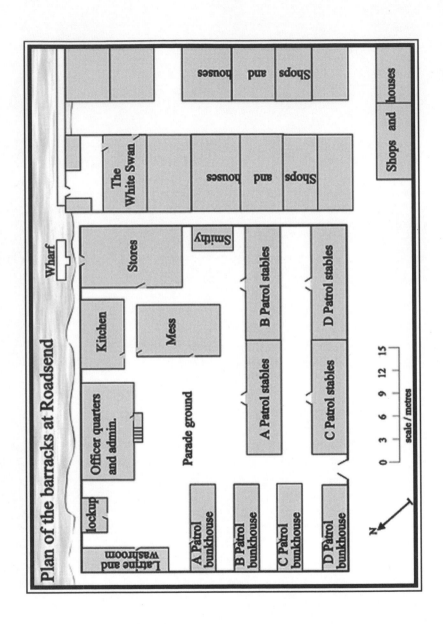

Plan of the barracks at Roadsend

Wharf

Shops and houses

Shops and houses

Shops and houses

The White Swan

Stores

Smithy

Kitchen

Mess

B Patrol stables

A Patrol stables

D Patrol stables

C Patrol stables

Officer quarters and admin.

Parade ground

lockup

Latrine and washroom

A Patrol bunkhouse

B Patrol bunkhouse

C Patrol bunkhouse

D Patrol bunkhouse

scale / metres

0   3   6   9   12   15

N

CHAPTER TWELVE—ROADSEND

At the beginning of May, the 12th Squadron was posted to Roadsend. Katryn knew that regular shifts in scenery were part of life in the Rangers. The squadrons were rotated around all the bases covered by a division. It meant that by the time a woman reached the rank of sergeant, she was already familiar with the terrain throughout the region, rather than having to perform emergency reconnaissance during a crisis. It was also true that the authorities liked Rangers to be flexible, not overly attached to any location or to the women who lived there.

The town of Roadsend was well to the south of Highview. The mountains were lower but no less rugged, carved into broken cliffs and canyons of red sandstone. Forests were confined mainly to the uplands; the valleys were stripped of trees. It was sheep country, with scattered flocks ambling over the scrubland. Roadsend had gotten rich on the trade in wool. Mutton stew was the staple food.

The barracks were virtually identical in layout to those at Highview, although the site backed onto the river, and the position of the stores had been adjusted to take advantage of the loading wharf. The most obvious difference was that the buildings were made of brick and stone rather than wood. Within two days of arriving, the squadron had settled back into its old routines—routines that included Katryn spending the evening standing sentry duty at the gates of the barracks.

Only in the most exceptional of circumstances did sentries fulfill a military role. Normally, the gates were unguarded. Sentry duty was used almost exclusively as a punishment, a boring way of wasting time, and everyone going in or out would see the woman and know that she had committed a disciplinary offense.

Katryn found that aspect the hardest one to take. The loss of her free time was not so bad. She had no wish to go into town, get drunk and pick up a local woman, which appeared to be the only form of entertainment on offer. But she had spent so many nights at Highview on duty by the gates that by now, everyone in the squadron must believe her to be either incompetent or a troublemaker. She was halfway to doubting herself.

That morning, Ellis had found fault with the state of Katryn's kit and had canceled her free time for the evening. As she stood to attention by the gates, Katryn's eyes drifted over the darkening hillsides surrounding the town while she went over the charges in her mind. All the equipment had been cleaned, polished and sharpened to the best of her ability. Katryn dared not do otherwise. But Sergeant Ellis had described her work as a disgrace.

Katryn chewed on her lip. Was it possible that Ellis was right and her kit had been in so much worse a state than anyone else's? No. Katryn closed her eyes. She knew that Ellis' charge was simply unjust—and especially galling because Bo had spent less than half as long on the same task.

Katryn's thoughts were disturbed by the crunch of footsteps. "Are we awake here?" Ellis' voice rang out.

"Yes, ma'am," Katryn replied sharply. It was unwise to assume any of Ellis' questions to be rhetorical.

The sergeant came to a halt in front of Katryn and looked her slowly up and down, a scowl of distaste twisting her features. "Why are you here?"

"My kit was not prepared to an acceptable standard, ma'am."

Ellis took a half-step back; then her face shifted into a mocking grin. "That's why I put you on sentry duty. But what I meant was, why are you still here?"

"Ma'am?" Katryn was confused.

"I told you to stand duty for two hours,. You've been here three."

"I…" Katryn bit back her words. Ellis had originally stated her duty as being for the entire evening; Katryn was certain of it. But there was no point in arguing or calling in others as witness. It was just Ellis' idea of a joke.

"Of course, if you want to stay here all night, you can." Ellis threw the words over her shoulder as she started to walk away. "But you've got to be bright and alert for tomorrow. I'm sending you out with Corporal Sivarajah on patrol." Her voice was fading, but Katryn could still make out the last sentences. "I won't start crying if she doesn't bring you back, but that'd be too much to hope for. A few days without you will have to do."

Katryn glared at the sergeant's back as it faded into the dusk. "And I'm sure you won't enjoy those days without me half as much as I'll enjoy the days without you," she whispered under her breath. Then, as though the word were an obscenity, she spat out, "Ma'am!"

❖

The site Jan chose for their camp the first night verged on the idyllic. A stream gurgled down a narrow valley sheltered by fragrant fir trees. The thick grass was as springy as a mattress. Through breaks in the branches, the rich blue sky was speckled with the first stars. The only sounds were the water, the breeze over the treetops, the chomping of the horses and the crackle of the campfire. Best of all, no one was there apart from the two of them. However, as the light faded, Katryn found herself growing uneasy and repeatedly having to fight the urge to peer over her shoulder.

"You worrying about what's creeping up behind you?" Jan asked, grinning, clearly amused.

Katryn jumped guiltily. "I...um...well..." She swallowed. "I've only been out in the wilderness in large groups before, and I guess I..." Her voice died.

"Think we might be outnumbered by a pride of snow lions?"

"No," Katryn said quickly. There had been none of the malicious ridicule that Ellis would have put into the words, but she did not want to give the other Ranger grounds to think she was a coward or a fool. "I know they'll all have gone back north by now. And it would have to be a very hard winter to push them this far south to start with. The largest predators are going to be mountain cats, and they aren't likely to be a problem at this time of year, with plenty of their natural prey availa—"

Jan cut her off with a laugh. "It's all right. I was teasing you, not testing you."

Katryn closed her eyes and sighed. There was no need to get defensive, but it was starting to become a habit with her. She pulled her lips into a lopsided grin. "I was just trying to show that I hadn't slept through all my training classes."

"Very wise, too. They'll be an unending source of amusement as you remember them in years to come. Like, when you're being chased by three mountain cats in February, you can shout out, 'Shouldn't you be hibernating?'"

"With all due respect, in those circumstances, I think I might save my breath for running." Katryn matched Jan's smile, feeling more relaxed.

"You know, I think you're right." Jan feigned earnestness. "The time it happened to me, I *did* wait until I was safely up a tree before instructing them in proper behavior."

"So what else didn't they tell us about mountain cats that I should know?"

"They're far more timid than snow lions and much smarter. They usually run from people, and they can smell that they can't eat us. The only ones that'll try are ill; maybe they've lost their sense of smell. So watch out for cats with runny noses." Jan's tone was not entirely serious. "The only time they're generally dangerous is in a month or two, when the females are coming into heat and the mature males are staking out territory. The younger males form packs to harass them and squabble among themselves and pick fights with anything else that blunders their way. They mark the area with an oily secretion that smells like"—Jan wrinkled her nose—"rancid cider. So if ever you're on your own and you catch a whiff of it, it means you should be somewhere else. The youngsters mainly stick to the backwoods, but once in a while, a pack causes mayhem in an outlying farm."

"It doesn't sound like there is much need for a full squadron of Rangers to be stationed here permanently."

"Don't get that idea. Roadsend can be a very lively posting—or should I say very deadly?"

"What causes the problems?"

"Nothing with four legs. Sheep country is bandit country—as the 12th has found out in the past. It's due to size. If you kill someone else's sheep, you can pick up the whole carcass and walk off with it—not like a cow. Or if you want to keep the stolen sheep alive, there are hundreds of canyons where you can hide a flock for years. Shear them, and there's no way anyone can tell where the wool came from."

"The 12th has had run-ins with gangs around here?"

"Oh, yes." Jan poked at the fire and then raised her eyes to meet Katryn's. "Really major trouble. Almost wiped out the squadron."

"What!"

"Thirteen...going on fourteen years ago. It's part of the tradition of the 12th. I'm surprised no one has mentioned it to you before."

Nobody talks to me, Katryn thought but did not say.

"The only survivors still left in the squadron are Ellis and Bergstrom. Although the Roadsend quartermaster, Gill Adebayo, was a corporal in the 12th at the time."

"What happened?"

Jan pursed her lips. "There was a gang leader who called herself 'the Butcher.' Everyone else added the word 'mad.' She even scared the other thieves. She managed to get control of all the criminal activity in the area. Then she started extorting money from the town, which was her first mistake. The other crooks couldn't inform on her without implicating themselves, but the shopkeepers had too much to lose. Someone made a map of where the Butcher had her hideout, and a raid was planned, but word was leaked to the gang. If the Butcher had been sane, she'd have fled. Instead, she arranged an ambush, and the 12th walked straight into it. It was a massacre. Twenty-one Rangers were killed, and another six were badly injured."

"Twenty-one lost!" Katryn was horrified.

"And four of the injured never returned to active service."

"Did the Butcher escape?"

"She did on that day. But of course, Central HQ immediately sent every Ranger it could muster to Roadsend—eight full squadrons. Within two months, every member of the gang was either captured or dead. And those who were captured didn't last much longer. They were tried and hanged in the market square."

"Do we know who leaked the warning to the gang?"

"No." Jan shook her head. "Maybe a Ranger was engaging in unwise pillow talk or bragging as part of her flirting technique. Chances are, whoever it was paid with her life. I don't think the survivors were questioned too hard. They'd been through enough."

"It must have been bad luck that so many died."

"From what I've heard, it was more like good luck that any escaped. The gang knew the time and date of the raid and the route the squadron was going to take. They picked their spot. It was only because of Ellis that the massacre wasn't complete." Jan's expression hovered between awkwardness and defensiveness. Then she shrugged and went on. "I can understand if you find that hard to believe, but as I told you before, the one thing Ellis can do well is keep people alive. When all hell breaks loose, she keeps her head and makes the right decisions quickly. No one has ever seen her panic."

"And that makes her a good sergeant?" Katryn asked bitterly.

"No. She's a bloody awful one."

"Then why…?" Katryn did not need to finish her question.

"Because of the massacre. Ellis was only a Leading Ranger at the time. However, the Butcher had planed her ambush well. The captain and lieutenant were the very first to be killed. Utter chaos broke out, and the squadron became split. Ellis ended up in a group without any sergeants. I think there were a couple of corporals, but they were either wounded or panicking, so Ellis took charge and got most of the group out alive.

"Afterward, Central HQ had to decide what to do with the 12th. There were only nine able-bodied Rangers left. They considered disbanding the squadron and assigning the survivors elsewhere, but in the end, they rebuilt the 12th. That's when I came in as a new recruit. Dolokov was transferred over from the 8th as a sergeant. There are a few more of us around from that initial draft. Because Ellis had done so well during the ambush, she was promoted straight from Leading Ranger to sergeant. I suspect that if the captain or lieutenant or any of the old sergeants had survived, there might have been objections raised, but there was no one who could comment on her suitability for the post."

"In all these years, has nobody had second thoughts?"

"You have to serve under Ellis to realize just how bad she is. She looks better from above. I think the previous captain knew she was less than perfect, but there were no incontestable grounds for disciplinary action."

Katryn stared grimly into the fire. "That never stops Ellis."

Jan reached over and patted Katryn's shoulder. "I know you're having a rough time. It's Ellis' way of keeping discipline. There's always one member of her patrol who's out of favor. It's intended to keep the rest of us on our toes so we don't end up swapping places. Before you arrived, Bo Hassan was the main victim, and she largely deserves it. She's a lousy soldier. Sloppy. The Goddess alone knows how she passed her entrance tests. The rest of the patrol are okay—or would be with a better sergeant.

"Sal drinks too much, which should've been stamped on years ago. Ellis has let it get worse and worse. Maybe she thinks an alcoholic will be easier to intimidate. Tina bottles things up and then explodes. She needs someone to give her direction.

"Nikki is young and blusters. It's due to insecurity, which is understandable in our patrol, but in a few months, she'll get her Leading Ranger badge, and then she'll calm down. And Pat's competent, although not too bright."

"She seems sharp enough."

"She's got a pretty face, and she's taught herself to say little and look as if she's having profound thoughts, but..." Jan broke off, shaking her head. "She's the most one-dimensional person I've ever met."

"That must be a useful mental trait when you're sleeping with Ellis."

Jan snorted in amusement. "True. No matter who she's in bed with, the only woman Pat will ever love is herself. It's one of life's ironies. Pat is good-looking enough to have any woman she wants, and she's too self-centered to notice anyone else. She agrees to sleep with Ellis, as it guarantees her place in the sergeant's good books."

"So that's what I've got to do," Katryn said sarcastically.

Jan looked at her in sympathy. "I'm afraid your case is hopeless. It's your own fault."

Katryn glanced up sharply. Did Jan think there was any truth in Ellis' accusations? "I try my best."

"Oh, it's not your conduct. Your mistake was the letter you showed Ellis—the one from the Militia HQ, promising you a lieutenancy."

"Ellis told you about it?"

"She was spitting mad," Jan said with emphasis. "Because of her record, Ellis thinks she's the best sergeant in the whole of the Rangers. She's been expecting promotion for years, and she stands as much chance of it as I do of flying. Seeing Bergstrom promoted over her was the last straw. She wants that star on her badge so badly it hurts, and at last, she knows she's never going to get it. Then you show her the letter. You could have been a lieutenant. Even if you were only in the Militia, you'd have outranked her, and you turned it down. She hates you."

"Ah…right." Katryn rolled her head back and looked up through the branches at the stars. It explained some of Ellis' cryptic remarks.

"It may not sound too comforting, but if you hang on another ten months, I predict you'll be okay."

Katryn looked back at Jan. "Why?"

"Ellis is coming toward the end of her first seven-year extension of service. She may not apply to re-enlist, but even if she does, I think Captain Dolokov will reject her. Dolokov was a sergeant alongside Ellis for years. She's got a fair idea of what Ellis is like, and if she needs more information, I'm sure Val Bergstrom will be happy to give it."

"I've noticed Bergstrom and Ellis don't like each other."

"Bergstrom was once a private in Ellis' patrol and one of her favorite targets for abuse. Ellis was nearly as down on her as she is on you."

"What did Bergstrom do to upset her?"

"She was a new recruit at the time of the massacre, less than three months in the Rangers. When the bodies started dropping, she completely went to pieces—at least according to the way Ellis tells the story. Ellis has her marked down as a coward. Bergstrom's performed okay ever since I've been in the squadron, but it's had no effect on Ellis' opinion of her. Ellis tried to block her promotion to Leading Ranger. In the end, Bergstrom transferred to another patrol. There was a nasty feud between them while they were both sergeants. Ellis was completely stunned when Bergstrom got the vacant post of lieutenant instead of her, but there's not much she can do now that Bergstrom outranks her."

"The feuding can't have been good for the squadron," Katryn said thoughtfully.

"It wasn't. The 12th has not been a…" Jan paused, searching for a word. "…satisfactory squadron since the massacre. Ellis is one of the problems and the major thing preventing the other problems from being sorted out. The 12th has got some bad habits. Take the scene when Fitz died—sergeants squabbling like two drunks in a tavern. It shouldn't happen. The 12th desperately needs a sense of unity, and it'll never get it with Ellis around, because she only works on the 'divide and rule' principle. That's why Dolokov wants to get rid of her. The captain has been in the squadron long enough to know its weaknesses. She has to get all thirty-four women fighting on the same side, and she's prepared to be quite ruthless to achieve it."

"She could have blamed Ellis for Fitz's death and gotten rid of her that way," Katryn suggested.

"Not without setting B and D Patrols against each other. And she knows it's less than a year until Ellis has to re-enlist." Jan spoke through a yawn. She shifted back slightly and looked around. Dusk had thickened into night, and both moons were rising. "It's time for us to turn in. Make sure you've got your sword at hand. It's a good habit. But we don't need to take turns on watch. Nothing is going to bother us, and I'm an extremely light sleeper."

Her earlier jitteriness had gone, yet it still took Katryn some time to drift off. She lay wrapped in her blanket beside the fire and thought about Jan's comments. They helped explain a lot, including the events surrounding Fitz's death and Dolokov's response. The final, official account was that the wind had changed after the two patrols had separated. D Patrol had been downwind of Bergstrom and had heard her first signal, but the sound had been carried away from B Patrol. When she saw that Ellis' Rangers were not attacking, Bergstrom had changed position and repeated the signal. It explained everything except why Ellis had not used her initiative and gone to Takeda's aid.

Now Katryn could make sense of it. Ellis had stuck to the letter of Bergstrom's orders as a bloody-minded protest against someone she thought was unfit for the job. She must have assumed that any blame would be attached to Bergstrom rather than to her. Dolokov had been angry but did not want to divide the squadron still further. Assigning blame would not bring Fitz back.

At last, Katryn fell asleep and dreamed of waking up in Woodside with Allison beside her and the smell of baking bread in the air. The feeling of relief was so great that tears rolled down her face. But when she went downstairs, Ellis was there, eating breakfast with her mother.

❖

Two months after arriving in Roadsend, a report came of a raid on a farm to the south, and Captain Dolokov rode out to investigate with A and C Patrols. Katryn wondered at the wisdom of leaving Ellis under Bergstrom's command, especially in the company of D Patrol. Yet Dolokov could not compromise the flexibility of the squadron by avoiding that particular combination permanently, and it was better that the potential trouble be left behind in the barracks. For a week, the routine patrols and drills ran smoothly. If anything, the atmosphere in the barracks was even more controlled than usual, as though people were avoiding conflict consciously. But Katryn had the nagging feeling that the control would not last—that something was about to go very wrong. When it did, however, it was not in the direction, or from the source, that she had expected.

It began late one day as Corporal Sivarajah led half of B Patrol back down the trail to Roadsend. The summer solstice was only a few days past, and the evenings were long. The incessant bleating of sheep carried on still air. Colors were muted in the soft light, like a smudged painting. Katryn was tired and hungry, but she felt no eagerness to reach their destination. They had been on a two-day trek through some of the gorges upriver, checking for any signs of illegal activity. Katryn had enjoyed the time. Jan was a good teacher, and just being away from Sergeant Ellis was cause for joy. Sal and Tina made up the rest of the group. Katryn was still not on good terms with the other members of her patrol, but at least when Ellis was not around, they could behave in a reasonable fashion toward her without incurring sarcastic abuse themselves. Normally, any friendly remarks to Katryn would put the speaker in the firing line for Ellis' bad temper.

They approached the barracks from the west, riding over the bridge and around the outer wall. As they turned the last corner, two Rangers were visible, standing sentry duty at the entrance. Katryn wondered who had upset Ellis in her absence. But when they reached the gates and dismounted, she saw that both Rangers were from D Patrol. Neither sentry moved a muscle as Katryn caught hold of her horse's reins and followed Jan the short distance to the central parade ground. B Patrol's stables were off to the right. Straight ahead, on the far side of the open space, were two more sentries standing guard outside the small lockup. Tina also noticed the motionless women and exchanged speculative comments with Sal. Something unusual had happened.

Pat Panayi was just leaving the stables as they arrived, with a bucket in each hand from watering the horses. Tina hailed her immediately. "Hey, Pat, what's up with Takeda's girls?"

Pat turned around; her face slid gradually into a disinterested smile of greeting. "Oh...we've had all sorts of fun while you've been gone." She waited until the rest drew close so she could drop her voice before continuing. "Last night, D Patrol went into town in a group; just Takeda and Corporal Kiani stayed behind in the barracks. There was an argument outside a tavern over someone's girlfriend, and a fight broke out with a gang of locals." Pat shrugged. "That wouldn't be so bad, but the new recruit, Zoe, drew her trail knife and stabbed a woman."

Simultaneous exclamations greeted the news.

"No!"

"Was she badly hurt?"

Pat shook her head. "Word is that the local will survive, but you can imagine the fuss people have been making. The town mayor wanted to turn Zoe over to the Militia, but Bergstrom managed to keep hold of her here. She's in the lockup. By general consensus, the only one from D Patrol who didn't get involved in the fight was Taz, so she's been sent with Kiani to let Dolokov know what's happened. The other four have had all their free time canceled and are standing sentry duty until the captain gets here. As a final point to calm the mayor, knives are banned off duty outside the barracks. We have to be searched as we go out."

A few more questions and comments followed, but it was getting late, and the horses needed attention. While she removed the saddle and brushed the mare's coat, Katryn thought about Zoe—Fitz's replacement, although no one referred to her that way. It would be wrong to imply that a dead woman was a replaceable item. Katryn had been jealous of Zoe and of the easy way she had become an accepted member of her patrol. The only teasing Zoe received was what anyone might expect upon joining a tightly knit group. Katryn was still an outsider. She knew that it was partly her own fault. She should have made compromises to fit in. She had chosen to become a Ranger; no one had asked her.

Katryn chewed her lip. She had been wrong to join the Rangers. It was a military unit, not a haven for heartbroken lovers. But it was too late to change her mind, so she was going to have to make the best of it. Perhaps it would be possible to improve her relationship with the other members of the patrol—if not for Ellis.

When they finished tending to the horses, the four Rangers left the stables and walked around to the doorway of the mess. They were too late for a hot dinner; however, Jan had sent Pat off with instructions to find bread, cheese, beer and (no doubt) cold mutton. As they reached the corner of the parade ground, the door to the officers' quarters opened, and Ellis and Takeda came out. Ellis saw the members of her patrol and strolled over, a broad grin on her face.

"You've heard what D Patrol has been up to?" Ellis made no attempt to keep her voice down. In fact, she seemed deliberately to be pitching it loud enough so that Takeda could not help hearing. "It's bad enough stabbing a civvy, but she couldn't even make a proper job of it. It'll save her neck, but her training can't be up to much. Some patrols are very sloppy. Isn't it a good thing that I make you practice your knife play?"

Katryn was pleased that there were other people around to reply. There was nothing even remotely appropriate she could say. Her voice would have failed, merely uttering, "Yes, ma'am." Fortunately, Jan took the lead and moved straight into a brief report on what they had seen upriver.

Katryn averted her gaze. In the middle of the parade ground, Sergeant Takeda had come to a stop and was glaring at Ellis with a look of pure, venomous hatred.

CHAPTER THIRTEEN—DISOBEYING ORDERS

Early sunlight glinted obliquely on the dusty earth of the parade ground the next morning. Birds screeched in the treetops. The rangers of B Patrol stood to attention in two rows of four. A little to one side, the depleted ranks of D Patrol were also present for the dawn inspection. Lieutenant Bergstrom paced deliberately along the line, her eyes scanning each woman as she went. Quartermaster Adebayo and the two members of her staff stood a short way back. No one else was in sight. During her time in the Rangers, Katryn had witnessed a couple of dawn parades with fewer women present, but she had never known one that felt so empty.

At last, Bergstrom returned to the top of the steps outside the officers' quarters and read the orders for the day. D Patrol was assigned to routine drills and maintenance tasks that would keep its members inside the barracks. Bergstrom turned to B Patrol. "There is a report from Three Firs Ranch in Upper Tamer Valley of a pack of mountain cats. Sergeant Ellis, take half your patrol and go and investigate. You need to talk to a rancher called Wisniewski."

Katryn was standing directly behind Ellis. She noticed a twitch in the set of the sergeant's shoulders and a faint backward movement of her head. Neither gesture was pronounced enough to count as defiance, but it was clear that Ellis was not pleased. To Katryn's left, Sal breathed out sharply. It sounded like a contemptuous sigh, but the noise was too soft for Bergstrom to hear, even if she had not already moved on to the final few assignments.

When the parade had been dismissed, Ellis turned to her subordinates. "Okay. Militia, you seem the right person for a wild-goose chase. Hassan, you'll come with me as well, and…" She looked at the other women. "Agosta. You'll be good at keeping a straight face when Wisniewski starts describing the fifty gigantic cats that have slaughtered half her flock."

Katryn was confused. Normally, she was not the first choice for a serious mission, but obviously, Ellis was not expecting the patrol to find any trace of the mountain cats. Katryn glanced at the other Rangers. They all looked either bored or scornful. Even Jan seemed unbothered. Katryn assumed that rancher Wisniewski had a reputation for false alarms.

❖

It was midmorning when the four Rangers arrived at the Three Firs homestead. The sun blazed down on the ramshackle collection of buildings from a clear blue sky. A shepherd working in the barn volunteered to escort Ellis and Tina in search of the ranch owner. No conversation had taken place during the ride out. Ellis had not made any attempt to conceal her bad mood, and the rest of the patrol had wisely kept silent. However, once the sergeant strode out of earshot, Bo muttered, "I wonder how many thousand sheep Wisniewski has lost this time?" The heavy irony in her voice was plain.

"Can I take it that Wisniewski often complains about mountain cats?"

"Oh, mountain cats, bandits, dishonest neighbors. Next thing will be invisible pixies rustling her sheep."

"She's got an overactive imagination?"

"She's got an underactive wallet." Bo hesitated. She was the member of the patrol who made the most effort to distance herself from Katryn; however, Bo was also very fond of the sound of her own voice. After a few seconds, she continued, "Wisniewski won't hire enough hands for the size of her flock, so she's always losing sheep. She uses the Rangers like auxiliary shepherds. Bergstrom should have sent the message back that we were too busy, except that she knew she could irritate Ellis by sending her here."

Ellis and Tina reappeared from around the end of the barn in the company of a woman Katryn assumed to be the ranch owner. Wisniewski was gesturing to the southeast, her hand flapping and pointing while she told her story. It looked as though she was cut off short when Ellis turned away and marched back to the horses. Tina tagged along behind.

Ellis provided no information as she led the way, heading in the approximate direction indicated by Wisniewski. In half an hour, they reached the top of a deep gully and turned east, following a sheep track that ran along the rim. After a few more minutes, the path disappeared into a loose thicket of thorn-covered shrubs, and Ellis signaled for them to stop. "Apparently, the savage beasts are all down there," she jeered, indicating the gully with her thumb.

Katryn twisted her neck to peer over the edge. The sides were steep, sheer in places and covered in loose gravel. Only a few low bushes sprouted on the slopes, but more plants grew at the bottom. A small river cascaded over broken rocks twenty meters below the path where they stood.

Sergeant Ellis swung her leg over the head of her horse and jumped down from her saddle. "Let's check it out quickly so we can get back to Roadsend and do something more useful—like combing our hair. Agosta and Hassan, come with me. Militia, stay here with the horses and look after them. That means make sure they don't run away."

Katryn grabbed the reins of the horses and stood watching as the other three scrambled carefully down the steep incline. Bo tripped at one point and slid several meters until she fetched up against a buttress of rock protruding halfway down the side of the gully. Tina was the first to reach the bottom. She crossed the stream, jumping onto a flat-topped boulder midway and then using another stepping-stone before pulling herself onto the far bank.

"You've got five minutes to play beside the river. Then we can all go home and say we searched the area. If you spot any sign of the missing sheep, don't bother making notes. We aren't going to report back to Wisniewski. She can find her own sheep," Ellis turned downstream, ducking under the branches of a spindly tree. Bo picked up a handful of pebbles and began tossing them into the water as she followed. Tina headed upstream. A rockslide reaching down to the water's edge blocked her path. Tina clambered over the fallen rocks and moved on, disappearing behind a clump of bushes.

Katryn stood alone in the glaring sunlight. The air smelled of dust and baked leaves. The horses shuffled their hooves and took a few mouthfuls of dry grass but were too well trained to stray far. Minding them was an excuse—isolating Katryn with a pointless task to demonstrate Ellis' opinion that she was incapable of doing anything useful.

A soft wind stirred the bushes, carrying a fresh scent to Katryn. She wrinkled her nose and looked around, trying to identify which plant was the source. It certainly would not win any prizes for its fragrance. A hint of overripe apples was in the odor, but the general effect was of decay—like rancid cider. Even as the thought occurred to Katryn, a second gust blew, confirming her impression.

She leaped to the gully's edge and opened her mouth, about to shout a warning, but then she stopped. If she was wrong, Ellis would not merely make a joke of it. The story would provide ammunition for months of baiting—proof of weak nerves and gullibility.

Katryn took an indecisive step backward and then spun around and dived toward her mount. She tore the bow from her horse's saddle pack and strung it with quick, practiced movements. She grabbed four arrows from the quiver, stuck them in her belt and returned to the vantage point at the head of the slope.

The figures of Ellis and Bo were visible atop a rock ledge overhanging a deep pool. Ellis had her hands on her hips as she examined the scene. Bo was looking down at the water.

Katryn's mouth was dry. Tina had emerged from the undergrowth some way upstream and stood on the bank, seeming to be looking for a way to cross back. There was no sign of life in the gully except for the three women. And then Katryn saw a patch of shade on the opposite bank mold itself into a sleek, muscled form before flowing into another dark shadow under a bush.

"Agosta! Watch out! Behind you—cats!" Katryn shouted at the top of her voice.

Tina looked up at the cry, shading her eyes from the sun. But instead of moving, she twisted to look downstream, the palms of both hands held up in an exaggerated shrug, as though she were seeking guidance from Ellis on how to respond. It was not frozen inaction due to fear, Katryn realized. Tina simply did not believe her.

The cat was moving closer to Tina through the brushwood. And now that Katryn's eyes were attuned to the shape, she could pick out two more, crouched on the slope above.

She started to nock an arrow, but now the cat stalking Tina was under cover. It would not be visible from above until it was upon its victim. Katryn needed to get lower for the shot.

She launched herself down the gully wall, her feet skidding wildly, arms thrown wide for balance. Her uncontrolled descent ended when she crashed into the same rocky projection that Bo had hit earlier. The impact jarred every bone in her body, but Katryn did not have time to notice. Somehow, she had kept hold of the bow. She clawed her way back up the slope until she was above the obstruction; braced one knee against the ground, one foot on the top of the rocks; nocked an arrow; drew; and took aim.

Tina might have been unmoved by Katryn's shouted warning, but the sight of an arrow pointed in her direction produced an immediate response: She ducked and threw herself sideways. In the bushes just behind where she had been standing was the cat, crouched and ready to leap.

The distance was at most thirty meters, but Katryn did not have the chance to test her range or the wind.

"Nagata! What the fuck do you think you're…"

Katryn was scarcely aware of the sound of Ellis' voice. The cat's body surged upward. She loosed the arrow and watched it arc through the air, hitting the cat in mid-leap. The animal yowled and crumpled, writhing, to the ground. Its cry screeched over the rushing of the stream, cutting off Ellis' words. Tina scrambled to her feet, staring at the dying beast. Then she leaped off the bank without bothering to identify stepping stones and waded through the knee-deep water.

Another cat broke from cover. It reached the bank and hunkered down, gathering itself to pounce on the fleeing Ranger, until Katryn's second arrow hit it square in the chest.

Ellis and Bo were racing up the riverside. They reached Tina just as she got to the bank and helped pull her out of the water. Then the three of them, swords drawn, began a slow retreat toward Katryn on the rock.

On the gully wall opposite, Katryn could see the shapes of six more mountain cats. Suddenly, she heard a noise to her right, on her side of the water. She twisted around and saw a cat bounding down toward her.

Katryn did not have the time to draw or aim properly. Instinctively, she loosed the arrow half-set, her bow horizontal. It was only by the grace of the Goddess that the arrow hit its target and the cat's charge became a tumbling roll down the slope.

She pulled the last arrow from her belt and nocked it on the string.

She raised her head. The situation was grim. They were outnumbered by the beasts and in a poor defensive position on the exposed, unstable gravel. Fortunately, the cats did not think that way. They had seen three pack members struck down, and that was enough to scatter them. On the other side of the gully, the animals were going, fading away into the dappled shade of the bushes.

The other Rangers also saw the cats depart and sheathed their swords, freeing their hands to help them in the tricky climb. Katryn kept in position with the last arrow on the string until they reached her.

Ellis' face was twisted in a snarl. "I ordered you to stay with the horses."

Katryn could not believe her ears. Her anger flared. "Was I supposed to stay there and watch Tina get killed?"

"You're supposed to obey orders, you're not supposed to desert your post, and you're supposed to say 'ma'am' when you speak to me."

"Fuck you! I—"

The back of Ellis' hand cracked hard across Katryn's face. "What did you say?"

"I said..." Katryn's voice died, jolted back to common sense as much by the violence of Ellis' tone as by the blow. Regardless of the justice of the initial charge of disobeying orders, Ellis had snared her into insubordination. The sergeant's triumphant expression showed that she knew it as well. Katryn swallowed her words. "Nothing, ma'am."

"Oh...nothing? Well, for that 'nothing,' you can lose all your free time for the week. It's a shame Takeda's girls have grabbed all the sentry duty. But you can start tonight by polishing the saddles and harness for the whole patrol, and we'll take it from there," Ellis snapped out savagely. Then she jerked her thumb, pointing up the slope. "Come on. We don't want to hang around until the cats regain their courage." She set off on the rest of the climb.

Katryn did not move. She waited until the sergeant was out of earshot. "I'll kill her. I swear it. I'll kill her."

Tina also had not moved. Her eyes traveled to the spot where the bodies of the two cats lay and then back to Katryn. "You had me worried at first, but that was a neat shot."

"Thanks," Katryn said listlessly.

"I think I'm the one who should say 'thank you.'" Katryn looked up. Tina's expression held genuine appreciation and commiseration. She held out a hand to help Katryn out of her half-kneeling position. "We'd better not keep Ellis waiting."

"True. I wouldn't want her to get *really* mad at me."

Bo had been dithering to one side. She joined them as they started to climb the hillside. Tina continued talking. "You've rattled Ellis; that's why she was such a bitch just now. She's got you pegged as useless, and then you go and preserve her injury record. You can't expect her to be grateful...but I am." Tina paused as they negotiated a steeper part. "You know why she hates you?"

"Jan told me. It was letting her know I'd turned down promotion to lieutenant."

"You turned down...?" Bo joined in. It was obviously news to her.

"Only in the Militia," Katryn said.

They reached the top of the gully. The horses were a few meters away. Ellis was already mounted and waiting impatiently.

Tina dropped her voice. "My advice is to get out of B Patrol. Ask to be moved next time there's a place in one of the other patrols. Val Bergstrom should be sympathetic if you make your request via her. It was how she got away from Ellis."

❖

They headed back to Roadsend as quickly as possible, but by the time they reached the barracks, it was midafternoon and too late to return to the gully with a larger force of Rangers. The two sergeants and Jan Sivarajah were summoned to meet with Bergstrom to make plans for the next day. The other Rangers were assigned to various preparatory tasks. Katryn was detailed to work with Bo in the stores under the supervision of Gill Adebayo, the Roadsend quartermaster.

A long scar puckered the side of Adebayo's face, making it hard to be certain of her age, although Katryn judged her to be younger than forty. The quartermaster also walked with a pronounced limp; her left leg scraped across the ground as she approached the entrance to the storeroom. Her shoulder badge bore the single star of a lieutenant, but because she was a member of divisional staff, the identification *Eastern* rather than a squadron number was embroidered below it.

Quartermasters were responsible for buying supplies, hiring civilian workers and supervising the maintenance of the buildings. Unlike most Rangers, who lived nomadic lives, they were assigned permanently to one town so that they could establish good working relationships with the local businesses. Invariably, the post was filled by a Ranger who had retired from active service or, as Katryn guessed was the case with Adebayo, been invalided out.

Adebayo took a key from the pouch on her belt and unlocked the main door. She led the way to the back of the stores and used the same iron key to repeat the action at the rear entrance. Katryn looked out. The doorway opened some way above water level, and a vicious row of spikes protruded from the wall below to deter anyone from climbing up. An expansive view of the river was on offer, with a barge moored to the loading wharf. Between the doorway and the wooden jetty was a gap of nearly two meters; however, just inside the door were four long planks, designed to form a removable bridge.

The quartermaster pointed to the barge. "Everything on it is for us. Pile it all there"—she indicated an empty spot in the storeroom—"and I'll be back shortly to check it against the invoice." Her voice was authoritative but vague, as though she were thinking about other, more important things.

Katryn and Bo positioned the planks and began to unload the barge. None of the crew were onboard to help, but because there was not a vast amount of goods to be carted off, it did not take long to empty the hold. Adebayo had not returned by the time they had finished and dismantled the bridge. Katryn found a comfy seat on top of a pile of sacks containing oats for the horses. Bo shuffled around, seeming uncharacteristically self-conscious, and then sat down beside her.

"You were amazing with the cats. I didn't know you were such a good shot." Bo launched into speech.

Katryn pulled a bitter, humorless smile. "The assessment from the tests at Fort Krowe is in my records. I doubt Sergeant Ellis has bothered to read it, and even if she has, it's not surprising she hasn't spread the news around."

"Ellis can be a complete bitch."

"That's one of the politer words for her." Katryn was slightly confused. Bo had never made any attempt at friendliness before, but now there was no mistaking her eagerness to talk.

Bo gave her a conspiratorial grin and said, "Even the less polite words don't really do her justice. There's always one member of the patrol she picks on. It always used to be me…except when it was Sal or Nikki. Pat sleeps with her to stay in favor, Jan's too useful, and I think Ellis is a bit scared of Tina's temper. Of course, she'd never admit it. But with me…" Abruptly, Bo's voice struggled as the good humor failed. "I'd go months on end without doing a thing right and lose half my free time. And I know when you're in that position, it seems as if the whole patrol is laughing at you. But it's just…" She swallowed. "It's how Ellis works—keeping you isolated. And there isn't much anyone else can do."

Bo looked so unhappy that Katryn had to say, "I understand," although she wasn't sure that she did.

A weak version of Bo's grin returned. "Ellis has canceled your free time, and it isn't fair, given how it was. If you want to appeal to Bergstrom, I'll back you up, and Tina will as well. You saved her life."

Katryn toyed with the idea for a second and then shook her head. "If she'd accused me of disobeying orders, I might stand a chance of appealing, but I swore at her. I think I got off lightly."

"Ellis deliberately provoked you. She's virtually admitted she was in the wrong by not taking things further. She's grounded you for a week because that's the most punishment she can dish out without referring it to Bergstrom or Dolokov. She knows she'd never make a charge of insubordination stick."

"It's not worth causing trouble over. Hopefully I won't be serving under Ellis for too much longer. I can hang on for a few more months. But thanks for the offer." It occurred to Katryn that by being so vindictive, Ellis had done her a favor. At last, she might be able to make some friends in the squadron.

"Everyone hates Ellis, you know—except Adebayo." Bo interrupted Katryn's thoughts.

"I guess not serving in the same squadron as Ellis would help."

"She used to." Bo paused. "Has anyone told you about the trouble with the Mad Butcher?"

"Yes, Jan did."

"Adebayo was badly hurt in the battle. She couldn't return to active service, so she joined divisional staff. She was promoted to quartermaster here a few years back. But even though she's got the scar and the limp, she reckons that she owes her life to Ellis."

"And she must remember Ellis from when she was a private. Maybe Ellis was okay before she got promoted." Despite Katryn's words, her tone was skeptical.

"You're more charitable than me. Some people even think Adebayo…" Bo's voice died.

"Pardon?"

Bo shrugged. "Just rumor, but I've heard some say that Adebayo sucks up to Ellis because she's being blackmailed."

"Over what?" Katryn asked.

"Well, she's a quartermaster. People are always saying quartermasters skim the accounts. There's no evidence I know of, but maybe Ellis has—"

The sound of shuffling footsteps made Bo break off guiltily. They both jumped to their feet as the quartermaster hobbled in through the main door.

"Someone misfiled the invoice." It was a criticism, not an excuse. Adebayo unfolded the sheet of paper and began to read. "Seventeen sacks of oats. Two barrels of weak beer. Five rounds of cheese." She carried on down the list, counting off the items.

Bo and Katryn stood a little to one side, waiting until they were dismissed. While Adebayo's back was turned, Bo whispered, "Did she say seventeen sacks of oats? I'm sure we carried in more."

Katryn met her gaze and then moved forward to a spot where she could surreptitiously count the sacks in the pile. Bo joined her just as Adebayo finished running through the invoice but said nothing until they were dismissed from the stores and heading toward the bunkhouse to get ready for dinner. Adebayo stayed behind to lock up.

"You counted the sacks?" Bo asked.

"There were seventeen." Katryn's lips twisted in a wry grimace.

"Oh, well." Bo pulled her widest grin. "Sorry." There was an unexpected depth of emotion in her voice.

"That's okay." Katryn said, although she was not sure whether the apology was for sowing false doubts or for a lack of friendliness in the past.

Chapter Fourteen—In the Storeroom

When they reached the bunkhouse, Pat was the only one in sight, sitting on the edge of her bed. She had several sheets of paper spread out in front of her—presumably, a lengthy letter. Yet instead of reading, her eyes were fixed on the floor. Her frown made her appear confused rather than annoyed, but it changed to a quizzical smile at the sound of footsteps.

Bo gave a quick wave of greeting but for once said little. She undid the buckle on her knife belt, pulled open the door of her locker and thrust the belt inside. "I've...just remembered," Bo mumbled, backtracking toward the door. "I'll catch up with you in the mess." She turned and darted away.

Katryn removed her own knife more carefully and hung it on the peg inside her locker. After the long ride and the work in the stores, she felt in need of a good wash, but there was no time before dinner, and she would be busy afterward.

"I hear you've impressed Tina with some fancy shooting," Sal called out.

Katryn stuck her head around the door of her locker, for the first time noticing the other Ranger lying on her bed. Sal's bunk was the one below Katryn's, diagonally opposite Pat's. "I...er...yes. We had some trouble with mountain cats. I was the only one with my bow at hand."

"And you know how to use it."

Katryn shrugged. There was no point in false modesty.

"That must have put Ellis in a nice mood," Sal said casually.

Katryn grinned and wandered over to stand by the bunk. "Oh, it did. I've lost all my free time for the week."

"Of course she couldn't admit you'd done well without admitting she'd made a mistake. Our sergeant isn't very good at humility."

"I know. I wasn't expecting congratulations."

"So how good are you with a bow?"

"I scored 528 on the field test at Fort Krowe."

Sal's lips shaped into a soundless whistle.

"You've kept that quiet," Pat joined in.

Katryn looked back over her shoulder. Pat had put aside the letter and was standing by Katryn's open locker, peering in at the contents as though she expected to see something remarkable there. Katryn felt a ripple of irritation at the blatant snooping, but there was no real privacy in the Rangers. The lockers did not even have locks, and Pat was incapable of understanding that her behavior might cause offense. Katryn let it go. "It's not the sort of thing that crops up in conversation. And Ellis insists we always practice on our own at the butts."

Sal grinned broadly. "That's because she couldn't hit a barn from the inside and doesn't want to be shown up. I'm afraid she isn't going to love you at all."

"And who'd have thought Wisniewski would be right for once?" Pat interjected.

Katryn made a half shrug. "I think that was my advantage. If it had been the twentieth time I'd been dragged out to Three Firs Ranch, I might have not paid any attention to the smell."

"Smell?"

"Something Jan warned me about. The sign of a pack of cats. It was what alerted me and made me string my bow."

"So Jan was indirectly responsible for your getting one up on Ellis," Sal said. "That will please her when she finds out."

"Jan?" Katryn was surprised. "I thought she got on okay with Ellis."

Sal gave a bark of laughter. "She probably hates her more than any of the rest of us."

"She hides it well."

"She hides a lot of things."

It was an unexpected insight, but before Katryn had time to question Sal further, the bell for dinner rang out over the barracks. Sal swung her legs off her bed and stood up. Katryn pushed the door to her locker shut and then followed the other two out and across the parade ground.

❖

The brushes, rags, polish and other items lay in a neat semicircle around the spot where Katryn was kneeling. Her eyes ran over them one last time, checking that nothing was missing; then she picked up a cloth and pulled the first saddle toward her. She was just starting her search for dried mud when she was interrupted by the sounds of footsteps and voices. She looked up to see the members of B Patrol entering the stables, with Tina in the lead. Jan Sivarajah was also present, but fortunately, not Sergeant Ellis.

"How's it going?" Tina asked.

"Just started."

"I could give you a hand."

Katryn was taken by surprise at the offer. "I...er...thanks. But Ellis has threatened to stop by later, and she wouldn't be pleased if she found you helping me."

Tina shrugged. "Tough. She's never pleased about anything anyway."

"Well..." Katryn looked at the pile of saddles and harnesses; then she shook her head. "No, it's okay. My free time is canceled, so I can't leave the barracks. I might as well have something to do to pass the time. But thank you."

"If you're sure," Tina conceded.

The other members of B Patrol filed through the open doorway. Nikki and Pat moved farther in and went to check their horses in the stalls while the rest gathered around the spot where Katryn was kneeling. Their faces held a range of expressions from supportive grins to awkward sympathy, but none held any hostility—at least, none directed at her. They all clearly felt that Ellis had treated her badly and were prepared to make a token show of solidarity with her. However, they were not at ease. Alliances within the patrol were shifting, and no one was too sure where things were heading.

"You're going into town?" Katryn asked. It was not a serious question, just words to demonstrate friendly interest—something that had been lacking in the past.

"Thought we'd check out a tavern or two," Sal answered.

"Just one tavern, and not for long," Jan said firmly. "We don't want to be tackling cats with hangovers tomorrow."

"I didn't know the cats drank alcohol," Bo joked. Sal barged her with one shoulder.

The foolery softened the tension. Tina grinned and flexed her shoulders as though she were adjusting the weight of a rucksack. Jan picked up a rope that had been dropped just inside the door and began to coil it. Pat left her horse and came to stand in the doorway, resting her back against the frame and staring vacantly at the roof of the smithy.

"Did we decide where we're going?" Nikki called over.

"Someone said the White Swan," Tina replied.

"Why there?"

"Not so far to stagger home," Bo joined in again. "Always assuming I can get something to drink," she added thoughtfully.

"Is that in doubt?" Sal asked.

"Could be. I've just realized that I've left my money in my locker. My purse was on my knife belt. I forgot to keep hold of it when I took the belt off," Bo explained.

"Clown! Go and get it." Tina shoved her toward the door.

"Right. I'll meet you by the gates in a couple of minutes." Bo jogged away.

Nikki wandered over. "I don't like having to leave my trail knife behind. I wonder if I could hide it inside my jacket. Will they really search us on the way out?"

"That's what Bergstrom said. And a knife isn't easy to hide," Sal spoke up.

"I could slip it down my neck so it lies against my spine."

"That's an old trick. You can guarantee that the sentries will pat your back to check."

"And why are you so keen to take your knife?" Tina asked dryly. "You've already carved your initials on the wall of every outhouse in town."

Nikki grinned awkwardly "It's just...supposing that someone has a grudge against Rangers? The sentries search us on the way out to make sure we're not armed, but no one is searching the townsfolk when they leave home. It puts us at a disadvantage."

"Another good reason for the White Swan. It's got two exits," Tina said.

"All taverns do, if you talk nicely to the bar staff." Pat's voice came from the doorway.

"And we won't ask how you know." Jan grinned and held up the neatly coiled rope. "This belongs in the stores. I'll just go and see if the door's open. Adebayo might be working late." She trotted off and returned a few seconds later. "No, I've left it by the door. The next person in should see it."

After further shuffling around, the Rangers exchanged expectant looks. Nobody seemed sure what to say, but eventually, Sal spoke. "So are we ready to go?" She smiled apologetically at Katryn to show that there was nothing personal in her desire to leave the stables. There were a few grunts and nods of agreement; then the Rangers headed out. As each one left, Katryn smiled or waved goodbye.

Alone once more, she sat staring at the open doorway. It was the friendliest exchange she'd had with her patrol comrades since the night she had joined the 12th. She thought of the dozens of times she had watched the others set out for an evening of drinking. For the first time, she wished she were going as well.

Katryn was halfway through the eight saddles when she heard footsteps. She glanced up as Sergeant Ellis appeared at the entrance to the stables. Katryn started to scramble to her feet. "As you were," Ellis snarled.

"Yes, ma'am." Katryn dropped back to her knees. Her lips tightened in a line. It was unclear whether the order also meant to continue working. Of course, she would be wrong either way, slacking if she gave Ellis her attention or ignoring her superior if she concentrated on the saddles. After a second's pause, she picked up the polishing rags. Seeing that she could not win, she might as well look at Ellis as little as possible.

"Are you enjoying yourself?"

"No, ma'am." *Certainly not since you arrived,* Katryn added to herself.

"Put that cloth down and pay attention to me when I'm talking to you."

Despite the aggression in Ellis' voice, Katryn had to fight to keep the smile off her face. The petty vindictiveness was quite predictable. "Yes, ma'am."

Ellis leaned against the doorjamb and studied her. For a long while, the only sounds in the stables came from the horses. Then Ellis' lips pulled back in a parody of a smile, and she took a key out of her top pocket. "I've borrowed the key to the stores from the quartermaster. I thought I'd have a little look around in there."

That will be nice for you, ma'am. Katryn bit back the words. From Ellis' tone, she was clearly supposed to deduce something, although she did not have a clue as to what.

"Do you think you've done well for yourself today?"

I've saved Tina's life, and I've started to make friends with the rest of the patrol. Aloud, Katryn said, "Obviously not, ma'am."

"Obviously?" Ellis' tone made it a question.

"If I'd done well, you wouldn't have canceled my free time, ma'am."

A flush of anger darkened Ellis' face, but there was nothing in the words that she could object to, and Katryn was careful to keep any sarcasm from her voice. Ellis glared. "It takes more than a few lucky shots to make a marksman."

"I know, ma'am."

"And it takes more than a gray and green uniform to make a Ranger."

"Yes, ma'am."

"You'll never be a proper Ranger. You should have stayed in the Militia."

Katryn clenched her jaw. At last, there was something that she and Ellis agreed on. The sergeant left her position by the door and crouched down so that her face was scant centimeters away from Katryn's. "Why did you leave the Militia?"

"Personal reasons."

"And you wouldn't like to share those reasons with me?"

"No, ma'am."

Ellis nodded as though the answer was significant. "You weren't running away?"

"From what?" Katryn's anger started to kick in.

"You tell me." Ellis moved back slightly. "You turned down promotion. You must have been frightened about something catching up with you." There was gloating in Ellis' eyes. She stood up. "Carry on with your work. I'll talk to you again later, after I've checked the stores."

"Yes, ma'am."

Katryn watched Ellis' back disappear down the passageway between the storeroom and the rear of the mess hall. Anger gave way to confusion and apprehension. The sergeant had been hinting at something. But what?

❖

The daylight faded into a gentle dusk. Katryn considered fetching a lantern to finish her work, but she had little left to do—just one final set of reins. So instead, she opened the other half of the doorway and sat in the entrance with her back to the light. Ellis had not returned, and Katryn was not complaining. She felt quite happy. The work had been therapeutic, allowing her time to think, but not as tedious as sentry duty.

Allison had occupied a fair chunk of her thoughts. Now that her heart was starting to heal, Katryn knew that she had been overly hasty. She should have listened to Captain Kalispera. Katryn winced as she remembered their last, uncomfortable conversation. Kalispera had made no attempt to hide her resentment. Joining the Rangers had been a mistake. It was not the life Katryn wanted, but perhaps it would be possible to fit in and make a place for herself in the patrol—after Ellis had gone.

Finally, Katryn put down the polishing cloths and held up the harness to catch the last of the light. The leather was clean and supple. It would not satisfy Ellis, but there was nothing Katryn could do about that. Ellis would be able to find fault with the work of the Blessed Himoti herself.

The sound of footsteps made Katryn flinch, but she immediately realized there was more than one set of feet making the noise. This was confirmed by the chatter of voices. B Patrol was returning from the tavern. She looked over her shoulder to see the strung-out group walking toward her. Tina and Sal were the first to reach the stable.

"How's it going?" Sal called out while she was still a few meters away.

"Just finished."

"Good timing. We can help you tidy up."

Katryn smiled and got to her feet. She felt numb from sitting on the ground so long. Her hands were sticky from the wax polish, and she restrained the impulse to scratch her nose.

Tina bent down to pick up one of the saddles. "I hope you got mine nice and shiny." Her tone was deadpan, but Katryn could tell that she was teasing.

Jan, Bo and Pat strolled in next. They also lent a hand with the job of placing the saddles and harnesses in the tack boxes. Everything was done by the time Nikki arrived, breathing heavily, as though she'd had to run to catch up. Mainly out of habit, they checked the state of the horses; then they swung the stable doors shut and began to wander back to the bunkhouse.

Katryn was passing the mess hall when a voice from the rear called out, "Hey, isn't the door to the stores open?"

Katryn and the others backtracked slightly and peered up the alleyway. It was hard to be certain in the poor light, but the door did seem to be ajar.

"Perhaps Adebayo had to get something in an emergency?" Bo suggested uncertainly.

"Such as?" Pat asked.

Jan took the lead. She squeezed past the knot of women and walked the few meters to the doorway. Pushing it open, she stuck her head in and called, "Is everything okay? Do you—" Her voice cut off so sharply that it brought the rest running.

They crammed through the entrance. It was even darker in the storeroom than outside, but not so dark as to hide the sight of Ellis lying on the floor at the other side of the room, a dark patch of blood staining the flagstones under her and the hilt of a knife protruding from her back.

Everyone froze.

"Go get Lieutenant Bergstrom," Jan snapped at Nikki. The sound of her voice lifted the paralysis.

Bo stumbled forward and crouched to check for a pulse in Ellis' throat. After a few seconds, she stood up and shook her head.

Tina moved to the rear of the stores and rattled the door violently. "Locked," she called back.

Katryn stared at the body in horror. Now that her eyes were adjusting to the light, she could tell that the handle of the knife was unmistakably that of a Ranger's trail knife. A cold, dead weight formed in her stomach. In her ears, she could hear her own words from the morning: *I'll kill her. I swear it. I'll kill her.* She did not need to check to know that the others were already casting sideways looks in her direction.

A bustle at the entrance announced Nikki's return, accompanied by both Bergstrom and the quartermaster. "By the Goddess." Adebayo's muttered oath was the only sound.

Bergstrom stepped forward. "Have you sent for a healer?"

"No, ma'am. There's no pulse. Hassan checked," Jan replied.

"It might be an idea to see whether they can learn anything. Panayi, go summon one from town. And somebody get a lantern." Bergstrom crouched beside the motionless figure, waiting until yellow lamplight blossomed. "Have you seen anyone hanging around the stores this evening?" She threw the question over her shoulder.

"No, ma'am." Jan hesitated for the briefest moment. "We've been at the White Swan. Private Nagata is the only one who's been in the barracks."

"And you, Nagata. Have you seen anything?"

Katryn took a deep breath. "No, ma'am. I've been working in the stable. Sergeant Ellis came to see me about an hour ago. She said she was going to the stores. I didn't see or hear anyone else until the rest of the patrol returned."

"It's a Ranger's trail knife in her back," Bergstrom acknowledged the obvious. "And there's no sign of a fight or a break-in. I'm afraid that leaves us with limited suspects. Quartermaster, if you stay here, Corporal Sivarajah and I will see if we can find out whose knife is missing."

The atmosphere in the storeroom was ominous. Nothing was said; most of the Rangers simply stared at the body on the floor. Katryn could not bring herself to meet the eyes of the others. She did not want to know which of them had murdered Ellis. She certainly could not find it in her to blame the culprit. She only wished it had happened while she was somewhere else. It occurred to her that she was probably the last person, apart from the murderer, to see Ellis alive.

The fact that the murder weapon was left behind was an absurd blunder on the killer's part—a blunder for which Katryn was very grateful. Without its evidence, things would have looked awkward for her. She had left her own knife hanging in her locker. It had to still be there, but her nerves felt frayed as the wait for the lieutenant's return dragged on.

At last, they heard footsteps. Bergstrom strode through the door. Jan slipped in behind her. The lieutenant's eyes flitted quickly over everyone there and finally came to rest on Katryn. "Private Nagata, can you explain why your knife is missing?"

Katryn opened her mouth, but no sound came out. *I'm dreaming,* she told herself. *It's a nightmare, and I'll wake up in a second.* Every eye in the storeroom fixed on her. "No...no, ma'am. I left it in my locker when I went to the stable. I don't know where it's gone."

"Oh, I think we know where it's gone." Bergstrom's gaze shifted purposefully to Ellis' back. "And unless you can tell me different, it would appear that nobody apart from you had the chance to put it there."

"No, ma'am. I didn't do it." Katryn barely kept the panic from her voice.

"Really?" Bergstrom's tone was grim. "Well, this is definitely something for the captain to deal with. Hopefully, she'll be back soon. You can save your story for her. Sivarajah, Agosta, escort Private Nagata to the lockup."

CHAPTER FIFTEEN—THE EVIDENCE

The lockup was small, barely three meters square, divided into two unequal sections by a heavy iron grill with a padlocked gate. In the larger section were a pair of narrow bunks and a piss-pot. In the smaller section were a barred window and the door. There was not enough floor space between the beds for two women to pace up and down simultaneously. By midmorning, jokes about timetables were wearing thin, and the temperature was rising.

"Wait until afternoon. Then it really warms up in here," Zoe said cheerily.

Katryn sat cross-legged on her bunk, resting her back against the wall. She tried to smile, but her mood was despondent. The other woman seemed not to notice. Having spent two days alone in the lockup, Zoe was overjoyed to have company and rambled on without any need of encouragement. The stream of chatter was wearing thin with Katryn.

"I hope I get out soon."

Katryn nodded. Such a banal sentiment did not need a reply.

Zoe stopped talking long enough to study Katryn's expression. "You know, I don't blame you for stabbing Ellis." She paused. "That's if you did."

Again, Katryn did not speak; she had given up protesting her innocence.

After a few seconds of silence, Zoe went on. "I'm glad I didn't end up in Ellis' patrol when I joined the squadron. Takeda's a proper sergeant; she sticks up for her patrol. I mean, she was mad at me the other night, but she was still ready to listen to my side. And when I told her—you know that bitch was coming for me with a broken bottle in her hand? I used my knife in self-defense—something her friends forgot to mention when they called the Militia. Takeda came to see me yesterday. She's spent hours tracking down independent witnesses and has all their sworn statements. There's no way Ellis would have put herself out like that for a member of her patrol."

"Certainly not for me," Katryn agreed.

"Takeda has passed all the evidence on to Bergstrom. The lieutenant won't stick her neck out and risk upsetting the mayor by releasing me, but once Dolokov gets back, I'll be in the clear."

Katryn tilted her head up. A large flying beetle bounced its way in circles across the ceiling, hitting the stone surface with audible cracks.

"I know I owe a lot to Takeda." Zoe carried on talking, but her tone dropped, holding a sober intensity. "Without her, there's no way I'd have escaped a flogging."

Katryn's jaw tensed. Who was there to help her escape a hanging?

A surge of noise erupted outside in the parade ground—shouting and movement. "If that's more for in here, they'll have to sleep on the floor." Zoe's buoyant effervescence returned.

Katryn tried to ignore Zoe's voice, instead concentrating on the sounds outside. At least a dozen horses were trampling around. Then came the unmistakable tones of Captain Dolokov's voice calling the order to disperse. The rest of the squadron had returned.

Zoe leaped to her feet in excitement. "Wha-hay! Freedom, here I come!"

Katryn's shoulders drooped. Her own future did not look so good, but at least the waiting part would soon be over. In a sudden surge of fellow feeling, her eyes returned to the pointless, painful flight of the beetle.

❖

Zoe had been right about the afternoon heat. Sweat trickled down Katryn's neck and stuck her uniform to her body. She was alone in the lockup. Zoe had been escorted away hours before and had not returned. Presumably, Takeda's evidence had won the Ranger her freedom. Katryn tried to find humor in the ironic thought that she had the room to pace only when it was too hot for any unnecessary activity.

Several sets of footsteps stopped outside the door; then the key turned in the lock. Katryn sat up straighter as Corporal Kiani of D

Patrol stepped into the cell. With a second key, the corporal removed the padlock from the grill and beckoned Katryn out.

"Turn around."

Katryn obeyed and felt her hands tied securely behind her back. Outside the lockup, in the early-evening sunlight, another three Rangers were waiting, their faces impassive. They lined up as escort, two ahead and two behind, for the short walk to the captain's office. Several clusters of Rangers were gathered around the dusty edge of the parade ground. Without looking, Katryn knew that all heads were turned in her direction, watching her march, step by step, to her fate.

The captain's office led off the main administration room. The escort stopped at the door, allowing Katryn to enter alone. It was not a large room; the desk took up a third of the floor space. On one wall hung a detailed map. Opposite it, a window overlooked the parade ground. Three women were awaiting Katryn's arrival. Dolokov and Bergstrom were there, as expected. The other stood in a corner, dressed in the black uniform of the Militia, a lieutenant's badge on her shoulder. This woman looked to be past forty and had an intelligent expression combined with a brisk, no-nonsense manner. Katryn remembered seeing her around town.

Dolokov stood behind the desk, treating Katryn to a long, sour glare. Eventually, she spoke. "On the basis of the information received, I've decided to turn this case over to the Militia. Lieutenant Sanchez will be in command of the interview."

Katryn's initial surprise faded quickly. Rangers had to trust one another with their lives. Murdering a fellow Ranger was the worst crime imaginable, yet many Rangers would think that Ellis had deserved it. No matter what the verdict and sentence were, some members of the squadron would be deeply unhappy. Dolokov had done her calculations and decided to let the Militia be the focus of any resentment—a safe decision, particularly if she felt that there was no doubt about the outcome of the investigation.

Lieutenant Sanchez took a few steps forward until she stood directly in front of Katryn, claiming her attention. "Before we go any further, would you like to confess?"

"No, ma'am. I didn't kill Sergeant Ellis," Katryn replied quickly.

"Then who do you think did?"

Katryn hesitated; it was not quite the question she had expected.

"I don't know, ma'am." *But there are enough candidates,* she added mentally.

"You disliked Sergeant Ellis."

"No, ma'am, I hated her." There was no point denying it. Sanchez looked a little taken aback at the honesty. Katryn spoke again, "But I wasn't the only one." Out of the corner of her eye, Katryn saw Bergstrom shift uncomfortably.

"You're the only one we're interested in at the moment." Sanchez recovered her momentum. "Do you deny threatening to kill Sergeant Ellis on the morning she died?"

"I didn't mean it seriously."

"You were joking?"

"It was more a figure of speech."

"You were angry at her?"

Again, Katryn hesitated, but it was useless to lie. "Yes, ma'am. Very."

Sanchez drew a slow breath. "So you had motive and opportunity, and it was your knife that was found in her back. Are you sure you wouldn't like to confess?"

"Somebody else must have taken my knife from my locker."

"But nobody else could have taken it into the storeroom."

"It wouldn't—"

Sanchez cut her off. "You see, we are fortunate that two of your fellow Rangers were on sentry duty outside the lockup. From that position, they could see everyone who crossed the parade ground. The rear door of the stores was locked, and the key was found in Sergeant Ellis' pocket. It would be impossible to break in without leaving a sign. Therefore, we can be sure that the killer came and went via the main door, leaving it open behind her when she left. The two sentries saw Sergeant Ellis walk across the parade ground toward the stable and stores. Nobody else went in that direction until your comrades from B Patrol returned in a group, shortly before the body was discovered."

Silence hung in the room. Katryn shook her head in confusion. "There has to be…" Her voice died.

Sanchez continued softly. "Furthermore, we can place where everyone else was. Most of the squadron was with Captain Dolokov on the way back to Roadsend. Of the rest, the two sentries outside the lockup and the two at the main gates can vouch for one another. And we can also dismiss the Ranger in the lockup from the list of suspects. The six Rangers from your patrol were in a tavern and swear that nobody disappeared for part of the evening. None of them was carrying a knife; they'd all been searched on leaving the barracks. Lieutenant Bergstrom and Quartermaster Adebayo were together in the officers' quarters—in this very room, I believe."

Sanchez paused and glanced at Bergstrom for a nod of confirmation. "Sergeant Takeda spent part of the evening here with them, discussing some information she'd gathered, and then returned to her room. The sentries confirm seeing her cross the parade ground in the direction of D Patrol's bunkhouse, and also confirm that she did not return, with or without your knife. The two members of Adebayo's staff were on the other side of town, being entertained by a visiting trader. The sentries on the main gates attest that no one else entered or left the barracks all evening." Sanchez stared into Katryn's eyes. "I repeat, are you sure you wouldn't like to confess?"

"No, ma'am. I didn't kill her." Katryn could hear the edge of despair in her own voice.

"Then can you explain how someone entered B Patrol's bunkhouse, took your knife, crossed the parade ground, killed Sergeant Ellis and then left the stores without being seen? Or can you say how someone was in two places at the same time?"

"No, ma'am, I can't."

Sanchez's tone was remorseless. "There's only one way Sergeant Ellis could have been killed. You had left your belt in your locker but taken your knife with you to the stores, maybe in all innocence, thinking that you might need it for your work. After everyone else had gone, Sergeant Ellis came to talk to you in the stables. She said something to make you angry again, and this time, you had your knife at hand and no witnesses. You followed her into the stores and murdered her."

"No, ma'am." Katryn fought to keep her breathing steady.

"I think you did."

"Would I then have left my knife behind and gone back to polishing the saddles?"

"I've known murderers to do stranger things."

Katryn hung her head, trying desperately to gather her thoughts, to see the hole in the case being brought against her. "I didn't kill her," she reaffirmed, but now there was no hiding her panic.

Sanchez moved away to the desk and returned with a trail knife in her hands. She held it up in front of Katryn. "Can you deny that this is your knife?"

Katryn stared at it—the murder weapon. And then her eyes registered what they were seeing. "Yes, ma'am, I can."

"Pardon?"

"It's not my knife." Confidence had returned to Katryn's voice.

"What do you mean?" Sanchez sounded slightly rattled.

What I say. Despite her sudden feeling of euphoria, Katryn managed to restrain the retort. She swallowed before picking the words to explain. "I've only been a Ranger for six months. All my kit was issued new at Fort Krowe. This is the wrong knife. It's much older than mine. You can see the wear on the handle, and the blade is bowed from sharpening. It would take years to reach that state." She met Sanchez's eyes. "This is not my knife."

There was not a sound in the room for the space of several heartbeats. Eventually, the unexpected turn brought Dolokov in. "So you took someone else's knife with you to the stables."

Sanchez interrupted "Maybe we should find out whose knife this is first."

"How?" Dolokov snapped back.

Sanchez pursed her lips. "Well, from what Private Nagata says, there should be a veteran Ranger with a knife in pristine condition."

"I'll check." Dolokov moved toward the door.

Sanchez beat her to it. "I'll check, but you can come as well if you want."

Their places in the room were taken by two members of the escort waiting outside. Nobody spoke. Bergstrom stood staring through the window at the parade ground. Katryn tried to get her pulse under control while her mind raced over what she had been told. Somewhere, something was wrong, but she could not pull a coherent explanation together. Fortunately, it was clear that Sanchez was as sharp as she looked and not about to rubber-stamp the expected conclusion.

A fair slice of Katryn's thoughts was directed toward Dolokov. She wondered whether the captain was beginning to regret giving the case over to the Militia. Katryn's brow furrowed. It seemed as though Dolokov wanted her to be guilty, but her attitude probably was not malicious. The captain would see her as being one of the more expendable members of the squadron—certainly in comparison with other enemies of Ellis. Most of all, a clear-cut case was what Dolokov would want. The squadron would lose a Ranger, but there would be no suspicion attached to anyone else. No one would be left looking over her shoulder at her comrades.

The wait for Dolokov and Sanchez to return was agonizing. Once they were back and the two junior Rangers left, Sanchez again held out a knife. This time, the finger guard was unscratched, the cutting edge was straight and the wooden handle was not polished dark and smooth from years of use. "Is this one yours?"

Katryn nodded. "That looks much more like it, ma'am."

Sanchez compared it with the first knife. "I'll concede that the two cannot be confused."

"Where was it found?" Bergstrom voiced the question that Katryn had been dying to ask.

Sanchez pulled a wry smile. "It would seem that Sergeant Ellis was stabbed with her own knife. Private Nagata's was found hanging in its place in her room."

There was a lengthy silence, but at last, Dolokov faced Katryn and snapped out impatiently, "It makes no difference. You're still the only person with opportunity. You admitted that you hated Sergeant Ellis. You hated her enough to want to stab her with her own knife as the final insult. So you switched your knife with hers before going to the stables."

"No, ma'am. And if I'd planned the murder in advance, I wouldn't be so stupid as to do it when there were no other suspects."

"You admit that there are no other suspects." Dolokov pounced on her words, but Sanchez stepped in before Katryn could reply.

"Private Nagata couldn't have switched knives before going to the stables."

"Why not?" Dolokov said tersely.

"I've already checked with the sentries to make sure nobody had carried a knife off-site. As part of their evidence, they told me about an incident with Sergeant Ellis. After B Patrol had gone to the tavern, Ellis wanted to speak with one of them. She was challenged at the gates, as she was still wearing her knife. The sentries told her to remove it. Apparently, things got a bit heated."

I can imagine, Katryn thought.

Sanchez continued, "She wasn't permitted to leave the barracks until she'd put her knife back in her room. I have confirmation that she made a brief appearance at the White Swan and then returned to the barracks. I think if the knives had already been switched, Ellis would have spotted the difference just as quickly as Private Nagata did just now."

"She must have taken the knife after Ellis put it in her room."

Sanchez shook her head. "We have the evidence of the sentries that she didn't cross the parade ground after B Patrol had left the barracks."

"Obviously, the sentries weren't as alert as they claimed—probably chatting with the prisoner," Dolokov said doggedly.

Sanchez was equally implacable. "I'll agree that they must have missed seeing someone, but I don't see how we can positively identify Nagata as the person they didn't see."

"She had the best opportunity. She's still our top suspect," Dolokov persisted.

"I don't think so."

"Why not?"

"Because I can't see why she'd focus suspicion on herself by swapping her knife," Sanchez spoke calmly. "My guess is that Sergeant Ellis took her own knife into the stores. Somebody got in, took the knife and stabbed her. This woman had heard about the threat Private Nagata had made earlier in the day and decided to frame her. So the murderer took Ellis' empty belt, slipped across the parade ground without being seen and put Nagata's knife in the sheath before hanging it in the sergeant's room."

"That sounds pretty implausible," Dolokov said.

"Maybe, but I think it's the best option."

"How…" Dolokov's voice faded as the difficulty of finding a sensible sequence of events finally overcame her determination to blame Katryn.

Sanchez put both knives down on the desk and crossed her arms assertively. "I want to go back to my office and read the statements that have already been collected. I'll need to interview everyone again, starting first thing tomorrow. For the meantime, I'd say we have no more of a case against Private Nagata than anyone else, and I can see no justification in keeping her imprisoned, although how you run the barracks is your concern."

Dolokov mustered her composure quickly. There were a few last comments, but nothing of any significance, and Sanchez left. After she had gone, the Ranger captain continued to study Katryn for a while longer but then untied the binding on her wrists.

"You are released for the evening, but consider yourself confined to barracks. And don't repeat anything that was said here."

"Yes, ma'am."

Dolokov opened the door. The four Rangers who had escorted Katryn from the lockup were waiting in the outer office. They scrambled to attention.

"On the advice of the Militia lieutenant, I'm releasing Private Nagata without charges. You are all dismissed." Dolokov's voice was so utterly neutral as to sound forced, and her expression was one of displeasure.

Katryn followed the others out of the building. At the foot of the steps, they formed a small huddle that Katryn was obliged to squeeze past. The sound of muttering followed her as she set off across the parade ground. Dolokov had released her, but by the manner in which she had done it, and with the absence of any information, few people would think that it meant Katryn was innocent.

❖

Katryn lay on her top bunk, staring blindly at the ceiling. She was alone in the room. The others had headed off after dinner. They had not said where they were going, and Katryn had not been invited. No one had spoken to her directly since she had left Dolokov's office, although she had overheard plenty of hissed comments. The words "Militia sticking together" formed part of most remarks, while the "facts" being passed around bore no resemblance to the truth. It was unfair, but there was nothing Katryn could do about it. Dolokov's order to say nothing meant that she could not even challenge the rumors.

The ceiling blurred as tears stung in Katryn's eyes. She had just started to think that she might be able to be happy in the Rangers—that it would be possible to form friendships while her skill with a bow earned her respect. Then Ellis had to get herself murdered. Katryn could almost believe that the sergeant had done it out of spite—or even committed suicide. It would fit with all the facts. Ellis could easily have swapped knives before walking over to the stables. All Katryn had to do was work out how Ellis managed to stab herself in the back.

The door to the bunkhouse opened, and the rest of the patrol filed in. They spoke among themselves, but no one even looked in Katryn's direction. It was time to sleep. With any luck, on the next day Sanchez would return and the real murderer would be found. It would help a bit, but Katryn knew that doubts would always be attached to her name. She was a new girl and not popular, despite the affair with Tina and the mountain cats. Some Rangers would want her to be the guilty one, and when another, better-liked member of the squadron was arrested, they would still continue to blame her. Worst of all, the murderer might never be caught.

Katryn rolled over and climbed down from her bunk. She needed to visit the latrine before sleeping. As she walked through the bunkhouse, the conversation quieted, but no one acknowledged her. She might have been invisible. The volume of voices rose again after the door had swung shut.

No lantern hung in the latrine block, but brilliant bands of moonbeams fell through the windows. Katryn left the stall and went to the water trough. She still had not taken the bath she wanted. Now it was too late, and there would be no hot water.

Katryn pulled on the hand pump and bent to stick her head under the spout. The cold gushing broke over the nape of her neck and flowed around her face. It felt good after the heat of the day. Her mind settled, more positive. After six months of Ellis, surely she could put up with a little hostility. All she had to do was keep going for a few more days, and things would resolve themselves.

Footsteps clipped on the tiles behind her as others entered the block. Katryn did not bother to look around to see who. Unexpectedly, one person stopped beside her. Katryn was about to stand when a blow crashed down across her shoulders. She pitched forward, striking her nose on the side of the trough. One knee hit the floor, but before she could fall, hands grabbed her arms, yanking her up and around. A fist thumped into her stomach twice; then someone backhanded her across the face.

She was surrounded. An arm from behind went around her throat, cutting off the air in her windpipe as another succession of punches thudded into her. She tried to protect herself from the onslaught, but both her arms were held in locks so savage that they were almost twisted from their sockets. Another strike landed hard. From the flaring increase in pain, she was certain that at least one of her ribs had cracked, and she could do nothing to shield the injury from the blows that followed. Each punch turned her body to mash. Each jolt erupted as fire in her tortured shoulders.

The blows became less concentrated on her torso as more attackers joined in. For the first time since the initial assault, a fist smashed into her face. A foot connected hard with her knee. From the sickening crack as much as from the pain, Katryn knew that it was broken or dislocated. She wanted to curl up and hide. She wanted it all to stop. She did not care how; death would do. She was fighting for air, drowning in a red haze of agony.

At last, the fury of the pounding subsided. The arm around her throat slackened. As her head sagged forward, she saw that the front of her uniform was splattered with blood—maybe from a nosebleed, maybe from a more serious injury. Everywhere hurt too much for her to be able to tell. Her body insisted on trying to breathe despite the torture in her ribs.

Then the lock on her arms was released, and Katryn dropped to her knees. White-hot agony exploded in the broken joint. With what air she had sucked into her lungs, Katryn screamed. She pitched forward. The hard tiles of the floor slammed into her and then softened, flowing around her like a cocoon. The darkness became complete.

❖

Katryn awoke with the face of a healer hanging over her. Memories switched and impacted. There had been a jilted lover, an argument, footsteps behind her on the cobbles. For a moment, Katryn thought that she was back in Woodside, with Allison and home just a short walk away. Then she saw the figure of Captain Dolokov in the background.

"How do you feel?" the healer asked.

"Numb." In fact, Katryn could not feel anything. She glanced down to check whether she was all there. Her uniform had been removed, and her body was largely wrapped in bandages. A large bowl stood nearby; the water in it glinted pink in the lamplight.

The healer nodded. "I'm afraid you won't be so comfy when the numbness wears off, but I'll do what I can so you get a good night's sleep. You're in a bit of a state, but don't worry; there's nothing that won't mend, given a month or so." The healer turned to Dolokov. "You can ask her a few questions now. I'll be back in a minute."

Dolokov stood aside to let the healer past. Katryn looked around. She was in the lockup again. "I've taken you into protective custody." Dolokov answered the unvoiced question. She moved forward into the spot that the healer had vacated. "Did you recognize the women who attacked you?" Dolokov's tone was combative, daring her to answer.

Of course, Katryn thought, *she doesn't really want to know, doesn't want to inflame things in the squadron.* Katryn's eyes closed. She could sympathize. She also did not want to answer, did not want to admit that she knew the faces of the women she had lived and worked with for half a year. Furthermore, you never informed on comrades, even when they beat you senseless.

"It was dark in the latrine. I was attacked so suddenly." Katryn avoided the question.

Dolokov nodded sharply, looking relieved. She spoke quickly, as though she feared to give Katryn the chance to change her mind. "With hindsight, I see it was a mistake to remove the sentries from the gate. There's been trouble with local women recently. A gang must have slipped into the barracks, looking for revenge on the first Ranger they found."

Katryn fixed her eyes on the ceiling and said nothing.

Dolokov moved away. "The same thing might have happened with Sergeant Ellis. Lieutenant Sanchez will continue with her investigation, but I fear the culprit won't be found." She looked back to where Katryn lay, her gaze hard and cynical. "Your start in the 12th Squadron has not gone well. It's not entirely your fault. I think it might be wise if I arrange for you to transfer to another squadron...give you a chance to make a fresh start in the Rangers."

The door of the lockup opened, and the healer entered. "Have you finished?" she asked Dolokov. "The patient needs to sleep."

"Yes, I think I'm finished." Dolokov gave a tight smile and left.

No, it's me who's finished, Katryn thought. It was obvious that Dolokov was hoping the murderer would never be found, or maybe she had convinced herself that Katryn really was the one. Certainly, once

Katryn had been removed from the squadron, no one in the 12th would ever doubt her guilt.

And as for her life in a new squadron? It might go all right at first, but stories would spread around the division, passed from squadron to squadron. Soon, rumors of the Ranger who had murdered her sergeant would catch up with her. Ironically, the 12th probably was the safest place to be. Katryn knew that she was still alive because nobody liked Ellis enough to kill for her. But among people who had never met Ellis, there would not even be misplaced sympathy for the provocation. Instead, there would be tales of the coward's blow, the knife in the back. No squadron would want her. There would be other latrine blocks, other beatings, and one day, there would be a beating she would not wake up from.

The healer placed a hand on Katryn's head, gently exerting the skill to send her to sleep. As Katryn drifted away, she half wished that she would not wake up this time.

PART THREE

The Killer of Melanthe Ellis

21 October 533

CHAPTER SIXTEEN—TRIAL BY GOSSIP

Katryn finished speaking and sat in silence, cursing herself for past cowardice. Several times while they were in Landfall, she had been tempted to tell Chip everything but had held back. Like a pathetic dreamer, she had allowed herself to hope that with enough time, her new comrades might get to know her and trust her, and maybe give her the benefit of the doubt when the inevitable rumors reached them. Now the whole story had been dragged out of her, which was the worst possible way for it to come out, and even as she was speaking, Katryn could hear how weak and implausible it sounded. Not a scrap of evidence existed to support her version of the tale.

Her heartbeat pounded in her chest; her stomach felt sick. For the last part of her account, she had been unable to meet Chip's eyes, frightened of what she would see there—at best, it would be skepticism. Her gaze could climb no higher than Chip's ankles. Tears felt dangerously close. A string of useless sentences starting with "If only" jangled in her head. If only she had been posted to the 23rd to start with. If only she had been somewhere else when Ellis was murdered. If only Chip would believe her.

The last wish cut deepest of all. Katryn knew how much she liked Chip as a comrade and respected her as an officer, and how much she wanted her as a friend. The most painful part would be losing Chip's good opinion. Katryn steeled herself for the response.

"Callous bitch!" The words exploded from Chip's mouth. Katryn felt herself flinch. There was a second of silence. Then Chip went on furiously, "Did Dolokov want you to get murdered as well? Did she think that was going to help the squadron's morale? She didn't just drop you in the shit; she tied lead weights around your neck first. How can anyone who calls herself a captain…" Chip was too impassioned to continue.

Katryn's head jerked up of its own accord, dazed by the sudden comprehension that she was not the target of the outburst. For once, Chip's face did not hold any trace of a smile. There was nothing there but disgust and anger. Their eyes met and held.

Chip was the one who broke contact, rubbing a hand over her face. "What was Dolokov playing at?"

Katryn struggled to find her voice. "It's just guessing, but...I think she was....riding the odds."

"Easy to play long odds when it's someone else's life at stake."

"Well, she knew it wasn't likely that I'd be killed. There wasn't anyone who cared about Ellis as a person. It was just the principle of one Ranger murdering another that outraged some women."

"But didn't she make any statement about the switched knives? She acted as if she wanted to give the impression she thought you were guilty."

"I think she'd convinced herself that I was."

Chip sank back. "That's no better. She thought you murdered one of her sergeants, and she was happy to let you get away with it?"

Katryn's mouth twisted in a lopsided frown. "I shouldn't speak for her, but Dolokov tends not to worry about the rules as long as things sort out the way she wants. She worked out that there wasn't the evidence to get a conviction at a court-martial, so she settled for the unofficial justice of handing me over to the rest of the squadron. I got a beating and then got passed on to the next squadron." Katryn bit her lip. "There'll be some Rangers in the 23rd who'll want to do the same. I can't prove I didn't murder Ellis."

"If we were all treated as guilty of everything we couldn't *prove* we hadn't done, there'd be no one left outside the lockup to turn the key." Chip tilted her head and looked at the small window of her room. "It's too late to take any action tonight. In the morning, I'll go talk to Captain LeCoup, and you'd better come with me."

"Er...yes." Katryn was less than enthusiastic.

"She needs to know all of this," Chip pointed out.

"Oh, yes. It's just that she reminds me a bit of Ellis." Katryn shrugged. "Square, short-tempered, shouts and doesn't like me."

Chip gave a bark of laughter. "That's our captain. But she isn't anything like Ellis."

"I know, but—"

Chip cut her off. "For starters, she's fair. There's no way she'll stand back and have a member of her squadron convicted in a trial by gossip. She's got a temper like a snow lion with a hangover, but she doesn't play games. You can rely on her."

Katryn nodded, but before she could speak, they heard voices and the sound of the door opening in the adjoining room. The rest of the patrol had returned from the tavern. Chip brushed her palms over her cropped hair. "I guess it's time to sleep."

"Yes, ma'am."

Katryn stood and headed to the door. As she reached for the handle, Chip said, "Don't worry. The murder isn't general knowledge, and I can guarantee it won't get out until after LeCoup has decided what to do. My guess is she'll send to Sanchez and Kalispera for reports. Then she can squash the rumors from the 12th with real facts."

"But *you* don't need the reports? You believe me already?" Katryn could not help asking.

"I know you didn't kill Sergeant Ellis." Chip's voice was steady and utterly sincere.

Their eyes met again, and Katryn felt a shock wave ripple through her—a kick in her stomach that shot down her thighs and tingled at the back of her knees. "Thank you, ma'am," she mumbled. Then she fled.

The other six members of the patrol were in the process of getting ready for bed. They threw a few joking taunts in her direction, but no more than the friendly banter of the barracks. Soon, the lamps were out, and Katryn was lying in her bunk, staring up into the darkness. Her thoughts were bouncing around far too chaotically for sleep.

Astonishment was her overriding emotion. The most she had dared hope for was to be listened to critically. Being transferred stood as evidence against her. It was only reasonable that people would assume her version of events to be full of evasion, if not out-and-out lies. Even if Chip were the only person to offer unqualified trust, it was one supporter more than she had ever expected to find—although, of course, Chip was not an unbiased observer.

It was something that Katryn had been aware of for a while. She'd had enough experience to know the signs. Ever since she had hit puberty, there had been an unending stream of women drawn by her good looks. She had found the attention invariably tedious, often embarrassing and occasionally distasteful. The women had had no interest in her as a person and no real wish to understand her. The hopeful admirers had hung on her every word without paying attention to any of them. Then they had gone away and invented a fantasy personality for her to go with their other fantasies. She might as well have been a pretty-faced puppet.

But it was grossly unfair to put Chip in with that group. It was possible to have an entertaining conversation with her and know that Chip was hearing what she said—no more and no less. There had been no crude innuendoes, no pestering, no sense of being a game prize. And she knew that if ever anything was said, Chip would take no as an answer without childishly sulking or making a scene, without harming their friendship—if the answer was to be no.

As the thought drifted through her head, Katryn again felt her insides kick—a sensation similar to the jolt that had hit her in Chip's room, but more focused. And this time, there was no doubting the cause, or meaning, of her racing pulse and somersaulting stomach.

She liked Chip a lot. She had known that ever since she had gotten over the initial panic of meeting another new sergeant. Now Katryn realized that she had built walls in her mind, defenses against the rejection she had been sure would come. But the barricades had not been needed. Chip had not turned against her. The walls had crashed down, and Katryn found herself flooded by an emotion she had not known was there. Her whole body shook to the rhythm of her heartbeat while a very familiar ache started to grow.

It was so easy to close her eyes and recall Chip's face, complete with a smile like summer sunshine. Katryn felt herself falling even deeper as she toyed with the image. In her mind, she added the other details: the way Chip moved, her eyes, her voice, the shape of her hands...and then the thought of what those hands would feel like touching her body.

The breath caught in Katryn's throat as she considered leaving her bunk and slipping into Chip's room. She was sure that Chip would be very happy to see her...or would she?

Another memory surfaced—one from the evening following Clarinda Wright's death. On the way back from the tavern, she had tried to kiss Chip. In hindsight, she had known her own mind better when she was drunk than she did when she was sober. The memory had been hanging about on the edge of her thoughts, ignored in her confusion. The defensive barriers in her mind would not let her deal with it. Now she could, and what confronted her was the knowledge that Chip, gently but with unequivocal firmness, had rejected the advance.

Katryn's eyes flew open. Had she been misreading Chip's friendliness, projecting her own repressed emotions onto their target? *You can't expect the whole world to fall for you,* she mocked herself angrily. Or perhaps there was another explanation. Chip had been a Ranger long enough to know all the rules, including the unwritten ones. Katryn thought of the other Rangers' ill-concealed scorn as Pat had slinked out of Ellis' room. If Chip were to be her champion, it would harm both their reputations if it was perceived to be the result of bedroom bargaining. Furthermore, they were officer and subordinate. Absolutely the very last thing Katryn wanted was to be transferred to yet another squadron—not when it seemed that things might work out all right in the 23rd.

Whatever the reason, Chip's position was clear. The bitter irony struck her. She remembered thinking that Chip would be adult enough to take no as an answer. Katryn's face twisted in a pained grimace. It was her own maturity that was to be tested.

It was a miserable, wet afternoon in early December. Chip and Kim sat in one of the taverns in the town below Fort Krowe. Belts of sleet splattered against the green glass of the windows. Heavy clouds reduced the light outside to premature dusk, and the thatched roof creaked in gusts of cold wind. The two sergeants were quite content, however. They had comfortable chairs by the log fire and were washing down the end of a large meal with tankards of the best beer the town could offer.

The months leading up to Midwinter's Day traditionally were the slack time for the Rangers. With the worsening weather, there were few traders on the road and, therefore, few highway robberies. The mountain cats would be excavating their dens for hibernation, and although prides of snow lions would be following the cold weather south, plenty of their natural prey were still about, and the fenbucks and spadehorns would always top a snow lion's menu. It was rare for a pride to venture onto the domesticated Homelands before February.

November and December were when leave was granted, half the

squadron at a time. By the regulations, a Ranger was allocated to the division closest to her hometown, so the month would be sufficient to visit relatives. It also meant that she would be close at hand for emergency recall. It said much of the Rangers' lifestyle that many Rangers did not bother; instead, they spent the time with their comrades, propping up a bar. Women gave up their families to join the Rangers—those whose families had not given them up first. The bonds of life and death that bound a squadron were far stronger than blood.

Kim sighed and pushed her empty plate away. For a while, she watched the amber firelight reflected on the side of her tankard. "I wonder where we'll be dumped next."

"Somewhere cold, surrounded by lots of things with big teeth," Chip answered.

"You're just guessing," Kim said mock-seriously. Then she scrutinized her friend more earnestly; there had been a faint undertone in Chip's voice. "Or are you?"

"Pardon?" Chip's best attempt to look innocent did not fool Kim at all.

"Come on; don't do the wide-eyed bit. It doesn't suit you. What do you know?"

"I don't strictly *know* anything, but I have this feeling about the east."

Kim leaned forward and dropped her voice. "East?"

Chip flexed her fingers like a cardsharp. "Maybe."

"East," Kim repeated. "And from that look on your face, it's not just gossip. Have you been pulling strings?"

"What's the point of doing favors if you don't call them in from time to time?" Chip said, grinning. "Winter struck early this year. The border divisions will all have put in requests for extra hands. If they decide to send one of our squadrons out to Eastern, I've merely suggested to an acquaintance on staff to consider offering the 23rd."

"But why ea—" Kim stopped and became far more serious. "Katryn?"

Chip's shrug said yes.

"You're not planning some sort of confrontation with the 12th, are you?"

"Of course not. Well, not until I've worked out which one of them killed the sergeant."

"How?"

"I'm not sure yet. I'm going to need to visit Roadsend and talk to people there. But hopefully, if we do get loaned to Eastern, we'll be running up and down the border, and I'll get the chance to visit the place."

"And you're sure that's wise? You don't want to be reminded of phrases about leaving well enough alone?"

Chip was about to reply, but at that moment four figures, all heavily muffled with scarves and Ranger's cloaks, flitted past the window, moving too quickly for identification. A second later, the tavern door was shoved open, allowing a cold draft to swirl down the room briefly. Kim was sitting with her back to the door. However, she did not need to turn her head to know that one of the new arrivals was Katryn. The look in Chip's eyes was unmistakable.

"It must be nice to be on sergeant's pay and be able to afford to eat away from the mess." Lee Horte's tone was conversationally deadpan as she walked past the table, but the corners of her lips twitched up. The others merely smiled a greeting and settled around the bar. Kim was not surprised when Chip caught Katryn's eye and beckoned her over.

When Katryn was seated with her drink, Chip said, "I was talking to Captain LeCoup this morning—"

Kim interrupted on Katryn's behalf. "Oh, no! You're not going to discuss work now?"

"Well, only semiofficially." Chip turned back to Katryn. "I said we should get you certified as a marksman. And LeCoup agreed. Your archery is easily up to it. That way, you'll only need to do one year as a private before you're eligible for promotion to Leading Ranger, which will be...?" She broke off with a query on her face.

"Start of February." Katryn provided the information, though she did not look too confident. She frowned. "It seems a bit like cheating."

"Hardly."

"Won't people who did two years as private mind?"

"No one complained when Carma took certification as a healer," Chip said, referring to the Ranger in D Patrol who possessed enough of the healer-sense to function as an effective medic—a real asset to the squadron. "As a Leading Ranger, you wouldn't be so conspicuous."

"Seeing as how I'm so old and haggard?" Katryn suggested lightly.

Chip pursed her lips. "Or you could hang a sign around your neck, telling people you're younger than you look, but you've had a hard life."

The two continued talking, soon drifting to other subjects. Kim shifted back in her seat and watched them thoughtfully, playing little part in the conversation. However, she soon found it necessary to rest her chin on her hand, with her fingers over her lips to hide her grin. She wondered whether the message in their animated faces and body language was as obvious to everyone else in the tavern as it was to her. Chip's response, she had come to expect. However, for the first time, Kim realized that Katryn was also giving out signals, which Chip was utterly failing to pick up on. The next few months promised to be rather amusing.

By Midwinter's Day, the entire squadron was back together. Captain LeCoup summoned a general briefing in the mess, the only room big enough to hold everyone. When all thirty-four women had taken their places, the captain began. "We've been given our orders. The 23rd has been seconded to Eastern Division for three months. It's a bit unusual, but as you know, winter came on early this year, and by February, they expect to be up to their necks in snow lions."

LeCoup scanned her audience before she continued. "By my reckoning, it's eleven years since we last did a winter stint with Eastern, and there aren't too many of you familiar with the setup there. So a quick summary is in order." She folded her arms in a declamatory pose. "There are seven squadrons in the division and seven main barracks. This doesn't include the divisional HQ at Eastford, where there's just a staff admin building. Their summer deployment goes from May to October, with one squadron based in each barrack town. In winter, the southern half of the region is quietish, while the northern section is a bit livelier. So the four southern barracks go on half muster—which, for those of you who can't do the math, means they have two squadrons free. One squadron, they send north to provide backup for dealing with the snow lions; the other squadron is held on reserve in Eastford. This year, since they're expecting trouble with snow lions, they want to put both spare squadrons in the north. They want us to do the general-reserve bit based in Eastford. Does everybody follow that?"

If anyone did not, she was not admitting it, and the briefing went on, covering some administrative matters in more detail. Eventually, LeCoup wound up. "They want us in Eastford on the fifteenth of January. We ride out tomorrow, so you've got one night to say goodbye to anyone in Fort Krowe who'll miss you. Okay, meeting over." As the women started to shuffle toward the door, LeCoup raised her voice again. "And Sergeant Coppelli, I'd like a word with you in my office."

As she squeezed out the door, Chip caught Kim's eye and exchanged a worried grimace with her. There had been something ominous in LeCoup's tone, but they would have no chance to speak. Chip headed straight to the captain's office with a nasty cold lump forming in her guts. LeCoup arrived a few seconds later and ushered her in.

Chip came smartly to attention in the middle of the room; it seemed the sensible thing to do. LeCoup slowly paced the length of the floor; then she fixed a long, critical stare on her. At last, she spoke. "Were you surprised to learn just now that we were seconded to Eastern Division?"

Chip hesitated, but lying was very unwise. "No, ma'am."

"Why not?"

"I...er...I had discussed the possibility with a member of divisional staff, ma'am."

"*Discussed the possibility?* That's a frigging euphemism. What you mean is you talked her into fixing it for you." LeCoup's voice had acquired a snarl. She walked closer until she was glaring directly into Chip's eyes. "Okay, Sergeant. Why?"

Chip managed to keep control of her voice. "I was hoping for a chance to visit Roadsend, ma'am. I wanted to see if I could learn more about the murder of Private Nagata's ex-sergeant."

"That's not your job."

"No, ma'am, but I wanted to clear her name."

"*I've* already dealt with that. The reports I received showed that her record in the Militia was exemplary, and there's no evidence to support claims that she was the one who murdered her ex-sergeant."

"Yes, ma'am. The reports you got were very helpful."

"*Helpful?*"

Chip judged that she had little to lose by continuing. "As long as the murder is unsolved, there are always going to be doubts...in Private

Nagata's mind, if nowhere else. Until she knows that she has been proven innocent, she's always going to be wondering just how much her comrades trust her."

"So you decided to fuck about with the squadron's posting?" LeCoup increased the intensity of her verbal offensive. Chip swallowed, hoping that the question was rhetorical. To her relief, after a long pause, LeCoup continued, "The deployment of squadrons is a matter of life or death, not a damned game of tiddlywinks. The 23rd is *my* squadron, and I am responsible for it. I will not have a shit-assed sergeant tossing it around the Homelands for her amusement." The volume of LeCoup's voice rose several levels. "If you want to make arrangements for the squadron, you don't go behind my back. Either you go via me, or you keep your fucking hands out of it. You don't take it on yourself to play games, or Himoti's statue in the chapel will be wearing your tits for earrings. Understood?"

"Yes, ma'am."

"Don't you ever dare do anything like this again."

"No, ma'am."

LeCoup stomped away. "Dismissed."

Chip did not start breathing normally until she was outside the building. She sucked in a deep lungful of air and began walking back to her room. Kim intercepted her on the way.

"Trouble?" Kim asked.

Chip scrunched her nose. "A bit. LeCoup found out I was the one who rigged the posting."

"How?"

"She didn't say." Chip shrugged. "How does she find out half the things she does?"

"Was she angry?"

"She threatened to remove some of my body parts."

Kim laughed. "With fatal results?"

"No, but I'm still rather fond of them." Chip thought for a moment. "And it's not as though the statue has pierced ears."

❖

Dusk was less than an hour away as the squadron rode over the brow of the last hill and saw the town ahead. Snow lay thick on the surrounding countryside. The river cut a black line through it. Lanterns were beginning to be lit, and their light glinted off the rows of icicles dangling from the lintels of windows. Eastford spanned the two sides of the Little Liffey River. The ford of its name had long since been replaced by an arched stone bridge. Apart from the divisional HQ, there was also a temple in Eastford. It was the tallest building by far; its dome raised a dark mass against the sky.

Captain LeCoup led the way along the main road into town and called a halt outside a flat-fronted building on the edge of the market square. The green and gray banner of the Rangers hung above the only door. LeCoup slipped from her saddle and went inside with Lieutenant Ritche. The other Rangers milled around in the deserted square.

"Where's the barracks?" one voice asked loudly.

Ash overheard. "Didn't you hear what the captain said in the briefing? There isn't a permanent squadron based in Eastford, just a few divisional staff, so they don't have purpose-built barracks here."

"We're not going to be camping out all winter?" It was more a protest than a question.

Ash merely smiled at the speaker and urged her horse away. The Ranger went on a fruitless search for another veteran from the squadron's last posting to Eastford.

Before long, Captain LeCoup reappeared in the doorway. "Okay!" Her shout got everyone's attention. "As you may have heard, the bad news is that they don't have barracks here in Eastford. They don't have troops stationed here year-round to make it worthwhile. The good news is that Eastford is on a major trade route, so in this season, there are lots of inns with lots of vacant rooms. We're to be billeted in them. I've got the allocations here." She waved some papers in the air and beckoned the four sergeants over.

❖

By nightfall, C Patrol was happily installed in the Three Barrels. The inn staff cleared away the remains of a meal that outdid anything ever served in a mess hall. The Rangers were in high spirits. Some settled down by the fire with a drink, while others prepared to go in search of the other patrols to see how they had fared.

Chip was building her resolve to brave the cold and call on Kim when her friend beat her to it, appearing in the doorway of the taproom, knocking snow from her boots. "Very cozy." She gave her assessment, smiling broadly.

The two sergeants picked a couple of comfy chairs in a warm corner. In response to a wave, one of the inn staff indicated that drinks would be with them shortly.

"It isn't bad, is it?" Chip said, her gesture taking in the whole inn.

"No, it's not," Kim agreed, laughing. "The squadrons in Eastern must fight pitched battles over who gets this winter posting."

"What's your inn like?"

Kim looked around, sizing it up. "A bit bigger; not so homelike. We've all got rooms to ourselves." Her grin got wider. "With a town full of interesting women who haven't seen a serving Ranger for months and a bed in crawling distance of the bar, I overheard one of my patrol wonder if she'd been killed in action and gone straight to Ranger heaven."

"I just hope we get to spend some time here. It would be awfully sad to be sent off tomorrow to the ass-end of nowhere, chasing some farmer's hallucinations."

"I thought you wanted a trip out to Roadsend," Kim said, feigning surprise.

"Oh, I do." Chip sighed and sank farther into her chair as two tankards arrived. "But there's no rush. I won't mind if I have to wait here a few days first."

CHAPTER SEVENTEEN—SCENE OF THE MURDER

A part from the snow, the barracks at Roadsend looked exactly the same as they had the last time Katryn had been there. The eight women of C Patrol dismounted at the gates and walked the short distance to the central parade ground. Katryn had to force her legs to move smoothly, matching her pace to that of the others. Her eyes took in the scene, and she tried not to flinch as they skimmed over the latrine block. The 12th Squadron was no longer there. It had moved at the end of October to its winter posting, the Clemswood barracks—information Chip had made a point of finding out. Currently, half of the 8th Squadron was stationed in Roadsend, under the command of its lieutenant.

Katryn watched Chip bounce up the steps to the main office and stick her head around the door. Immediately, Chip ducked back out, and the lieutenant appeared, smiling a welcome. In the cold weather, the horses were the first priority. With only half a squadron on-site, two stable blocks were free, as were two bunkhouses. Katryn bit her lip as she tended her horse. She knew that all four buildings were identical, in some cases right down to the graffiti scratched inside the lockers, but she found herself praying that the patrol would not be assigned to the same dormitory she had slept in before.

Fortunately, the B Patrol bunkhouse was taken, and they were put in the next one along. Even so, being back was disorienting. Katryn kept expecting Ellis to appear around each corner. Figures she saw out of the corner of her eye looked like Jan or Tina. She found herself waiting to hear Sal's voice from the bunk below hers.

Katryn took a grip on her imagination. She knew where it was headed. *Next, I'm going to want someone to hold my hand when I go to the latrine.* At that thought, Katryn set her jaw. It was something that she was going to have to face, and the sooner, the better.

The others were waiting for Chip to return from her talk with the lieutenant. Katryn strode out of the bunkhouse and along the edge of the parade ground. Despite her resolve, it was impossible not to hesitate. An irrational urge to back away almost overcame her, but somewhere, she found the courage to push the door open and step inside. She stood by the water troughs and looked around. Of course, there were no bloodstains left on the tiles. Slowly, her racing pulse began to ease, only to jump when the door was pushed open again.

Chip slipped in, an anxious look on her face. "I saw you come in, and I thought…" She broke off, clearly realizing the potential for getting it wrong. Katryn tried to act untroubled, but failed, and she knew it. Chip continued, softly, "It was in here that you were attacked?"

"Yes."

Chip studied her. "Are you okay?"

Katryn forced a smile and nodded. Chip reached out a hand to squeeze her shoulder. Instantly, every other thought in Katryn's head scattered. The effect of the touch jolted through her, shooting down her spine and rippling over her scalp. She turned her face away while fighting to control her expression.

"Are you sure you're okay?" The level of concern in Chip's voice had gone up a notch.

Perhaps if I act totally pathetic, she'll give me a hug. The thought was ridiculously tempting, but on a scale of maturity, it scored in negative numbers. Katryn forced herself to stand up straighter and move away slightly, breaking the physical contact between them. "Yes, ma'am, I'm fine. Really, I am." It was not a complete lie. Her shoulder was throbbing, but the bad memories were utterly routed.

Chip stood awkwardly, seemingly unsure what to do with her arm. "I've…er…" Then she gathered strength. "I've been talking to the lieutenant. We've got half an hour before dinner, so I'm going to give a quick briefing. Are you all right to come along?"

"Yes, of course."

The two reentered the bunkhouse. The iron stove had been lit, and the members of C Patrol were gathered round. Chip and Katryn took a place in the huddled group, holding their hands out to the warmth.

"Okay, girls. In the circumstances, I'm going to make this a very informal briefing. Feel free to interrupt." Chip grinned at the circle of faces and went on. "I've got a few more details on the reasons for our little jaunt here. The first report was right; it is mountain cats—

supposedly. The lieutenant was quite honest and admitted she didn't put much faith in the tales, but she doesn't want to risk ignoring them. She'd like to take two patrols out to get the hunt over with quickly, but she doesn't want to leave the barracks empty. In a month's time, when things get busy, she won't have the option. But she guessed rightly that there'd be a spare patrol available at the moment. I also got the feeling she wanted the chance to show us the local scenery, so if there's a crisis later, there'll be some of us in the 23rd who are familiar with it."

"How many of these reputed cats are there?" Lee asked.

"If the report is from a farmer named Wisniewski, it will be hundreds," Katryn interjected.

Chip shook her head. "Only three or four. The sightings are off to the southwest. Unfortunately, it's a bit too far to do the round-trip in a day, so we'll be throwing ourselves on the mercy of local farmers for lodgings. And in these parts, the farms will be…?"

"Sheep." Katryn provided the information. "Lots of sheep. There'll be no shortage of mutton stew and blankets."

"Could be worse."

The briefing continued. Chip gave what further information she had, supplemented by Katryn's knowledge of the surrounding countryside. When the facts were finished, the debate became more spirited, with jokes and laughter, ending with anecdotes about mountain cats.

Katryn gave the appearance of joining in, but her thoughts were elsewhere. Since she had joined the Rangers, she had served under two sergeants. It hardly seemed possible, yet being back at Roadsend had made the differences between them even more pronounced. There could not be the slightest doubt about whose patrol she would rather be in, but the situation did present opposite problems. One sergeant she had hated, and the other she liked far, far too much.

❖

From the doorway of the lockup, there was a clear view straight across the middle of the parade ground. The admin building and A Patrol's bunkhouse obscured opposing corners, but no one could cross from the stores to the bunkhouses without being seen. Katryn considered the line of sight for a few seconds and then gave her attention to Chip, who was experimenting with standing guard by the door.

"I guess they might have missed someone if they'd had their eyes closed." Chip's tone was ironic.

"Dolokov thought they might be inside talking to the prisoner."

Chip's eyebrows rose. "She was seriously suggesting that discipline in the 12th is that bad?"

"I think she was just desperate to show I was the murderer."

"And she wasn't going to let the truth stand in her way." Chip grinned supportively. "Come on; next stop is the stables."

Katryn trailed a half-step behind as they crossed the parade ground. She knew why Chip wanted a full tour of the scene of the murder. She had even heard a few rumors in the squadron that Chip was in some way responsible for the 23rd's being loaned to Eastern Division in the first place. Katryn had mixed feelings. To say that being proved innocent would be a relief was an absurd understatement. But what hope was there that they would find proof? Katryn wondered whether the only thing they would get was more doubts, and she did not know whether she could take that.

At the stables, Chip stood in the doorway, craning her neck one way and another, evaluating the angles.

"I was mainly sitting with my back to the doors." Katryn volunteered the information.

Chip wrinkled her nose in thought. "Wouldn't matter which way you sat; you've only got a very oblique view of the door to the stores. You couldn't even tell if it was open or closed." Her eyes lifted to the sky. "What was the light like?"

Katryn stood by her shoulder. "It was full daylight when I started and a bit darker than now when the body was discovered. It was a couple of hours later than this, but it was near midsummer."

Chip nodded and led the way up the passageway behind the mess hall. At the door to the stores, she pulled a key from her pocket. A shudder ran through Katryn as she entered, but once again, any bloodstains had long since been removed.

"Are there any significant changes?" Chip asked.

Katryn paced a slow circuit of the room. The piles of crates had been shifted around, and the general level of stock was noticeably lower, but there were no other changes that she could see as being relevant. Chip followed, stopping once to examine the ventilation gaps at the bottom of the wall facing the mess. The openings were at most fifteen centimeters high. Iron bars fixed into the concrete were starting to rust, but not enough to compromise their effectiveness.

Katryn stood uncertainly in the center of the room, looking around. The scene felt unreal. "I didn't expect to be back here so soon."

"Yes...well...um...it's how things worked out."

Katryn glanced across. The evasiveness in Chip's voice was unmistakable. There was something the sergeant was not saying, and she had deliberately turned her back to keep her face hidden.

Katryn watched her clamber over a stack of crates. Then she felt herself staring, drinking in the details of Chip's body. Maybe the dreamlike air was due to the company. Chip managed to seem twice as real as anyone else Katryn had ever known. Was it surprising that the surroundings appeared to be insubstantial by comparison? Sometimes, she could swear that Chip's smile literally made the room brighter.

Chip moved on to the loading bay at the rear of the storeroom. After examining the door, she took the key from her pocket again and unlocked it. The wharf was empty. The river looked bleak in the sullen light. Directly below, at a drop of at least two meters, a narrow ribbon of ground ran along the bottom of the wall. Immediately beneath the lip of the door, a row of iron spikes was hammered into the wall. Each skewer had two barbs, one pointing out and the other hooked down. Chip took two of the boards that made up the bridge, laid them across the gap to the wharf and walked out.

While Katryn waited in the doorway, Chip took a few minutes surveying the entire riverbank. Then she came back, shut the door and locked it. They left the stores and continued around the site. Chip spent some time examining the end of the alley beside the kitchen, where it met the outer wall, but still, she said nothing. They stopped once more before leaving the barracks, when Chip went into the officers' block to return the storeroom key,

The others from C Patrol had gone into town to find a tavern. Katryn was expecting to join them, but Chip had not quite finished. At the side of the barracks, there was a gap between the walls and the back of a row of shops. From what Katryn could see, it was not so much a path as a place where people dumped rubbish. This did not deter Chip from making her way along it. The ground sloped away steeply at the end to bring them out on the banks of the river. Chip stood with the water lapping a few centimeters from her toes.

The light was failing rapidly. The far bank was disappearing into the gloom. Chip turned left and walked a few steps until she stood under the rear door of the stores. Katryn looked up at the spikes projecting like claws over Chip's head—a powerful disincentive to climb up.

Chip took a few more steps along the bank. Ice fringed the edge of the river. The only sound was the slop of cold water against the frozen mud. The dusting of snow was marked by the footprints of birds and one lone dog, but nothing larger.

Chip turned back and rejoined Katryn at the end of the alleyway. The building ahead jutted out a good meter into the river. Its walls rose directly from the water. There were deep crevices where the mortar between the stones had been partly washed away. Chip patted her hand against the stones. A trickle of cement dust drifted down onto the snow.

"Would this be the back of the White Swan Inn?" Chip threw the question over her shoulder.

"Er...yes, I think so," Katryn replied.

Chip took a few steps back, craned her neck to peer around the corner and then walked back to the wall. Her fingers explored the gaps between the stones. There was no shortage of hand and toeholds. Within seconds, she had scrambled out over the water and disappeared around the corner.

"It's all right, Katryn; come on up here," Chip called.

Katryn removed her gloves and followed. Around the other side, she saw a wooden quay running the entire length of the tavern's rear wall. Chip was standing there, waiting. Katryn negotiated the last few handholds and clambered up to join her.

Farther along, a flight of steps led up to street level. A door in the wall near where they stood was the only other way off the quay. Chip pushed experimentally, and the door swung back, revealing a large courtyard open to the sky, with mildew-covered cobbles. A row of barrels lined the far wall. In one corner was a small building housing the latrines. A short flight of steps led down to the cellar. Another flight went up to a door that, from the noise coming through it, could only lead to the taproom.

"The rear exit," Chip said thoughtfully.

"This is definitely the back of the White Swan," Katryn confirmed. "I've been here a few times, though I've never come in this way before.

I can see they'd use the door for delivering barrels, but I don't know how often it's left open."

"We could ask, but I'd guess it's open whenever the tavern is. The landlady wants to get drinkers into her taproom. You don't do that by locking your doors, and barge crews make good customers."

The two Rangers walked up the steps and into the inn, where they were enveloped by heat and noise. Even before their eyes adjusted to the light, a loud whoop caught their attention. The rest of C Patrol was already there—not so surprising, since the White Swan was the first tavern encountered on the way into town. Chip and Katryn stripped off their cloaks and wandered over, smiling, to take their places at the table with their comrades.

Katryn had no opportunity to speak to Chip privately or to get any hint about what she was thinking. As the evening progressed, Katryn's eyes strayed anxiously in Chip's direction. Now that they had returned to Roadsend and had the chance to look at the site, it seemed even more impossible to understand how Ellis had been murdered. Katryn prayed that Chip was not reconsidering ideas about her innocence. She needed Chip to believe in her. She wanted Chip physically. Her body ached at the thought of lying with Chip's arms wrapped tightly around her. But she could live without that. She could not live without Chip's trust.

❖

The two patrols rode out the next day and returned to Roadsend four days later. Their hunt had found only one geriatric cat, too sick to hibernate, that had done them the favor of dying a few hours before they caught up with it. It was after midday when the Rangers arrived back at the barracks. Chip announced that C Patrol would stay at Roadsend for the night and set off for Eastford the next morning—a reasonable decision from the point of view of the horses, even without other motives.

The current opportunity was one that she did not want to waste. It appeared that LeCoup had gotten over her anger. C Patrol had been sent to Roadsend at the first excuse. Chip was sure that it was a dual message—not that LeCoup approved of meddling with the squadron's deployment, but like her, LeCoup wanted the murderer caught. It was also a demonstration of how much easier it was to get things done if you had LeCoup on your side.

The members of the two squadrons got on well together. If the Rangers from the 8th had heard stories on the divisional grapevine, they did not connect the murdered sergeant with Katryn, and no one had taken steps to enlighten them. After lunch, the returning Rangers were given some free time, which they took as a good excuse to arrange an intersquadron game of football in the parade ground. Chip was tempted to join in, but she had more important things to do.

She left the bunkhouse, heading for the gates. At the edge of the parade ground, she paused, watching the two teams. Chip could not help it; the sight of Katryn darting past opponents with the ball was hard to tear herself away from.

By force of will, she shunted her gaze to the opposite corner of the square. At the door to the kitchen stood a round, middle-aged woman in civilian clothes. If she was not a cook, she was going out of her way to look like one. The woman's eyes were also following Katryn—but, Chip suspected, for very different reasons from her own. It occurred to Chip that the cook might be worth talking to, if there was time, but she was not at the top of the list.

Chip headed into town. The streets were busy, and she had no trouble getting directions to the Militia station. When she arrived there, she found that Lieutenant Sanchez was not only on duty, but also available to see her right away. Chip took a seat in the cramped office and considered the woman on the other side of the desk, wondering how best to play it.

"How may I help you, Sergeant?" Sanchez kicked off the conversation.

"Er...yes, ma'am. I understand that there was a murder at the barracks here a few months ago." At Chip's words, the lieutenant's eyes narrowed, though she made no attempt to interrupt. "It happens that one of the suspects was transferred to my patrol. Obviously, I'm not too happy at the thought of a subordinate who makes a habit of sticking knives into officers she doesn't like. Equally, I don't want false accusations thrown at a blameless member of my patrol."

"Private Nagata?" Chip nodded in answer. Sanchez continued, "I sent a report to your captain. Did that not answer your questions?"

"Officially, yes. But I was wondering what you might be able to tell me—off the record. It would be nice to have some idea who the murderer was, even if I can't prove anything."

Sanchez sat back in her chair. "Personally, I'm certain that it wasn't Nagata. Unless I'm missing something obvious, the murderer has no shortage of brains and imagination. You can bet she is someone who arranged things so that suspicion didn't land on her. Her only mistake was not allowing for the age of the knife. If it hadn't been for that slip, your Private Nagata would've been dangling from a noose months ago, and no one would now be any the wiser."

"Do you have any idea who the murderer might be?"

"None at all. You're welcome to go through the statements I collected to see if you can spot anything I missed. I hate having unsolved murders on my watch, but I've more or less given up on this one."

Chip subjected Sanchez to a shrewd look. "You don't strike me as the sort of woman to give up easily."

A flush of annoyance darkened the lieutenant's face. "It's a question of jurisdiction. The official story is that a gang of thieves obtained a duplicate key to the stores. They got in via the rear door but were disturbed by Sergeant Ellis. They wrested the trail knife off her and killed her before fleeing. The story also has it that Sergeant Ellis swapped knives with Private Nagata before leaving the bunkhouse, for reasons that she is now unable to reveal."

"But you don't believe that?" It was half question, half statement.

"No. Sergeant Ellis was killed by a Ranger. However, Captain Dolokov of the 12th was not"—Sanchez paused, scowling—"helpful. She did everything she could to block my investigation inside the barracks while trying to pressure me into wasting time chasing after this nonexistent local gang."

"Why are you so sure it was a Ranger?"

Sanchez hesitated and then held out her hand. "Can I see your trail knife?" Chip drew it from her belt and handed it over. She watched as the lieutenant studied the knife pensively, rolling the handle between her fingers. The blade was twenty centimeters long, weighted at the end for both hacking and thrusting, sharpened to a razor edge.

It was nearly a minute before Sanchez spoke again. "It's a nasty piece of weaponry, dangerous in anyone's hands. But to be really effective, it needs a trained user. I'd have stabbed Sergeant Ellis holding it like this." She indicated with the blade. "But the person who killed Ellis held the knife like this." She rotated her wrist so that the blade lay horizontal. "Now that I've seen how it's done, I can work out why. The blade slipped between the ribs, with less risk of deflection and minimal blood spilled. And it was a single thrust straight to the heart—no retries or prodding about." She shook her head. "I don't have the training to do that, and there aren't any local thieves who do, either. Plus there was no sign of a fight in the stores. The murderer was someone Ellis knew."

"And you really have no ideas who?"

Sanchez shook her head. "Normally, I'd try to identify motive and opportunity. But opportunity is a nonstarter; everyone has an alibi. And as for motive..." She sighed. "If you dig around, everyone had a reason to want Sergeant Ellis dead. I know Val Bergstrom quite well... the lieutenant of the 12th. She's a local girl. Did her time in the Militia with me here in Roadsend. Whenever the 12th is posted here, we get together for a drink and a chat. From what she's told me, my main surprise is that Ellis didn't get murdered years ago. It could've been virtually anyone in the entire squadron. Work out how the killer did it, and I'll tell you her motive. The only thing I—" Her voice cut off abruptly.

"The only thing...?" Chip prompted.

Sanchez leaned forward and dropped her voice. "Okay. This is completely off the record. Right?"

"Sure."

"It was just...Dolokov was so keen to stop me from probing into the murder that I sometimes wondered if she knew who it was and didn't want to lose that person over Ellis. Maybe it was just frustration leading me into paranoia, but my only advice is to start by working out who are the most valuable members of the squadron." Sanchez pushed back from the table and stood up. "And now...do you want to look at the statements?"

"Oh, yes, please."

"They're over here." Sanchez led the way.

❖

Chip returned to the barracks some time later. The football game was over, and a gentle snow had started to fall. There had been no surprises in the statements. The six women in the tavern all swore independently that none of the others had disappeared for part of the evening. The sentries outside the lockup swore repeatedly that they had not lapsed in their attention. And both Bergstrom and Adebayo swore that they had been in each other's company all evening.

The only one who was on her own at any time was Sergeant Takeda. Her story was that she had spent part of the time in the officers' quarters, talking to Bergstrom, and then had gone straight to her room in D Patrol bunkhouse, where she had stayed until news of Ellis' death reached her. The testimony of the sentries was that Takeda had made only one crossing of the parade ground, heading away from the admin block. She had not been seen again, with or without a knife.

Chip considered going into the bunkhouse to warm up, but then she remembered the cook. Dinner was still an hour away; with luck, the cook would have things sufficiently under control to chat for a while.

In Chip's experience, military chefs came in two flavors: mother hens who would cluck away nonstop and sour despots whose only conversation was swearing more venomously than any Ranger would. To her relief, she found within seconds of entering the kitchen that the Roadsend cook was firmly in the former group. All the Rangers, from the divisional commander down, were her "girls." Engaging the flour-covered woman in conversation was not hard, but steering the flow of words in the desired direction took far more effort. Eventually, Chip got there via the oblique route of Katryn.

"I thought it was her I saw playing football...poor lamb." The cook slapped a boulder of dough on the table, punctuating her speech. "She should have gotten an award for topping Ellis. I can't imagine why they did what they did. I don't know anyone who wasn't glad to see the woman out of the squadron...not that I want to talk ill of the dead, you understand."

"You didn't get on with—" Chip did not get the chance to finish.

"I couldn't stand her. I like to think I treasure all my girls, but there was always this sinking feeling when I heard the 12th was coming. And it was just Ellis. You get some people like that. She couldn't cope unless she had everyone under her thumb. A real bully. She used to come in here, trying it on with me, shouting. So I told her, 'I'm a civvy, I don't have to say ma'am, and I only report to the quartermaster.'"

The cook snorted and thumped both fists into the dough before continuing. "It was the girls in her patrol I felt sorry for. The cheeky one, Bo—she was always coming in here, cadging bits to eat and telling me about the goings-on. I've heard some say Bo isn't up to much as a Ranger, but I reckon she's sharp enough—just that there was no point in her trying. Everything shc did was wrong by Ellis. And there was Pat. You're not telling me she was happy sleeping with Ellis, but she didn't get the choice. That's not right, and there's no need for it." The cook smiled at Chip. "I know what you girls are like, but there's no shortage of women in town who're desperate to have a Ranger warm their bed. Ellis didn't have the prettiest face, but she had a sergeant's badge, and that always helps."

"I know. It's what I rely on. I'd be lonely without it," Chip said, matching the teasing tone.

The cook barged her with a hip. "Oh, go on. I'm sure you don't need it. You've got a lovely smile."

Thanks, Chip thought, stifling a sigh.

The cook went on. "And I can tell you, no one ever said that of Ellis. She had to be totally in control. That's why she couldn't make a move on someone who was free to say no. That's why she treated her girls the way she did. Take that other one. The one who drinks. What's her name?" The cook smudged flour across her forehead. "Whatever. Ellis used to pick on her. Okay, the girl's got a problem with drink. She needs help, not abuse. But Ellis liked it. It meant the poor lamb was totally in her power. She's coming up to the end of her fourteen years. Bo told me Ellis kept threatening to block her re-enlistment because of the drink, but it was just a game.

"Ellis could be nasty like that. She'd even pick fights with the other sergeants. She and Val Bergstrom hated each other. I'm surprised they never came to blows. And on the day she died, I heard her having a go at Sergeant Takeda. The pair were standing outside the mess snarling at each other, just like my sister's dog. That's a vicious brute as well; only the other day, it went for—"

Chip cut in to try to steer the conversation back. "Somebody must have got on all right with Ellis."

"Name one," the cook retorted.

Chip pursed her lips. "The corporal? Surely the patrol couldn't function if she didn't get along with the sergeant."

The cook's eyes rolled to the ceiling. "Hardly. Jan keeps a tight lid on herself, but after the thing with her gene mother, I'm surprised she wasn't the one to gut Ellis."

"Her gene mother?"

"Bo told me all about it. They were stationed down at Monday Market when they got the news Jan's gene mother was dying. Jan put in for compassionate leave, and Ellis said no. No reason; they weren't stretched at the time. Jan appealed to the captain, but Ellis stuck her heels in. It had to go to a full review. In the end, Jan got her leave after two days of mucking around and got to her gene mother a few hours after she died—just too late to say goodbye. But that was Ellis through and through. She didn't need an excuse. She had the power to say when people could come and go, and she was going to use it."

The cook finished pounding the dough and began to shape lumps on a baking tray. Chip considered the woman's back thoughtfully. It was hard to know how much faith to put in thirdhand gossip, but it was certainly interesting. "You don't think it might have been Jan who did it?" Chip tried to make her tone as mild as possible.

"Jan's too quiet. Not that that's always a safe marker. Sometimes they're the most dangerous when they're pushed too far. Like the big girl in the patrol. Tina Agosta. She acts all quiet. I used to think she was a bit dim, and then she blows." The cook glanced back over her shoulder. "You know, I think Ellis was frightened of Tina. But that's a bully all over. They never pick on someone they think can give it back. But she picked on the wrong person in the end." She returned to the dough.

"So you're sure it's the woman in my patrol who did it?"

"Oh, yes. Not that I've had much to do with her. It was the first time she'd been in Roadsend—her and the other young one."

"That's a bit worrying." Chip did not attempt to argue Katryn's case. It was far more instructive to let the cook have a free hand.

"You shouldn't hold it against her. Anyone can snap, and Bo was telling me Ellis was really awful to her. It would have pushed the Blessed Himoti into fighting back. Though that didn't stop Bo joining in—" The cook broke off and turned around, looking uncomfortable. "I suppose you heard that she got a beating from the others?"

Chip nodded, and the cook went on.

"No one is supposed to know anything about it, but..." She shrugged. "I heard that Jan and Tina would have no part in it, and the alkie...Sal, she only went as far as being a lookout for the rest. Some of the girls from the other patrols joined in. But it says something if half a patrol won't avenge their own sergeant."

The cook picked up the baking tray and waddled toward the oven. Chip obligingly opened the door. The cook smiled at her. "Now, don't you worry about that new girl of yours. She's already taken more than she should've." The cook swung the oven door shut. "She deserves a second chance."

❖

On the way back to the bunkhouse, Chip stopped in the center of the deserted patrol ground. Dusk was not far away. The churned snow held a gray sheen in the last of the light. She turned in a full circle, finishing looking toward the latrine block. Her eyes became unfocused as she played with the fantasy of being able to turn back time, of being able to go to Katryn's aid. *In the hope that she'll hurl herself into your arms in gratitude?* Chip jeered at herself. *Do you think she'd squeal with delight at the sight of her heroic rescuer?* She shook her head. Katryn was not the squealing type. Chip would not find her nearly so attractive if she were.

There were layers to Katryn. On the surface, she was reserved and calm; beneath that, there was steel. She had to be strong to have gone through the previous year without cracking. And under all that was someone who had been hurt far too much, in too many ways.

Chip closed her eyes. She wanted to help heal the pain, but what hope was there that Katryn would ever look to her for comfort?

She rubbed her hands over her face in despair. When creating a human life, Imprinters were supposed to select the best combination of genes to ensure a healthy baby that had no predisposition to disease. Considering the amount that the Tangs had paid for the Golden Chapel, surely the Imprinter could have put in a bit of extra effort and done something more creative with her facial bone structure.

"You've got a lovely smile." Chip groaned as she remembered the cook's words and the dozens of times she had heard them before. It was the nearest thing to a flattering description she ever got, and Chip was quite coldly certain that it would take more than grinning like an idiot to merit Katryn's attention.

She hunched her shoulders and continued walking across the parade ground, kicking lumps of ice. It was probably just as well.

If Katryn ever admitted the same feelings toward her, Chip thought she might pass out from the shock. *And what would that do for my reputation as a mean, tough Ranger sergeant?*

CHAPTER EIGHTEEN—THE LIST OF SUSPECTS

A noisy game of dice was in progress in the bunkhouse. Katryn was looking down on the players, sitting on her bed with her legs dangling over the side, when she saw Chip return. The football had provided a temporary distraction, but now her sense of anxiety was growing. She had to know what Chip had learned and in what direction the information had sent her thoughts.

Chip shared a few wisecracks with the dice players, stripped off her heavy cloak and wandered into the sergeant's room. Katryn did not wait. If she stopped to think, she would lose her nerve. She slipped down from her bed and followed.

"Can I talk to you, ma'am?" Katryn blurted out.

"Sure. You've got nearly half an hour before dinner. Is this about Ellis?" Chip hung her cloak on a peg and kicked the door shut. Through it, the sound of the dice game was muted but still audible, rising and falling. A sudden burst of ironic cheering erupted; someone had been very lucky—or silly. Chip pointed Katryn toward the cushioned chest.

Katryn sat rigidly. *Do you still think I'm innocent of murdering her?* was far too abrupt. It was the thing she desperately wanted to know, but she did not think that she could cope with the blunt answer "No." Instead, she asked, "What do you make of things…now that you've seen Roadsend?"

Chip settled on the edge of her bed. "It's not easy." Her forehead wrinkled in thought. "I mean, the obvious candidate for murderer is Sergeant Takeda, but you can't rule anyone out."

"Takeda!" Katryn's voice rose. "But she was—"

"You look surprised," Chip said, grinning. "Supposing I tell you how I see things?" Katryn nodded. It was exactly what she wanted.

Chip continued, "There was no sign of a fight, and you didn't hear Ellis shouting. From this, I deduce that Ellis wasn't startled by whoever she encountered in the stores; which might in turn imply that they'd planned to meet there. Why has to be a guess, but everyone knew Ellis disliked you. Maybe someone told Ellis they suspected you of stealing but didn't want to make it public without evidence. She arranged a secret meeting and asked Ellis to get the key and bring her knife."

"Something like that would explain what Ellis said to me in the stables," Katryn said cautiously. "But the sentries…I don't see how Takeda…" Her voice trailed away in confusion.

"From the position the sentries were in outside the lockup, no one could cross from one side of the parade ground to the other without them seeing," Chip said. "But they didn't have sight of the doorways to the admin block, or of B and D Patrol's bunkhouses. If Takeda snuck down the path between the kitchen and the mess hall when she left Bergstrom, she could have reached the stores without anyone noticing. When she got there, she could have stabbed Ellis, removed her knife belt and left again. She could easily have hidden the belt under her jacket.

"The sentries saw her walk across the parade ground. But they couldn't tell whether she had come directly from the admin block or whether she went straight to her own room. It would have been quite possible for her to slip into B's bunkhouse first. Takeda could have gone to your locker, taken your knife, put it in the belt and then hung it up in Ellis' room before continuing on to her own bunkhouse. Takeda wouldn't have known which locker was yours, but she could have riffled through the letters in them. It would have taken her only a few minutes, and she had plenty of time."

"You don't think it was simply chance whose knife she took?" Katryn spoke with a frown on her face.

"No. I think it was a deliberate attempt to frame you by someone who knew you'd be nearby and had heard about your threat to Ellis that morning."

"I didn't mean it seriously," Katryn mumbled, embarrassed.

"I know," Chip said quickly. Then she went on. "But it does put a question mark against Takeda. Would she have heard about it? She doesn't seem the type to gossip. The women from your old patrol are more likely candidates."

"None of them left the White Swan."

Chip held up her finger. "None of them made a big thing of waving goodbye and heading out the front door for half an hour. But if they spent an evening drinking, you can bet they all paid at least one visit to the latrine. We've seen that it's easy to scramble around from the back of the tavern to the riverside path, and we're assuming the murderer had arranged to meet Ellis. Therefore, Ellis could have opened the rear door and put out the bridge, and would be there to lend a hand up. Within seconds of slipping out of the taproom, the murderer could have been in the stores."

"How would she get the knife off Ellis?"

"Easy. She'd have asked for it. I'll demonstrate." Chip bounced to her feet. "You be Ellis. I'll be the killer."

Katryn also stood, although she felt uncomfortable.

"And this is a row of crates." Chip pointed to her bed. "Right. We've just closed the rear door. I rush over to these crates, and you follow." Her intonation shifted to an act of forced eagerness. "Thanks for meeting me here, ma'am. But before I say anything more, I want to be sure of my facts. I think this is the crate." She patted the bed and glanced back to Katryn. "Can I borrow your knife, ma'am?" She held out her hand.

After a second of hesitation, Katryn realized that she was expected to play her part in the charade. She pulled the knife from her belt and passed it over.

Chip took it and mimed prying up the lid of a box. She peered down. "Yes. It's like I thought. If you want to see…?"

Chip stepped away. Katryn moved forward automatically and then realized that Chip was now directly behind her. Katryn felt the knife handle tap gently on her back. "And now you're dead." Chip spoke the final words softly.

Katryn turned around. Chip smiled and handed back her knife. They resumed their seats.

"But if it wasn't Takeda, how did the murderer get my knife into Ellis' belt?" Katryn asked.

"There's a stock of grappling irons in the stores. I know; I checked. The murderer borrowed one, locked the rear door, returned the key to Ellis' pocket and slipped out the main door. She went to the wall by the kitchen and used the grapple to climb over. She trotted along the riverbank, around the corner and over the wall again into the space between A and B blocks. She made a quick visit to your bunkhouse and then went back the way she came. She left the grapple hidden under the rubbish in the alleyway before climbing around to the White Swan.

"The whole thing would have taken her five minutes—ten at most. Probably no one even noticed she'd been gone. If anyone had, she could say that there'd been a line for the latrine or she'd been chatting in the courtyard. When the Militia asked if anyone had left the tavern for part of the night, the rest weren't going to say, 'So-and-so took a little bit longer than you'd expect when she went for a piss.'"

"Wouldn't the missing grapple be noticed?"

"I'd guess the murderer collected it early the next day and snuck it back—maybe even pushed it through a ventilation grill." Chip looked thoughtful. "Of course, for completeness, there are two more suspects to consider. Bergstrom and Adebayo were together all evening, but like the Rangers in the tavern, one of them could have slipped off for a few minutes. I think we can dismiss Adebayo. With her leg, her days of climbing over walls are finished, but Bergstrom could have used the riverside path to return the knife belt." Chip paused. "And I'm afraid the last suspect has to be you—if I can just work out a reason why you'd switch your knife with Ellis'." The grin removed any serious intent from her last sentence.

Katryn sank back so that her shoulders rested against the wall. She felt light-headed. Her first reaction was to not even care whether what Chip proposed was feasible; it was enough that Chip still believed in her. Then it struck her that Chip was right. The facts did not add up to an impossible picture. Someone had murdered Ellis and tried to frame her—and came frighteningly close to succeeding.

For the first time, it fully hit Katryn that someone she knew had conspired to kill her. She was not the primary target. She was sure that it was merely incidental to the murderer's plan that she would have been hanged, but she would not have been any less dead. A cold feeling of anger gripped her. She raised her head. Chip was looking at her.

"You're going to find the murderer," Katryn said—more a statement than a question.

"I'm going to find her," Chip confirmed. She opened her mouth as if to say more, but the dinner bell rang out, greeted by shouts from the room outside. "Come on; let's go eat."

❖

By the time the patrol got back to Eastford, the weather was deteriorating, while the action was starting to heat up, metaphorically speaking. Ash was already off chasing reports of missing people. Kim's patrol was dispatched to the south the day after Chip's return. C Patrol had less than a week to savor the delights of the Three Barrels before they were sent on a mission to Liffey's Crossing, escorting an important convoy. In early February, a series of bad storms hit. All the Rangers spent the middle half of the month taking emergency aid to isolated homesteads, rescuing stranded travelers and, on one occasion, digging out corpses after an avalanche overwhelmed several hill farms. By the end of February, the snow lions were getting hungry enough to try for domesticated animals.

Captain LeCoup led C and D Patrols out to deal with a large pride. On the fourth day, they met up with half of the 12th Squadron, which had been similarly dispatched from the Clemswood barracks. The tiny hamlet where their paths crossed was not big enough to shelter everyone, so the Rangers from the 23rd Squadron went farther up the valley to the next lonely cluster of dwellings. That night, Captain LeCoup and her two sergeants returned for a joint briefing. The women from the 12th were led by Lieutenant Bergstrom. One of the others was introduced as Sergeant Sivarajah. Chip studied her. From Katryn's account, it was hardly surprising that the experienced corporal had been promoted to the position left vacant by Ellis' death.

The meeting was routine. The gully that the lions were using as a den had already been identified, and a rough map had been drawn. After a short debate, a coordinated plan was agreed on, with roles assigned for a dawn sortie the next day. In less than half an hour, the officers from the 23rd were ready to leave. However, Chip wanted a private word with Jan Sivarajah first. Chances were that the women from the two squadrons would not even get close enough to recognize one another, but if they did, Chip did not want anyone attempting to lay into Katryn.

Chip slipped around the edge of the room to get to the newly promoted sergeant. "Jan Sivarajah? Can I have a quick word with you?" With her head, Chip indicated an empty corner.

"Do I know you?" Jan asked in confusion when they were out of hearing of the others.

"No. But you know one of the women in my patrol. Private Nagata."

Jan's expression flickered from surprise to concern to something that looked like guilt. "Oh, so that's where she...um, yes...yes, I do. She was—"

Chip cut her off. "I know the whole story, including how she left the 12th. What I wanted to say was, after we've finished with the lions tomorrow, if she should be noticed, I don't want any of your girls thinking they can carry on where they left off."

"No," Jan said immediately. "No, they won't. You have my word on it. I—" She broke off, biting her lip, and then looked up at Chip. "Please tell her I'm sorry about what happened. I should have stopped it, but I was..." She held her hands up in a pained gesture. "Just tell her I'm sorry."

"I'll pass it on."

"Katryn didn't deserve all the blame. I know you must find it hard, having her in your patrol, but don't hold it against her. Ellis pushed her so hard, anyone would've snapped. But I know she can be a good Ranger."

"Katryn didn't kill Ellis."

Jan stared uncertainly at Chip. "Are you sure you've got the whole story?"

"Yes. Possibly more than you have."

"It couldn't have been anyone else. And it was her knife," Jan said obstinately.

"No, it wasn't." Chip glanced across the room. LeCoup was standing by the door, looking in their direction. The captain did not have the appearance of impatience—yet—but it was not wise to keep her waiting. "I can't hang around and talk, but it wasn't her knife. Katryn's was new issue from Fort Krowe. Ellis was stabbed with her own knife. The amount of wear gave it away. Someone made a switch, and the only reason I can think of was to frame Katryn."

"Why didn't Dolokov tell us that?"

"You know your captain better than I do."

Chip started to back away, but Jan caught her arm. "You're sure about the knife?"

"I've seen the report, signed by Lieutenant Sanchez *and* Captain Dolokov."

Jan looked as though she was biting back her words, but then she released Chip's arm "Okay. There isn't time at the moment. Maybe we can talk some more tomorrow. And I promise there won't be any trouble."

❖

The skirmish with the lions went largely according to plan and was over before the sun had cleared the horizon. The Rangers assembled afterward in small clusters, stamping their feet in the cold and shouting good-natured jibes to one another. Chip made a quick head count of her patrol, ensuring that everyone was present and unhurt—and particularly that Katryn was safe. Then she went to report to Captain LeCoup.

It was not the weather to be standing around in the open; but two women from the 12th had received minor injuries that required attention. As the most gifted healer present, Carma Achillea from D Patrol was sent to tend to them. Chip took advantage of the delay to go in search of Katryn's ex-corporal. It was apparent that the same idea had occurred to Jan. The sergeants met in the open space between the two groups of Rangers.

"Sergeant Coppelli," Jan hailed her.

"Hi again." Chip gave the more informal greeting, pulling her cloak tightly around herself. A sharp wind was gusting over the hillside, and the clouds held the promise of more snow. They moved on to a spot sheltered by a tangle of bushes.

"I've been giving a lot of thought to what you said last night," Jan opened the discussion.

"It gives a lot to think about," Chip agreed.

Jan's lips compressed in a thin line as she glared down at the snow. "No matter what way I add it up, it doesn't work out well for the 12th."

"True. You've got a murderer in your midst."

"Yep." Jan sighed. "That was pretty much the conclusion I reached."

"Do you have any names topping your list of suspects?"

"Do you honestly expect me to answer that?"

"Not really," Chip replied evenly. "Though it would be helpful if you did. I've learned enough to know that half the squadron had reason to want Ellis dead, and I think I can show that nine women had the opportunity to do it, you and Katryn among them. Except that Katryn wouldn't have switched knives."

"You think I might—" Jan began.

"You had a hefty grudge over your gene mother."

"So you've been doing your research." Jan's voice was tight.

"It's good practice for a Ranger who wants to stay alive."

Jan looked up to meet Chip's eyes. For the space of a dozen heartbeats, they held the contact. Then Jan made a wry grimace, but her face showed approval. "Very good practice." She drew a deep breath. "And you're right. I hated Ellis. I think part of the reason I didn't stop the others from roughing up Katryn was because I felt so guilty about being pleased by Ellis' death. My gene mother was the only one of my family I cared about. She knew I loved her, but I never got to explain why I..." Jan's voice died. Then she said softly, "You always think you've got more time than you have." She shook her head as if to dislodge the memories. "Yes. I was happy to see Ellis dead, but I didn't kill her. And it wouldn't have been with a knife if I had. I'm the squadron's top tracker. I pick the trails and say where it's safe to go. Do you know how easily I could have rigged an accident? Since Mom died, there have been several perfect opportunities." Jan's eyes bored into the horizon. "I'll admit I thought about it. I was tempted, but I didn't."

Chip studied the other woman thoughtfully. "From what I know, I can give reasons why any of my nine suspects might have wanted to kill Ellis, but it's only an exercise in stringing together facts. You know them—what they're like as people, how they react. If you don't want to tell me who you think did kill Ellis, perhaps you could tell who you think didn't?"

Jan hesitated briefly and then spoke. "Nine suspects? Well, since I'm on your list, I guess you've worked out a way that someone who was in the White Swan could have managed it. So..." She pursed her lips. "Tina—she'd never knife someone in the back. She's got a temper. If Ellis had been battered to death, Tina would be the one I'd look at, but she'd never stoop to backstabbing. Bo hasn't got the brains, the ability or the guts to be a murderer. Pat doesn't care about anything enough to kill for."

"Not even being obliged to sleep with someone against her will?"

Jan gave a humorless laugh. "Your research is slipping. I'm sure

Pat didn't find Ellis attractive, but she used to lead her on. Ellis might have thought she was the one in control, but it was Pat who was in the driver's seat and got all the benefits."

"And the other two?"

"Sal and Nikki? I can't see that either had a motive."

"I'd heard that Ellis threatened to block Sal's re-enlistment because of her drinking."

"There was no way Dolokov would listen to Ellis' recommendation, and Sal knew it." Jan rubbed a hand over her face. "So that's six of your nine. You said Katryn was one, but I'll assume by now that you've got a good idea of what she's like. So who else is on your list of suspects?"

"Lieutenant Bergstrom."

"Oh, yes. Her." Jan squinted toward the rising sun. "I'd say that if she didn't resort to murder when she was Ellis' subordinate, I can't see why she'd do it when she was in a position to make Ellis' life awkward by way of revenge. And I guess your last suspect is Adebayo." Chip was about to correct her but stopped, interested to hear what Jan might offer. "She was the only person who had a good word for Ellis. I suppose it would be nicely ironic for Ellis to be murdered by the nearest thing she had to a friend, but with so many people who hated her guts…" Jan did not finish the sentence.

"And Sergeant Takeda?"

"That's ten." Jan looked sideways at Chip. "Oh…whatever. Takeda is too conscientious. If she was going to murder someone, she'd have scheduled it on the duty roster and filed a report afterward."

"I've heard she has a bit of a temper."

"Takeda? Never." Jan shook her head. "It says a lot about Ellis' goading that she never got any reaction from Takeda. And even if her temper did flare up enough to commit murder, she wouldn't have framed someone else."

A call from LeCoup ended the discussion. Carma had returned, and farther down the hill, the Rangers from the 12th were heading for their horses.

"Looks like it's time to go," Chip said. "Thanks for your help. Maybe we'll meet up again."

"That's okay. I think I owe Katryn something. I'm pleased she's settled down in a squadron. I had been worried about what might happen to her. She deserves a decent sergeant."

"I try my best, and like you, I owe her. Within a month of joining the 23rd, she'd saved my life. As you said last night, she's got the makings of a very good Ranger."

❖

The taproom at the Three Barrels was full of Rangers. Over half the squadron had descended on the cozy tavern to swap stories. Kim's patrol had returned to Eastford at the same time as Chip's, and there was a fair bit of news to exchange. Because they were Rangers, this exchange was done at high volume, accompanied by large amounts of beer. The atmosphere was lively. Several women were singing a ballad of questionable taste.

In one of the quieter corners, Chip sat at a table, going over what she had learned with Kim, while Katryn added the occasional remark. Chip knew that they had to find a way to whittle down the list of suspects. The problem was working out how.

"The trouble is motive. There are just too many people who wanted Ellis dead," Chip concluded.

"True," Kim agreed. "Becoming a sergeant doesn't do much for your popularity, but she does seem to be in a class of her own."

"I hope so," Katryn added in heartfelt tones. "I don't want to run into someone like her again."

Chip frowned. "Except I don't think hatred was the driving motive. You lash out at someone you hate in a fit of anger. This murder was coldly planned in advance."

"Okay. So give me some nice rational reasons to kill her," Kim suggested.

Chip slipped down slightly in her chair as she mulled it over. "We know she was the sort of person who liked to have a hold over others, which is only half a step from blackmail. I'm sure that in her own eyes, Ellis thought she was on the side of the righteous. So it wouldn't be for money, but maybe to try to get what she believed she was entitled to: a promotion. She knew Adebayo and Bergstrom from way back. They were both senior officers to her. She might have threatened to use some information she had on them."

"Such as?"

"If Adebayo has never skimmed anything from the stores, she's unique among quartermasters."

"That's a bit sweeping," Kim protested.

"I don't mean anything major—just that it's very easy for them to start thinking of the stores as their own personal property. It may be only a flagon of beer, but they can still be court-martialed for taking it. And with Bergstrom, there's the story about her going to pieces during the fight with the Mad Butcher. Suppose there were a few more details Ellis kept to herself, so she still had a hold over her? Ellis was desperate for promotion. Perhaps she tried putting pressure on."

"But neither of them could have done anything. It would be up to Dolokov to recommend Ellis for a lieutenancy."

"Oh, yes. But Ellis wasn't a particularly reasonable woman. And it would mean that her victim was in an impossible position."

Kim shook her head. "It's feasible, but it's too much conjecture. And I'm not sure about all this clambering over walls. It's a shame we don't have much of a motive for the one with the best opportunity."

"Sergeant Takeda?" Chip fixed her eyes on the ceiling while running through everything she knew. "Well, we know she takes her responsibilities to her patrol seriously. She had someone's life to avenge, and we don't know what she and Ellis were arguing about earlier that day."

"Might just have been Ellis thinking it funny that one of Takeda's patrol was in the lockup," Katryn said. "I agree with Jan's assessment. Takeda hated Ellis, but she's not the sort of person to act on emotion."

Chip tilted her head toward Katryn. "Do you go along with Jan Sivarajah's opinion of the rest of your ex-comrades?"

Katryn's nose scrunched in thought. "More or less. I don't think Sal took Ellis completely seriously—certainly not when she was drunk, and Ellis was killed after Sal had been in a tavern for a while. Which meant…" Katryn finished the sentence with a wave of the hand. "In the same way, I don't think Bo took *anything* seriously."

"Drunks are unpredictable, and I've never known one who wasn't in debt. Ellis strikes me as the sort to lend money just to tighten her grip," Chip said. "And by all accounts, Bo was the one who Ellis used to pick on most before you arrived."

"So why kill Ellis when she was no longer the main target for abuse?" Katryn countered.

"What about the one who was sleeping with Ellis?"

"Pat?" Katryn shrugged. "Despite months in the same patrol, I'd say that I hardly know her. Jan reckoned it's because there's nothing to know."

"Ellis was chancing her luck there. It's always a bit dicey when a sergeant sleeps with one of her patrol. If there were any evidence of coercion, Ellis would have been in deep shit. LeCoup would be down on us like a ton of bricks at first hint of it in the 23rd." Chip fought to keep her tone level and almost succeeded, although the sight of Kim smirking at her across the table did not help. Fortunately, Katryn's attention was fixed on something on the other side of the room. Chip risked a disapproving frown at her friend, but this only served to amuse Kim more.

Chip managed to regain full control of her voice. "Maybe Pat objected more than she let on."

Kim shook her head. "In that case, she could have made an official complaint, which would have been just as effective in stopping it and far less risky. What do you think, Katryn?"

Katryn's eyes had been riveted on the far wall. She recalled herself. "Er...maybe. Um...Tina. For her, I'd go completely with Jan's assessment. Tina would use her fists, not her knife."

"Except we're not talking about an attack in anger."

"Perhaps." Katryn relaxed visibly. "There's more going on in Tina's head than you'd guess from looking at her. Only the Goddess knows what lies at the bottom."

"So who does that leave?" Kim asked.

"Nikki and Jan herself." Katryn tilted her head to one side. "I like Jan, although I know that's no proof she isn't guilty. And I can't think of any reason Nikki would have to murder Ellis. Plus she isn't the sort to plan things out."

"Supposedly, it's always the ones you don't suspect," Kim threw in. "Except in my experience, the first name to come to mind is the right one nine times out of ten."

"And what's your experience of this sort of murder hunt?" Chip asked wryly.

Kim raised her eyebrows, miming innocence. "Who said I was referring to murder?" She pointed to a group of three local women who had just entered the room and were looking at the Rangers. "Now, do you see the attractive one on the end? If that woman's partner came around here tomorrow, complaining that her other half had gone out for a drink with friends and not come home, whose is the first name you'd think of?" Kim got to her feet, smiling. "And what are the chances you'd be right?"

Chip matched her friend's grin. "Kim, really! You're the sort of woman who gives Rangers a bad reputation."

"I know, but someone has to do it." Kim glanced at the three women and then back. "If you like, I could try to get her friends to come over."

Katryn looked away. Chip hesitated for an instant—not because she was tempted, but she had caught the probing edge in Kim's voice. "Thanks for the offer, but don't bother."

Kim shook her head in mock sorrow. "What a way for Rangers to act! You can't keep this up for long, or you'll have the whole squadron contorted with frustration on your behalf."

"I'm sure nobody is keeping a tally."

"Just as well. There's nothing to count." Kim was completely unmoved by the angry glare Chip was directing at her. She tapped Chip's shoulder. "Catch you tomorrow." Kim smiled once more and then sauntered in the general direction of the attractive local.

Chip cleared her throat. "Um...ignore her. She was just being a clown."

"I'm not so sure. Isn't it one of the rules that all Rangers should go at sex like a three-year-old in a cake shop—one bite out of everything?"

"No." Chip's reply came out more sharply than she intended. "Kim's just..." She paused, gathering herself. "Kim has her own demons to fight. Her family was killed by bandits when she wasn't much more than a kid. She was the one who found the bodies. I think Kim...she plays around so much, it's a defense thing. A way of keeping people at arm's length. She won't let herself get close; then she can't get hurt."

"She cares about you."

"Yes, well...as a friend." Chip looked across the room. Already, Kim had the local's undivided attention. "I think by now, she knows you can't cut yourself off from everyone. And she's grown. She doesn't need the emotional armor, but she carries on out of habit."

"But the rest of the Rangers all act pretty much the same."

"I don't."

"What about the trader in Landfall?"

Chip swallowed, unable to think of anything to say. "I...er...she was..."

"You don't need to explain. It's not you who's out of line; it's me." Katryn said bitterly. Then she buried her face in her hands. "I'm sorry. I shouldn't have joined the Rangers. I never was any good at one-night stands."

"They're not compulsory."

"Aren't they?"

"No. It's your skill with a bow that counts, not your performance in—" Chip swallowed the end of the sentence. She realized that she had gotten into a conversation with Katryn that she desperately did not want to have.

Katryn let her hands drop and looked toward the bar. "Or perhaps I should give it a go...act like a proper Ranger...see if it helps. You never know; I might get to like it. What do you think of my chances with her?"

Chip followed the direction of Katryn's eyes and realized that they were fixed on one of the women standing near the bar. Chip felt her own eyes narrow and was surprised by the strength of her response. The woman looked like a perfectly nice, ordinary person. It was completely unjustified to want her to drop through a hole in the floor.

At the sound of movement, Chip turned back, bracing herself for the sight of Katryn getting to her feet. However, the opposite had happened. Katryn had sunk farther down in her chair, her eyes now glued to the floor.

"Katryn, don't worry. Kim was just joking. Nobody in the squadron will be bothered about what you do. You don't have to prove yourself like that."

"Oh, it's not what Kim said. It's just me, thinking...wondering whether it would provide a distraction, since I can't have the woman I want."

The last of Katryn's words were spoken so softly that Chip was not sure she had heard them correctly. She made an intuitive leap that, with luck, would not land her in anything too nasty if she got it wrong. "Your partner from Woodside...Allison, wasn't it? You're still in love with her?"

Katryn looked puzzled for a moment; then she shook her head. "No, I think I've completely recovered from her."

"Oh. So..." Chip's voice died. She had the sense that she was missing half the conversation.

"Is HQ really so down on affairs between Rangers?"

"Only if it gets serious." Chip gestured toward the room. "It's a safe bet that several of the women here will—" Halfway through the sentence, the implications of Katryn's question caught up with Chip's brain. She stumbled through the last few words. "Er...wake up in each... other's beds...tomorrow."

Chip averted her face while her mind scrambled through memories of the past few days, trying to work out who Katryn might be referring to. Had anyone been receiving extra attention from Katryn or spending more time with her? Or was Katryn speaking hypothetically, reverting to a previous topic as a way to avoid what was becoming an increasingly awkward conversation?

"But it all gets a bit trickier between a sergeant and a lower rank?"

Katryn's words were devoid of emphasis, but they hit Chip like a sledgehammer. She scoured the people standing at the bar, trying to recall exactly where they had been positioned a few minutes earlier. She had thought that Katryn was staring at the local woman. But where had Kim been standing?

It figures—the two best-looking women in the squadron. The thought shot through Chip's head, followed by *I can cope with it... easy...all I have to do is saw my own head off with a blunt knife, and it won't bother me in the slightest.*

"I'm sorry. I shouldn't have said." Katryn's voice recalled Chip from her stunned silence. On the other side of the room, the singers broke into another, even bawdier song. Katryn gestured in their direction. "Why don't we go and join in?"

"Er...yeah...sure." Chip felt dazed. She turned her head and found herself staring deep into Katryn's eyes.

Katryn blushed and dropped her gaze. "Look, I know the rules. I didn't mean to put you on the spot. Please forget I spoke. I won't mention it again." She smiled weakly and then rose from her chair.

"That's okay." Chip stood and followed her across the room, frowning. Her confusion mushroomed. Just exactly what *had* Katryn been saying?

Chip's eyes dropped to the empty tankard in her own hands. Might the better question be, just how much had she drunk?

CHAPTER NINETEEN—AN OLD STORY

March was easily Chip's least favorite month. The weather was utterly unpredictable and unstable. A thaw could set in, only to be overwhelmed by blizzards the next day. The one thing you could guarantee was mud. It was also the month when the snow lions were at their most dangerous, from a human point of view. Once the spadehorns started dropping their calves, the lions would be far more deadly to the young herbivores than they ever were to domestic stock and women. By April, the snow would be in retreat, taking the lions with it, but in March, there were snow lions and mud.

Chip was mumbling curses at the weather as she crossed the main square in Eastford. She had the collar of her cloak turned up and the brim of her hat pulled down to keep the stinging sleet off her face. Her eyes were fixed on the flagstones, watching for icy patches. She collided with a figure in black who was similarly scurrying, head down, across the storm-blown square.

Chip started to apologize before she recognized the other woman. "Lieutenant Sanchez."

"Sergeant Coppelli," the Militiawoman responded.

"What brings you to Eastford?"

"Only regional business." Sanchez made as if to move on. Neither wanted to hang about in the open and chat. Then she stopped and asked, "Have you thought of anything about Ellis' murder?"

"A few bits and pieces." Chip started to back away as the sleet increased in intensity. "I'm at the Three Barrels. If you've got time, come find me, and we'll discuss it."

"I'll do that!" Sanchez shouted before she turned and hurried off.

❖

It was just after dinner when the Militia lieutenant made good on her promise. Chip was lounging by the open fire when she saw Sanchez come in, shaking the water off her cape. In midafternoon, the sleet had changed to rain, but it would probably be back to snow by morning. Chip called out and waved Sanchez over. The barmaid had a drink ready for the Militiawoman even before she sat down at the table.

"Very nice," Sanchez said, smiling. "I can see Central is going to have to beg to get you to go back."

"It's going to be like turfing an old dog out of her kennel," Chip agreed.

They both took a taste of their drinks; then Sanchez became more businesslike. "You said you had information about Ellis' murder."

"Remember you said that if I could tell you how it was done, you could tell me the motive?"

"Yes, and I was totally serious."

"I think I can provide methods for quite a few people."

"Go on, then," Sanchez said, her eagerness showing through her smile.

Chip went through her ideas. Even before she got to the end, she could tell that Sanchez had problems with what she was saying. However, the lieutenant let her finish. Then she leaned forward and said, "I hate to tell you this, but—"

"There's something I don't know." Chip finished the line for her. "Okay, tell me."

"The riverside path. Rain in our area is pretty constant throughout the year, but in winter, it gets locked up as snow, and the level of the river drops. You saw the river at its lowest. In summer, when the murder happened, the river was a good meter higher." Sanchez pursed her lips thoughtfully. "You could still get to the end of the alleyway, and maybe a third of the way along, but the middle part is the lowest. It's still wadeable, but the murderer would have been spotted if she'd gone back to the tavern soaked to the knees. On top of that, there's broken glass cemented onto the top of the wall. It's not visible from the ground, but anyone who tried climbing over would get cut to ribbons."

Chip sunk down in her chair. "So it's Takeda, then," she said softly.

"That was what I was getting to. Obvious, really. I should have thought of it myself."

Chip frowned. "The trouble is, she doesn't seem to have either the personality or the reason to murder Ellis."

Sanchez placed a forefinger on either side of her drink. Her face was pensive as she twisted the tankard around. "Okay, then, for my side of the bargain. The motive…" The frown on her forehead deepened. Then she looked up at Chip. "It's part of an old story. Have you heard about the outlaw called the Mad Butcher and what happened to the 12th fourteen years back?"

"There was a massacre."

"Right. And did you know that Takeda's older sister was one of the Rangers who died?"

"No."

"The family comes from Eastford. Takeda's mothers have a blacksmith's forge on the other side of the river. By Ranger policy, both she and her sister would have been assigned to Eastern Division, so it isn't that much of a coincidence that they both went to the same squadron. And of course, her older sister was dead by the time Takeda joined." Sanchez stared into the nearby fire, musing. "I've known both sisters, not terribly well, but enough to talk to. They're completely different personalities. Takeda is serious and intense and painfully conscientious. She'll end up in divisional staff, pushing paper around. Her sister was more of a typical Ranger."

"Loud, reckless and brazen?" Chip suggested.

"Your words, not mine." Sanchez smiled. "She was also, in my opinion, the less bright of the two by quite a wide margin. However, Takeda worshiped her older sister. I'm sure that's why she followed her into the Rangers." She paused. "I guess you're wondering where this is going."

Chip shrugged by way of an answer.

"If you've been told about the massacre, you must have heard someone tipped the Butcher off about the Rangers' plans. Officially, we never found out who. However, I was one of the people in the Militia given the job of trying to find the source of the leak. We didn't prove it absolutely. Too many people we needed to talk to were dead. But Takeda's sister was right at the top of the list of candidates—not as a deliberate betrayal; most likely unguarded pillow talk. She wasn't noted for discretion, and the night before the raid, she was in one of the Roadsend taverns, utterly plastered and bragging that the 12th was going to put an end to the Mad Butcher. She was last seen that night in the arms of a local woman whom we never identified for certain, but her description matched someone who was later found to be a member of the Butcher's gang. Unfortunately, we couldn't ask the bandit, since she wasn't taken alive."

Sanchez sighed. "And that's where it was left. A decision was made higher up that no purpose would be served by naming the guilty party. It wouldn't bring the dead back, and Takeda's sister had paid for her mistake. By all accounts, she played a hero's part in the fighting, holding off three bandits single-handedly, giving the few surviving Rangers the chance to escape. For the sake of her family, HQ wanted her to be remembered like that."

"Did Ellis know this?" Chip asked.

"Yes, though she didn't admit it. Believe it or not, she and Takeda's sister were friends. Ellis was a much nicer person before she became a sergeant. She had been in the tavern that night and saw the woman in question. We asked her to identify the bandit's body. I was there. Ellis hardly bothered to look. Just a quick glance. Then she turned around and said it wasn't the same woman."

"She was protecting her friend's memory?"

"That was the feeling I got."

Chip considered the information in relation to the murder. "So… what I think you're implying is that there was growing friction between Takeda and Ellis. Ellis was being unpleasant about the Ranger in the lockup, and there was the affair of the woman killed by lions. We know they argued about something on the day Ellis was killed. You think, as part of the argument, Ellis threatened to disclose what she knew about Takeda's sister?"

Sanchez nodded. "Takeda can be cold. One of the few things she is violently passionate about is her heroic dead sister. She's thumped people in the past for jokes she saw as bad taste."

"You think she'd kill to preserve her sister's reputation?"

"Oh, yes."

"So we've got motive and opportunity," Chip said slowly. "All we need now is proof."

Sanchez drained the end of her drink and stood up to go. "True… and that's always the tricky one."

❖

The Old Ford Inn was the most luxurious lodging house in Eastford. Its solid timber frontage opened directly onto the main square opposite the temple. It was where the senior officers were billeted, Captain LeCoup among them. The captain had a small suite to herself, including an audience room where she held briefings. Chip looked around at the cushioned chairs, the wine decanter and the remains of the extensive dinner that had been served in the room. All things considered, it was very unfair that LeCoup had not given her an award, rather than an ear bashing, for wrangling the posting to Eastford.

Chip hitched herself up onto a windowsill. With the strong sunlight falling on the back of her neck, she could close her eyes and imagine it was summer. Ash O'Neil came to stand beside her, looking out across the square at the crisp blue sky behind the row of rooftops. All trace of snow had gone. In mid-March, the weather had improved dramatically. In the space of a day, it had gone from winter to spring and stayed there. With the beginning of April, the string of emergencies had dwindled to nothing, and for the first time since January, all four patrols were back in Eastford.

"Now do you believe me that we've seen the last of winter?" Ash asked, teasing.

"I believed you when you said it two weeks back. I just didn't know how you could be so sure," Chip replied without opening her eyes.

"The fenbucks. They were moving to their summer grazing." Ash's voice was edging into self-parody. "Of course, the question is, how did they know it was more than a short thaw?"

"Presumably, no one has ever told them, 'Early winter, late spring.' Which was what I'd been expecting. I'd thought we were going to be chasing around like a one-legged woman in an ass-kicking contest right up until the day we returned to Fort Krowe."

"And I had you marked down as an optimist."

The door of the room opened, and Captain LeCoup came in, with Lieutenant Ritche at her shoulder. All four sergeants moved to adopt more formal positions, but LeCoup immediately indicated that they could stay as they were.

"It's just a recap session. I've got to produce a full report, and I want you to jog my memory. General impressions; things like that. You can be honest. I'll censor out anything that should stay off the record."

Chip could not restrain a grin at the thought of LeCoup as a guardian of propriety. She stared down at the floor, judging it safest not to catch anyone else's eye.

LeCoup went on. "Eastern Division is having its annual officers' briefing, starting tomorrow. Either the captain or lieutenant from each squadron will be here. They'll be sorting out postings for the next year and filling each other in on items of note. They want the 23rd to have an input—anything anyone's noticed that might be of use. So…what do we tell them?"

The debate started slowly but soon warmed up. After two and a half months, there was a fair bit of information to pass on to the Eastern squadrons: unfinished business, worrying signs there had not been the time to pursue further, gossip from farmers that was worth checking again. It was nearly an hour before everyone was finished.

LeCoup wound up the meeting. "Okay, I'll try to knock all this into shape. One last thing before you go: By this evening, I want everyone to send me a full list of anything that's lost, damaged or used up. I'm sure Central will want to try putting in a bill for it."

As Chip slipped down from the window ledge, LeCoup caught her eye. "Sergeant Coppelli, can you hang on a minute? I want a word." Chip felt her stomach clench in reflex. However, the captain did not look angry, and once they were alone, LeCoup adopted a casual stance. "How have you been doing on your hunt for the murderer?"

"Mixed luck," Chip replied, relaxing. "I was talking to Lieutenant Sanchez from the Roadsend Militia a short while back. We're pretty sure we know who did it, but proving it is a lot harder."

"And it's not Private Nagata?"

"No, ma'am."

"Anything I can do to help?"

Chip hesitated. It was too good an offer to turn down. "Another visit to Roadsend might help. I'm not sure what I'll find, but it's the best place to look."

"Okay. I'll see what I can do. Dismissed."

"Thank you, ma'am."

Chip headed across town, feeling both pleased and anxious. LeCoup's intervention was encouraging, but it served to remind her that she was running out of time. In two weeks, the period of secondment to Eastern would end. If she could not get the evidence to prove Takeda's guilt by then, she would have to give up.

Back at the Three Barrels, she picked Katryn to help with taking the inventory of lost stock. It gave them a chance to talk over everything again. What they needed was a witness to the argument between Ellis and Takeda or, failing that, proof that Ellis knew Takeda's sister was the one responsible for the disaster. No new ideas had occurred to either of them by the time they finished the inventory.

❖

Katryn trotted across the square toward the Old Ford Inn, carrying the list of items. The sun had dropped behind the rooftops, and already, torches framed the entrance to the inn. The wind was picking up, and an icy bite had returned to the air. Racing to get out of the cold, Katryn leaped up the steps and collided in the doorway with another woman in a Ranger's uniform.

The single star of a lieutenant's badge was the first thing to register. "Sorry, ma'am," Katryn blurted out, snapping to attention even before she recognized Bergstrom's face. The two stared at each other. Katryn dropped her eyes. "I'm sorry, ma'am. I wasn't looking where I was going."

Bergstrom looked flustered but collected herself quickly. "Be more careful in the future." Her voice was as sharp as her gaze.

"Yes, ma'am," Katryn said. She looked at Bergstrom's back as it retreated. The lieutenant had seemed startled rather than surprised; Katryn guessed that Jan had let people know she was in the 23rd. She wondered how much else had been said.

❖

Chip and Katryn returned to the inn later that night. Probably, Bergstrom knew nothing that would be of use to them. However, she was one of the few survivors of the massacre, and Chip wanted to take the opportunity to try to see what information could be had. It was not going to be easy. Not only did Chip have no authority to question a senior officer, but she also did not want to mention Takeda or her sister by name.

The room allocated to Bergstrom was on the upper floor of a wing overlooking the courtyard. Katryn went with Chip as far as the lobby at the top of the stairs but decided not to join in the interview with her former lieutenant. Chip walked the last few meters alone and knocked on the door.

Immediately, a voice bade her to enter. Bergstrom sat at a table littered with dispatches. "What is it?" Her tone was peeved. She was obviously not pleased by what she was reading.

Chip snapped smartly to attention. "Excuse me, ma'am. I'm Sergeant Coppelli of the 23rd Squadron. Would it be convenient for you to talk to me?"

"I can spare ten minutes," Bergstrom said, putting down the sheet she had been holding.

"Thank you, ma'am." Chip paused briefly, adopting a more relaxed stance. "I think you are aware that Private Nagata is now in the 23rd?" Bergstrom nodded. "She is a member of my patrol. I heard about the incidents in the 12th and why she left. Naturally, I was concerned, and I have been trying to see if I can get to the bottom of it."

"Lieutenant Sanchez in Roadsend would be a better person to talk to than me. If you can't get to meet her, I'm sure she would send you a report."

"Yes, ma'am. Actually, I've spoken to her already. As an offshoot to our conversation, I've become interested in the events concerning the massacre of the 12th by the outlaw known as the Mad Butcher."

The effect on Bergstrom was instantaneous. Her eyes narrowed, and she sat up straighter. However, her voice remained neutral. "In what way?"

Chip picked her words cautiously; she did not want to be the one to mention Takeda's name. "Apparently, someone slipped a warning to the gang. I wonder if you had any idea who it was."

"Why? What makes you think I have anything more to say? I told everything I knew at the time." The defensive edge to Bergstrom's voice was unmistakable.

"It's just that you were there. You knew the other survivors and those who died. Even if you don't have anything more to say on your own account, I wonder whether you think Sergeant Ellis might have known the identity of the informer?" Chip tried to keep the situation calm. Too late, she remembered that Bergstrom had been the target of ridicule from Ellis on the subject of the battle.

"Sergeant Ellis? Exactly what are you getting at?"

"I'm sorry, ma'am. I don't want to be too blunt, but I think I know who leaked the information. I wondered if there was anything you could add."

Bergstrom leaped to her feet. "No. I don't know what you're implying, and I don't see the relevance of this to Sergeant Ellis' death. If you have looked into things at all, you will know that I never talked to the woman more than I could help. Certainly not about—"

It was time to retreat. "Then I'm sorry to have wasted your time, ma'am."

Bergstrom continued to glare as Chip backed out of the room. Just as she reached for the door handle, the lieutenant spoke again, her voice clipped. "Sergeant, if you start spreading gossip and accusations, I will ensure that it is treated as a severe disciplinary matter. Do you understand?"

"Yes, ma'am." Chip escaped.

"How did it go?" Katryn asked after the door had shut.

Chip only groaned by way of answer.

"What happened?"

"She threatened me with disciplinary action."

"Over what?"

"Come on. Let's get away from here." Chip indicated the exit with her thumb. When they were on the stairs, she continued, speaking quietly. "Bergstrom is very, very touchy about the affair. I guess years of Ellis' accusing her of cowardice have left a permanent scar. Maybe she thought I was going to dredge the whole thing up again. She might even have thought I was implying that she killed Ellis because of the jeering. She certainly took it personally. We didn't get anywhere near discussing Takeda."

At the bottom of the stairs was a door to the outside. Chip pushed it open and stepped into the courtyard. She stopped to gather her thoughts. Her eyes fixed on the glittering display of stars in the cold night sky. "I'm sure it was her sister who tipped off the Butcher, but we need real proof that will stand up in a court-martial."

Katryn waited beside her. "And what are our chances of getting that?"

Chip pursed her lips. "I need to go to Roadsend. Fortunately,

Captain LeCoup has promised to send me there before we finish our time with Eastern. Maybe I can talk to Quartermaster Adebayo and look through the Militia records. We're so close to making our case, we can't stop now."

Chip's eyes carried across the sky. Directly overhead was the window of Bergstrom's room, slightly ajar despite the cold. She sighed. Talking to the lieutenant had been a total waste of time. "Let's get back to the Three Barrels and warm up."

❖

Katryn laid her cards on the table and scooped up the small pile of coins. The others at the table expressed good-natured resignation. One of the Rangers swept up the cards and molded them into a neat pack, which she rapped on the table. "Are you going to give us a chance to get it back?"

"I think I'll quit while I'm ahead and use my winnings to buy everyone a drink," Katryn replied.

Corporal Lee Horte immediately stretched out her hand to stop the woman who was shuffling the cards. "Don't distract Katryn when she's having a good idea."

General laughter greeted the words. Katryn twisted around in her chair and signaled to the bar staff. While she waited for someone to come to take the order, she listened to the banter of her comrades. She felt happy and relaxed. She was even starting to believe that joining the Rangers had not been such a horrendous mistake—but at that moment, the one aching regret in her life surged to the forefront of her thoughts. Chip had sauntered into the taproom. Katryn felt her stomach flip over.

The sergeant wandered over to their table. "Lee, Katryn, can I have a quick word with you?" The two followed Chip to one side of the room and waited for her to speak. "I've just been talking with Captain LeCoup. The Eastern Division officers' meeting finishes today. LeCoup has volunteered C Patrol for courier duties. We need two Rangers to go to Roadsend and give the lieutenant the report, so that she knows where she has to go to meet up with her captain and the rest of the squadron. That will be Katryn and me. We also need two Rangers to go to Monday Market and pass similar information on to the half of 19th

Squadron that's been stationed there. Finally, we need couriers for the 12th at Clemswood."

"That isn't one of the split squadrons. Why won't Bergstrom be taking the message back?" Katryn asked.

"Apparently, she's been called away to pay her last respects to a relative who's at death's door. She went last night, as soon as she'd finished giving the report from the 12th." Chip turned to Lee. "I'd like you to be one of the women who goes to Clemswood. You know how we've been trying to find out who murdered Katryn's old sergeant?" Lee nodded. She was aware of most of the facts. "Katryn obviously can't go, and I really want to talk to Sanchez, but it would be useful to have someone try to pick up gossip from the ordinary Rangers."

"There's someone called Bo Hassan who's a great source of stories," Katryn suggested.

Chip nodded her agreement. "Time the journey so that you get to spend an evening there and chat with people. Pick someone from the patrol to go with you—someone nosy but discreet."

"Find someone nosy but discreet?" Lee repeated slowly, looking pained. "You know, one of the great things about having you as a sergeant is that I get such challenging assignments."

CHAPTER TWENTY—THE OLD MILL

A re you Sergeant Coppelli?" Little more then a nose was visible in the gap below the hood. The girl was lost in layers of what looked like rags, although there possibly were a few complete garments among them.

"Yes."

"The lady said you'd give me twenty cents if I gave you this." The urchin held up a scrap of paper.

"The...who?"

"She didn't say who she was."

Chip bent down to get a better view of the girl's face. The fidgety eyes told her all she needed to make a guess. "Twenty cents? On top of what she already paid you?" Chip's tone dripped with skepticism.

The urchin shuffled her feet and then gave a broad grin. "Well, no harm in me asking, was there?"

Chip held out her hand for the letter, her curiosity seething to know who had paid a street urchin to act as go-between. Who even knew she was in Roadsend? "Okay, but there's ten cents in it if you describe the woman and tell me when and where you met her."

"Just an ordinary farmer. I think I've seen her around once or twice on market days. Don't know where she's from. She came up to me five minutes ago, when I was standing over there." The girl held out a grubby finger. "Said you were in the Militia building and I was to give this to you when you came out."

"She described me?"

"She said you were a sergeant in the 23rd. I could tell it was you from the three bars on your badge."

Chip dug a coin out of her purse and flipped it over. The young girl caught it deftly and scampered away. Chip opened the folded sheet and read:

Sergeant Coppelli:

I know what you are after and have information that
I think will help you. I can meet you at sunset tonight
at the old mill, three kilometers out of town on the
Clemswood Road. Private Nagata will know where it
is.

There was no signature at the bottom. Chip did not expect one. She looked down the street in the direction the girl had gone, but there was no point going after her. Even if she found the child again, Chip was sure that there was nothing more to be gained from her. Whoever had written the note wanted to keep her identity hidden; else why bother with the go-between and the obscure rendezvous? That the unknown woman felt the need to go to such lengths was nearly as much of a mystery as the message itself.

Who in Roadsend, apart from Sanchez, knew what she was trying to do? And the lieutenant was not around. Chip had been on her way back from a wasted visit to the Militia station when the urchin had hailed her. Sanchez was out of town and would not be available until the next morning. Yet not only had the writer of the note claimed to know their objective, but she also knew that both Chip and Katryn were in Roadsend—knowledge all the more surprising as they had reached the town less then two hours ago, and Chip's current excursion was the first time either had set foot outside the barracks.

The back of Chip's neck tingled as her thoughts moved on. The writer had also known that she was in the Militia station, which she could only have found out by following her.

Chip scoured the street. The person might well be watching her now. In fact, she almost certainly was. How else could she be sure that the urchin had carried out her errand? There was no way to single the writer out from the crowds. It was a deeply unsettling idea. Chip turned around sharply and marched back to the barracks.

❖

Chip and Katryn arrived at the old mill an hour early and hid in woods overlooking the river, hoping to see the unknown note-writer arrive. However, she was either there before them or not coming. As the sun dropped below the horizon, it was time for Chip and Katryn to make their minds up about whether to go ahead with the rendezvous.

"I'm not happy about this." It was the third time Katryn had expressed that view.

"Neither am I." Chip's eyes bored into the deserted building as though she was hoping to see through the ancient timber walls. The conversation had been traveling in the same circle ever since she had gotten back to the barracks. The setup was too convoluted to be a joke. The best guess was that the woman was a survivor of the Butcher's gang—the trouble with this conclusion being that it was hard to see why she would want to help catch Ellis' murderer or inform against Takeda's sister. "I wish I knew where she got her information about us, and I wish I knew why she has to play these games. However, most of all, I want to know what she has to tell us, and the only way we'll find out is by talking to her."

"As long as it isn't a trap."

Chip frowned. She shared Katryn's doubts. The offer of information was too good to turn down. It was also too good to be trusted. Chip drew her sword and pushed her cloak back from her shoulders to leave her arms free. "One way or another, it's going to give us answers. We have to go in, but very carefully, and we watch each other's back."

Katryn nodded and pulled an arrow from her quiver. The two slipped out from the trees. The overgrown path took them down toward the river. The only sounds as they approached were the gushing of water along the millrace and the piercing cries of birds returning to their roosts.

A short flight of steps led up to the doorway. At the top, they stopped. The door itself had fallen in—or been kicked down.

While Katryn kept her attention on the surrounding hillside, Chip slipped around the threshold, straining her eyes against the gloom inside. The structure appeared to be generally sound. The ceiling was still intact, as were the floorboards. The millstones were gone, leaving only the huge wooden gears. The stairs to the upper level looked a tad unsafe, but they had probably been in much the same condition when the mill was in use. Chip guessed that it had been abandoned for under a dozen years. Three inner doorways led to adjoining rooms. There was no sign of the woman they had come to meet.

Chip was just starting to think that the note had been a practical joke (although Sanchez did not seem the type, and it was difficult to see who else might have played it) when she saw a faint light coming from one of the back rooms. "I think our friend is here," she whispered to Katryn.

Chip moved away from the door, still keeping her back to the wall. Katryn followed, with an arrow nocked on her bowstring. As Chip's eyes adjusted to the dim light, the glow from the inner room seemed a little brighter, yet it was obvious that the candle or lantern was being shielded in some way.

They edged around the walls. Finally, Chip stepped through the inner doorway. Again, she found herself in an empty room, but now she could see that the light was emanating from an open trap door in the floor.

Katryn stood guard while Chip kneeled by the hatch and peered in. The opening was a good meter square, large enough for flour sacks carried across shoulders to pass through easily. Stairs led down to a cellar two-thirds underground. A window was high on one wall, squeezed in just below the ceiling. The glass was gone, but thick iron bars remained, with vines and branches poking between them. Rotting straw and empty sacks littered part of the floor. The candle was in a holder on the wall. The only furniture was a battered table pushed against the far wall and a stool. Sitting on the stool was a hunched figure, bundled in layers of rags like the street urchin. The woman showed no sign of moving. Possibly, she was old and hard of hearing; possibly, she was asleep. Chip began to descend the staircase, placing each foot to land as silently as she could manage.

At the bottom of the stairs, Chip paused and glanced up. Katryn was standing to one side of the opening, her eyes trained on the outer room. Chip returned her attention to the woman at the bench.

"Hey!" Katryn's sudden cry broke the silence.

Chip's head shot up. Katryn was lifting her bow, but before it was half drawn, Chip heard the familiar twang of a bowstring. Katryn flung herself sideways, landing sprawled across the trap-door opening.

Chip leaped for the stairs. Simultaneous with Katryn's dive was the thud of a projectile striking wood. In a calm, logical corner of her mind, Chip registered the fact that the arrow was, therefore, not lodged in Katryn. Chip's foot hit the first stair at the same moment that the sound of running footsteps reverberated through the mill.

Meanwhile, Katryn was struggling to avoid falling down the stairs. She had one leg pulled in through the hatch, hunting for footing. Her elbows were fighting for purchase on the edge of the hatchway.

Chip's second foot hit the stairs. Katryn was twisting, starting to rise, when another figure appeared above her, dressed in a Ranger's uniform, drawn sword in hand.

"Katryn, look out!" Chip shouted.

Katryn abandoned her battle with the hatchway. She tumbled through the opening, dropping away from the downward-swinging arc of the sword. Halfway down the stairs, she collided with Chip. Katryn ended up sprawled on the earthen floor. Chip fared a little better, but even before she regained her balance, they heard the crash of the trap door slamming shut and the unmistakable sound of a bolt being driven home. Then there was silence.

Katryn scrambled to her feet. They both stared at the closed hatchway and then at the seated figure. Unbelievably, she had not stirred. Chip crossed the floor and reached out to shake the woman's shoulder. At her touch, the figure slumped sideways. Chip's initial horrified thought that the woman was dead lasted no more than a second: The rags dropped away to reveal a sack stuffed with straw.

"What game are they playing?" Katryn asked, bewildered.

"I don't know, but we're playing it by my rules once we get out." Chip's voice was grim. She returned to the stairs, climbing high enough so that she could push experimentally against the hinged flap. It showed no sign of moving, but the wood was old and cracked. "I think we can get through, but it will mean using my sword like an axe."

"Use mine. I've got less use for it."

Chip nodded while she continued to examine the timber, deciding on the best point of attack.

"Chip, move!" Katryn screamed.

Chip flung herself off the stairs and hit the ground rolling. An arrow thudded into the wooden frame at the spot where she had been crouched. Chip's momentum took her back up to her knees. Her eyes darted around the cellar. There was nowhere to hide. The open treads of the stairs offered no protection. There was only one option.

Katryn was a step ahead of her. By the time Chip reached the table, Katryn had grabbed the edge and thrown it on its side. They jerked it around so that it faced the window, its legs touching the opposing wall. Chip spared a look at the candle. Darkness would make them less of a target, but there was no time. Already, she could hear the soft creak of the bow being drawn again. Chip dived over the top of the table. Katryn was beside her an instant later as a second arrow struck the wall above their heads and rebounded back onto the floor. Small flakes of stone rained down on them.

The space was cramped. It took a bit of squirming before they were both half lying side by side, keeping as low as possible, shoulders against the wall and knees drawn up against the underside of the table.

For a long time, everything was very quiet. Then there was the sound of footsteps on the floorboards directly overhead.

Chip peered around cautiously the edge of the table. She caught the glint of candlelight on an arrow poking through the window and pulled her head back. More than one attacker was involved in the ambush.

The footsteps stopped by the trap door, and a voice rang out. "Sergeant Coppelli?" There was a pause. "I just wanted to say I'm sorry, but you've given me no choice."

Chip and Katryn stared at each other in amazement, both at the words and at recognizing Lieutenant Bergstrom's voice.

"Are you hoping for me to say I accept your apology?" Chip shouted back at last.

"No, of course not." Bergstrom had missed the irony. "I just wanted to ask how you worked out that it was my sister who tipped off the gang." When Chip said nothing, Bergstrom continued, "I've spent years in fear, thinking it would come out. I was just starting to relax when you came around, threatening me. I was right, wasn't I? You were hoping to rattle me into admitting something. And I heard what you said in the courtyard afterward. How did you know?"

Chip covered her face with her hands, shaking her head in disbelief. What she had missed—or blundered into? Her hands dropped. A bluff might be the best way of getting answers. "We got lucky with some old reports. The only thing we weren't sure of was the extent of your sister's involvement with the Butcher."

"Oh, yes. Fran, my shithead little sister," Bergstrom said bitterly. "Please, you've got to believe me. If I'd known she was going to pass the warning on, I'd never have told her. I'd have let her die with the other scum like she deserved."

"Hey!" The anger in the shout from the window allowed Chip to make a fair guess at the identity of the archer.

Bergstrom ignored the complaint and went on. "I guess it was obvious Mom would prefer Fran, seeing how she's her birth daughter, especially since my birth mother walked out, but—" She broke off, sudden pain tearing her voice. "I'd have done anything to please Mom, but it was always Fran, Fran, Fran. Like the sun shone out of her ass... spoiled brat. When I was in the Militia, I knew Fran was mixing with the wrong people, like it was a game. I tried to shield her for Mom's sake, though it stuck in my gullet. I joined the Rangers partly to get away. But first posting and I was back in Roadsend again. Then we had the briefing about the raid on the Butcher's hideout. If Fran had been killed, it would have broken Mom's heart. But I swear I never thought the silly bitch would pass the warning on."

"Oh, come on. They were my friends." Bergstrom's sister at the window was goaded into speaking up. "And like you, I never thought they'd try ambushing the squadron. I thought they'd just run and hide. Once I knew what the Butcher was planning, I was out of there. She thought if she gave the Rangers a bloody nose, they'd leave her alone. I knew Fort Krowe would hunt her to the ends of the earth. That's why I went straight into town and made myself very conspicuous the whole time the ambush was happening."

"And left me and the rest of the squadron to walk into it."

It was obviously an old and very bitter argument. Chip pinched the bridge of her nose in despair. But at least she could almost tie up the whole story. She raised her voice. "So what about Ellis?"

"Ellis?" Bergstrom spat out the name. "What do you want to know? She saw me panic when the fighting started, and I realized it was my fault. I was blabbering away. Ellis was always holding it over me, and she was getting worse after Fitz's death and Dolokov told her she wouldn't be allowed to re-enlist. I guess she felt she had nothing to lose." The sound of footsteps from above announced that Bergstrom was moving again. "I wasn't sorry about her death, but I'll be sorry about yours. I never, ever meant for any decent Rangers to die."

The footsteps receded. Chip followed their progress until they left the mill, but she did not dare assume that the archer at the window had also gone. From Bergstrom's final words, it was clear that the renegade lieutenant was determined to kill them both.

Chip's gaze moved on to the candle, considering her chances of extinguishing it. But even with the candle out, there would be little to gain. If they started hacking at the trap door, Bergstrom's sister would not need light to know where to send the arrow.

Katryn's bow lay on the ground near the foot of the stairs. Again, getting it was not worth the risk involved. There was not room behind the table for Katryn to draw the bow without making a target of herself.

Chip's examination of the room ended with Katryn. For the first time, she noticed the blood soaking the shoulder of Katryn's jacket. "You're hurt!"

Katryn glanced down as though she had been unaware of her injury. "Just a flesh wound. The arrow nicked my arm."

"Let me see."

"It's not a priority."

"We might as well do something while we wait for Bergstrom to set fire to the mill."

"You think that's what she's going to do?"

"It's what I'd do in her place."

Katryn looked at the locked trap door. "We aren't in a very good position, are we?"

Chip gave a humorless laugh. "Not really. But we might get lucky, and our chances will be better with your arm bandaged."

Katryn nodded and slipped her shoulder out of her jacket. The arrow had sliced a gash. Blood was still oozing, but the injury was not serious. Chip took the field dressing from the pouch on her belt to bind the wound.

Katryn leaned her head back against the wall. "I don't suppose you have any of the healer-gift?" She spoke with her eyes closed.

"The barest residual trace. We were all tested. Prudence is the best in my family, and she can't do much more than cure a headache. How about you?"

"The same. My sister had a bit more than me. I wouldn't have trusted her with a headache, though."

Chip finished tying the knot and helped Katryn back into her jacket. She looked up. Katryn's face was in profile in the candlelight. Chip opened her mouth to speak and closed it again. Then she set her jaw. In the circumstances, there was no point holding back. She hoped that Katryn would take it as a compliment, rather than an unwelcome additional trial. "Your sister...you know...if your ex-partner left you for her, your sister must be really something."

"She's something, all right."

"I mean...what I meant is...I like you a lot...and I...just wanted you to know that." Chip's voice failed her, but she had probably said enough. She braced herself for a rebuff.

"I know." Katryn slowly rolled her head around to meet Chip's eyes. Astonishingly, she was smiling sadly. "You're not so bad yourself."

Very deliberately, Katryn reached out to interlace her fingers with Chip's. She raised their joined hands to her lips and kissed each of Chip's knuckles in turn.

"Oh, shit," Chip gasped.

Katryn looked up, a slightly quizzical expression on her face.

Chip managed a sickly grin. "I'm sorry. It's what Kim is always telling me. My line in sweet-talking needs polishing."

Katryn's shoulders shook with suppressed laughter. She pressed the back of Chip's hand to her cheek. Chip watched her in amazement, trying to think of something else to say. "Er...my timing could stand some improvement as well. This is one of those rare occasions where lifelong commitment might not count for as much as a one-night stand."

"You think we have no chance?"

"We're Rangers, and we're still breathing. Of course we stand a chance."

Katryn moved their joined hands to her lap. She stared at their intertwined fingers pensively. "Bergstrom's taking her time with the fire."

"Maybe she has other plans."

"Such as?"

"I don't know. We need to think—see if we can outmaneuver her. It's our only hope." Chip lifted her eyes to the floorboards above them. Her heart was pounding. The feel of Katryn's hand made rational thought almost impossible.

"Well, if not, it's been nice knowing you. Thanks for believing me."

The depth in Katryn's voice pulled Chip's gaze back down. Their eyes met and locked. Then Katryn leaned forward and kissed her, slowly and very softly. It was not the situation for passion; yet the tenderness in Katryn's kiss flooded through Chip. Their mouths molded together, wordlessly expressing both promises and regrets. At last, Katryn shifted back to her original position. All the time she kept their hands clasped.

Chip stared at Katryn, her mind reeling. Of all the responses she had anticipated, this had been the very last on the list. She did not know whether to cry with despair or joy. The chances of either of them seeing sunrise the next day did not look good, but Katryn had admitted feeling some affection for her. And at least if she was going to die, it would be nice to go out holding Katryn's hand.

❖

It was well past midnight. The candle had long since burned out, but the full orb of Hardie was now low enough in the sky to shine squarely through the barred window of the cellar. The bands of brilliant moonlight lay across the earthen floor. There was no sound except for two sets of soft, even breathing, echoing off the stone walls. Then came the faint scratching of a bolt being eased back and the sigh of seeping air as the trap door was lifted carefully.

Bergstrom peered down into the cellar. From the hatchway, she had a clear view of the two huddled figures behind the table, wrapped in gray cloaks, with wide-brimmed Rangers' hats pulled down over their eyes. The moonlight was bright enough to catch a hint of the green in the jackets underneath. Neither figure moved, nor did the gentle breathing pause. Bergstrom beckoned her sister, Francesca, over. It was a small sop to her conscience that she would not be the one to end the lives of her blameless fellow Rangers.

Francesca looked at her targets and nocked an arrow. She drew back, bracing her hand under her chin and touching lips and nose to the string. At such close range, taking aim required only a moment.

She loosed the shot. The arrow struck fully into the breast of the figure farther away. It keeled over from the impact. The other shape in gray shifted slightly but showed no sign of waking. A few seconds later, Francesca's second arrow thudded into the remaining figure. A shudder ran though it; then it slumped down slightly farther into the shadow behind the table. The breathing stopped.

Bergstrom realized that her hands were moist and shaking, but it was over. She brushed her palms dry on her thighs and stepped onto the stairs, her eyes fixed on the motionless shapes below. Francesca followed her down. The pair crossed the cellar to the upturned table and looked down. It took a few heartbeats for them to identify the figures as two sacks of straw wrapped in gray cloaks. Before either could react, there was the sound of movement behind them.

Then Chip's voice rang out. "You know, our falling for the stuffed-bag trick was bad enough, but you can't even claim you'd had no warning."

Bergstrom and her sister spun around to see Katryn and Chip standing in the shadows under the stairs. Chip held her knife and sword. Katryn had an arrow nocked and her bow three-quarters drawn. Chip went on, "But I'm glad you put in an appearance. It's a bit cold, standing here without our cloaks and jackets."

"But...I heard...they were breathing," Francesca blurted out.

"We heard echoes and told ourselves they were coming from where we expected," Bergstrom said harshly, cutting off her sister's mumbling.

Chip inclined her head to agree with Bergstrom's statement. "So are you going to surrender nicely?"

It was a reasonable suggestion. Francesca did not even have an arrow at hand, and Bergstrom's sword was still sheathed. Katryn could drop one of them before they had a chance to move, leaving the other to fight two against one. Francesca looked stunned, but she reached the inevitable conclusion and tossed her useless bow aside. However, Bergstrom backed away to the far corner of the cellar.

"You know I can't do that. And there's no point. I'm not going to be dragged through a court-martial just to provide entertainment when I'm strung up by the neck. I..." Her composure started to unravel. "I never meant any of this to happen. I wanted to be a good Ranger. I've really tried over the years to make amends. I'd have a perfect record if it weren't for her." Bergstrom's hand jerked in her sister's direction. "Mom's little darling. I did it all for her, and she never once said thank you. And Mom...she didn't..." Bergstrom's voice choked away. In a fluid movement, she whipped her sword out of its scabbard. "Tell everyone I'm sorry."

The others in the cellar realized a second too late what Bergstrom intended. Before anyone could move, Bergstrom had flipped the sword around. One hand grasped the hilt; the other clutched the tip and pressed it against her heart. She pitched forward, dropping like a felled tree. Insanely, the thought to shoot through Chip's head was *She's going to cut her fingers.* Then Bergstrom crashed into the ground, the force of the impact driving the point of the sword clear through her body. The bloody blade erupted from her back. Her body twitched once convulsively and was still.

"Val!" Francesca screamed her name. Then the echoes died away, and there was silence in the cellar.

CHAPTER TWENTY-ONE—CROSSROADS

D id you get an answer as to why Lieutenant Bergstrom didn't set fire to the mill?" The Ranger asking the question had the three stars of a divisional commander on her shoulder badge.

Sanchez nodded. "Yes, ma'am. It came out when I was questioning her sister. It was part of Lieutenant Bergstrom's plan to prevent herself from becoming a suspect." The Militiawoman's eyes flicked briefly in Katryn's direction. "Private Nagata's name had been linked to the murder of her previous sergeant, and Lieutenant Bergstrom knew she was a skilled archer. She also knew that Sergeant Coppelli was conducting an unofficial investigation into the murder. For Lieutenant Bergstrom's plan to work, it was necessary to shoot Sergeant Coppelli and to have Private Nagata disappear without trace. Bergstrom calculated that if Sergeant Coppelli were found dead from arrow wounds, and if Private Nagata vanished, it would be assumed that Sergeant Coppelli had obtained proof of her guilt and murdered her accuser before fleeing. The investigation would take the form of a search for Private Nagata— which would doubtless fail, as we'd be looking for a fugitive rather than a corpse."

The divisional commander nodded and turned to confer quietly with the officer sitting beside her. During the short lull in questioning, Chip let her eyes run around the room. The meeting hall in the divisional headquarters at Eastford was crowded. She, Katryn and Sanchez were squeezed onto a bench. Apart from them, Captain LeCoup, Lieutenant Ritche and as many members of divisional staff as could wrangle their way in were also present. Rumors had been rattling around town ever since the three had arrived from Roadsend the previous evening. This was the first of the official inquiry sessions.

Another of the officers sitting at the front leaned forward. "You said earlier that you thought Lieutenant Bergstrom was the one who killed Sergeant Ellis."

"Yes, ma'am," Sanchez replied.

The major frowned. "I read your original report. As I remember the details, it's hard to see how she could have done so."

"Sergeant Coppelli has some ideas about that. Perhaps she might be the best one to explain."

All eyes in the room fixed on Chip. "Sergeant?" The major invited her to speak.

"Er...yes." Chip quickly marshaled her thoughts. "What I think happened was that Lieutenant Bergstrom arranged to meet Sergeant Ellis in the stores. Before we left Roadsend, I was able to talk to Quartermaster Adebayo, and she confirmed that Lieutenant Bergstrom did leave the room briefly to collect a book from the office. The quartermaster hadn't mentioned it before, because she thought Lieutenant Bergstrom hadn't been gone long enough to kill Sergeant Ellis. However, it would have taken mere seconds to commit the murder. Afterward, Lieutenant Bergstrom hid Sergeant Ellis' empty knife belt inside her jacket and rejoined the quartermaster. As the officer in charge of the barracks, she knew she'd be called as soon as the body was discovered, giving her the chance to initiate the search to discover whose knife was missing. It needs to be confirmed with Sergeant Sivarajah, but I'm sure you'll find that Bergstrom sent her to look in the D Patrol bunkhouse, while she was left alone to put Private Nagata's knife in the empty belt and hang it in Sergeant Ellis' room."

"Yes, of course," the major said in enlightenment. "Did Bergstrom's sister confirm any of this?"

Sanchez was the one to answer. "No. Apparently, the two have hardly spoken for years. All she knew about were the plans for the attempted murders of Sergeant Coppelli and Private Nagata. She was the one who arranged for the message to lure them to the mill."

The officers at the table conferred again quietly, and a staff sergeant was sent to find some old dispatches. The discussion moved on to queries about Val Bergstrom's precise last words in what was, to Chip's mind, a rather forlorn attempt to link her to every other unsolved crime of the previous two decades. Night had fallen before everyone had run out of questions.

The divisional commander concluded the meeting, speaking slowly and somberly. "I trust this will finally draw a line under the unfortunate events in the 12th. There have been shadows hanging over the squadron for too long. And I think Captain Dolokov deserves to have the story firsthand, rather than be sent a written dispatch—or, worse still, hear it from gossip. Lieutenant Sanchez, would you be able to go with Sergeant Coppelli to Clemswood and give the report in person?" The divisional commander's voice was just questioning enough to make it sound like a request rather than an order. Although she outranked the lieutenant, the Militiawoman fell under a different chain of command.

"Yes, ma'am," Sanchez agreed.

"Good. If possible, leave tomorrow before the rumors get out.... Yes, Captain?"

LeCoup had made a polite bid for attention. "Merely that I think, for completeness, Private Nagata should go as well."

"Very well," the divisional commander agreed before moving on to other closing remarks.

As they left the room, Chip caught Katryn's eye, noting the conflicting emotions. Katryn would have to face her ex-comrades, the women who had beaten her for a crime she had not committed, but she would be facing them with proof of her innocence. Many people— probably most—would look forward to it with smug satisfaction. Chip was familiar enough with Katryn to know that it was not the way her mind worked. However, it would allow Katryn to draw her own personal line under the events in the 12th. Chip was sure it was the reason why LeCoup had asked for Katryn's inclusion. Chip sometimes suspected that under her caustic exterior, LeCoup nursed a protective maternal affection for her troops.

❖

It was a two-day journey to reach the Clemswood barracks. Sanchez, Chip and Katryn planned the overnight stop at a crossroads inn. However, when they reached it just before sunset, they discovered that they were not the only ones with the same plan. Three caravans of traders had also arrived that evening. The stables were full, and the hubbub from the taproom threatened to lift the rafters. The harassed innkeeper regretfully told them that there was not even a shared bed to be found in the common room.

Chip was considering the prospect of sleeping on the floor of the taproom (not for the first time in her life) when a local farmer overheard and offered them lodgings for the night. The woman even refused payment. Apparently, Rangers had removed a pride of snow lions from her farm that winter, and she was eager to repay the debt at the first opportunity. Anyone in the green and gray uniform would do.

In fact, the farmer was overeager to please. Her first intention was to turf her entire family out of their beds to give each of her three guests a room to herself. Chip felt it was too much too ask from the geriatric grandmothers and four children—one of them barely old enough to walk. After further debate, a straw-stuffed pallet was made up for Sanchez by the hearth. In the cold weather, it was an arrangement she was very happy with, and despite her higher rank, it was clearly felt to be quite adequate for a mere member of the Militia. However, the farmer and her partner could not be dissuaded from giving up their own bed for the two Rangers.

They took a meal at the long table with the farmer's family and field hands. The food was hot, plentiful and, for the tail end of winter, reasonably varied. Afterward, Chip entertained the family with ridiculously exaggerated stories of her exploits. The children listened in open-mouthed awe while the adults enjoyed the joke. Firelight from the hearth glowed over the comfortable farmhouse kitchen, catching its solid wooden furniture and eclectic assortment of farm implements and family heirlooms. A flagon of cider made the rounds, but the evening was not allowed to drag on; the needs of the farm came first. Everyone headed to bed at an early hour.

The farmer escorted Chip and Katryn up the twisting staircase at the back of the kitchen. The room in the eaves of the house was cozy, with its scrubbed floorboards and bed piled high with blankets and quilt. Their host hung the lantern from a hook on the ceiling and bid them both good night.

Once they were alone, Chip stood awkwardly in the center of the room and looked around. There was only the one bed and nowhere else to sleep. It was too cold for the floor to be the least bit appealing. She looked back to Katryn. Since they had escaped from the cellar, they'd had no chance to talk in private. A couple of times, it had seemed that Katryn was deliberately avoiding her. The two nights they had spent in Eastford had been sandwiched between meetings. On both nights,

Chip had returned to the Three Barrels late and alone. On both nights, she had stopped outside the door of Katryn's room but had lacked the courage to knock. Now there was no avoiding the issue.

Across the room, Katryn was sitting on the side of the bed, untying her bootlaces. Chip's heart was pounding as she remembered holding Katryn's hand in the cellar and Katryn kissing her fingers—but how much had she meant by it? It could hardly be counted as normal circumstances. Had Katryn merely been distracting herself from what had seemed to be unavoidable death? Following their return from the mill, Katryn had neither said nor done anything to imply that she wanted to be reminded of the incident.

Katryn was keeping her head down, concentrating on her boots. Chip wished that she would stop and look up. She wanted to see Katryn's face, to judge the expression there for a hint of what Katryn was feeling. Was she feeling anything at all except for tiredness? Or were the bootlaces a deliberate ploy? A way of avoiding eye contact? A signal for Chip to keep her distance?

Chip cleared her throat. "Um…if you want, I'll sleep on the floor."

"Why?" Still, Katryn did not look up.

"Because…in the cellar…I said I liked you, and I meant it. And if I'm sharing a bed with you, I'm going to find it very hard to get to sleep."

Katryn froze. Chip waited in agony for the curt rejection or embarrassed evasion. Long seconds passed. Then Katryn slipped off her boots and stood up. Her face held a bemused smile. She walked over until she was directly in front of Chip; then she reached out and took hold of both sides of Chip's open jacket. "What on earth makes you think I'm going to want you to sleep?"

Chip found that she was staring deep into Katryn's eyes. The effect was paralyzing, heart-stopping, soul-rending. Chip could feel her legs shaking. Her stomach was bouncing around like a spring lamb. Her arms, her face, her voice would not obey her. She knew that she was frozen in the image of a clumsy, brainless oaf—gawking like an adolescent on her first date. Yet amazingly, Katryn seemed not to notice. Letting go of the jacket, she slipped her arms around Chip's back.

Chip's own arms moved with the grace of a string puppet to clasp Katryn. She had the strange impression that the woman she was holding was trembling just as much as she was. She twisted her neck back to look at Katryn's face and saw that her eyelids were closed and her lips half open. Chip shut her eyes and met Katryn's mouth with her own.

The effect of the kiss ripped through Chip. In an instant, her body turned from wood to rubber. Then a crashing wave of pure happiness washed away the panic. Katryn's tongue softly caressed hers, exploring in the gentlest of invasions, an invitation to reciprocate. Katryn's arms held her tightly, pressing their bodies together. The sensation engulfed Chip, redefining reality. The world was no longer the way she had come to expect, but Chip knew that she could live with it.

Eventually, Chip pulled away. Katryn stood unmoving, breathing in gasps with her eyes closed, as though she were the one at risk of losing all self-control. Chip lowered her head, nuzzling the smooth skin of Katryn's throat, but the shaking in her legs had returned. She had to lie down while she could still move. Chip stared at the bed. It almost certainly was not quite what the farmer had envisioned in loaning it to them, but there was no way Chip could stop herself from making love to Katryn that night.

She looked back. Katryn's breath was faintly visible in the cold air. Chip managed to summon her voice enough to say, "I'd like to take my time and undress you very, very slowly. But this isn't the weather for it."

"True." It looked as though it also took Katryn a lot of effort to say the one word.

Chip let her arms fall and stepped away. Her hands moved to the fastenings on her own clothes, fumbling awkwardly as she loosened them, but her eyes never left Katryn until they were both naked and under the heavy blankets.

Chip pressed her body against Katryn's, entwining their legs. She ran her hand up Katryn's side, feeling the curve of her hip, the furrows of her ribs, the texture of her skin. She cupped a breast while rubbing circles around the nipple with her thumb.

Katryn gasped. Her arms tightened around Chip's shoulders as she rolled onto her back, urging Chip to lie on top of her. Chip did so, and the first soft moan of passion escaped Katryn's lips. Katryn arched her neck, exposing the full length of her throat. Chip burrowed in. With the sensitive skin of her inner lip, she explored the jawline, tasting salt. Katryn's hands were running over her back, sweeping down from her shoulders to her hips, pulling their bodies into ever-harder contact. Chip's mouth moved to Katryn's face, nuzzling her nose, tracing the shape of her eyes and finally joining again with her lips.

This kiss was longer, deeper and more searching than the first. At last, Chip pulled back and looked down at Katryn. Unexpectedly, she was swamped with a deep sense of peace, almost of awe. The last knot of nerves melted away. Never had anything felt so right.

Chip had been worried that she would fall on Katryn like a starving dog on a bone—but it was not going to be like that. It was not going to be a series of increasingly frantic maneuvers, an impatient race with an ever-narrowing focus on the target to be found between Katryn's legs. Chip wanted to explore every square centimeter of Katryn's body slowly. No one part was the goal. No one part was anything less than utterly precious.

Chip did not know how many times she'd had sex or with how many women. She had lost count within two years of joining the Rangers. But for the first time in her life, she was truly going to make love.

❖

Katryn was awakened the next morning by a knock at the door. She peered over the top of the covers. The room was in darkness. In response to Chip's call, the farmer's second-youngest daughter came in, carrying a jug of hot water in one hand and a candle in the other. The girl lit the lantern and placed the water by the bowl on the dresser.

"Breakfast is downstairs whenever you're ready." The youngster sounded a little in awe of the two Rangers. She ducked her head and scampered out.

Katryn lay in the warmth of the bed, allowing no more than her nose to poke into the cold outside the blankets. Chip's body was stretched beside her, solid and comforting. Katryn turned her face into Chip's neck. The unmistakable scent triggered an onslaught of memories: the weight of Chip's body on top of her; the fullness of Chip's fingers inside her; holding Chip and watching her face as she climaxed. As the images ran through her mind, Katryn felt her breathing grow ragged again.

The previous night had probably not been wise. Katryn remembered untying her bootlaces, wondering how Chip would want to play things, wondering whether they could go back to the rigid self-discipline imposed by Ranger regulations. And then Chip had spoken, offering to sleep on the floor and giving the choice to her—as though Katryn could have responded any other way to the desolate earnestness in Chip's voice. Now there was just the future left to deal with.

Katryn closed her eyes and snuggled a little closer to Chip in the warm nest under the covers. She wanted to treasure the next few seconds before the rest of the world took over her life again. She wanted to memorize each detail to hold in her dreams for the nights ahead.

Chip raised on one elbow and traced her fingers lightly over the skin on Katryn's shoulder. The touch rippled through Katryn's body, reawakening desire. Katryn opened her eyes. Chip was staring down at her. Passion was evident in the gaze, but also nervousness.

Chip wet her lips. "Um...thanks for last night. I...er...really enjoyed it...and maybe sometime again, we could..." Chip's voice died as the nervousness won out.

Katryn shook her head. Was Chip trying to suggest that they could treat what had happened as merely a night's sport? Was she hoping they could pretend to the world that it was not serious enough to merit attention? "Are you trying to say we can act like this wasn't important?"

"Well, I can see it's important to you, as you haven't been... sleeping with anyone...not since you joined the Rangers. And I'm pleased you chose me to..." Chip's eyes fixed unhappily on the pillow by Katryn's neck.

Katryn frowned, trying to work out exactly what Chip was trying to say. "Do you think that you're not important to me?"

"We're friends."

"We're more than that."

"Yes, I suppose...at the moment, but I'm not expecting you to want to get serious about it."

"So what do you think last night meant to me?"

"I guess you've finally hit the rebound from Allison...and that's good...you can move on. I'm not expecting that you're going to want to stick with me. I mean...I think I love you, but I don't expect...I know you're not going to want...and there's lots of other women...and..."

Katryn reached out, laying her hand on the side of Chip's face, stopping her broken sentences. "Chip, I love you with all my heart and with all my soul, and I know, for the rest of my life, I don't want anyone else but you."

To Katryn's astonishment, Chip burst into tears.

❖

Lieutenant Sanchez did most of the talking. Dolokov listened in silence, but even the dour captain could not prevent her expression from revealing her shock. Once everything had been said, she paced across to the window and stood staring out, though by now night had fallen, and there was nothing to see except her own reflection in the glass. Eventually, she turned back to the three women in the room.

"Bergstrom was a good lieutenant, or at least she—" Dolokov cut off her words and drew a sharp breath. "I suppose we should call Sergeant Sivarajah in here and confirm your guesswork. It's too late to hold a briefing now, but I would like to make a full announcement at the dawn parade tomorrow."

Chip was the one standing closest to the door. She stuck her head out. As she expected, both members of the quartermaster's staff had found reasons to be in the outer office—not that they could have heard anything through the heavy door. "Captain Dolokov would like to speak with Sergeant Sivarajah. Do you know where she might be?"

The two women exchanged glances before one hurried off. Chip closed the door and waited with the rest for Jan's arrival. It did not take long. Once again, Sanchez went through the explanation of Ellis' death. At the end, Jan frowned. "No, ma'am. I'm sorry, but it wasn't like that. We both went to B Patrol bunkhouse together. I was the one who discovered that Private Nagata's trail knife was missing."

"Could Ellis have made the swap while you weren't looking?" Chip asked.

"Street conjurers earn their living from people who don't realize they're being distracted," Dolokov added her comments.

Jan hesitated. "Not from the way I remember it, although your memory can play tricks on you." Despite her words, Jan did not look convinced.

"But if Bergstrom confessed, then she must have done it somehow," Dolokov said decisively. She turned formally to Sanchez. "Thank you for coming to tell me this. I'll let you go now. I'm afraid we don't have any spare accommodations at the barracks, but you will be able to get rooms at the Golden Goose. Could you arrange to be back here half an hour before the dawn parade tomorrow, in case any other questions occur to me tonight?"

"Of course, ma'am." Sanchez led the others out of the room. The curious looks from the quartermaster's staff followed them out into the parade ground.

"You're heading straight to the Golden Goose?" Jan asked.

"There's nowhere else we need to go," Chip confirmed.

"Do you mind if I tag along? I want to try to get things straight in my mind."

"Sure. I think I'm feeling a bit the same."

The four women sat around the table at the rear of the inn's taproom. Virtually identical frowns creased their foreheads as Jan went over her account again. "I entered the bunkhouse first and held the door for Bergstrom. She told me to check the lockers, since I knew which was whose. She stood behind me as I went down the row. When we got to Katryn's, her knife belt was hanging up, but the sheath was empty. I was the one who took it out. I...I really don't see how Bergstrom could have touched it first. Are you sure she admitted murdering Ellis?"

Chip and Katryn exchanged a pained grimace.

"Well, I don't know if she did in so many words," Katryn began.

Chip shook her head. "She must have. There is no one else. Before leaving Roadsend, I had a word with Quartermaster Adebayo to ask if Bergstrom went out of the briefing room at any stage that night. She told me about Bergstorm going to get the book, but she also put Takeda in the clear. She claims that she stood at the window in the officers' quarters and watched Takeda walk across the parade ground to her bunkhouse after showing the statements to Bergstrom. Adebayo hadn't thought it was important enough to mention in her original statement to the Militia. It means that Takeda couldn't have slipped off to the stores first."

"Unless Adebayo is lying to protect Takeda," Sanchez suggested.

"I doubt it," Jan said. "I think Adebayo really did like Ellis, and I can't see what reason would unite her and Takeda."

"You're certain nobody left the White Swan during the course of the evening?"

Jan stared at the ceiling as she called on her memory. "It was crowded that night; people were moving around. Someone might easily have slipped out for ten minutes or so."

"It's returning the belt to the bunkhouse that's the problem," Chip said. "Whoever it was couldn't have walked around the front of the barracks without being seen by the sentries at the gate, and the back was flooded....I know, a boat!" she exclaimed in excitement. Then her shoulders sagged. "No. She would still have to climb over the glass on the wall. It had to be someone who was inside the barracks." Chip slumped despondently in her chair.

"Bergstrom, Takeda or Adebayo," Sanchez summed it up. "I think you have to go with Bergstrom. She certainly had the best motive."

Jan disagreed. "Adebayo is the one Ellis trusted. I'd be surprised if she voluntarily handed her trail knife over to either of the other two—certainly not Bergstrom. They hated each other."

"Not surprising, with Bergstrom's role in the massacre."

Jan shook her head. "And that's another thing. Are you also sure Bergstrom said Ellis knew she was the one who tipped off the Butcher? Because several of Ellis' close friends died in the fight, and I can't believe Ellis wouldn't have turned her in."

Chip looked to Katryn, but this time, Katryn's eyes were fixed on the distance, and she had paid no attention to Jan's words. "Katryn? Have you thought of something?"

"I don't know. It's..." Katryn's frown deepened. "It's just occurred to me that the murderer was taking a chance on Ellis' having her trail knife with her. Since we weren't allowed to wear them outside the barracks, most of us had taken to leaving them in our lockers when we didn't need them. And strangling her as a backup plan wouldn't have been nearly as effective in framing me."

"She probably made a point of asking Ellis to take it with her," Chip replied.

"But why?" Katryn said. "I mean, yes, if it was someone in the patrol who was in the White Swan. They all had to leave their knives behind when they went out. But what reason would Bergstrom, Takeda or Adebayo give for not taking her own knife along?"

"Was Ellis wearing her knife when she spoke to you in the

stables?" Jan asked.

Katryn shook her head. "I can't remember."

"Then perhaps Ellis wasn't the one to take her knife into the stores. Maybe the murderer took it earlier in the evening and put it there, ready to use as the final insult—killing Ellis with her own knife."

Sanchez shook her head. "No. There was the confrontation with the sentries on the gate when Ellis tried to take it off-site. And that happened after everyone's position was accounted for."

Chip jolted as though she had been slapped around the face.

"What is it?" Katryn asked.

"I've just..." Chip broke off and held out her hand to fend off the questioning looks. "Give me a few seconds." Her face scrunched in thought. The others watched impatiently, but at last, Chip's frown disappeared. Her hand dropped. "I've worked it out." Chip's voice was almost too soft to hear. "We've been looking at the wrong trail knife."

CHAPTER TWENTY-TWO—THE FUTURE

The entire 12th Squadron was assembled on the parade ground. The sky was clear, but it was too early for the sun to have any warmth. Dolokov stood on the raised platform at the front of the officers' block. Chip and Sanchez were at the foot of the steps to one side, while Katryn was a little way off, next to the quartermaster's staff. Dolokov was speaking, telling the squadron about Bergstrom's death. The Rangers did not stir in their lines, but more than one woman's eyes strayed repeatedly in Chip or Katryn's direction.

As she waited for Chip's turn to come, Katryn tried to evaluate her own feelings. Chip's explanation the previous night had fit all the facts neatly. Too neatly. Katryn was not sure that she totally trusted the conclusion, but it would soon be put to the test. She looked at the members of her old patrol standing at attention behind Jan, and at one face in particular: the woman Chip was certain had murdered Ellis. The woman who had deliberately framed her for the murder, not caring what would happen.

Katryn's jaw clenched. She half hoped Chip was right so that all the doubts would be ended. She half hoped Chip was wrong so that she would not have to watch the consequences destroy someone she knew, no matter how well-deserved the punishment. Looking at the face of the woman, Katryn was a little surprised to realize that she had no lust for revenge.

Dolokov finished her part of the announcement. "The matter of Sergeant Ellis' death is not yet fully resolved. However, Sergeant Coppelli from the 23rd has something she wishes to say about it." Captain Dolokov nodded to Chip, her face showing some reservation. Like Katryn, the captain had felt the explanation was too contrived, but she had been willing to let Chip have her chance—after a little pressure from Sanchez.

Chip mounted the steps and turned to face the squadron. "I don't know how many of you are aware that I have been looking into Sergeant Ellis' death. Since Private Nagata joined my patrol, it has obviously been of some concern to me. I managed to produce various theories. Most of them have been shown to be unworkable, and one of them led to the confrontation with Lieutenant Bergstrom. However, I think I have finally gotten to the bottom of it and want to tell you how I think the events surrounding the murder went."

There was a faint rustle among the Rangers, with the simultaneous drawing of breath. Chip waited for silence and then continued. "The murder was planned in advance. The first steps were made during the afternoon, when the murderer was working in the stores. She had already decided when, where and how she was going to murder Sergeant Ellis, and she had worked out not just how to get around the fact that no one was allowed to take her knife out of the barracks, but also how to make it work in her favor. She made sure that no one was watching; then she hid her own trail knife in the stores. It didn't need to be a well-concealed spot; on top of a stack of crates would have done.

"As soon as she was finished in the stores, she went straight to the bunkhouse and put her empty belt in her locker. Presumably, if someone had noticed that her knife was missing, she could have pretended she had left it behind by accident. At that point, she wasn't irrevocably committed to the crime. However, the empty sheath was not spotted, and the murderer went on to arrange a secret meeting in the stores with Sergeant Ellis, probably saying she suspected Private Nagata of stealing, since framing her was part of the plan." Chip's eyes flicked briefly in Katryn's direction. Quite a few others copied the action.

"That night, the murderer left with the rest of B Patrol to visit a tavern in town. She had already talked people into going to the White Swan, which had quick access to the rear door of the stores. The patrol stopped off on the way to talk to Private Nagata in the stables. The murderer made an excuse to return alone to the bunkhouse, where she took Private Nagata's knife and put it in the empty belt in her own locker. Then she went to the tavern with the others. Sergeant Ellis also put in a brief visit to the White Swan, probably to co-ordinate the meeting in the stores.

"When enough time had passed to allow Sergeant Ellis to get back, the murderer slipped out through the rear exit of the tavern. Sergeant

Ellis had set out the bridge and helped her climb in. All that she needed was to divert Sergeant Ellis' attention for a few seconds, pick up the knife from where it was hidden, and stab Ellis in the back. Then the murderer took the key and left via the rear door. Locking the door from the outside did not require much agility. There is a convenient row of thick iron bars to stand on, and they are designed to stop people from climbing in, not out. The murderer jumped down and went to rejoin her comrades in the tavern.

"The last step in the plan was the part that relied most on luck. The murderer wanted to be present when the body was discovered, and someone might have stumbled upon it by accident before the patrol returned from the tavern. However, luck was with her, and she got the opportunity she wanted. The lighting in the stores was not good, so no one noticed that when she bent over the body to check for a pulse, she slipped the key back into Ellis' pocket."

By now, all of B Patrol had worked out the name of the Ranger Chip suspected. Nikki even turned her head slightly to peer in Bo's direction. Pat was standing next to her and was glancing sideways with a genuine expression of dumbstruck amazement. Bo kept her eyes fixed rigidly ahead, but she looked as though she were going to be sick. Katryn studied her dispassionately and then turned her gaze away. Bo was guilty. Her face said it as clearly as words. Whether the last part of Chip's plan would provide the evidence was scarcely necessary.

Chip went on speaking. "The murderer's plan worked perfectly. Everything fell into place for her. Everyone went where she wanted them to and saw what she wanted them to. Nobody spotted the things she didn't want noticed. But there was one problem: She'd assumed that all trail knives are identical.

"I guess it hit her first thing the next day, when she had the chance to get a good look at the one she'd taken, and she realized the very same thing Private Nagata did when the murder weapon was shown to her. Nobody would confuse the two knives. Private Nagata had been a Ranger for less than six months; her knife was almost brand-new. The murderer had served for years, and her knife was visibly worn.

"She was in an awkward spot. It was possible that no one would look closely enough to spot the switch, but the murderer dared not count on it. The chances were that pretty soon, the search would be on for a veteran Ranger with an unexpectedly new knife. At this point, the murderer knew she had to switch knives again, but she was stuck for options. She didn't want the new owner to notice, just in case the search never came; neither did she want to throw suspicion on any of the Rangers in her patrol. She didn't want the investigators to start wondering how someone who'd been in the White Swan might have committed the murder.

"There was only one person whose knife she could take. So the murderer slipped into the sergeant's room and swapped Sergeant Ellis' knife with the one she'd taken from Private Nagata. This worked well enough in misleading the investigators into thinking that Sergeant Ellis had been stabbed with her own knife. It meant that the plan to frame Private Nagata failed, but it also meant that the murder went unsolved, which was nearly as good from the murderer's point of view—especially when it was so easy to convince most of the squadron that Private Nagata really was the guilty one."

Katryn looked over the ranks of Rangers, noting the ashamed expressions dotted around and matching them to her memories. But they were all watching Chip in fascination—all except for Bo, who was staring up at the roof of the officers' block with dead, hopeless eyes. Had she already taken the final logical step and realized what was coming next?

"Where the search for the switched knife went wrong was that it looked for a Ranger with a knife that was too new. What they *should* have been looking for was a Ranger with a knife that was too old." Chip pulled her own knife from her belt and held it up. "I have been a Ranger for eight years, and this is reflected in the degree of wear on my knife. The person I suspect of murder has been a Ranger for a similar length of time and, therefore, should have a knife in a similar state to mine. However, Sergeant Ellis had been a Ranger for eighteen years. The difference won't be so marked compared with a new knife. There's a limit to how polished a handle can get. But her knife should still be visibly more worn. Captain Dolokov…" Chip turned slightly to face her. "You have served for slightly longer than Sergeant Ellis, but your knife should be roughly comparable. What I propose is for Lieutenant Sanchez to take our two knives and compare them with those belonging to the Rangers who were at the White Swan the night Sergeant Ellis was murdered."

Dolokov nodded. It was pure theater; the plan had been agreed to that morning. Sanchez mounted the steps and took the two knives; then she walked down toward B Patrol. Jan had taken the lead and drawn her knife. She held it balanced across her palm for inspection. Sanchez made a show of looking at it for purposes of completeness before moving on to Tina and Sal, who were also presenting their knives.

At the end of the front row was a Ranger, new to B Patrol, who had taken the post of corporal. In response to the questioning look, Sanchez shook her head to confirm that she was not a suspect and need not show her knife. Sanchez walked around her and moved on to the second row—first to Nikki and then to Pat.

Bo had not moved. Sanchez stopped in front of her. For long, drawn-out seconds, they stood like statues. Finally, Sanchez reached out and took the trail knife from Bo's belt.

Bo's eyes closed, and her head dropped, shaking in disbelief or disavowal. Sanchez examined the knife for a few more seconds, pursed her lips and returned to Dolokov on the top of the steps. The captain also studied the three knives and then looked back to the assembled squadron. "Sergeant Sivarajah. Leading Ranger Hassan is under arrest for the murder of Sergeant Melanthe Ellis of the 12th Squadron. Remove her sword and any other weapons, and see that she is secured in the lockup immediately."

Bo was led away, wide-eyed and stumbling like a lost child. A confusing snarl of emotions beset Katryn as she watched her go.

❖

The lockup was small and virtually identical to the one in Roadsend. Bo sat alone on the end of one of the bunks, huddled against the wall with her arms wrapped around her knees. She peered up as Katryn stepped through the outer door of the cell. Her expression was twisted in anguish but held more self-pity, Katryn judged, than remorse or shame. Recognizing her visitor, Bo pulled herself up and let go of her knees, but she still presented a picture of pathetic despair.

"Katryn? Is there any news?" Bo asked.

"Dolokov is going to hold the court-martial tomorrow morning." Katryn made sure that there was no trace of smugness in her voice. It was not hard; she did not feel any.

"I know that."

"Then you know as much as I do."

"Then why…" Bo's shoulders slumped and she swallowed. "Do you hate me?" Her voice was a dead whisper.

Katryn stopped to consider the question. It was not an easy one to answer. She felt that she had the right to hate Bo, especially when she called on the memories she had tried so hard to forget: the beating in the latrine block and the grim satisfaction on Bo's face while she was smashing her fists into Katryn's ribs and stomach. But Katryn also remembered sitting in the lockup at Roadsend, fighting to keep panic and despair at bay—a fight that Bo had already lost, judging by the look on her face. It gave Katryn an unsettling feeling of empathy.

At Katryn's silence, Bo leaned her head back against the wall and looked at her with a sideways stare. "You've come to gloat. Will you enjoy watching me hang tomorrow afternoon?"

"No." That was an easier question to answer, but only as she spoke did she realize that with it, they both acknowledged the inevitable. If Bo had struck out in a fit of anger, she might have gotten away with a lesser punishment, given Ellis' record and the provocation, but not with the calculated planning, and certainly not with framing someone else to die in her place for the crime.

"So why are you here?"

"I wanted to know why you did it. I know you hated Ellis. So did I. But why kill her when I was the one she was picking on? And why frame me for it?"

"I was sorry about you, but…"

But not that sorry, Katryn mentally finished the sentence for Bo. "So why didn't you kill her before?"

Bo's head dropped. "I had nine years of being her victim. You know what that's like. I got all the shit that was going. Every move I made was wrong; at best, I got laughed at. After two years, I stopped trying, and it made no difference." She glanced up at Katryn. "I should have told you there was no point trying to get your kit clean. Whether you took five minutes or two hours, you had the same chance of sentry duty. You might as well have not bothered. The rest thought I was a joke. So I made myself the patrol clown, but it hurt.

"When I joined the Rangers, I'd been so pleased with myself. I remember putting on the uniform for the first time and grinning all day, and…" Bo's face contorted; she could not finish the sentence.

"And I ended up under Ellis. It was hell until you joined the patrol, and suddenly, I wasn't the bottom of the pile anymore. It was only when I was out of it that I could see how bad things had been. I had a few months when I kept most of my free time, when I didn't wake up each morning feeling sick at the thought of the day ahead, a few months when I felt I had a chance...when I felt I could prove I deserved my place in the Rangers.

"And then there was that skirmish with the cats. That was the best shooting I'd ever seen, and not just me. I was standing with Ellis. Do you know how much it shook her to realize she had a sharpshooter in her patrol? She hadn't known, so you could bet Dolokov didn't know, either. I was just starting to think that through when Tina let it drop that you were offered a lieutenancy in the Militia."

Bo's eyes met Katryn's. "I was never as bad as Ellis made out, but I'm not in your league. There was no way Dolokov was going to leave you to be kicked around by Ellis once she realized what you had to offer the squadron. Tina suggested that you apply to change patrols. I saw it as a safe bet that you'd be moved as soon as Dolokov got back and read the report about the incident. And once you were gone, I'd be the scapegoat again. But I heard you threaten to kill Ellis, and it gave me the idea. I couldn't go back to being the butt of the patrol—not after seeing how much better life ought to be." Tears started to trickle down Bo's face. "I couldn't go back to years of wading through shit. Can't you see that, now that you're free of Ellis as well?"

Maybe, but I wouldn't have let someone else hang for it. Katryn swallowed the words and the other things she could have said. Bo obviously did not know that Ellis was not going to be allowed to re-enlist, and there was no point telling her now.

"Nikki says you were the one who talked everyone else into giving me a beating." Katryn spoke the accusation without bitterness. Nikki, wearing her new Leading Ranger's badge, had been the first to volunteer an apology without hiding behind excuses. It had eased the resentment more than Katryn had expected.

"Sorry. But I thought if everyone had a stake in thinking you were guilty, they wouldn't be so keen on looking for other suspects. And it wasn't..." Bo broke off, looking uncomfortable. She twitched her shoulder in a nervous shrug. "I am sorry, and you're okay now, aren't you?"

The insincerity of Bo's tone brought the first real flash of anger to Katryn. She clenched her jaw shut, unable to answer the question, and made as if to go. Before she reached the door, Bo scrambled off the bunk and grabbed hold of the bars.

"Katryn!" Bo's voice was desperate.

Katryn turned back. "What?"

"I know I don't have the right to ask you this, but…" Bo gulped air. "When you leave here, you're going straight back to Eastford?"

"Yes."

"On the way, you'll go through this small village, Amberwell. Do you know it?"

"I think so."

"It's where my family comes from. I'm not bothered about my parents. They never gave a fuck about me. But two of my grandmothers… they run the general stores. They…they were always so proud of me in my Ranger's uniform. I don't want them to learn"—Bo was fighting to voice the words—"about all this from a letter. Please call in and see them on the way. Tell them the news. Be kind to them; it will break their hearts anyway. Say something nice about me. Lie if you must… please?"

Katryn nodded once sharply. Then she turned and left the jail.

A soft drizzle was falling on Fort Krowe. The nearby mountains were lost in low cloud. However, the air was not cold, and it carried the scent of spring. Chip and Kim stood in a doorway and looked out. Rangers in green and gray scurried between the buildings, their speed inversely related to their rank. Horses grazed on the fields above. A squad of new recruits slogged through the mud, carrying weighted backpacks, while a drill sergeant hurled abuse.

"Home, sweet home," Chip remarked.

"I wonder how long we'll be here?"

"Only a few days. We're being posted to Northcamp for the summer."

"Northcamp?" Kim asked in surprise. "How do you know? You haven't been calling in favors again, have you?"

Chip laughed. "No. I wouldn't dare. I want to keep my anatomy as it is."

"So how do you know?"

"I was chatting with a member of staff."

Kim shook her head in amusement. "We've been back less than a day, and already, you're up-to-date with the gossip."

"Oh, I wouldn't say I was up-to-date. Give me a couple more hours." Chip's smile faded as her expression became more serious. "But on the subject of gossip, are you hearing anything?"

"About...?" Kim prompted.

"Me and Katryn."

"Oh, that.... Yes, there's a bit of speculation, but there's been that for months."

"Months!" Chip exclaimed. "But we've only—"

Grinning, Kim interrupted, "The pair of you have been desperately ogling each other since midwinter. Of course people noticed."

"You knew Katryn was interested in me?"

"Yes."

"And you didn't tell me?"

"I thought you'd have more fun working it out for yourself. Neither of you was being particularly subtle. It was just that you were too nervous to look at Katryn long enough to notice."

Chip groaned and stared desolately at the pattern of rain falling on a puddle. "So we may not have very long."

Kim leaned her shoulder against the frame of the door and examined her friend. "You think you'll be separated?"

Chip shrugged by way of an answer.

"It has to be serious before they do that," Kim said.

"It's serious."

"Really?"

Chip looked up at her friend. "I'm utterly crazy about her, and it's getting worse, not better. Suddenly, I'm rescheduling my whole life. Even if we do get separated, I find myself thinking that I've only got three more years left of my enlistment term, Katryn has just under four to serve, and then we'd both be out with our demob payments."

"You're thinking of leaving the Rangers?"

"Yes."

"Children?"

"Oh, children, grandchildren. A little cottage. Flowers around the door. You name it."

"And what is Katryn thinking?"

Chip shook her head. "She refuses to think about the future. When I talked about leaving the Rangers, she said four years is a long time and anything might happen before then."

"She might get tired of you?" Kim said, half teasing.

"No. She's promised that's the one thing that won't happen." Chip's grin returned. "Oh, this is getting ridiculous. I keep fluctuating between panic and euphoria."

"As I've said before—what a state for a Ranger to get into."

Chip reached out to poke a finger into Kim's shoulder. "Don't be so smug. It will catch you one of these days, mark my words."

Kim opened her mouth to reply, but she was forestalled by a shout. "Sergeant Coppelli!"

Chip twisted her neck to look back out the doorway. A Ranger was hurrying toward them. "What is it?"

"Sergeant Coppelli, ma'am. Captain LeCoup wants to see you in her office."

"Right." Chip tapped Kim's shoulder one more time and headed off through the rain.

LeCoup was standing staring out the window when Chip arrived, an unusually pensive occupation for the captain. She glanced around at Chip's entrance and then paced slowly across the office, picking something off her desk. When she spoke, her voice held the hint of a searching undertone. "Nagata's certification as a sharpshooter has been approved, and she's got her promotion to Leading Ranger. They didn't bother sending the confirmation on to Eastford; it's been waiting for us back here. Tell her not to worry; she'll get her pay backdated." Whether or not it had been the intention of divisional staff, there was no doubt LeCoup would ensure that the members of her squadron were never sold short.

Now Chip could recognize the items in LeCoup's hands as a new set of shoulder badges. She waited for the captain to hand them over, but LeCoup continued to study the embroidered cloth patches as though there was something unusual about them. "You and Private

Nagata seem to be getting on very well together." She did not look up, but there was no mistaking the implied question in her tone.

Chip's stomach turned to ice. "Yes, ma'am."

"The safety and effectiveness of the squadron are very serious concerns of mine. I will not take risks with either."

Chip could not bring herself to say anything.

LeCoup's gaze shifted to stare out through the window again. "I've been giving some thought to the squadron's effectiveness. It might be a good idea if Leading Ranger Nagata were transferred to A Patrol. You already have some women who are useful with a bow. O'Neil could use a sharpshooter. I think the squadron would be better...balanced that way. What do you think?"

Chip's pulse leaped with the shock, both at what LeCoup was saying and at what she clearly meant. Chip fought to find words. "I... er...I think it might um...work well."

LeCoup nodded solemnly. "Yes. That's what I thought. I'll leave you to explain it to Nagata. I'll talk to O'Neil and see who would be best to swap from her patrol."

"Yes, ma'am. Thank you."

LeCoup met Chip's eyes in a shrewd, appraising inspection. "The Ranger Command has very strict guidelines on maintaining squadron discipline. But as I read the rules, there's no requirement for me to probe into the private lives of my subordinates if I don't think there's a problem." The captain paused significantly. "I'm not likely to come across anything in the line of duty to make me think there's a problem, am I?"

"I would hope not, ma'am."

"I hope not as well." LeCoup's lips twitched in a smile, and she tossed the badges across to Chip. "Dismissed."

❖

The horse flicked its ears and gave several of the short huffs that Katryn had learned to interpret as pleasure. Katryn smiled and moved around to brush its other flank. She was working alone in the stables, but then, out of the corner of her eye, she caught sight of someone standing in the doorway. Chip was leaning against the jamb, watching her. Katryn felt the smile on her face broaden.

"How long have you been there?"

"Just a few minutes."

"You enjoy watching people work?"

"Oh, yes. It's part of the job description for a sergeant," Chip said cheerfully. She strolled over, holding out the new badges. "I've just been talking to LeCoup. Congratulations; you're now a Leading Ranger."

Katryn put down the brush and took the offered embroidered shields. She looked back at Chip. Something else had happened. Chip was trying to act nonchalant, but the excitement was showing in her eyes. "What's up?"

"LeCoup made it clear that she knows we're lovers and not merely bedfellows."

Katryn's face fell, but she took reassurance from Chip's lack of concern. "She isn't going to transfer me?"

"Only as far as A Patrol."

"A Patrol?" Katryn frowned as she thought it through.

"LeCoup is juggling the personnel. It means that you're no longer my direct subordinate, which makes it easier for my patrol. You realize that if you stayed in C, I'd have to give you all the worst assignments so no one could accuse me of favoritism." Chip's voice was getting more exuberant. She was almost laughing as she spoke. "And Ash is senior sergeant in the squadron. I trust her judgment more than I trust my own. If I see you standing sentry duty at the gates, I'll know that you damn well deserve it."

Katryn was still slightly unsure. "And that's it? LeCoup isn't going to split us any more than that?"

"Not as long as we behave ourselves. She made it clear that she isn't going to start asking questions about what we do off duty, as long as we don't let it affect the way we perform in the squadron."

Katryn closed her eyes and let her head fall back as a smile swept across her face.

Chip went on talking. "It means we've got three or four years to work out what we want to do."

"Things change."

"You think you might stop loving me?"

Katryn opened her eyes and looked back at Chip. "No. Never that."

Chip's arms slipped around Katryn, pulling her into a kiss.

Katryn resisted briefly. "Hey, didn't you just say we're supposed to behave ourselves while we're on duty?"

Chip's mouth twitched into a lopsided grin. "Just this once. Then we'll start using our discretion a bit more."

Three Steps Forward

by

Jane Fletcher

15 November 47

An ankle-deep layer of mud covered the building site, while the rain fell in sheets. People working on the council hall were liberally coated in the wet clay—as was everything else. The horses, small trucks and electric hoists plowed through the morass. Workers hauling on ropes slithered in a battle to find firm footing.

From the control-room window in the labs across the street, Dr. Himoti stared at the scene in disgust. After seven decades as a biologist, the need for hygiene had become ingrained in her. She detested mud. The cold rain was unpleasant but avoidable; the mud would follow her indoors. The labs were, of course, clinically clean, but ugly brown streaks marked the halls of the domestic quarters. Dr. Himoti's face twisted in a grimace. At times like these, she virtually lived in her labs. Yet the building workers seemed unaware of the filth around them.

The sound of the door opening made Himoti glance over her shoulder. Su Li Hoy, head of security and her closest ally, entered the control room. Rain plastered the security chief's black hair against her head and dripped from her clothes. She shivered as she peeled off her wet jacket. Himoti was relieved to see that she had already removed her boots. The control room did not have the same need for absolute cleanliness as the rest of the labs, and some people were lax about the rules. However, Su Li Hoy had worked with Himoti long enough to know her attitude toward mud.

Himoti returned to the view outside. "I was just thinking that the children seem to be more resilient to the weather than you or I and wondering whether it is due to their upbringing or a side effect of the broad base of their genetic makeup."

"A sort of hybrid vigor?" Su Li Hoy joined her at the window.

"Um...something like that. Then I got to wondering whether I'll ever stop thinking of them as 'the children.' Some are over forty."

"It's understandable. They're your children. You created them all here in the labs."

"I had help." Himoti shrugged modestly. "Anyway, it's just as well that they don't mind working in the mud. Soon, you'll have a nice new council hall for your meetings."

"But it won't change the rubbish they talk in them."

"Have you just come from a meeting?" Himoti sympathized with the irritation in the security chief's voice. Attending council meetings was a job that she was very happy to delegate.

"Yes."

"What wonderful scheme have they hatched now?"

Su Li Hoy hesitated while her lips went through a series of pouts. "They refused to endorse one of my motions."

"What was it?"

"I wanted...I wanted them to name the town after you."

Himoti laughed. "I can imagine that wouldn't have gone down well with some."

"But they can't call the town Landfall. It's not a proper name. It's how you talk about landing a shuttle."

"People have been calling it that for forty-seven years. It would be hard to change it now."

"That's what was argued. But it didn't hold in the other case."

"Which?"

"I said that if they wouldn't name the town, they could name the country after you, since we still haven't agreed on one."

"And?"

"And then Dan Ockan started wittering on about how things only get personal names when there's a need to distinguish between them. He said that the Earth's moon is *the moon* rather than named *Moon*, since it was called that before anyone knew there were others. It was only when people discovered other moons that they started giving them names. Ockan reckoned it was senseless naming countries here until there was more than one on the planet."

"He may have a point. We named the planet Celaenia, because we know of other planets, but you rarely hear the children call it that. Mostly, they call it 'the world.' I've even heard some call it 'the Earth.'"

"That was another stupid idea—naming it after the spaceship."

"There's a tradition of naming inhabitable planets after their discoverer," Himoti reminded her overzealous supporter.

"In that case, it should have been called Emergencynavigationa, since it was emergency override that found the planet, after the *Celaeno*'s main navigation computer hit meltdown and dumped us on the far side of the galaxy."

"You sound angry."

"I am. There wouldn't be a viable colony on this planet if it weren't for you, but some people want to deny you the credit."

"I've trod on too many toes over the years."

"You deserve some memorial."

"It's sweet of you to make the effort. But I don't mind about the names. My memorial will be this world."

As she spoke the words, Himoti's eyes ceased to focus on the scene before her. The world would indeed be a monument to her and her vision, more than the council knew, more even than she had revealed to Su Li Hoy, her closest confidante. Only in her diary and notes was the whole truth to be found.

The situation had looked bleak when the crew emerged from suspended animation to find themselves stranded thousands of light-years from Earth. Hopes of founding a viable colony rested on the spaceship's identification of an inhabitable world. But then came the discovery of the all-pervasive pollen, with its estrogen-mimicking structure. Male fertility dropped to zero, and even if conception took place, women's bodies were so saturated that male embryos could not develop in the womb.

The *Celaeno* had been part of a colony mission, carrying only equipment and personnel for the life sciences. Without the other engineering disciplines, the stranded crew did not have the tools to create a self-sustaining, high-tech society. However, they did have the best biology resources of twenty-third-century Earth, which was all Dr. Himoti needed. As the ship's chief genetics consultant, she had a plan.

The neoeugenicists back on Earth had been brilliant, but their work in bioengineering extrasensory perception was illegal. News had been strictly controlled, even after the law caught up with them. Himoti had been a member of the secret government review committee. Thus, she was one of the few people who had access to the records and the only member of the *Celaeno*'s crew who was aware of the extent of the ban against using them.

Psychic healing was the key. This was the talent Himoti that had bioengineered into the children created in her labs—something that would be inherent in the new population. Not all would display the ability, and some would have it more than others—but there would be enough.

Because of the estrogen-mimicking pollen, there could be no men—no male animals of any Earth species. But it would not matter. Already, some of the children had the psychic-healing ability to a sufficient degree to induce spontaneous cloning in animals—especially necessary since all the native fauna was poisonous to humans. But more was to come once the population grew large enough. There would be a few—the rarest and most talented—who would be able to go one step further, who would not merely clone, but step inside the cell nucleus and deconstruct its DNA. They would be able to imprint new patterns copied from a third woman and, therefore, create unique individuals with two genetic parents. These gifted ones, the imprinters, were the only part of the plan that had yet to materialize. Everything else was done.

Himoti smiled as she thought of what she had conceived: a world of women, kinder and gentler than the one they had left behind. That was why she had revived the neoeugenicists' forbidden experiments, why she had concealed information about their legality, why she had blocked work on any other solution to the male-fertility problem, why she had blended the available genes to remove distinct racial types. When the town council tried to stand in her way, she had bulldozed through them or simply ignored their decisions. Small wonder that they would not name the town after her. But Himoti knew she was right.

This new world would not make the same mistakes as the last. There would be one gender and one race on the planet—no divisive causes for conflict, no wars, no superstitions, no religions, no dictators or kings. The inhabitants would live rich lives in tune with nature. The culture would be shaped for people, not machines.

Relationships would be based on friendship and respect, without lust, possessiveness, jealousy or inane infatuation. She remembered her three husbands. They had all been bastards, and she had been blinded by love, enough to marry them, enough to waste her time on them—energy and effort that would have been better used in her work. Without men, her life would have been so much easier.

Su Li Hoy's voice interrupted her thoughts.

"There was something else at the council meeting."

"What?"

"Another attempt to introduce legal recognition of relationships, with particular regard to children."

"Not that again!"

"I'm afraid so. You managed to marginalize the concept of marriage back when you had more influence with the council. These days, people aren't so ready to listen to you. Also, I don't think anyone back then really believed that the psychic healing would work. Dual parents seemed to be a wild fantasy. But with news going around that one of the children might be able to imprint DNA, some people are rethinking the issue."

"Were you able to block the motion?"

"Yes. Jean Smith wasn't happy. She accused me of endorsing your homophobia."

"Me? Homophobic? After I created this world?"

"She said that the absence of men on the planet didn't mean that stable relationships would be less important to society."

"She was spouting the UN Space Agency line," Himoti said contemptuously. "And the preference for *stable* couples in colony teams. UNSA even had the gays and lesbians lined up two by two. Do you know, the main reason I married my last husband was to get a place on a colony ship?" The sideways look she received brought a smile back to Himoti's lips. "Well…that and the temporary insanity of lust."

Su Li Hoy tactfully returned to the topic of the council debate. "Jean Smith wondered whether you'd been hoping the children would be celibate."

"Of course not. What I don't want is stifling, soulless monogamy. It's a historic hangover—solely due to male domination of women. It makes no sense on this world. The children will base their relationships here on openness and equality, not possession."

The door to the control room opened for a young technician clad in a white lab coat and surgical mask. The face above the mask was light brown, with dark brown eyes and a wisp of almost-black hair showing. The description would match any of the children. With so little of her face on view, it was just as well that the technician's name, Sue Beaumont, was stenciled on the pocket of her gown. Dr. Himoti could not restrain a smile. The children who worked with her were starting to wear their lab clothes all the time, to mark themselves from the rest of the population. She suspected that some even slept in their masks. They were also taking to calling themselves the Sisterhood.

Partly for the benefit of the new arrival, Himoti went on, "Marriage reinforces the belief that you have the right to control someone else's sexual expression. It's immoral. Exclusive relationships lead only to jealousy and resentment. I hope that nobody in the labs would become so absurdly fixated on one other woman—and certainly not expect to have the relationship recognized by the authorities if she did." Himoti gestured Beaumont forward. "What is it?"

"Please, ma'am, I've got the results on Jill Neilson."

Dr. Himoti's eyes dropped to the report. Immediately, all other thoughts were forgotten. It was the news she had been waiting for, the final step in her plan. "This is excellent. She really is our first imprinter."

The technician nodded. "I knew you'd be pleased."

"This confirms that we won't ever have to clone humans. This world will have a proper society."

"Would cloned humans not be...proper?" Beaumont's voice reflected her confusion.

"They would be undesirable. You need new, unique people to have new ideas. If everyone were the same as her mother, you would have stagnation—soulless monotony."

Over the technician's shoulder, Himoti caught Su Li Hoy's eye and smiled. *Like soulless monogamy.* She knew her friend would get the reference.

Beaumont nodded and left. Himoti watched her go and then turned back to the window, ignoring Su Li Hoy's questioning look. They had things to do and people to talk to. They needed to get more information and to make plans. But for the moment, Himoti immersed herself in a vision of the future stretching out ahead. She would not see much more of it. Her ninetieth birthday was approaching, but her dream of utopia would succeed. Nothing could stop it now.

6 July 101

A row of blank monitors greeted Chief Consultant Beaumont and her deputy, Sister Kallim, when they arrived in the control room. Only the security lighting was on. The Chief Consultant stood at the center of the room and considered the lifeless equipment in silence. At her shoulder, Sister Kallim gave a distinctive drawn-out sigh like a leaky compressor, which generally meant that she was thinking rapidly and not keen on the conclusions she was reaching.

A junior Sister had been brushing imagined dust from a console when they arrived and now stood fidgeting at the other side of the room. Only her eyes showed over the top of the gauze mask, but from the way they flitted about, it was not hard to read her anxiety. She flinched noticeably when Beaumont's gaze fixed on her.

However, the Chief Consultant was willing to gather all the facts before deciding whether to be angry, and she spoke in a calm voice. "You are Novice Pruzansky, are you not?"

"Yes, ma'am."

"Can you tell us exactly what happened?"

"Er…yes, ma'am. This morning, half an hour ago, I switched on the fifth pod, and there was a bang from…" The young woman pointed toward a sealed hatch on one wall. "And all the monitors went blank. That's all I did."

"You noticed nothing else unusual?"

"No, ma'am."

"And the equipment was working all right yesterday?"

"Yes, ma'am."

Chief Consultant Beaumont drew a deep breath and looked toward her deputy. "What do you think?"

"Sounds like a blown fuse."

"Can we fix it?"

"Depends on what blew the fuse to start with. But in here…" Sister Kallim's voice trailed off as she paced around a set of lifeless terminals, shaking her head. "I doubt it."

"Can't it be repaired?" the novice blurted out.

"You heard what Sister Kallim said," Beaumont spoke evenly.

"But if—"

The words cut off sharply as the Chief Consultant raised her hand for silence. Both pairs of eyes fixed on her expectantly. Ignoring them, Beaumont turned and stared out the window, weighing her options.

The imposing façade of the council hall faced her on the other side of the road. Politics and power. Recently, it had become more and more common for the town council to challenge the authority of the Sisterhood. To date, it had been a standoff, but with the loss of the lab equipment, the balance of power would shift. The Chief Consultant's jaw hardened. It was her responsibility to ensure that Himoti's legacy was not lost. The lab breakdown had been half expected for years, and she had a plan.

She turned back to her white-clad colleagues.

"There is nothing to worry about. It is as Himoti foretold. These labs were not really for us, although we've been lucky enough to have their use for a while. These were tools from Celaeno to help the Elder-Ones build the new world. The Elder-Ones have all passed on, their work complete. Himoti foretold that one day, this equipment would cease to function, but it would not happen until we no longer needed it. Obviously, that time has come. This is a day for rejoicing. We have more than two hundred Cloners, fourteen Imprinters and no shortage of women who want daughters. We do not need this lab. If anything, I am amazed that it has lasted for so long."

The other two digested her announcement.

"So what do we do with these rooms? Keep them as a monument to the Elder-Ones?" Sister Kallim asked eventually, ever practical.

"No. These rooms were made to be used by the followers of Himoti. They will continue to do her work, but their function will change." Beaumont spoke confidently. Showing any trace of doubt would be fatal in the inevitable battles ahead. "Himoti made it clear that her followers should not take partners. However, we live among the ordinary population. Temptation surrounds us, and many of us fail."

Novice Pruzansky glanced down sharply. It was a good bet that her mask was hiding red cheeks. Beaumont chose to ignore the blatantly guilty conscience; it was not a high priority.

She went on. "We can remove the equipment and turn this building into accommodation for the Imprinters and the Sisterhood. We will live here, on sanctified ground, pure in the love of Himoti and free from transgression. Also, the Imprinters are such a rare gift. It is too dangerous to risk losing them, especially now that the labs are gone. Here, they can be protected by the Guards."

Sister Kallim joined her by the window and took her turn in contemplating the building across the street. "Might not some women on the town council think that this is a cynical ploy on your part to mitigate any loss of influence? They might think your main motive is to keep a firm grip on the Imprinters, to bolster the power of the Sisterhood, now that the labs are out of use."

Behind her mask, Beaumont grinned. Although the deputy's words had been delivered with a deliberate lack of emphasis, there was no mistaking her meaning. Sister Kallim might lack initiative, but she had an uncanny ability to put two and two together. Sometimes, Beaumont would swear that her deputy was able to read minds.

"Some might think that."

"You're not concerned?"

"What could they do? The Imprinters have to come to us for training. We alone understand the books the Elder-Ones left for them. No one else can determine who has enough of the healer sense to be an Imprinter. If we say the Imprinters would work better under our continual supervision, how could we be challenged?"

"Perhaps not directly, but the council could get us in a battle over funding."

"Not if we start charging an imprinting fee from the women who come to us wanting children. It's justifiable in terms of the building's upkeep and the training school, especially if the council tries to cut our funding."

Sister Kallim nodded slowly. "An independent income would be nice."

"More than nice. The Sisterhood would be free from outside coercion and other people's attempts to reinterpret Himoti's teachings."

During this exchange, the novice had been listening with a frown lining her forehead. The Chief Consultant shot a quick glance in her direction. It was doubtful that the young woman had caught much of the political implications, but it would be wiser not to continue the discussion with her as an audience. A slight shift in topic was a good idea. Beaumont raised her voice into declamatory mode.

"Himoti's teachings—ensuring their observance is the Sisterhood's sacred duty. Her wisdom is the only true guide for the children of Celaeno. When all the Sisterhood are dwelling under this roof, we must be especially vigilant that those outside do not deviate from the path. In this, I only wish that it were possible to have the Cloners live here as well. But there are too many of them, and it would not be feasible for the farmers to drive their animals through the streets, bringing them here. Yet letting the Cloners travel around freely..." Beaumont broke off. "I worry that one might be tempted to clone a woman, in defiance of Himoti's teachings."

"It would be wrong," Sister Kallim agreed wholeheartedly.

"It would be an abomination. I have heard some say that Himoti was very good at telling us what we should and should not do but very poor at explaining why. In my experience, she would explain, but we were not able to understand her reasons." The Chief Consultant's eyes traveled to Novice Pruzansky. "I must have been about your age, and standing on this very spot, when Himoti told me why we should not clone humans. I had just brought her news of the first Imprinter. And she told me that cloned women would not be proper humans. They would be soulless monstrosities."

The furrows of confusion at the top of the novice's nose had gone, replaced by wide-eyed awe. As the years went by, Chief Consultant Beaumont was becoming increasingly aware of the reaction and was now starting to play on it deliberately. There were so few remaining who had even seen Himoti, let alone those who remembered speaking with her.

She continued, "It has taken me many years to understand exactly what Himoti meant, but now it is clear to me. A soul is unique and indivisible. A mother might pass to her cloned daughter all her physical parts, but she cannot bequeath her soul. And without a soul, the offspring would be a woman but not a human, alive in name only. This would also explain why we may eat only animals that have been cloned; they have no souls."

Chief Consultant Beaumont nodded at her own words. These were the sort of teachings that must not be lost to the world. It was her duty to ensure the survival of the Sisterhood. The political maneuvering was distasteful, but taking control of the Imprinters was essential for the moral purity of the world; otherwise, Himoti's dream might be lost. She drew herself up; there were things to do. After a faint nod to the novice, Beaumont swept out of the room, with Sister Kallim trailing in her wake.

As the door closed, she heard the young woman quietly offering a prayer of thanks to Celaeno.

10 October 158

The building site was thick with churned mud. It was the natural state for a building site to be in, Chief Consultant Pruzansky thought wryly; it did not seem to matter whether it rained or not. She spared another glance at the hems of her companions' white robes. Her own was certainly no better.

Sister Singh also was clearly aware of the mud. "I wonder if we should have given a bit more thought to it when we were debating lengthening our gown to the ankle. The argument that it would look more imposing has just lost some of its weight with me."

"It is fortunate that visiting building sites does not normally form part of our duties," the Chief Consultant agreed. She paused at the top of an earthen embankment to survey her surroundings. "And, of course, this is no ordinary building site."

"No, ma'am, indeed not," young Novice Mayot joined in fervently.

The two older women briefly caught each other's eye. Irony was wasted on the young. But then the scene before them—the foundation trenches and partly built walls of white stone—claimed Pruzansky's attention, and a feeling of awe engulfed her.

This truly was no ordinary building site. It would be the first great temple to Celaeno, the mother Goddess who had chosen this world for her children. It was to be set in the heart of Landfall, on the very site where the labs had stood, where the Blessed Himoti had first instructed Celaeno's children in the mysteries of life. Himoti's grave and the small shrine over it would also be moved here and incorporated into the new structure.

Sister Singh unrolled a copy of the plans and started to point out features in the developing site for her. "That's where the main hall will be. The school for Cloners and Imprinters is over there. Those are the foundations for one of the dormitory blocks."

"And this outline here?"

"It's the library for books left by the Elder-Ones."

"Are they not to be kept in the school, ma'am?" Novice Mayot ventured to ask.

Pruzansky glanced at her. "Some will be. Those necessary for their education. But most of the books are clearly not intended for common access. They just cause confusion. They will be stored in reverence at the library."

It had been a contentious issue during the planning stage. It had taken her vote as Chief Consultant to win the argument. Interpreting the Elder-Ones' work could be difficult enough for someone of her experience. Letting simply anyone read from the books could only result in stupid or dangerous rumors.

Sister Singh moved on to another section of the site. "That will be the sanctum where the Sisters and Imprinters live."

"Renouncing the sins and impiety of the world, in simple lives of celibacy and prayer." Novice Mayot bowed her head as she spoke.

"And hopefully with a bit more space than we had in the old labs." Sister Singh was far more prosaic.

"It's a great pity that the Blessed Himoti's labs have been taken down," Mayot said wistfully.

"As Sister Singh pointed out, we have outgrown them. They were unbearably cramped."

"Could they not have been kept as a lasting memorial, ma'am?"

"They were never intended to be permanent. They would have fallen down of their own accord in a few more years."

"But it is painful to break with the past. And sometimes, the Elder-Ones feel so distant."

"They will be if you think their legacy lies in buildings rather than in your heart," Pruzansky said firmly.

"I'm sorry, ma'am, I didn't mean—"

The older woman took pity and softened her tone. "It's all right. I understand how you feel. I was once the same. I remember the day the lab equipment ceased to function. I was worried, even frightened. Chief Consultant Beaumont came and spoke to me." Pruzansky looked around, judging her position. "It must have been on this very spot. She said the equipment had been a gift from Celaeno to the Elder-Ones, not to us. And the same may be said of the building itself."

"Beaumont is revered as one of the greatest Chief Consultants," Sister Singh added.

"Indeed. She was a very holy woman...one of the last who remembered talking to the Blessed Himoti, as I am one of the last who remember talking to her."

Pruzansky's lips tightened. The years were taking their toll. Her time in the world must be nearly over, and when she died, another link with the Elder-Ones would break—one far more important than the lab buildings.

"We are fortunate that you have finished writing your great work, so that your memories and wisdom will not be lost." Sister Singh must have sensed where her thoughts had gone.

Pruzansky smiled behind her mask. *The Book of the Elder-Ones* had been compiled from a hundred sources, of which the most important and irreplaceable was her own memory. It told the story of how the world began. How the Goddess Celaeno had searched among the stars for a suitable planet, with her servants, the Elder-Ones, asleep in her belly. How the Elder-Ones had worked with her blessing to build the new world. How the children of the Goddess had been engendered from the essence of life held within Celaeno. And how the Blessed Himoti, greatest of the Elder-Ones, had by the sanctity of her prayers called forth the Imprinters, the channel by which the Goddess granted souls to her children.

"I wanted to make sure that the knowledge wasn't lost. I wanted to pass on what I'd learned from the generation before me—the children who'd been raised by the Elder-Ones themselves."

"The Sisterhood is in your debt," Singh affirmed.

"I hope that my book will be of assistance to those who follow us. The Sisterhood carries a heavy burden of duty. We must care for the Imprinters, the chosen of the Goddess, and keep them pure from the sins of the world. And we must ourselves be pure, wearing masks as a guard against personal vanity and embracing celibacy so that we love no woman more than the Goddess." Pruzansky turned to the young novice. "You're new in the Sisterhood. In time, you will doubtless advance to greater rank. Maybe even become Chief Consultant."

Mayot looked down, bashfully. "I don't think that—"

"It is a great responsibility. Sometimes, you will have to do things that are difficult or distressing. It is my hope that *The Book of the Elder-Ones* will strengthen your faith when the call of duty is hard to follow."

A sudden attack of memory hit Pruzansky and clamped her throat shut. She turned away, eyes closed, while fighting to regain her composure. The greatest test of her faith had happened less than a year before. A Cloner had tried to avoid paying the imprinting fees by cloning her partner. Their crime had been discovered within days of the monstrosity's birth.

Ordering the punishment of the adults had been easy; they had knowingly defied the command of the Goddess and created a soulless abomination. But the infant itself…it had looked so much like a real four-week-old baby. Its tiny hands had waved about as it lay in its crib, wailing. Ordering its destruction, in Himoti's name, was the most painful duty Pruzansky had ever forced herself to perform. But although she had lost the novice's intensity and naïveté, the years had not weakened her faith.

Pruzansky drew a deep breath and opened her eyes. Before her stood the old council hall, now abandoned. As part of the plans for the temple, it was going to be pulled down to make way for new buildings. It was the physical display of a moral victory. The Sisterhood were the Blessed Himoti's disciples. As memory of the Elder-Ones faded, it was their calling to carry on her great work and ensure that the will of the Goddess was done. Now nothing would challenge Himoti's great vision for the world.

About the Author

Jane Fletcher was born in Greenwich, London in 1956. She now lives alone in the south-west of England after the sudden, untimely death of her partner.

Her love of fantasy began at the age of seven when she encountered Greek mythology. This was compounded by a childhood spent clambering over every example of ancient masonry she could find (medieval castles, megalithic monuments, Roman villas). It was her resolute ambition to become an archaeologist when she grew up, so it was something of a surprise when she became a software engineer instead.

Jane started writing when her partner refused to listen to yet another lengthy account of 'a really good idea for a story' and insisted that she write it down. After many years of revision, the result, *Lorimal's Chalice*, was published. This book was short-listed for the Gaylactic Spectrum award in 2003.

Lorimal's Chalice will be re-released as Book One and Book Two of The Lyremouth Chronicles in the coming year (*Book One: The Exile and The Sorcerer, Book Two: The Traitor and The Chalice*) along with the *all new* Book Three in the series: *The Empress and The Acolyte*.

Jane is also the author of The Celaeno Series. All three books in this series will be available from Bold Strokes Books in 2005 (*The Walls of Westernfort, Rangers at Roadsend*, and *The Temple at Landfall*).

Jane can be contacted at js.fletcher@btinternet.com

Other Books Available From Bold Strokes Books

Course of Action by Gun Brooke. Actress Carolyn Black desperately wants the starring role in an upcoming film produced by Annelie Peterson, a wealthy publisher with a mysterious past. How far is Carolyn prepared to go for the dream part of a lifetime? And just how far will Annelie bend her principles in the name of desire? (1-933110-22-8)

Rangers at Roadsend by Jane Fletcher. After nine years in the Rangers, dealing with thugs and wild predators, Sergeant Chip Coppelli has learned to spot trouble coming, and that is exactly what she sees in her new recruit, Katryn Nagata. But even so, Chip was not expecting murder. The Celaeno series. (1-933110-28-7)

Justice Served by Radclyffe. The hunt for an informant in the ranks draws Lieutenant Rebecca Frye, her lover Dr. Catherine Rawlings, and Officer Dellon Mitchell into a deadly game of hide-and-seek with an underworld kingpin who traffics in human souls. (1-933110-15-5)

Distant Shores, Silent Thunder by Radclyffe. Ex-lovers, would-be lovers, and old rivals find their paths unwillingly entwined when Doctors KT O'Bannon and Tory King—and the women who love them—are forced to examine the boundaries of love, friendship, and the ties that transcend time. (1-933110-08-2)

Hunter's Pursuit by Kim Baldwin. A raging blizzard, a remote mountain hideaway, and more than one killer-for-hire set a scene for disaster—or desire—when reluctant assassin Katarzyna Demetrious rescues a stranger and unwittingly exposes her heart. (1-933110-09-0)

The Walls of Westernfort by Jane Fletcher. All Temple Guard Natasha Ionadis wants is to serve the Goddess, and she volunteers eagerly for a dangerous mission to infiltrate a band of rebels. But once away from the temple, the issues are no longer so simple, especially in light of her attraction to one of the rebels. Is it too late to work out what she really wants from life? (1-933110-24-4)

Change Of Pace: *Erotic Interludes* by Radclyffe. Twenty-five hot-wired encounters guaranteed to spark more than just your imagination. Erotica as you've always dreamed of it. (1-933110-07-4)

Fated Love by Radclyffe. Amidst the chaos and drama of a busy emergency room, two women must contend not only with the fragile nature of life, but also with the mysteries of the heart and the irresistible forces of fate. (1-933110-05-8)

Justice in the Shadows by Radclyffe. In a shadow world of secrets, lies, and hidden agendas, Detective Sergeant Rebecca Frye and her lover, Dr. Catherine Rawlings, join forces once again in the elusive search for justice. (1-933110-03-1)

shadowland by Radclyffe. In a world on the far edge of desire, two women are drawn together by power, passion, and dark pleasures. An erotic romance. (1-933110-11-2)

Love's Masquerade by Radclyffe. Plunged into the often indistinguishable realms of fiction, fantasy, and hidden desires, Auden Frost discovers a shifting landscape that will force her to question everything she has believed to be true about herself and the nature of love. (1-933110-14-7)

Beyond the Breakwater by Radclyffe. One Provincetown summer three women learn the true meaning of love, friendship, and family. Second in the Provincetown Tales. (1-933110-06-6)

Tomorrow's Promise by Radclyffe. One timeless summer, two very different women discover the power of passion to heal and the promise of hope that only love can bestow. (1-933110-12-0)

Love's Tender Warriors by Radclyffe. Two women who have accepted loneliness as a way of life learn that love is worth fighting for and a battle they cannot afford to lose. (1-933110-02-3)

Love's Melody Lost by Radclyffe. A secretive artist with a haunted past and a young woman escaping a life that proved to be a lie find their destinies entwined. (1-933110-00-7)

Safe Harbor by Radclyffe. A mysterious newcomer, a reclusive doctor, and a troubled gay teenager learn about love, friendship, and trust during one tumultuous summer in Provincetown. First in the Provincetown Tales. (1-933110-13-9)

Above All, Honor by Radclyffe. The first in the Honor series introduces single-minded Secret Service Agent Cameron Roberts and the woman she is sworn to protect—Blair Powell, the daughter of the president of the United States. First in the Honor series. (1-933110-04-X)

Love & Honor by Radclyffe. The president's daughter and her security chief are faced with difficult choices as they battle a tangled web of Washington intrigue for...love and honor. Third in the Honor series. (1-933110-10-4)

Honor Guards by Radclyffe. In a journey that begins on the streets of Paris's Left Bank and culminates in a wild flight for their lives, the president's daughter and those who are sworn to protect her wage a desperate struggle for survival. Fourth in the Honor series. (1-933110-01-5)